NEW MOON
RISING

BY D.A. GODWIN

Guardian's Prophecy
Book One: Eyes of the Blind
Book Two: Hunter's Moon
Book Three: Weaponforger
Book Four: New Moon Rising

NEW MOON RISING

GUARDIAN'S PROPHECY: BOOK FOUR

By

D.A. Godwin

For Jim,
and all the adventures we shared

CONTENTS

CONTENTS

CONTENTS

Westholm
Newlmir
The Wildlands
Lajor
Wastrog
Ironwood
Evermen's Forge
Kirchmont
Verone
Ronse
Viaden
Anovin
Tiridon
Orthonia
Fallhaven
Wiermist
Saxalm
Kenzing
Bexville
Durbris
Jonrin
Sandenmill
Rivermist
Bendin
Halisford
Glint
Braunton
Calvia
Merrywood
Small Sea
Ildalarial
Gyland
Kendenhall
Harlma
Iscar
Duraco
Actondel
Terent
Eitholmir
Rexford
Siderion
Lisiria
Locksall
Orcaster
Adair
Tornton
Briggenwell
Shirath
Sereburn
Merallin
Lightpoint
Dwarf Clans
Rossian Sea
Highfall
Kharni

Stoloc
Thess
Novalum
Dresia
Leppon
Ceringion
Reginum
Senarum
Brixonne
Mendara
Pon Druisi
Otalio
Arivell
Kavenna
Andoran
Gramaria
Nemiperra
Valedia
Palandan
Casarcium
Nassa
Cellavia
Entria
Iscaria
Mersania
Salinis
Tarnia
Siemtra
Avalta
Scaccin
Genotta
Tythir
Larnia
Consarus
Macharra
Namarin
Shab
Bahkla
Akham

Chapter One

Consequences

It was dark, and his mind was in a fog.

He could not say with any measure of confidence how long he remained in such a state before the chill of the stone beneath him began to permeate his awareness. That sensation was, somehow, not as it should be, though for no reason that he could name. Seeking to establish a frame of reference, he sought the missing inputs from his other senses, but they remained elusive. He drifted in and around such thoughts for an unknown time until, eventually, a new feeling forced its way into his consciousness: pain.

The sharpness of it brought focus, coalescing his sense of self. He had memory of neither what task he had been about nor why it was to be performed, but there had been an importance in its doing. His arms, if he had any, refused every instruction to alter his position, and so he set his attentions to resolving the darkness that enveloped him. After methodically discarding a number of less than satisfactory options, he concluded that his eyes were closed.

With care, Fellaxus willed them open.

The parting of his eyelids yielded only a blurry haze that solidified with agonizing slowness into shapes with which he was familiar: A vial bubbling softly as it steeped above a small flame. Shelves filled floor to ceiling with books and dusty tomes from every corner of the world. The ancient desk from which he fulfilled his duties as Grandmaster of the Conclave of Imaretii.

A demon.

He looked for the summoning circle that should have contained the creature, but if one existed, its location lay beyond his view and his head seemed unwilling to turn in the needed direction. For a man whose daily life was dependent on being in absolute command of his faculties, his paralysis was… disconcerting.

The demon lowered its goat-like head and crossed the room in two giant strides, as if to gore him with the horns perched where its ears should have been, but it stopped a handspan short of a collision. Sulfur assaulted Fellaxus' nose and terror squeezed his heart, even as his mind cataloged the tiny serrations on the edges of the creature's broad, flat teeth. The hatred emanating from its horizontally pupiled eyes was palpable. The goat creature gave a snort, then turned and spoke over its shoulder in a deep, rumbling string of sounds that were so surprising to hear they almost failed to register as language.

It was then that Fellaxus deduced he was caught in a dream; demons could not speak.

The floor trembled from a series of jarring impacts, and the goat's head was replaced by something completely different—and far worse. His entire field of view filled with a twisted visage of deep reds and mottled blacks, one dominated by rows of sharp teeth contorted in a wickedly eager grin. Fellaxus avoided the burning red eyes set above those teeth, focusing instead on the massive hooved foot planted next to his own, his left one, which was pointing in the wrong direction. With that realization came excruciating agony, shocking him sufficiently from his stupor to accept that this was no dream.

"Greetings, master of the tower," the demon spoke in a thick, deep voice laced with sarcasm. "It is well that you still live. You have, after all, done so much, and your efforts deserve a suitable reward."

His astonishment at the creature's command of his language rendered him mute. He tried to muster a spell to force the creature away, but his broken body responded with no more than an impotent twitch.

"I know your name," he mumbled. "You must obey."

"Ah, the master wishes to command me." The demon withdrew just enough to give a mocking bow. "That you and your predecessors believed such nonsense is a staggering ineptitude."

Fellaxus could not grasp its meaning. Someone else should have heard this catastrophe. Had the alarms been triggered? A dim memory of protocols that should have been followed after such a breach wormed its way into his mind. Where was Verelli?

"Come," the creature sneered, "we shall tell your world my name together."

A giant, taloned hand seized Fellaxus, lifting him as easily as a child but far less gently. He dangled helplessly, consumed by blinding pain as his bones grated against each other in ways they were never meant to. Struggling to maintain consciousness, he was taken up the broad stone stairs to his workshop, or at least to where his workshop should have been. Instead of the spicy scent of reagents and the bitter aroma of potions, salty winds blew across his skin, unslowed by walls or roof. Such constructs were gone, and with them the observatory and indeed the entire top of his tower. With a cold chill of dismay, he realized that almost nothing remained of his life's work—not the books, or experiments, or drawings—nothing.

The demon thrust Fellaxus aloft like a trophy, forcing upon him a view from one edge of the sky to the other. The rising sun burned angry and red through the ashen smoke which rose with it. Cool ocean breezes that had so often stimulated his thinking now carried aloft harsh screams and the scent of burning wood and flesh. Flashes of magic crackled amidst the flames, casting an otherworldly glow across the destruction being wrought upon the city of Tythir. Swarms of demons in every form imaginable draped the royal castle on the hill below, appearing like ants atop a disturbed nest. The people unlucky enough to reside within that fortress rushed about in terror. Some fought, most ran. Fellaxus' analytical mind ascertained that either course of action was an equally hopeless endeavor. Even those ships in the harbor that had dropped sails and fled towards the safety of the open ocean managed only a futile dash before meeting their end. Papers floated down from his tower, fluttering like dried leaves blown from a tree.

So much knowledge lost.

From their perch high above this horrific vista, the demon

threw back his head and smote his chest with a clenched fist, bellowing, "I am Sulfaxrhu!"

The roar of a thousand affirmations rose above the death of the city in answer. The demon spread its arms and wings wide, reveling in the exaltations, then drew Fellaxus close and whispered in his ear.

"You thought to use us, across the centuries, for your own petty goals and machinations." Its grip tightened like bands of iron around his chest, forcing the breath painfully from his lungs. "Know, then, that you were the ones who have been servants, and *this* is your legacy."

With that absolute failure forever burned into Fellaxus' mind, Sulfaxrhu clenched his fist, wringing the last vestige of life from the once powerful mage like water from a sponge.

Chapter Two

Loss

Enna wept in silence, alone.

The morning sun filtered through the leaves above to fall on her hunched shoulders, its warmth adding to the unbearable weight that had driven her to her knees and kept her there the entire night. Not even the delicate coolness of the grass between her clenched fingers could abate the burning anguish consuming her soul.

What had he done?

From the first hint of yesterday's dawn, every motion and moment of the entire day had gone exactly as it was meant to—a perfect end to a road that had been far too long and filled with far too much pain. When the ritual preparations of cleansing and contemplation had been completed, Shalindra at last donned Elurithlia's sacred armor, reuniting it with Shining Moon for the first time in centuries. Her blond hair curled about her shoulders like gold edging on the silver scales of that armor, and her impossibly blue eyes lost the edge of self-doubt that had followed her. Even the staunchest of detractors could not have denied her right to the Ascension that would forever mark her as Elurithlia's Guardian.

She had looked so beautiful as she had taken her place on the sacred stone in the center of Lana Aviaseer, the Glade of Ascension, the first human ever to do so. Elurithlia's blessings had rained down upon her with a joy so pure that there were no words in any language which could hope to describe its brilliance.

It was in that moment of absolute perfection that Tormjere had come forward, walking through a barrier that no living creature should have been able to cross, and had stood with Shalindra during the peak of a ceremony that belonged more to their goddess than to those imperfect mortals who participated.

That was when everything had gone terribly wrong.

Joy turned to torment, placidness to tumult, and light to darkness. Enna had watched helplessly as Tormjere convulsed in agony before falling limp. Shalindra spun to catch him, rising from her knees so quickly that she seemed not to have moved. The wards surrounding the pair, which should have sheltered them from any calamity, shattered. Multicolored energies had exploded outward, hurling every Sister from the sacred stone and bending the mighty trees encircling the Glade, trees that had stood unbowed by any force of nature for ages beyond memory.

Enna had watched from outside her own body as she forced herself to her feet, her white robes and equally white hair billowing behind her as she struggled against the primal wind to reach them. And, for the briefest of moments, she had stood with them in the presence of her goddess, bathed in the glory of Her magnificence, reveled in the rapturous purity of all that had been and all that could ever be.

Then everything was gone.

Enna's mother was screaming incomprehensibly, her face contorted into a horrific mask of unrestrained fury terrible to behold. Like a creature possessed, she had thrown herself bodily at Shalindra, only to be repulsed by a flash of silvery blue light.

Then Shalindra spoke, her voice imbued with authority unlike anything that those present had ever heard.

"Leave."

That word had been a command imbued with such weight and majesty that every elf in attendance, without consideration of disobedience, had scrambled over each other in their haste to flee. Enna felt it in the deepest fiber of her being as she ran with them, rushing from the Glade as if her life depended on it. When the curtain of vines draping the entrance had closed behind them, the other Sisters came to a sudden and panicked halt, locked helplessly outside their own sanctuary.

But Enna kept running.

She flew down the path that wound through the temple forest to the massive Glade of Worship, properly named Lana Clariandar, which was packed with thousands of the faithful. A cheer went up the moment she appeared, for there were none in all of Ildalarial who possessed the green eyes and pure white hair so closely resembling that of Illathalirial, the most powerful Guardian to have ever taken up the mantle.

It was a noisy and festive gathering still untouched by the chaos that raged just a short distance away. The worshipers pressed around her eagerly, knowing her role in the ceremony and hoping that she bore word of the new Guardian, but Enna wanted only to escape, and so she kept running.

She ran and she ran until she at last stumbled into an empty clearing somewhere in the forest, where she collapsed to her knees. She remained in that position throughout the night, barely noticing the chill in the air which heralded an early arrival of fall.

There had to be some sense to it all, some reason for this to have happened, but no matter what logic she sought to apply or how fervently she prayed for understanding, she was left floundering helplessly in a sea of questions.

No sooner had her thoughts rejoined her in the present than they were sent hurtling back to the ceremony once more—a horrible nightmare from which she could not seem to awake.

Tormjere had come forward with the casualness of someone on a pleasant stroll in the woods, yet Enna had felt uncertainty coil around her stomach immediately. Though she had been deeply committed to the ritual—the sacred and powerful request that linked Shalindra directly to the goddess of the moon, Elurithlia— she had risked the briefest glance at him. As his dark eyes met hers, she had known that, somehow, he would hear her silent question: *What are you doing?*

His answer came with such matter-of-factness that they could have been discussing the most ordinary of subjects.

What are you doing?
Visiting the gardens.
What are you doing?
Going to the baker for bread.

What are you doing?
Checking on the dogs.
What are you doing?
Tearing your goddess to pieces.
What are you doing?
Walking my path.

She recoiled from that answer, but the finality of his words was inescapable. His manner had been neither sad nor fatalistic, and he had shown not the slightest trace of fear. As always, he had known what he was about to do, and he had known what it would cost him.

And he did it anyway.

Hot tears dripped like embers onto her hands.

Mistress, why? Why did you allow such horror to happen?

It was a question for which she might never gain an answer, but the reply arrived as suddenly as it was unexpected.

~ There is much beyond my control ~

The divine voice of her goddess coursed through Enna's body, warm and reassuring, and, though she had never heard it before, as familiar as if she had been listening all her life.

Forgive my doubts, Mistress, but this price was too high.

~ Of him, I demanded no more than I have asked of you ~

He was to protect her as no other could. If you require a sacrifice for this ritual, then I beg you to restore his life and take mine instead. No one can replace him at her side.

~ You must try. Yet, at this moment, it is your mother who needs you. Go to her, that she may be saved from herself ~

A sense of dread filled her, both for her mother's safety and for the well-being of those around her. Enna's hand sought the silver disc of her faith that hung from her necklace, her fingertips tracing every detail engraved in the metal. There was strength to be found in the twist of the rope, which turned once for every cycle of the moon in a year; harmony could be felt in the twenty-eight orbs representing the days within each of those cycles; and in the peaks of the mountains representing the Three Sisters supporting the pearl of the full moon there came a sense of permanence. Her stiff muscles protested as she pushed herself to her feet, and her grip on the sacred talisman tightened as she committed herself once more to her goddess.

By your light, Mistress Shalindra.

Chapter Three

Awakening

Shalindra stood in the stillness of the forest dawn, kept company only by the life-sized effigies of the seven women who had served as Eluria's champion before her. The smoothly sculpted wooden statues appeared almost to have grown naturally in their nurturing arc around the perimeter of Lana Ariiliar, the Glade of Guardians. Beside her, and in perfect harmony with that arrangement, was a wooden dais upon which rested Tormjere's body, still clad in the layered greens and browns evocative of a Silvalarian Woodswarden, though with a style that was markedly unique. She had no memory of how the platform had arisen, but, as with the statues, it was so smoothly unblemished that it appeared to have sprung from the ground in such a shape.

She was even less certain of how either of them had arrived in this location, or why they had come to it in such condition. The evidence presented before her provided no clues to be unraveled. Her memories were a warring conglomeration of multiple pasts, of different histories and inconsistent sequences in which similar events had happened.

Or in which they *could* have happened?

Perhaps, even the way in which they might yet happen.

Though she stood as a solitary figure, she carried with her the distinct impression that there were multiple *hers* which had arrived to simultaneously occupy this current place and time, each the culmination of an alternate life guided by different decisions. If she thought about it too long, she became unsure of which Shalindra was the one standing here now, the one whose thoughts she was experiencing. It was difficult to tell them apart, especially since every one of them was insistent that they were her true self. There was no one else from whom to seek confirmation, and the statues of the prior Guardians regarded her in silence.

She wished fervently that her mind was as placid as her surroundings, but above the arguing *hers*, her ears were filled with the indecipherable shrieking of thousands of voices which were not her own, a cacophony of noise pulling and plucking at her attentions like tiny fish in a creek. It was without structure or reason, a deluge of sound that was visible to her inner eye as swirling streaks of color in a darkened void. The primordial assault pulled at her from every direction, unravelling who and what she was like frayed cloth. The more effort she put towards the capture and examination of these phenomenon, the more unstable the world around her became, twisting and lurching like waves driven before a storm but in patterns impossible to predict.

She attempted to ignore them, to close her mind off from the barrage, for even if they meant her no harm, their very existence threatened her ability to function. When that effort yielded no results, she shifted her awareness from their path as one would dodge a runaway horse, but that only caused them to arrive from disturbingly wrong directions. The harder she tried the more her vision twisted into increasingly abstract smears of color that blurred any sense of what was up or down.

To continue her efforts would call into question her sanity. If she could not remove herself from them, then they would have to be redirected from her. To this end, she began to construct a wall around her mind, a barrier of energy not unlike the divine shield she had manifested countless times for her physical defense, deflecting the inescapable torrent away. The glade with its statues righted itself, but while she stood once more on solid ground, the sky above remained filled with chaos.

She pressed more forcefully against it, pushing the sphere of protection outward until both land and sky appeared as they should. The edge between this reality and the one she had forced away remained visible if she stared upwards, but the boundary was fuzzy, less a solid mass than an accumulation of tiny vines of light reaching inward, each seeking to snatch a piece of her for itself. She judged the shield a limited success, because she was soon drifting closer to it once more. With a thought, she realigned the protective barrier around herself. This could have been required because the wall lacked the strength to remain in place. Or, it was equally probable that the point she was attempting to protect—herself— was in motion. Either way, she had provided herself sufficient clarity to devote her mind to other tasks.

Shaken but resolved to solving these puzzles, she set herself to finding an explanation to that overwhelming background noise.

Whatever its source, it was almost certainly tied to whatever events had deposited her here.

As no other suitable starting point presented itself, she began by considering her physical form in hopes of deducing an answer. The overlapping silver scales of her armor wrapped her torso snugly yet were as light as the white robes she had once worn. Her forearms and shins were protected by stiffer plates of the same material, but only the coolness of the air brushed against her thighs and upper arms. No helmet hid the striking blueness of her eyes or restrained her blond hair from curling gently atop her shoulders. Shining Moon, the sacred warhammer of the goddess Eluria, hung on her right hip, as it had for years. Its head was a sphere the size of her clenched fist, with smooth, circular striking faces on opposite sides. Elegant inscriptions and patterns were engraved upon it, elvish glyphs so old that they appeared to be decorative embellishments rather than the symbols that they were.

Given that she was incapable of creating any of it herself, the armor must have been given to her. A different memory interjected itself, adamant that she had stolen it. Yet another recollection insisted that such gifts were worn by a different person entirely.

As she considered the arguments each of the *hers* presented, she drifted between them, inhabiting each thread for a time before moving to the next. She again felt herself slipping into a debilitating uncertainty as she jumped from one Shalindra to the next, wondering which to inhabit. Despite the unpredictability of it, her condition was not as frightening as it should have been. Indeed, there were elements of this situation that logic dictated to be normal, at least at the moment, even though they probably were not.

A stirring deep inside one of the Shalindras demanded her attention. Something that was most assuredly *not* normal, no matter the frame of reference from which it was considered, though it seemed linked to the mystery of her armor. This potential relationship pulled at her curiosity. Her mind began to isolate the abnormality, drawing it together into a spikey, amorphous glob of discontent—a construct contained and held together by bands of her own determination. To her mind's eye, it was dark to the point of being black, and it flickered like glowing coals in the ashes of a simmering fire. As something distinctly unique she sought to identify it, to label it in a manner that made sense to the majority of *hers* that now weighed in on the subject. Their opinions seemed equally split on whether this singularity was a good thing or bad, and indeed if it was a thing at all or something entirely different. It was undeniably a part of her but somehow not, an influence that she recognized as well as any piece of her own body, an amalgamation of what had once been… Tormjere.

Many of the *hers* registered fright at that realization. Others expressed sadness, a few despair. The gamut of their emotions merged into a unified sense of disquiet, reflecting the incongruity of its current state. The mass shifted about while she examined it, as unhappy to be within her as she was to possess it. There was at least broad agreement on one aspect of the thing: it should not be in one place, but distributed throughout herself, as was everything else she had gained.

What had she gained?

She pulled that thought close. Obviously, whatever she had

received was more than she had been prepared for, even if that bounty remained as yet unmeasured. It frustrated her to the point of anger that she could recall so little of what had happened to her.

The calls from the various *hers* grew louder, demanding that this anomaly be rendered and processed—absorbed, as it was clearly meant to be. But she could not bring herself to destroy it so casually and vowed not to consume Tormjere as he had consumed so many demons.

Yet she had, hadn't she, for how else would this part of him reside within her when his body lay nearby? If she had consumed him, and gathered him inside herself, then this had taken place during… the ceremony. This thought brought about great argument from the *hers*, but before they could be addressed, their voices were swept away as she was again buffeted by the noisy, chaotic winds of sound as they curled around the edges of the shield wall as it drifted close to her once more. Everything inside her seemed in motion, necessitating a constant repositioning of the barrier she had constructed.

Everything except that which had been Tormjere. There was only one of those, and it remained where it was, a fixed point within the universe of her mind, bound tightly to only one of her. She centered herself on it, shifting and expanding the mental shield protecting her to radiate outward from it.

Once more insulated from the more tumultuous fringes of her awareness, the memory of the ritual she had participated in coalesced into a singular thread, and so she followed those thoughts as they drew closer to the present, certain it was where she belonged. Her Ascension had been well planned and flawless in execution, but… insufficient. That was it. The observation had importance but was not relevant to this mystery, and so she set it aside for later contemplation. He had been there, with her, and brought…

Pain.

Horrible, indescribable pain. He had hurt Eluria and he had gone, but the two events were not linked in the manner one would first assume. Whatever he had sacrificed had been for her, but her mind refused to focus long enough to produce meaning. Had he died? His body had gone lifeless behind her and she had spun to catch him, then…

The thread of those thoughts slipped away, replaced by a multitude of voices speaking atop each other. Although she was completely alone, she could no more concentrate than if she had been standing in the Glade of Worship, which now teamed with thousands of uncertain celebrants who were—

But how could she know that?

Something tugged insistently at her thoughts, dragging her attention back to the reality in which she stood, to one of the forest paths that linked this sacred clearing to the others. Elothlirial, Manalathlia of Eluria and titular head of all who worshiped the moon, charged angrily into the glade, preceding a flock of other Sisters who were equally impassioned. Armed soldiers poured in from the opposite direction, trapping Shalindra between the two factions. Yet every elf now surrounding her was incorporeal, a shifting figure painted in translucent shades of white upon white.

Was she now remembering her own death?

The ghostly figures began to separate and divide, blurring

around the edges as they fractured into multiple copies of themselves. The doppelgangers did not interact with their own copies but moved in conjunction with those around them.

Shalindra turned her focus to the Sister of Eluria closest to her. Its whitened visage grew more solid, as did the appearance of the other ghosts synchronized to it.

She felt a disconcerting tug on her body, like dough being stretched too thin, and saw that she, too, was separating into translucent versions of herself.

The ghostly Elothlirials spoke at almost the same time, their words slightly different and slightly out of time with each other, but the tone of their demands were all laced with the same unmistakable anger.

Shalindra's skin crawled as the ghost versions of herself answered, and she felt the brush of their lips moving inside hers. She stood as still as possible to minimize the sensation, terrified at the thought of being pulled further apart yet helpless to turn away. Perhaps in response to her lack of action, the number of her ghosts standing there reduced, as did a corresponding number of Elothlirials.

This exchange continued back and forth, the voices and ethereal bodies of the combatants overlapping. The echoes of their words became muddy and faint, though the desires in their hearts betold the ending they sought from this confrontation. No matter what direction she turned, she was greeted only with unavoidable hatred.

Shalindra screamed.

It was a cry against these ghosts tormenting her, a denial of the different versions of herself that argued about who she was, and rage against the uncertainty of all that had been done to her against her will.

Then the ghosts were gone, and she stood alone once more, breathing heavily.

Whether it had been the past or the future which had been forced upon her, Shalindra wanted no part of it ever again. Her wishes, however, had absolutely no effect, as Elothlirial stormed into the clearing in perfect imitation of the visions Shalindra had just witnessed. Her sleeveless robes, a shimmering white tinted with the palest of greens, billowed behind her with the force of her arrival, their delicate fibers now marred and scorched as if she had stood too long near the fire.

At least a dozen Sisters in the white robes of Eluria marched in and spread out behind her. Most Shalindra recognized from the ceremony or the preparations, and each face betrayed a differing mixture of resolve and reluctance.

Given what was about to happen, she counted it a blessing that the elderly Sister Superior Avrilia was not among them. Enna's former mentor, and one of the few in Ildalarial who had shown Shalindra unconditional kindness, did not deserve to witness this strife.

Shalindra glanced behind her towards the only other entrance to the sacred clearing. Soldiers emerged to stand shoulder to shoulder with weapons firmly in hand, exactly as she expected. It was as if she were caught within a lucid dream, reliving a future that had already happened.

Both groups of elves regarded Shalindra warily, perhaps

unsettled by her lack of reaction. She let her eyes wander back down the line of clerics, reading each woman's intentions and fears as if they were her own. One by one, they dropped their gaze, but Elothlirial was too consumed to heed the warning signs staring her in the face.

"You dare to desecrate this temple with his taint?" the priestess demanded, her eyes ablaze. "It is the least of the foul heresies you have committed—you who were bestowed our highest of honors, and against my better judgement—but it will be the last. I will see an end to this farce, and I will suffer no further offense!"

Shalindra had already heard these same words from the shadow version of Elothlirial, and they failed to convey the same venom on the second listening. No argument she raised in her own defense would change what happened next, and so she did not waste effort on it. This was as pointless as it was infuriating. The woman had no idea of what had happened or of what she placed at risk with this confrontation.

As Shalindra waited for the command that would plunge this holy place into chaotic combat, her anger brought the taste of bile to her mouth. How could Elothlirial be so blind? Shalindra wanted to shout at her, to force an understanding of what had transpired onto those who had long since ceased to listen. But she did not, and the present caught up to the future she had witnessed.

A flick of Elothlirial's wrist was the only signal needed to send the soldiers leaping forwards.

Freed of the binding premonitions that had led them all to this point, Shalindra's determination to end this farce overrode all logic. Her fury lashed out, a coiled serpent of mystic command,

and the elvish soldiers' weapons blackened and crumbled to ash, dissipating in their hands like pollen in the wind. To a man, they stopped, their legs rooted in all-consuming fear.

Elothlirial clutched her sacred symbol, her desperate plea for protection echoing faintly in some portion of Shalindra's awareness. But the elf deserved no validation of her actions, nor did the clerics with her who sought the aid of their goddess in her defense. Their invocations became open channels into their minds, granting Shalindra insight into their most private thoughts and feelings. Where they sought strength, she gave weakness. Where they begged for mercy, she supplied terror. Her mental assault was sharp and merciless, leaving every one of the women bereft of strength and even hope. One after another, they tumbled to the ground, too weak to stand. Elothlirial alone remained on her feet, though she wobbled uncertainly.

"You lack an understanding of what has happened," Shalindra stated, some part of her still trying to change the outcome which she knew to be unavoidable.

"He violated our goddess!" Elothlirial screeched, taking an involuntary step back. "Do not claim that you had no part in it, you vile abomination!"

"Neither of us knew. Eluria gave us—"

"Do not take Her name in vain! He was a thief who—"

"Gave himself!" Shalindra snapped in a voice that rolled like thunder between the trees. "Not his love, not his life, *his very existence*. Look upon me and tell me you could have done the same!"

The command hit Elothlirial like a slap. Her eyes widened in surprise, which turned to inescapable panic as Shalindra sent herself plunging into them. The priestess sought to turn away but could not, her numb fingers fumbling as Eluria's symbol slipped from them. The deepest crevasses of her soul were laid bare, and Shalindra bored into places the elf would never allow her own mind to go, seizing the secrets she had hidden even from herself. Dark wings of fear wrapped the elvish matriarch in an unearthly solitude as every sin and failing of her entire life was dragged screaming into the light and hung before her in a tapestry of shame.

A wail of abject terror was torn from Elothlirial's lips as she collapsed to her knees. "Forgive me! You know I could not!"

Shalindra did know, because she had lived exactly what Tormjere had subjected himself to. None of those around her could have endured what he had. None would have been willing, even had they been capable. They could not even comprehend such a selfless act, and so they would be shown the burning pain he had endured as he tore himself apart for her.

It was through the raw turbulence of her rage that a different note carried. It arrived from no discernable source—a voice as clear and cool as a mountain stream, and somehow familiar. Shalindra allowed her perceptions to narrow to that one sound. She examined it, turning it over in her mind like a smith inspecting his work, and with it she beheld herself clearly from a different perspective.

The Guardian stood as a figure of vengeance, radiant and filled with justified purpose. Light blazed from her eyes and from between the silver scales of her armor, the only brightness in the dark that blotted out everything around them and left those in attendance abasing themselves in blind terror. From this altered perspective, she felt a desire, a need—not for the power to change what was happening nor for protection from its effects. Only for mercy upon those who were beyond hope of seeking it themselves.

Shalindra shrank from such a depiction of herself. What was she doing? She had no cause to strike out so forcefully. The image of her Sisters cowering on the ground filled her with a sudden revulsion, and her anger broke. The glade resumed its pleasant atmosphere so quickly that all in it were left befuddled, wondering if what they had witnessed had really happened.

"Please, rise," she said kindly, taking Elothlirial's hand and helping her to her feet. "You have been a faithful follower of your goddess for so many years. There is no shame in our imperfections. Such sacrifices as were made are incomprehensible to all who have never given the same."

"I do not understand," Elothlirial said, clutching Shalindra's hand as a drowning woman would cling to a log.

Shalindra was mortified by the desperation in the woman's voice, but she forced herself to smile. She let her calmness radiate through them, easing their fears and dispelling their doubts, even though her ability to influence their emotions was frightening in its effortlessness.

"I have many questions, as do you," she said. "Please, allow me time to put order to all that has been changed. The continued well-being of Ildalarial is as important to me as it is to you."

They nodded as if it made sense, and perhaps it did in some way. Then they turned, cleric and soldier alike, and walked from the glade like sleepy children.

When they were gone, Shalindra sought the place from which

she had looked upon herself, and found Enna standing there.

Blue eyes met green, each woman searching for something from the other. Within those azure depths of Shalindra's eyes, Enna saw hints of the frightening turmoil inside the human woman who had become her closest friend before being converted to something far more. Yet what she had just witnessed was more akin to a toddler lashing out than a woman as in control of herself as Shalindra always had been, and that assault had rendered impotent the most powerful clerics in all of Ildalarial.

Enna approached her slowly, not out of fear but concern, fighting all the while to keep her eyes away from Tormjere. She would surely fall apart at the sight, and now was a time to remain strong. Whatever loss she was feeling, Shalindra must have felt tenfold more.

Before she could offer words of comfort, Shalindra flung her arms around her and cried with unconstrained anguish. The trees of the forest wilted with her like flowers in grief, and the agony of her loss threatened to swallow every glimmer of hope that existed in the world.

Enna clutched Shalindra to her with trembling hands as would a child consoling a parent who had collapsed unexpectedly into despair. She bit her tongue and screwed shut her eyes but, unable to stifle the torrent of emotion that Shalindra's sobs had released inside her, she succumbed to her own grief once more.

Around them, the statues of the former Guardians gazed down in silent compassion.

There was no telling how long they clung to each other in this way. When Shalindra at last withdrew, her face was unmarred by puffiness and her eyes without hint of the tears that lay wet on Enna's shoulder.

"What are we to do?" Enna asked, at last finding her voice, if not the conciliatory words she meant to offer.

"That is a question I continue to ask myself." Shalindra looked to the heavens. "My Ascension… was not what any of us intended."

Enna tried to force her thoughts to remain in the present but found herself reliving the events of yesterday yet again. "I do not understand what he thought to accomplish."

"Neither do I, though I know why he did it."

Enna waited anxiously for more, but instead Shalindra drifted distractedly in a circle as if she was participating in some silent conversation. The perplexing behavior left Enna suddenly alone, and her lip trembled as her head was pulled involuntarily towards Tormjere. A tightness in her chest stifled her breathing as her feet carried her to his side.

She wanted to hit him, to strike him hard enough to force him to cease this charade and get up, but all she could manage was to place her hand softly on him. There was still warmth beneath her fingertips, and firmness. He felt exactly as he should, except that his chest did not rise and fall. It was an unnatural stillness, an absence of life that was surreal in its undeniability. There was so much she wanted him to know, so many things that should have been said but now could not be. It was a minor comfort that at least he lay where he should, in a fitting resting place for someone so devoted to the Guardian he was meant to protect. Yet he deserved so much more.

She almost jumped at the sound of Shalindra's soft words at her shoulder. "What has happened here must be dealt with, but now is not the time."

"And for those who await their Guardian?" Enna asked, again surprising herself with the practicality of her question. It was not something that Shalindra should be worried about at a time like this, but the throngs who had gathered for her appearance had to be told something, and that message did not need to come from Enna's mother.

"Inform them that I seek Eluria's wisdom and will not emerge until it has been properly conveyed. That should buy us time."

"Time for what?" Enna asked, looking back at Tormjere. There was no need to see Shalindra's face to feel the anguish in her answer.

"I do not know."

Chapter Four

No Time for Sorrow

Enna barely noticed her surroundings as she carried the tray of uneaten food up the path through the gathering dusk. The evening was just as pleasant as the prior two had been, though the weather was the only thing in Ildalarial behaving as it should. She could have been locked within the conflicts of the human kingdoms rather than the tranquility which normally wrapped her homeland. Nothing had been the same since the ceremony.

The trail climbed gently away from Lana Ariiliar—the Glade of Guardians, in the human tongue—and up through the temple forest. It was odd that she switched between the names so easily. Though she had lived among humans for only a brief span of years, she was already more used to conversing in their manner than her own. Her people's ways were more open and free than those of the rest of the world, and tightly coupled to the natural rhythms of nature, but they had never *felt* different. Elvish temples of Elurithlia were not bounded by walls or roofs, nor did they contain statues or fountains. The human propensity for solemnity and decoration over openness and laughter was a constant source of both aggravation and amusement, though at times it seemed far more sincere than how she had been raised.

Her foot scuffed over a root—the same one that she had tripped over so many times as a child—pulling her from her reverie. The shadows of evening wrapped the forest around her, leaving the towering trees as quiet and contemplative as they had ever been. Yet the dry rustling of leaves carried with it a hint of unease, as if the woods themselves disliked the early changing of the seasons. She longed for a return to a simpler time when the reverent silence of this trail had offered its promise of wonder and majesty, but there was no way to reclaim that innocence.

A flash of white on the trail ahead signaled the approach of a trio of Sisters descending towards the sacred clearing she had so recently departed. The pair of young Sisters in the front worked quietly, one pushing poles into the ground and the other topping them with large candles. Enna recognized neither of them, but the wrinkled, grey-haired cleric who supervised their actions was as familiar to her as her own mother.

Avrilia, the most senior of the elder Sisters and one of the longest-serving women on Elurithlia's Calontier, evaluated the tray as Enna came to a stop before her. "She still does not eat?"

Enna shrugged as if it did not matter but was unable to force any lightness into her voice. "She will when she is hungry."

Avrilia waved the younger women forward. "Continue, Sisters, but do not enter Lana Ariiliar."

Enna stepped aside as the two clerics continued down the trail, both avoiding her eyes as they passed. She had no idea why, but the slight bothered her.

"I've never seen candles used within the temple," Enna said as she watched them place the next pole into the ground. Illumination on the path had always been achieved by divine lights rendered with the blessings of their goddess. The two girls lighting candles should have been honing their devotions by calling those lights into place.

"Much light has gone out of the world." Avrilia waited until the girls moved further away, then her manner shifted to one of concern. "Three days without food or water?"

"With all that has happened…" Enna did not finish, for whatever words she produced would surely come out like a lie. She looked away. "I don't know, Avrilia. I don't know why she doesn't eat, or sleep, or go anywhere."

"Well, you need to be doing all of those things even if our Guardian does not."

Enna managed a half-smile. "Thank you for naming her so."

"Our feelings pale in comparison to those of our Mistress. Shalindra was made Guardian, no matter what happened after." Avrilia plucked a grape from the tray and chewed thoughtfully. "Does she continue to speak to you?"

"It varies every day, and she is…" Enna almost said 'confused,' but that would have been unkind no matter how accurate. "…distracted."

"Have you considered your mother's offer?"

She shook her head emphatically. "I have no desire to speak to her. Not after what she tried to do."

"Emotions were raw," Avrilia cautioned, "and decisions were

made rashly."

Enna made no effort to keep the bitterness from her voice. "It was the opportunity she wanted all along."

"That may be, but you cannot deny that your mother put every possible effort into the Ascension, as did we all. Our Manalathlia she remains, and the faithful continue to look towards her for guidance. In the absence of other voices, they believe her when she says that Elurithlia has abandoned us because of our mistakes."

"By allowing a human Guardian, you mean."

Avrilia laid a hand on her shoulder. "Ennathalerial, you cannot refute all that has changed. Our world is altered. You need look no further than the candles we place along this path for proof. This is no false pretense—we are unable to call upon our Mistress as we once could. Not for Her guidance, not for daily blessings, nor even simple illumination. Our restorations have become so ineffective that they are barely possible, and we must struggle to make do with bandages and herbs like the healers of old. That She is absent is not in question."

"Perhaps this is a normal after-effect of the ceremony."

Avrilia remained patient. "There is no mention of such a condition in any account we possess, and you have studied them as thoroughly as I."

Enna did not want to believe any of it, though she trusted Avrilia more than any of her elvish kin. She lifted her eyes heavenward. Even in the dim glow of the candles she recognized branches that she had walked beneath countless evenings as a girl, calling forth the same lights that were now denied. She whispered the prayer for it almost without thought, and a small globe of soft, pure light appeared exactly where it should.

Avrilia marveled at that accomplishment. "You were always stronger in Her light than the rest of us, and it does my heart good to know She still listens."

"She is still here," Enna said. "She must be. Avrilia, I do not pretend to understand what took place between Her and Shalindra during the Ascension, and I am not certain that Shalindra knows either, but—"

Avrilia's eyes came alight with sudden intensity, and she seized Enna's arm. "Say that to no one else! It is enough of a strain on our faith that our Mistress is absent. We cannot afford weakness and indecision. There must be purpose to the Guardian's actions."

"But—"

The old cleric's face grew somehow more foreboding. "And the Guardian will not find answers in Ildalarial. You know your mother well enough to understand this. Should the Guardian remain here, there will be strife. It grows more certain with every passing day. The guards posted outside this temple are not there to ensure the Guardian's privacy."

Enna knew that her former tutor was correct. There was no telling what effect such an admission of indecision could have. That level of honesty might throw the entire church into despair. Enna was well aware of the whispered rumors that had begun to circulate, no matter how hard she tried to hold herself apart. Her mother would not allow the situation to continue as it was for much longer.

Not that they could stop Shalindra from doing whatever she wished. That much had already been made clear. Enna chastised herself for such unkind feelings, disappointed that the frustrations of the past few days were getting to her. But if Shalindra were to turn and run… "What else can she do but leave and be cast as a villain who has turned her back on Ildalarial?"

Avrilia looked past Enna's shoulder and spoke quickly. "We do not need a Guardian to save us from ourselves, and she does not need to be distracted by our petty jealousies. No Guardian has ever fulfilled their destiny by sitting here in Ildalarial. You are the only one of us whom she listens to. You must stay true to the old customs and remain at her side no matter what she chooses, or what is chosen for her."

Enna began to speak but held her tongue as the other Sisters returned.

"Never forget where you belong," Avrilia said, stepping back. "Stay strong, in Her light."

The two girls failed to meet Enna's gaze once more as they followed Avrilia up the path, but neither missed the glowing light now floating above their heads.

Enna looked up at it as well. Their Mistress had not abandoned them. She might not be responding as She should, or rather, as She normally did, but there had to be a better reason for it than anger at Shalindra's Ascension.

Enna dispelled the light with a thought, leaving only the ambiance of the flickering candles to stave off the night. With a final glance after the departed women, she spun on her heel and hurried back to Shalindra.

Chapter Five

What Must be Done

Enna's steps were quick as she returned to Shalindra, but she forced herself to slow to a pace more in line with the reverence that so holy a place demanded. There were no candles here to light the clearing. Other than herself, no Sister of Elurithlia had set foot in the clearing since her mother's disastrous attempt to confront Shalindra days before. Yet, as with every night since the Ascension, the clearing was illuminated by soft lights floating in the air above each of the past Guardians. Shalindra stood as motionless as those statues surrounding her, facing the depiction of Illathalirial, as she so often did.

Tormjere's equally inert body, as unchanged as the day he had been placed there, drew Enna's eye as she approached, causing her steps to falter beneath a sudden upwelling of emotion. No matter how grateful she was to see him so lifelike, it was unnatural. She still expected him to rise at any moment, to make some annoyingly accurate observation about their current predicament, as he always did. But he did not. The world was so empty without him.

"It is indeed," Shalindra said, turning to face her.

Enna started in surprise. Were her thoughts so transparent? The argument she had been prepared to make slipped away, forgotten, and her mind stumbled as a dozen questions tumbled over themselves. The one that reached her mouth was, as was happening far too often lately, uninspired. "How do you feel?"

Shalindra's gaze returned to the statue of Illathalirial, the fifth and most powerful Guardian, and the one for whom Enna had been named. "That is a surprisingly difficult question to answer."

Enna sat the tray of food on the grass. At least Shalindra was speaking today, which she considered a good sign. If Enna could not get her to eat, perhaps she would be able to get her to listen. "With everything that has happened since the ceremony, I am not surprised. It is so much to take in so quickly."

"Everything…" Shalindra's voice trailed off, and Enna worried that she would slip back into the distracted state in which she had stood for days. Shalindra blinked. "I am sorry. I did not mean to allow my thoughts to wander."

"There is much to think about."

"There is. I have stood before each of the statues, seeking to learn what I could from them."

"Do they speak to you?" Enna asked, curious and nervous at the same time.

"Not directly. They served to… bring back memories." Shalindra frowned at some thought, and her voice became distant. "I often wonder why I feel such an attachment to Illathalirial, more so than to any of the others. The bond is more intimate than kinship, but not one of true affection. It is one of a hundred mysteries that I possess no ability to unravel, for every thread reveals only a deeper secret. So much of me has changed that at times I hardly recognize myself."

"You are Shalindra," Enna said, trying to conceal how unsettling such comments were. She had expected Shalindra to emerge from her Ascension different than she had been—that was the intent, after all—but she was like an entirely different person now.

"I think I am. But I am also something more." She was silent for a time, and then gave voice to the question Enna had been too timid to ask. "You wish to know what was done to me?"

Enna did, more than anything. But even with so direct an offer she demurred, hesitant to intrude. "I want to know that what happened was for a reason and not for some arbitrary influence. We have been through so much, and for it to end like this…"

"Struggle is something we have all known and will be required to deal with again. Sit with me, please."

Shalindra took a seat in the grass and seemed to notice the tray of food for the first time. She took an apple in her hand and studied it before taking a bite, almost like she was remembering what to do with it.

Enna crossed her legs as she sat, welcoming the invitation even as her stomach fluttered apprehensively. She bit her lip, then plunged ahead. "When Tormjere… He should not have been able to join you. The wards surrounding you were impregnable, set by Elurithlia Herself to prevent any contamination of Her blessings."

Shalindra's eyes lost focus, then regained it before she responded. "You have just answered your own riddle. She told me he was coming."

"So, She allowed him in?"

"It would seem that way. It is what he did afterwards that I struggle to fully grasp."

"I confess my confusion as well, Guardian." Enna hesitated again, but Shalindra deserved to know what was being said about her. "My mother claims that he violated Elurithlia somehow, but he was a good man who would never—"

"She is correct, though not for the reasons she believes."

Enna could not have been more stunned. "Did he succumb to the demons' influence at last?"

"No. He was free of the darker desires that his time in their company left him. Our efforts were successful in that regard, at least. He knew exactly what he was doing, and I believe it was Eluria who asked him to do it." Shalindra's eyes shifted to hers with an intensity that seemed to burn right through her. "He wished for me to receive more than your ceremony was capable of providing, to have… to have what he thought I deserved. He took what he felt was needed from Eluria, in the same way as he drew strength from the demons he had killed."

Enna rocked back, mortified. That such a terrible thing was even possible left her weak and filled her with disgust. Her mouth worked silently as rage and sorrow competed to see which would burst forth.

"Such was my initial reaction as well," Shalindra said. "Though as terrible as that seems, in the end he did the same to himself."

"What!"

"Memory by memory, piece by piece, he tore himself apart.

For me."

"How could he have done such a thing?"

Shalindra's shoulders slumped. Her eyes grew moist, and suddenly she was the same woman as she had been before the Ascension: one who had lost every bit as much as Enna had. "He… It is painful to speak of."

"Then do not," Enna said hurriedly. "I should not have pried."

Shalindra wrestled to compose herself before continuing. "Though all of this may sound like an explanation, it is more accurately a retelling of events. You asked why, and that is the same question I have been attempting to answer without success. I have been changed in ways that I cannot measure or describe, nor can I guess at its ultimate effects upon me."

"Guardian?" Enna asked. "Have you sought Elurithlia's guidance?"

Shalindra's eyes closed, and a spasm of sorrow flashed across her face. Fearing that she had triggered some remembered pain, Enna rushed ahead. "While She has been absent for many, for you she would surely be able to…"

Chapter Six

A Meeting of Equals

Shalindra stood alone on the curving floor of an amphitheater seemingly cut from a single, immense block of the whitest marble. She did not know where she was, or rather, she knew where she was but not where the place itself existed. It was a curious paradox, but only a minor concern compared to *why* she was now here. Enna had given voice to exactly what needed to happen, yet Shalindra feared to confront a god who had been damaged by what she and Tormjere had unwittingly done.

But she could hide from it no longer, and that realization had brought her here.

The stone around her was clean and pure to the point of being sterile, yet it held an element of warmth and comfort. The temperature was neither hot nor cold, as the air was neither dry nor damp. Around the perimeter, smooth columns rose at pleasing intervals to disappear into the insubstantial fog above. Terraced steps from which an audience might gaze down upon her rose in concentric levels before fading into the same milky haze. The opaque whiteness surrounding the amphitheater did not mask her vision as would a morning mist in the forest, there was simply nothing further to be seen. It was as if she occupied a partial construction, a sliver of reality that was not fully realized yet was perfectly suited to her needs.

Dominating the stage behind her was an oval pool of water raised from the floor by a series of sculpted figures, each bent nearly in two as they carried its weight upon their backs. Shalindra wandered closer and leaned against the edge as she stared into it. Though contained in a vessel no deeper than her forearm, the liquid was as dark as midnight and as bottomless as the ocean, and in its mirrored reflections she beheld the movements of the celestial bodies on an incomprehensibly vast scale. The motions of the stars and planets were as slow as sap running down a tree in winter, but their travels were mesmerizing in their coordination. Each of the tiny objects possessed a name, which she was certain she knew, but remained unable to recall.

"Your arrival was surprisingly quick."

Shalindra turned towards the richly toned voice. On the opposite side of the pool, where before there had been no one, an elf now stood. Or, at least, something that had taken the form of an elf. His slight frame was garbed in the layered greens and browns that might have pronounced him a Woodswarden, though the patterns stitched into the materials were intricate enough to be considered formal. His beardless features were more finely chiseled than any elf that she had seen, and his ears tapered to a longer and more delicate point. She had never beheld him before, and yet she had known him since the beginning of time.

"Lithandris," she said, dipping her head politely to the god of the forests. "I did not expect to meet you here."

"The same could I say about you. You display a surprising amount of resilience given that which has transpired."

"You are aware of what has taken place?" she asked, matching his light tone as if she conversed with gods on an unremarkably frequent basis.

"I was shown enough. We do not commerce with our knowledge the way mortals do, yet some things are shared."

She knew that, of course. She was already aware of the means with which the gods communicated with each other, a fact that stood in sharp contradiction to the newness of this experience.

"I have come seeking Eluria. Where is she?"

Lithandris circled the pool with unhurried steps. "I find it fascinating that you did not first seek to learn where you are, or how you might return to where you should be."

"You avoid my question."

Lithandris stopped, his eyes sparkling with amusement. "And that you are not the least bit flustered in my presence. I confess that I normally elicit a more profound response from those of your race, when I have occasion to meet them. To answer you, then: she whom you know as Eluria cannot engage with you in the present."

"By her choice, or yours?"

His brow creased, though a raised eyebrow indicated his approval of the question. "Ours. She is badly depleted at a time when we can ill afford her weakness."

The thought of Eluria in distress was a cause for sorrow, but it was a sadness tempered by a multitude of perspectives. There were layers of reasons for this attitude—a few of which even made sense—but they did not need to be enumerated. That such a statement should have affected her more profoundly than it did was more distressing than the news itself.

"Harming her was never my intent," Shalindra said. "Had I known it was even possible, I would never have wished to become her champion."

"In this, we all of us were taken unawares," Lithandris said. "Your companion"—Shalindra felt a sharp twinge of annoyance at that reference—"possessed a singular ability to do the wrong things so perfectly well. What he gave to you, the gift which allows you to stand here in this place, impressed even us."

Shalindra struggled to hold her impatience in check. It was a hollow comfort that Tormjere had been able to surprise the gods, and irrelevant to why she had come. They had instigated a calamity, and it was something she intended to see resolved. "While this revelation is comforting, you remain other than who I need to see, and you do not strike me as a simple messenger."

"Yet a message is what I have to offer you," Lithandris replied with a cock of his head. "Combine what you know with the knowledge of those who have gone before you and of those who walk beside you, and you will come to the correct resolution."

"The wisdom of the fallen," Shalindra breathed. "Why can you not tell me yourself instead of giving me riddles?"

Lithandris smiled ruefully. "Because I do not know. You will find, as you spend time here, that we each keep our secrets."

She was convinced that he was keeping something from her now, and so she directed at him a question certain to cause discomfort. "Am I a god, then?"

His hesitation, though slight, revealed that she had been accurate in her aim. "Not yet."

"You say that as if the outcome was a foregone conclusion."

"It may be, or perhaps not. We find ourselves in a most peculiar situation. But you should know with all certainty that you are not the god Eluria was."

"And I do not wish to become the god she will continue to be." Her words were instinctive, but she found herself questioning them almost before they were said. Eluria had been wounded far more deeply than she had suspected, and if it had been to a degree that frightened the gods themselves, what would happen should Eluria not recover?

"A noble position, and yet already have you begun to fill the void of Eluria's absence."

"It has been only a few days since my Ascension," Shalindra protested, "and I have yet to do anything beyond attempt to understand what has happened within myself."

"Time is different for us," Lithandris reminded her, "as is life, and death, and distance. Many are the tasks we perform without conscious thought."

He remained outwardly calm, but she saw all the signs that he was worried. Shalindra felt like a pawn in a game she had never even known was being played.

"Am I such an abomination as to frighten you?" she asked.

"No," he answered, just a little too quickly. "You are, however, an anomaly."

"How then is this happening?" She allowed a trace of the panic he likely expected from her to lend a tiny quiver to her voice. "My purpose was not to become a god."

The barest relaxing of his shoulders betrayed his relief, though his words did not. "Nor did we desire such an outcome. And yet it is happening."

"I do not want it to." There was no subterfuge to that. She had taken on the mantle of Guardian with reluctance and had never imagined there could be any greater burdens to carry.

"Then set yourself to your task and follow it to its conclusion, whatever that may be. It is not given for me to know where you must go, but go you must, and soon. Yours is not the only interest at play here."

It was far less of an answer than she wanted, but she did not doubt the sincerity of his sentiment. She could not remain in one place, hoping to puzzle out who and what she now was. The time for waiting was past, and she felt the urgency of his words as if her world had told her itself. Something was not right, and that wrongness was hers to resolve.

"When next you see Eluria, you may tell her that I will continue my efforts to fulfill her prophecy, and I hope that she is sufficiently recovered to speak to me when I return."

"I am certain she awaits that meeting as eagerly as do you."

She dipped her head politely once more in parting, and the whiteness swept everything away.

Chapter Seven

Uncertain Direction

"…guide your direction," Enna completed her sentence.

Shalindra's eyes snapped open, and she was again in the Glade of Guardians, sitting in the grass beside Enna. Or, more probably, she had returned to the Shalindra who had remained there. It was equally possible that the entire exchange with Lithandris had existed only in her mind, something she would have considered delusional not long ago. The potential to exist in multiple places at the same time was a difficult concept to wrap her thoughts around but, as with so many things, she could only hope there would be more time to unravel that later. She rose to her feet, possessed by a need to act.

"What is it?" Enna asked, scrambling up with her.

"I know the nature of what has befallen Eluria, and I am aware of the direction I must proceed."

Enna frowned in confusion. "But, you just said… Do you not wish to speak with Her?"

"I did seek her out, though I was greeted instead by one who spoke in her name. There is good reason that she has not responded to the prayers of the faithful as she normally would, and it is a condition which has everything to do with my Ascension."

"My mother was correct then," Enna said, crestfallen. "We have angered Her with our actions, no matter how noble our purpose."

Shalindra shook her head. "She is not angry with any of us. She is wounded, drained. I suspect the damage she suffered was far more extensive than anything she had expected."

"How badly?" Enna asked, her face ashen. "Will Her strength return?"

There was a note of desperation in her voice, and one of disbelief. Shalindra could understand her dismay, and her unspoken plea for reassurance. The answer Lithandris had left her with was less than descriptive but terrifying in its ramifications. If there was even the possibility that Eluria could be replaced as the goddess of the moon, then it could only mean that she was dying. The chaos such a revelation would inflict would be cataclysmic. No one—not even Enna—could be told of that possibility.

"I am certain that it will," she said reassuringly, then turned the conversation in a safer direction. "But it is time for me to proceed in the direction I have been given. I must seek the wisdom of the fallen."

Enna took a deep breath as she composed herself, then glanced at the statues surrounding them. "The fallen Guardians? You will find no more authoritative record of their words than those texts we hold here in Ildalarial. I have read many of them myself and I'm at a loss to think of what they might reveal that has not already been discovered. The works span millennia, but much has been lost over the centuries, and some has simply faded to legend."

"In this I am not surprised," Shalindra said thoughtfully. "However, it was also made clear to me that I must not stay here nor attempt do this alone; rather, I must do so with 'those who walked beside me.' As you are already here, that could only have referred to others who have helped in the past."

"Surely that would mean Honarch or Birion?" Enna suggested.

Or Tormjere. That was who Shalindra needed most, but he was gone. If his aid was beyond reach, who then could possibly help them? Honarch's magical perspective might be helpful, and Birion was as practical and dependable as a knight should be, but neither was likely to hold the answer.

Perhaps she should seek Treven's aid. The blind Legitarso of Amalthee was as wise a man as she had ever met, and he was a conduit for knowledge that no other possessed. Honarch and Birion were, as Enna suggested, the obvious choice to help with that, and it was fortuitous as they were already on the way to—

"Yes! And they are already travelling in the proper direction."

Enna gave her a quizzical look. "Where are they going? They should've been back in Newlmir weeks ago."

Shalindra was unsure of where such a leap in logic had come from. She put her hand to her head. Enna was right. When the group had parted ways, the two men had planned to escort the Ildalarian Woodswardens north to the elvish nation of Silvalaria and from there return home to the valley beneath the Three Sisters. Why *would* she now think that they were elsewhere, and if they were indeed headed towards her, then what was their destination?

A memory brushed against a thought as it wove through a dream, then solidified into a mental image. A city nestled into the crook of a mountain, bordered on three sides by a river fed from a tall, thin waterfall. Honarch and Birion were there—or had been there? Would be there?—which meant they were heading towards...

"We must go to Fallhaven."

"Fallhaven? I spent a short time there the year before I met you, but it is an unremarkable place with only the tiniest collection of artifacts. What would they know of the Guardians that we in Ildalarial would not?"

"It is difficult to explain, but Honarch and Birion will be in Fallhaven soon."

"I will take you at your word, but why there? Fallhaven is not on the way to anywhere."

"Because that is where I told them to meet us."

Enna placed her hands on her hips. "Forgive me, Guardian, but when did you tell them this? We haven't seen either of them in months, not since boarding the boats in Rivermist to come here."

Shalindra began to pace, unhappy at the convenient randomness of these thoughts. Were they even hers, or was she being manipulated somehow? Neither of those possibilities seemed accurate, but she was at a loss for why she was thinking this way. "I am not entirely certain. My thoughts organize themselves in unusual ways, but I believe that I communicated with Honarch through the dohedron."

"That little sparkly thing Tormjere was always poking at?

When did you use it?"

Shalindra went to Tormjere's still body and plucked the device from a pouch on his belt. She could remember with absolute certainty having held it only once, and that was all the way back in Newlmir. Yet she also had a very distinct recollection of employing it to tell Honarch what needed to be done. But looking at it now, she was less certain.

She handed it to Enna. "Bring it with us, and we will use it to check with him again."

"When are we to leave?"

"Now," Shalindra said, already moving. Her feet were almost on the trail that led from the clearing when she realized Enna had yet to move. She looked back and saw Enna rooted in place, hurt and disbelief in her eyes.

"Is there to be no burial for him?"

And, just that quickly, Shalindra was brought slamming down into herself: a woman who had gained exactly what she had been seeking and lost what she cared about most in the process. The sudden shift left her woozy, and her trembling hand reached for something solid on which to steady herself. Her eyes squeezed shut, fighting to contain the tears as waves of emotion tossed her back and forth. What was happening to her? How could she care so little one moment and so much the next? It hurt so much that she desired nothing but to collapse upon on the grass and cry until she woke from this terrible dream which ensnared her.

When she gathered herself enough to open her eyes again, she found her hand resting against the statue of the first Guardian, a woman whose name so closely matched her own, and who had given the first words of the prophecy:

When Her gifts follow the blood moon west
A Guardian shall ascend
To walk as two where only one may tread
And with the wisdom of the fallen
End that which should never have begun

How much more of that prophecy would Shalindra be forced to endure? Mortified that she had come so close to leaving Tormjere lying there, she sucked a deep breath of air into her lungs and turned to face Enna. "He must have that. Enna, this thing that has happened to me…"

"None of us understand," Enna finished for her. There was sympathy, if not acceptance, in her words. Shalindra could not forgive herself either. No matter what had been done to her, she had to remember who she was.

She returned to stand beside him and gazed down at the man who had always given so much, and so selflessly, for her. He could have been sleeping, except that he rarely slept at all, and when he did so, he was always alert, and watching over her.

The thought brought a small smile to her face. She would not consign his body to the ground. He deserved better than that—deserved to be remembered here for what he had given. She brushed a tangle of his wild hair from his face and straightened the pouch she had disturbed when removing the dohedron.

In silent agreement, Enna began to do the same. Together they prepared him for his repose, working in silence to gently arrange his few possessions. At the last, Shalindra removed his sword so that Enna could fold his arms across his chest. Their work complete, their hands withdrew reluctantly from his body, but neither woman moved away.

Whether by command or of its own free will, the fibers of the dais grew like water flowing up a hill, slowly encasing him in a sarcophagus of carved wood that preserved every detail of the man who lay inside. Glowing lines of silvery blue traced their way across the highlights and edges of the tomb and pulsed softly before fading into the wood. Shalindra considered it a fitting tribute.

"His body will remain undisturbed until our return. He hates ceremonies, but when the time is right, everyone will know what he gave for us."

Tears streaked down Enna's cheeks, but her jaw tightened, and she whispered a silent vow. Shalindra went to dab at her own eyes and became aware that she still held Tormjere's sword in her hands. Unwilling to leave it behind and without anywhere to store it, she buckled it about her waist. It settled comfortably on her left hip opposite Shining Moon.

The balance of the two weapons was a marked contrast to how unbalanced her world now was. She was certain that order could be restored, she just needed more time. As always, the thing she needed most had been denied to her, and while her decisions might steer her in this way or that, she could no more alter her course than could a boat caught in the midst of a rapids.

Shalindra was already weary of it as she turned away from Tormjere and took her first steps towards an uncertain destination.

Chapter Eight

Once More Into the Night

The path they followed away from the Guardians was narrow and unlit, climbing a short hill towards the edge of the temple forest. Shalindra considered it odd that the other trails of the temple had been provided with candles while this one was left dark. Regardless, she could see where she was going, as the moon had waned only slightly from the fullness it displayed during her Ascension.

The trail emerged from a thin gap in the trees, nondescript enough that it could be easily missed from the outside were it not for the small wooden pedestal carved with the image of Shining Moon. Tonight, however, more than just a marker awaited them.

Fully a dozen elves armed with short blades and armored in padded leathers stood guard at the exit. Only one faced inward, and Shalindra was almost upon him before catching his notice. He leapt to attention with a terse warning to his comrades.

"Guardian," the senior elf said respectfully as he came to her. "I am Captain Engolar, at your service. How may I aid your travel?"

Shalindra suspected they were here more to keep tabs on her than to protect her solitude, and she had neither the desire nor time for an escort.

"I should be able to find my way on my own. I do not think I have anything to fear in this city."

"I agree, Guardian, but it will hasten your travel and ensure order if we assist."

Shalindra began to decline more forcefully but was stopped by Enna's hand on her arm.

"He's likely correct," she said, nodding towards the street beyond the guards. "They are all here waiting on you."

The streets, normally brightened by cool, pure light, were unusually dark, with flickering torches and makeshift fire pits casting an unfamiliar orange glow. Despite the late hour, the thoroughfare was far from empty. Hundreds of elves slept huddled beneath blankets or propped against each other to ward off the chill in the air. Others milled about or spoke quietly in small groups.

Engolar began to speak again but was interrupted by a shout from behind.

"Alta Suralia!" a woman cried, shattering the calm.

The crowd surged to its feet in excitement. Engolar barked an order, and the guards leapt in front of Shalindra, locking arms to form a barrier. The space before them became crammed full, and they were soon straining against the press of bodies.

Enna gave her a worried glance, but Shalindra was not about to retreat to her isolation.

"The nearest stables," she said to Engolar. "Sister Enna and I require horses."

Engolar signaled, and the guards folded back around her and Enna. Another command, and they were moving forward with both women hunched between them.

Many in the crowd did their best to allow room for them to squeeze through, but others pressed close, clamoring for her attention. Some shouted questions, while others pleaded for help.

The mass of people continued to swell, becoming so dense that the guards had to muscle their way through. The need for such force was upsetting. Shalindra should be doing something to justify their adoration rather than plowing her way through. She slowed, hoping to avoid injury to anyone in their path, but Enna's hand on her back kept her moving.

Shalindra stood erect and affected a cheerful smile, which had an immediate impact. She did not shy away from the arms that extended over and around the guards, and her brief touch to their hands spread a calming effect to those she passed. The press of the crowd eased, and the procession shuffled forward without further conflict.

The stables were only one street over from the temple, but it seemed to take forever to reach them. At Engolar's insistent knock, a bleary-eyed elf opened the door then snapped awake as he caught sight of Shalindra.

"Guardian," he said, bowing low. "This is truly a joy. You honor my humble stables with your presence."

"The honor is surely well deserved, Horsewarden Venorden." She surprised herself with her knowledge of his name but did not dwell on it. "I apologize for waking you."

He bowed again. "It is no imposition. How may I assist?"

A winged steed would be the most useful, but she caught herself before asking for anything so unreasonable. Such things lay in the realm of fairy tales.

"Sister Enna and I require two fast horses, though I am unsure when I might see to their return."

Venorden clasped his hands together. "You will have the finest that I own. When do you need them?"

"Now, if it is not too much of an imposition."

If her request surprised the man, he hid it expertly. "Not at all, Revered Guardian. I will see them readied myself."

He was lying about the imposition, but it eased her mind knowing that the temple would reimburse him for his efforts. Enna stood by a window, her brows knit in worry as she watched the crowds, which had thankfully remained in the street.

The Horsewarden returned a short time later leading a pair of saddled horses. "Not knowing how far you intend to travel, I've packed everything you need for their care in their bags. The sorrel carries two days' feed for both, though they'll be as happy to graze."

"Your forethought is much appreciated," Shalindra said, and they mounted quickly. "May her light shine over you and your family."

Venorden bowed again.

A clatter of hooves greeted them as they emerged from the stables, signaling the arrival of a troop of mounted soldiers. Engolar pulled himself into the saddle of a riderless horse that was brought to him and turned to Shalindra. "Revered Guardian, my men and I are again at your disposal. Where are we bound?"

Shalindra did not need an escort of such size and certainly did not want them accompanying her everywhere she went. The captain was only doing what he thought best, however, and it would serve no point to cause a scene here. She would have to find another way to separate from them. Once out of the crowds, it would be difficult to leave them behind.

"North," Shalindra answered.

Enna glanced at her, surprised, as the way to Fallhaven lay more to the east, but there was no time to convey the plan that was forming.

"Out of the city?" Engolar asked.

"Yes."

Engolar took the lead this time, maintaining a slow trot through the packed street.

Shalindra sat high in her saddle and did not avoid the gazes of the crowd. So much was written upon the faces staring up at her: hope, wonder, distrust, and unease. These people deserved to know that their Guardian was healthy and well, if not what business she was about.

And her business required her to be elsewhere, and soon. She pondered the best place to lose the soldiers as they rode, but she was unfamiliar with most of the elvish city and there was no way to tell Enna of her plan without the soldiers hearing.

She spied a darkened alley not far ahead and pondered a sudden dash down it to escape. No sooner had the thought crossed her mind than she felt an uncomfortable tug inside her as a ghostly double of herself separated and went riding ahead, surrounded by copies of the soldiers. Could those around her feel themselves being split apart as she did? They gave no reaction, so it seemed unlikely.

Her specter made a sharp turn left and galloped between two houses, but the ghostly version of Enna failed to react in time and was cut off as half the soldiers raced in pursuit of the ghost Shalindra.

The moment Shalindra discarded the idea, all of the projections vanished, only to be replaced with a different set as her eyes fell on a winding cross street. The tug of her projection separating from her body was not unexpected this time, but it set her teeth on edge. There were almost certain to be consequences to what she was doing. The ghost Shalindra raced into the side street, only to wheel about and return a moment later.

The separations continued without her control or consent until there were a dozen Shalindras, each exploring the turns and options as they were presented. Soon she was riding behind so many versions of the horsemen that she began to lose track of which were real. The possibilities overlapped in a hazy white fog, and Shalindra's head began to swim. She slumped in the saddle, her equilibrium distorted by the unnaturalness of witnessing multiple points of view.

She fought the disorientation by focusing on individual versions of herself. As she did, the associated duplicates of the horseman grew brighter and more substantial to the point she could make out voices and the sounds of horse and harness.

Determined to exert some level of control, Shalindra constrained the next projection of herself to emerge, allowing it to drift only slightly to one side rather than racing off. The ghost soldiers paired with it reacted, those closest to her shifting away while the ones on the opposite side drew closer. With a squeeze of her knees, she nudged her horse—hopefully the real one—into alignment with her ghost self, and the physical soldiers adjusted to perfectly match their own ghostly doubles.

It was the future she was experiencing, then, and there were ways to influence the potential events. She concentrated on the most promising escape routes, and the premonitions became more focused to match. At last, one turn ahead yielded a successful result. As the squad slowed on one side to avoid a cart in the road, an opening formed that allowed both her doppelganger and Enna's the exit they needed. But they were almost upon it, and her timing had to be perfect.

She caught Enna's eye, but there was no time to explain with anything beyond a pointed glance. Shalindra wheeled sharply just beyond the cart and charged between two buildings, emerging onto a quiet street. Enna was right behind her, but the soldiers were briefly clogged at the far end. With a snap of the reins, she sent her horse into a gallop. Wind whipped her hair as they raced through the torchlit streets. She continued sending her ghosts ahead to every approaching turn, watching which of them pulled to a stop and which continued. Their otherworldly guidance sent Shalindra zigzagging through side streets and along forested paths that she had never seen.

The riders crossed the bridge over River Annyre without slowing to acknowledge the startled sentries who stood watch. A smattering of houses occupied the eastern bank of the river, but their windows were dark, and few residents noticed the women's hasty arrival and even more hasty departure. They broke into the forest proper at last and lost themselves in the night.

Chapter Nine

Merrywood

"Foul creatures walk the earth, I tell you!" Betha exclaimed to whoever cared to listen, tossing her wet rag down on the table. It was pointless to clean the surface this early in the day as the common room of Conygate's Tavern was near to empty, but it gave her something to do and an excuse to talk to someone. If she sat still too long, her joints were liable to freeze up, especially with this early chill in the air. She cast a forlorn look at the fireplace, wondering if the warmth of another log was worth the effort required to put it there.

The sole patron at the table—one of her regulars—looked up from his drink. "You're retelling those stories again now, are you?"

"Bah! Put your head in the sand if you will, Dorven. I'll not be caught unawares. Armies everywhere, and then poof! Gone."

"It's because they walked off," Dorven said with a bored look.

"And what was it that made them do it? Not your elvish kin, no sir. And where've all the travelers run off to?"

"Maybe your king scared them away?" Dorven teased, lifting

his drink so her rag could pass beneath it. "I heard he made a personal appearance at the front and, upon catching his first glimpse of the natural world, ran screaming back to his castle."

Betha made an exasperated sound. "Believe what you will. You've seen the to-do those Sisters of Eluria are in right now. Doesn't that concern you?"

Dorven took a large gulp before conceding her point. "I say my prayers to the moon as infrequently as any of us who don't wear the white, but even I can tell something is wrong."

"There's always something wrong, especially of late." Before she could share her ideas of exactly what was needed to make the world right, or at least her part of it, the door banged open behind her. Betha turned eagerly to welcome the visitors.

Rather than her typical customers, such as merchants dragging their wares or families headed south towards a real city, there stood a pair of women in the white of Eluria, and Betha found herself staring into the bluest eyes she had even seen. Those eyes alone would have made the woman memorable, but her silver armor and weapons were every bit as unusual. The elvish Sister beside her was equally distinctive what with her hair as white as her robes, though her sparkling green eyes carried dark bags beneath them and she appeared ill-used by whatever road had brought them here.

"Welcome, Sisters. Welcome to Conygate's." Betha waved them in with both arms. Sisters of Eluria rarely visited, but when they did, they never argued over the prices like those misers of Amalthee, and they were generally good for business. Betha saw them to a table and began to tell them what was on the menu—most expensive items first, of course—but Dorven rushed in front of her to kneel before the one in the shiny armor.

"By Her light, Revered Guardian, my services are yours," he sputtered.

The armored woman blushed in embarrassment at the display, though her words were kind.

"Your services are appreciated but not required, beyond food for my Sister and a room for the night, if one is available."

"We've plenty of both," Betha said, giving Dorven a kick so he'd get up and stop groveling. "Stew's warm and our bread's fresh. Relax yourself and I'll bring you a hearty meal."

She hurried to the kitchen, giving Dorven a warning glare and hoping he wouldn't chase them off while she was out back.

Thankfully, both women were still there when she returned and set the bowls of stew before them. Dorven stared at the women from the other end of the table, as if they were here to make all his wishes come true.

"Allow me, please," Dorven said, slapping four coins down on the table before Betha could even name the price.

The clerics nodded their thanks, and the white-haired elf dug into hers immediately, as if she had not eaten in days.

"What beasts?" the blue-eyed woman asked, ignoring the food. "Just before we entered, you mentioned foul beasts and soldiers who disappeared."

"They're only rumors, my lady," Betha apologized, straightening her apron. "We're set off the road and out of the way by choice, like the rest of the town, and many pass us by without even stopping. The talk's enjoyable when we get it."

"We have been on the road for almost a week now and have

heard little news. Did any soldiers come this way?"

"Near a hundred," Doran said excitedly. "They passed a couple of days ago, probably returning to Jonrin or Kenzing, if I were to guess. They were full of talk about the war being called off, but they'd seen fighting and said there were horrible creatures about."

The clerics exchanged a glance.

"And our Sisters of Elurithlia here, are they well?" the elf girl asked, sounding like she expected the opposite.

"That's the funny thing," Dorven said. "They went out to help, as they always do, but they were an unsettled bunch when they came back. No one knows why."

"Well," Betha said, wishing Dorven would shut up, "you'd be knowing about the goings-on with your own order better than we would, of course, but the bigger word is that the king's been killed, and his son's taken over."

"You've got it backwards again," Dorven said. "It's his son who was knifed, and he's so distraught that now the other prince has to run the Kingdom."

"I heard it same time as you," Betha huffed, "so don't be changing things." She leaned closer to the clerics. "It's said that his own daughter had a hand in the murder. Right after he welcomed her back, no less. Ah, but who can say? Kings come and go, and all of 'em leave us alone, ain't that the truth?"

"May it ever be so," Dorven said, raising his drink.

Betha was pleased that Dorven had settled down, until she caught the worried looks the Sisters shared with each other. She patted the armored woman's arm. "Don't you worry about none of it, my lady. You'll have the peacefullest sleep of your life here, and nothing will trouble you tonight."

* * *

Shalindra did not sleep that night, the same as every other. It was impossible to quiet more than a handful of the voices in her head at one time, and the successes with one only allowed the others to grow louder. She still could not tell if these voices were an intended consequence of her Ascension, but it seemed unlikely. The more probable answer was that something had gone wrong during the exchange and that there were not more than one of her. On the one hand, this would be a good thing, since one of her was all she really cared to have; on the other hand, it could also mean that she was going mad, imagining all of it. After lying awake for the entire night thinking about it, she was still not sure which alternative was more preferable.

She woke Enna before the sun broke the horizon, and they rode from the sleepy village, following a winding trail through the trees to rejoin the road that ran north and south along the Merallin River.

No one noticed their departure, which was for the best. She wished fervently that people would cease bowing and offering her their services or beseeching her for this favor or that. She had a task to do, and their attention was more a hindrance than help. They rode in silence, though there was nothing quiet about the cacophony of voices in her head.

The *hers* were carrying on a spirited debate that bordered on argument, one centered on the effect her leaving had inflicted on Ildalarial. Some theories which they advanced were unrealistic, while others sounded so plausible that might have been offered by someone who was still there to witness it firsthand. At least the recent days had been free of the ghostly premonitions.

Enna was either contemplative or still half-asleep, and the morning hush was broken only by the soft clomp of the horses' hooves. She had spoken less and less every day since the pair had fled Ildalarial, a condition that was almost certainly Shalindra's fault. But at those rare times, when the voices in her head would settle to a low hum, Shalindra relished the almost-peace that silence brought.

They passed through a tiny village not far north from Merrywood, but beyond that the road was empty as it wound its way through wooded hills. As the day wore on, it remained quiet and oddly devoid of travelers. This late in the summer they could have expected more people going to the towns to buy things for the winter. People were either avoiding the road or had little desire to come this way to begin with.

The sun finally burned away the fog, but rather than heralding blue skies it revealed only clouds and circling carrion birds. Their appearance in such numbers filled her with a dark foreboding, but there was nothing to do but proceed.

The first sign of trouble came in the form of an overturned wagon, its cargo strewn across the ground. They slowed their pace, each woman alert for danger, but there was nothing beyond disturbed earth and stained grass to mark what might have happened there. A little further along lay the first body. The rancid odor of death assaulted their noses, and around the next bend they came to the aftermath of a battle.

Shalindra slid from her horse, causing a clutch of vultures to take wing. The tabards of the soldiers were a red, yellow, and white checkerboard pattern—colors that marked them as house troops instead of levies. The bodies were mangled and tossed about as if they had been savaged by some large animal. Broken spears and discarded shields littered the ground. From the way the bodies were clustered, it appeared that some of the fallen had intentionally remained behind to allow others their escape.

Shalindra recognized the angle and size of the wounds—she had restored similar injuries countless times before. She looked back to Enna. "It was a demon. Just one, thankfully."

Enna shook her head as she also dismounted. "They weren't prepared."

"None of them are. Not the Kingdom, not Ceringion, perhaps not even the wizards who summon them. But why an attack here? There is little of value in this corner of the world."

"Who can say? Do you think they were part of the army that meant to invade Ildalarial?"

It was plausible. Judging from the state of the bodies, the battle was at least two days old, and whatever had attacked them had likely left the area by now.

"Should we do something for them?" Enna asked.

"Their souls will appreciate a prayer, but we must move on."

Enna supplied a eulogy, and then the pair mounted and continued north.

Despite her words to the contrary, Shalindra wanted very much to stay and find out what had happened, to hunt down and destroy the creature responsible. Demons meant that wizards of the Conclave were not far off, and the evidence of their continued meddling set a seething anger burning inside her.

She was tired of both wizards and demons. She would discover the wisdom of the fallen, as she had been bidden, and when that task was complete, the Conclave would answer for all they had done.

Chapter Ten

Paths Converge

The whole of that day and part of another had passed without seeing another traveler on the road, an abnormality that was impossible to ignore. This stretch of the highway between Merrywood and Bendin was sparsely populated, to be sure, but either every last person had wandered off or there was some larger disturbance afoot.

The weather remained cooler than normal but not unpleasant, though Shalindra would have appreciated more of the sun's cheer. The shadows were edging longer, lending a more closed-in feel to the trees on either side of the road. It came as both a surprise and a relief when she at last spied another group of riders coming towards them.

"Well, it will be nice to have someone to talk to," Enna muttered.

Shalindra studied the approaching men. At first glance, there was nothing unusual about them, save that they were the first people they had seen since leaving Merrywood. Upon closer inspection, however, there was almost nothing normal about the four riders.

Two of the men, one close to Shalindra's age and the other older, were wrapped in the red robes of Toush, which was odd as those who walked the Sixfold Path took the walking part of that obligation literally and rarely rode. The third had a squarish head topped with short hair, a clean-shaven chin, and thick features that matched his solid build. He could have been a simple laborer from the manner of his dress, but there was vitality and precision in his motions that marked him as something other than what he was trying to appear to be. He held himself with an aloof properness that put her in mind of nobility—or of wizards. The last rider was a familiar-looking halfling with upswept hair who bounced uncomfortably on a mount several sizes too large for him.

Her thoughts skimmed past each of them faster than they should have and returned to the younger of the two monks. His dark hair was straighter than Tormjere's and pulled back in a knot, but the dark eyes that calmly took in the world around him bore a familial resemblance that was impossible to mistake. Enna's sudden intake of breath confirmed that she was not imagining anything.

The four riders slowed as they drew near, and the older monk wrestled his horse to a stop in front of them, smiling.

"It is good to see you again, Hammett," Shalindra greeted him, genuinely happy to see the enigmatic old monk once more. "Have you taken up riding now?"

"If Toush had meant us to gallop across the countryside, he would have given us hooves," Hammett said, wiping a thin hand across the grey stubble of his nearly shaved head, "but I can see the appeal for those in a hurry to get somewhere."

Shalindra could not be sure if that observation was meant to apply to her or the men with him. He was so eccentric that either could have been the case.

Hammett slid from his horse and hobbled about uncomfortably, shaking his legs. "I, too, hoped our paths would cross once more, and just in time for lunch, no less. Come join us?"

Shalindra almost refused, still anxious to reach Honarch and Birion. The man and halfling—Weeby, that was his name—looked equally uncomfortable at the thought, but Enna was more than eager for a break.

"Food is an excellent idea," she said, dismounting with a sideways glance at Shalindra.

The unknown man studied Shalindra expectantly, and his hands twitched as Shalindra hopped from her horse. Though they returned to the reins fast enough, the gesture had not been defensive.

Weeby slid to the ground with a forced smile. "Food is always good for conversation."

The man beside him dismounted stiffly, his eyes still glued to her every movement.

Hammett waved Shalindra to a seat on a nearby log and produced a loaf of thick, dark bread, seemingly oblivious to the building tension. "It is a sign of wisdom that you are never found walking your path alone, no matter the importance of your goals. I am Hammett," he said to Enna.

"Enna," she replied, though her attention remained fixed on Eljorn.

That was who the younger disciple of Toush had to be, after all. The odds of finding another monk who so closely resembled Tormjere were too improbable to contemplate. It was not age alone which separated him from Hammett. Hidden beneath Eljorn's robes was an efficiency of motion which belied his unassuming demeanor. Eljorn moved to secure the horses, but where Hammett's scrawny frame rattled about haphazardly, every action Eljorn took was fluid and purposeful.

"Where does your path lead you this time?" Hammett asked.

"We are meeting friends not far from here," Shalindra answered. Fallhaven was not exactly close, but the implication that they were not as alone as they appeared seemed an appropriate falsehood until she learned more of the stranger.

"Ah, Master Verelli is in search of friends as well, but I'll allow him to tell you why. It's terribly rude to speak for someone who's right beside you."

All eyes turned to the man who still stood beside his horse, regarding them warily in return. "I am not certain that now is the time for that discussion."

Hammett popped a piece of bread in his mouth contentedly. "The funny thing about the right time is that it often finds you instead of the other way around."

Verelli's silence began to stretch uncomfortably.

"You'll have to forgive the stoicism," Weeby spoke up. "He's come a long way in a remarkably short time, and the road to Merallin is not the happy journey it once was."

When they had last encountered Weeby, Tormjere had been more amused than worried, but the halfling's reappearance with someone Shalindra was now certain was a wizard put her on her guard. Enna must have reached a similar conclusion, for she brushed at her hair, using the motion to rest her hand atop her symbol of Eluria.

"If you have come from Ceringion, why not follow the Gold Road?" Shalindra asked. "It would have been weeks faster."

"There's a nice little brouhaha going on there," Weeby said, "so we chose to come upriver from the Small Sea."

"And from Halisford you did not turn south for Kendenhall?"

Weeby grimaced. "They have other no-less-nasty problems to deal with at the moment."

Verelli gave her a quizzical look. "You are surprisingly unaware of current events, given your influence upon them, Your Highness."

Enna shifted uncomfortably beside her. Shalindra had not made secret her ancestry but neither had she made mention of it.

"It is no longer my kingdom," she said warily, "and I have not been to any of those places in quite some time."

Verelli studied her like a specimen on a table, and she could almost see the methodical evaluation of options running through his mind.

"We had certainly not thought to meet you here," he finally said, "but it could be, as our friend says, a fortuitous encounter. I carry a message from the Conclave of Imaretii to His Majesty, your father."

"My family has had more than enough of the Conclave's threats. You may wish to reconsider."

"There have been some misunderstandings in the past, but I

am not here to repeat them. I have come seeking Actondel's aid."

He said it with a straight face, but Shalindra could not keep the incredulousness from her voice. "Misunderstandings? Your Conclave abetted one war against us and attempted to start another. You have made efforts to kill members of my family more than once, and me and my friends more times than can be counted. After all of that, you wish our help?"

Weeby shook his head. "I told you they wouldn't take it well."

Verelli ignored the halfling. "I will dispute none of your accusations, nor will I answer for them. There are more pressing events concerning the fate of this kingdom."

"Does King Gymerius intend to seize the rest of what he could not last time?"

"It is quite likely that the ruler of the Ceringion Reginum is dead, but before you take that as cause to celebrate, I would tell you that it is due to the emergence of an even greater enemy. As you have no knowledge of the events close to you, I will infer that you remain equally ignorant of the situation in Ceringion: an unchecked portal to a different realm has been opened in Tythir. The entire city is overrun with demons."

Shalindra found it impossible to believe. "You have seen this devastation yourself?"

"I was there when the breach occurred."

"And you escaped unscathed?" Enna asked.

"Would you be better off if I had not?" Verelli shot back. "I've given you more information in a few minutes than you could have gained in months on your own, and it is likely far more relevant to your plans than you let on."

"And I will not share those plans with you," Shalindra said, rising to her feet. "*If* such a calamity actually occurred, you might garner more sympathy had you not spent years trying to inflict that same devastation on us."

Verelli's voice took on a menacing edge. "If you had any clue what your actions could lead to, it wouldn't have been necessary."

"Yes, well," Weeby said, stepping between them. "Let's continue discussing this like rational people before you squash Master Verelli like one of those pesky little demons you're so good at disposing of."

Verelli threw him a withering look, but Weeby just smiled up at them both.

"We did not come here seeking conflict," the wizard reiterated. "As I have already stated, we came to ask for help."

"Yet conflict follows you everywhere, and it seems fitting that you suffer the ravages you have inflicted upon others."

Verelli's eyes blazed. "There comes a time for setting aside differences, no matter how deep. Ceringion has no defense against this. As their cities fall, the population will suffer the brunt of the destruction. When they flee, they will not chance the deserts of Namarin or the violence of Westholm. They will flood your lands, whether you wish them to or not. If you do not care about us, then you might care about them."

Shalindra did, in some way. But not enough to sway her from her task. "The uncaring always demand help from those they have trampled in their rush to power, but you will not find it here."

"Then you'll do nothing?"

"No," Shalindra answered as she walked to her horse. "I will hope that my family's greeting carries more kindness to you than what you have shown to them, but I will not save you from your own mistakes."

Chapter Eleven
Unexpected Obligations

The thud of her horse's hooves on the wooden bridge above the Merallin River jarred Shalindra from her thoughts, and she readjusted uncomfortably to the now. Her thoughts brushed against Tormjere's focus, assuring herself that she was again occupying her original self. It was good to verify, because without that reference it was often impossible to be certain. She had been arguing with the other *hers* again about what task she needed to accomplish, and once more without resolution or revelation. Her predicament was not dissimilar to the one she had undertaken years before as a fresh initiate into the following of Eluria, but Tormjere had been with her then.

The wood of the bridge turned into cobblestones, and she followed the road into the town of Jonrin, Enna trailing unhappily a short distance behind.

Shalindra struggled to recall why Enna was being so uncommunicative. Indeed, she remembered very little of the journey since encountering the Conclave wizard. She must have participated in whatever had transpired since then, but the details were fuzzy. Perhaps her mental wanderings had taken her too close to the barrier separating her consciousness from the swarm of voices flying past. Like standing too close to a roaring waterfall, they had the tendency to drown out any other thoughts.

There was something she needed to do, some great task worthy of a Guardian to accomplish, and simply reuniting with her friends offered no apparent progress towards that hidden goal. There had to be something more.

Over the tops of the houses, she spied the white marble roof of Eluria's temple. Unlike the modest temple at Merrywood where she and Enna would have been a burden on the Sisters, here there was no reason to avoid visiting the sanctuary. A place to pause and contemplate recent events could be just what they both needed. It certainly could not add to her confusion.

"Let us seek rooms at the temple," she said over her shoulder. "I see it there."

When no response came, Shalindra turned in her saddle. "Enna?"

"We should have told him," Enna said in a disinterested monotone.

Shalindra sighed, certain that they had covered this topic already, and probably without either of them being happy with the result. "I could not in front of our enemies. There will be a better time."

Enna just shrugged and returned to staring at the back of her horse's head.

Shalindra would keep them here only for the night and then

hasten on to Fallhaven. It was an understatement to say that she had not been herself of late, and that was not helping matters. Reuniting with their friends might bolster Enna's spirits. Once she could gain clarity on their direction, surely that would restore Enna's enthusiasm.

They passed through the gates at the south end of the city without incident and emerged into a bustling market square dominated by a red-roofed building with myriad chimneys. Shalindra's passage drew more than a few curious looks, and several people stopped to stare. The attention was different than the adulation of the elves, more a mixture of surprise and some disbelief. Enna nudged her horse closer to Shalindra's despite her earlier lethargy.

Shalindra guided them along a series of streets from memory, more cognizant of the stares than of where they were going. That changed abruptly when they came onto a long, eerily familiar thoroughfare. It was on this very street, while disguised and on a secret journey to Fallhaven, that she had been attacked years ago. The memories it rekindled were strong, and images of smoke and dead bodies overlaid her vision, not as ghostly premonitions but as tangible renderings that she could feel and smell. The shop in which she and Tormjere had hidden from the goblins still stood, though it now belonged to a shoemaker. She wondered if the house they had smashed their way into to escape over the walls was still the same. Her horse slowed, then drew to a stop at the exact place where Tormjere had saved her life, and she swallowed past the lump in her throat. Here on this very spot was where she had whispered her first true prayer, begging Eluria for salvation as her protectors were cut down by would-be kidnappers. Right before Tormjere had saved her.

"Guardian?" Enna asked. "Are you alright?"

The memories vanished, and Shalindra waved aside Enna's concern. "I am fine. My recollections of this town are less than pleasant and have caused us to miss our turn."

Enna's eyes narrowed, but she said nothing. Shalindra pulled her horse around smoothly, but her thoughts were as turbulent as a river. Who would she turn to, now that he was gone?

* * *

The temple of Eluria was smaller than she remembered, a rectangular building fashioned of white marble, edged with columns across the front. A short wall lent privacy to the orderly but unkempt gardens. Weeds sprouted where they should never have been allowed, and petals shed weeks earlier still collected beneath the flowers. A handful of the beds were well tended, but Shalindra could only shrug at Enna's questioning glance.

The stout door of the temple received their knock, and after a short delay came the sound of the bolt being thrown. The portal swung open, and they were met by a young woman in simple initiate's robes. Before Shalindra could say anything, the girl's hands flew to her face and she dropped to her knees.

"By Her light, it's true! Guardian, we are honored by your presence."

Shalindra looked at Enna in embarrassment and drew the girl to her feet. "Please, Sister, there is no need to worship me. We have come—"

A second Sister just as young as the first appeared from within and rushed forward. "Can it be? Bless Eluria for sending you! We've been so scared."

"Slow down, please," Shalindra said gently. "Everything is fine. Where is your Sister Superior?"

Tears welled in the first girl's eyes. "I am, Guardian. Sister Rosamund was killed in the streets over a month ago. We've barely left the temple since then, and only early in the mornings when the sun is out."

"Let us sit, and tell me what happened," Shalindra said, taking her by the hand. As with most of Eluria's temples, the interior of this one was given over to a large sanctuary with a statue of the goddess at the far end. The floor was left open to allow for freedom of movement during ceremonies, but benches had been placed against the walls. It was towards one of these that Shalindra guided the distraught girls.

Enna secured the entrance once more, then disappeared through an interior door near the statue to check the rest of the temple.

"Now," Shalindra said when the girls had settled, "what are your names?"

"I am Isabel," said the older of the two, "and this is Hannah."

Enna reappeared, giving a shake of her head to indicate that she had found nothing of note in the small building.

"Tell us what happened to your Sister Superior."

"We had gone out one evening," Isabel began. "Sister Rosamund didn't like to be out after dark, but someone had been injured and could not be moved. I went with her. Everything was fine, by Her blessings, but the restoration was tiring. We were on the way back here when…" She put her head in her hands, and Hannah hugged her close. "A man stepped out of the shadows, and… he was angry at us and said terrible things, but I don't know why. Sister Rosamund told me to run, and I did, all the way back. But she never returned. The next morning, we learned that she died."

Enna knelt beside her. "And you've been alone since then?"

"Yes," Hannah answered as Isabel struggled to compose herself. "There are a few who continue to worship here, and they bring us food."

Shalindra was shocked. Jonrin was not a large town and there was nothing unusual about a temple having so few Sisters, but the temple in Merrywood should have heard of the tragedy by now and sent someone more senior to take over.

"And nothing works as it should," Isabel added. "Eluria does not answer any of our prayers. I don't understand. Maybe we have done something wrong."

Shalindra placed a reassuring hand on her arm. "She is still there, but she has been sorely tested. When I—"

"What she means," Enna cut in, giving her a sharp glance, "is that She is still with us, as She always will be. We must have patience."

"But without Her, we are helpless," Hannah wailed.

Shalindra recognized the wisdom of Enna's approach, as neither girl needed anything but encouragement at this point. "You must have faith, and you must pray with her, and for her. She will return, with our help."

The girls were far more trusting of her fib than they should have been, but Shalindra supposed that, in their position, she would have believed just as readily. If only she knew Eluria's recovery as fact instead of a hope. Not wishing to dwell on the subject, she asked: "Do you have room for us here?"

"Of course," Isabel answered. "There is no one else but us. Are you going to stay in Jonrin long?"

Enna jumped in again. "Long enough to set this right. We must take care of each other."

Shalindra had almost given them the truthful answer that they would only stay the night, but Enna was correct. They could not leave these girls with nothing, no matter how pressing the task before them.

The remainder of the day was spent restoring order to the temple. She felt out of place tending to plants in her armor, but she had nothing else to wear and no real desire to remove it. Despite all the metal, it was as comfortable as the lightest robes, making it easy to forget she was even wearing it.

Enna escorted Hannah to the market, and they returned with almost more than they could carry. It was satisfying to see the pantries stocked and things organized properly, but Shalindra chafed at the delay, no matter how nice the flower beds looked when they were done. Only one person came to the evening prayer, an older woman who seemed to be visiting more to check on the girls than to worship Eluria. When everyone separated to go to their rooms for the night, Shalindra pulled Enna aside in the back of the sanctuary.

"What we did today was important, but I would like to stay no longer than we must."

"Of course," Enna said stiffly.

"Enna, tell me what is wrong."

She looked at her incredulously. "You really don't know, do you?"

Shalindra shrugged helplessly, which was clearly not the response Enna sought.

"I've done nothing but hold you back since we left Ildalarial. No, don't deny it. We barely speak, and when we do, it makes no difference to what happens. You already know everything, so what does it matter?"

That characterization was unfair, even if it was easy to understand why she would feel that way. Enna's counsel had always mattered and would continue to do so, but she would never understand the constant conversations Shalindra was engaged in every moment of the day. How could she? No one could fully understand what Shalindra was experiencing; it was difficult enough for her to make sense of it.

"Your opinions have always held value."

"Is that why you haven't listened to any of them? Do you even remember what I tried to talk to you about yesterday?"

Shalindra did not, which bothered her.

"Of course you don't. And now this. Do you think those girls can comprehend what has happened or find solace in your descriptions of Elurithlia's weakness? *You* are the one who should be giving them hope for a way forward."

Shalindra spread her hands, at a loss for how else to describe it—it was like trying to teach the intricacies of siege craft to an infant just taking her first steps. "I do not understand what was done to me. I cannot even begin to quantify how I have been changed. I have not forgotten—"

"He was everything for you!" Enna almost shouted. "And you don't even care that he's gone!" She pushed past Shalindra but paused at the doorway. "I liked you better the way you were. I wish you had never become Guardian."

Enna glared at her, daring her to respond, but Shalindra could not find any words that would make it better. Enna left in silence.

Alone in the room, Shalindra took a deep breath and let it out slowly. "So do I."

She could only wonder at what Isabel and Hannah thought of that exchange, for the temple walls were too thin to muffle raised voices. Becoming Eluria's Guardian had been nothing at all like she had imagined it might be, and the endeavor had cost far more than she would have willingly paid. She should be solving problems instead of creating new ones, healing those in need and guiding them in a better direction. Her decisions produced only questionable results, and she desperately wanted someone who could evaluate her options. It would probably behoove her to pray before the statue of Eluria, to seek guidance on the way forward, but it felt like it would be a wasted gesture. Their goddess was not listening and had much larger problems to deal with. She felt lost.

Shalindra walked to the tiny, austere chamber that had been given to her so she could at least pretend to sleep. She folded her legs beneath her as she sat on the bed and turned her attention inward, drawn back to what Tormjere had given her, to what he was, or would have been. It remained tucked away, contained within a lattice of energy like a bird in a cage. No, she thought, that was not right. Birds were far too delicate. More like a precious liquid kept in a bottle to save it from dilution or loss. But the bottle she had constructed was permeable, and she was forced to continuously patch it to prevent leaks. She had been unaware of such maintenance, but the evidence was there. Even that was a poor analogy which only served to cheapen his gift.

Shalindra cared greatly for it, but her feelings were buried deep beneath her newer self, like stones covered by the falling leaves of autumn. One memory she could never forget was the tearing of her very soul as she had collected him, taking the last of what he was when he had no longer been able to give it himself. He had to have known what he was doing, somehow. Eluria might have been the enabler, but it had been Tormjere who guided the outcome. It had not been an act of capitulation.

She wanted him back so desperately. If there was anyone who could gain the appropriate perspective from the jumble of options before them, it was him.

Her thoughts circled around his gift, examining its boundaries. The contents within shifted and swirled under her attention like black mists flecked with embers of fire. She could not begin to guess at what would happen should she release all that was contained within. The other *hers* might have opinions, but this particular problem was one she reserved for herself. When Tormjere had consumed the afterdeath of demons they had slain, it had never been the entire creature. He filtered what he could, growing in power while maintaining the essence of who he was. Even if she had known and understood every implication of consuming it fully, she lacked the desire to release what she held, to allow it to disperse into the finality that death would bring.

It was… she needed a name for it, this amalgamation of everything he had lived and learned, what he was and could have been. It was not Tormjere. No matter how much she wished it to be, or how much she needed it to be, she could not give it his name. Tormjere lay with the fallen Guardians. She could call it a soul, or perhaps a spirit, or essence, or… a focus. That seemed appropriate. He was always focused, always able to distill any situation to its most direct solution. It was his focus.

That simple resolution lifted her spirits more than she might have expected. He had been good at doing that, as well. His words were always what she needed to hear, even if not always what she wanted.

Her thoughts carried her back to that fateful morning of his end, and the question she wanted desperately to understand: Why?

I love you.

Those had been his final words. Was that it, then? Had it been some noble sacrifice done for love? She had little experience with love in her life, but that seemed unlikely. Not because he was incapable, but rather because it was an insignificant reason. If his sacrifice was not a premeditated act—an assumption she believed to be true—what then had prompted his decision? Surely, she would have known if anything had happened during her preparations to set him on such a course.

I love you.

She was kneeling on the sacred stone as she had that day, enveloped by a divinely magical experience beyond anything she could have imagined. The voices of the Sisters around her had ebbed and flowed in a melody as old as the forest, the ancient elvish words as beautiful as they were indecipherable. The glow of energy surrounding her obscured all that was outside it from her sight, but the world that opened above her had taken her breath away. Within that peaceful, silent dome of protection, they had created a window to the heavens. When the moon aligned itself and the stars began to fall around her, her spirit had been transported, rising to absorb Eluria's gift. It was potency and knowledge, ability and understanding. It filled her physical body, swelling it with strength and awareness such as she had never known.

I love you.

She had known he was coming. Whether by premonition or conversation, it had been no surprise when the ripples of energy parted, and she heard his intent. No, that was not correct. She already understood his intent, already knew he was coming, watched him as he walked towards her. Felt the surprise and shock as she slipped through the curtain of protection imparted by Eluria herself, and she approached him to… no, *he* had slipped through the barrier. She had been the one kneeling.

Probably?

I love you.

The words were his. They had to have been. He had never said it before. Had never made an attempt at affection, not by touch or by glance or by any expression of attraction. But he must have felt something, or the words would never have been spoken.

Her mind pressed more tightly against his focus, testing it, plucking at a tiny bit of what kept it together. Could she find that love within? Retrieve the memories of it as if they were her own?

Before she could debate the wisdom of it, she peeled back a sliver of the web holding his focus together and slipped inside. Love should be powerful, a strong memory easy to call forth. Find it she did, almost immediately, as if it had been waiting for her. Affection mixed with an urge to protect bobbed before her like a cork in the ocean. She plunged deeper, following the threads of that desire. But when she reached her confirmation, it was a pair of green, elvish eyes that sparkled in the darkness.

Shalindra jerked back in surprise, colliding hard with the wall at her back and nearly tumbling off the bed. How could that be? Could she have heard wrong, and could those feelings have been for…

No.

She shook her head, casting aside any thoughts of jealousy. With a burgeoning sense of guilt, she told herself that such emotions were a silly thing to have gone looking for. Of course he loved Enna. *She* loved Enna. No one but Tormjere had remained closer to her than Enna. No one but Tormjere had given of themselves so consistently, had taught without reservation, or sacrificed so much on her behalf. Shalindra considered everything she loved—her mother, her true friends, the ocean. If she looked farther, she would surely find in Tormjere similar affections for his dog, his parents and brother, and for the mountains and forests he called home.

This had been a foolish thing to do. Setting aside her doubts, she leaned back against the wall and waited for the night to end.

* * *

Shalindra rose before the sun, allowing time to reorient herself once more in her true body. It was a morning ritual which was fast becoming habit. No one else stirred, though they too would wake soon and prepare to mark the end of Eluria's nightly vigil that came with the dawn. Shalindra had remained in her armor overnight, even though fresh robes had been offered. While she could not call her period of inactivity 'sleeping,' she emerged from it without the discomfort such an oversight should have brought. Whether that was an attribute of the armor or of herself was unknown.

She tiptoed from her tiny room, careful not to wake the others, and returned to the sanctuary, empty but for the statue of Eluria.

A small sound caused her to turn, and she found Enna standing in the doorway.

"I did not mean to disturb you," Enna said with resigned annoyance.

"You of all people are never an intrusion," Shalindra said. "If anything, I might wish for you to disrupt my thoughts more frequently."

Enna almost turned away from the invitation, then changed her mind and came closer. "Are they truly so jumbled right now?"

"The simple answer would also be the most inaccurate. It is impossible to describe the things happening inside me, every moment of every day, but it takes so much effort to maintain control. I do not feel like myself anymore."

Enna chewed her lip but was unable to maintain her angry façade. "About my words last night…"

"Oh, good morning, Sisters," Hannah said, smiling as she entered the room. "I should have expected you to be awake already."

Shalindra wished the girl had slept just a little longer, but the moment they had shared was gone. Enna was already retreating to stare at the statue in annoyance. Isabel arrived moments later and went to unbar the door.

"Do you expect many worshipers?" Shalindra asked her.

"Only two or three come on a regular basis," Isabel answered. "The mornings are easier for them to hide the nature of their visits."

"Are we still persecuted?" Enna asked, spinning to face them.

"At times," Isabel stammered, taken aback by the intensity of the question. "Not directly, but the respect we held was lost last year after the King's proclamation."

Shalindra felt the heat of Enna's accusatory glance, though she recognized that it was directed more at her father than at her. Whether he or the Conclave wizard sent to watch him had been the instigator of that militant fervor, the decision to brand Eluria as an elvish goddess unworthy of human worship had brought about many disastrous consequences.

Hannah went to light more candles, but Enna called a light into existence above the statue. The room was so small that the single globe was sufficient to illuminate its entirety. Both girls looked at Enna as if she had performed a miracle.

"Neither of us have been able to do that in over a week," Hannah marveled.

"It is through no fault of your own," Enna assured them.

She was correct in that. The fault lay entirely with Shalindra, though she did not believe Enna's words to be an intentional reminder of that fact.

Shalindra moved to the side to await the morning congregants, content to let the girls run their temple as they usually did. Much to their surprise, there were almost a dozen people instead of the handful they expected.

"We have not seen so many in forever," Hannah whispered to her. "This is wonderful."

More than a few of those in attendance paid more attention to Shalindra than to the ritual. Both the girls bustled about, putting forth their best effort.

When everyone was ready, Isabel turned unexpectedly to Shalindra. "Would you honor us by leading the prayer?"

Shalindra began to decline, but Enna's warning glance at the sky reminded her there was no time to wait. She knelt before the statue of Eluria, and the assembly followed her action.

Shalindra closed her eyes and took a deep breath. It was a shock to realize that she could not feel Eluria as she had every time before. It was her first prayer since her Ascension, so she must be experiencing the same emptiness as everyone else. Yet the words were ones she had recited thousands of times, and so she began to speak. The voices of the other women joined in, Enna fervently, the others in fits and spurts, reciting the parts they remembered. The dawn ceremony was as brief as the sunrise, but Shalindra took strength from those around her even in that brief span.

"That was beautiful," Hannah said to her afterwards.

"Incredible," Isabel agreed. "I wish I could speak elvish as you do."

Shalindra stopped short, as she had not realized her words were in anything but the language of her birth. The odd look Enna gave her confirmed that the girls spoke the truth.

Most of the worshippers hurried from the temple, but a few lingered. Shalindra walked them to the door, not wishing for her presence to detract from the purpose of the ritual.

As the group emerged outside, they were confronted by an officious looking man accompanied by two soldiers in the baron's colors, waiting just inside the courtyard. Both Isabel and Hannah became unsettled the moment they caught sight of him. The worshipers hurried past with nervous glances at the official, but they were not the target of his attentions. The man was balding and grey, but he moved towards Shalindra without any slowness of age.

"Princess Shalindra?" he inquired with a short bow.

"I am she," Shalindra answered. At least he had not used her birth name, though she would have been happier had he omitted her family rank as well.

She heard excited gasps behind her. Both girls already idolized her as Guardian, and it would be doubly worse now they knew that she was royalty. Was there any part of her life that her heritage could not interfere with?

"It is a pleasure to meet you, Your Highness. I am Steward Bolton, master of His Lordship's house. Lord Halthon wishes to extend his greetings and to convey his most sincere apologies for not realizing you were guesting in our city."

"No apologies are needed, and thank you. Our visit here will be short, of necessity, and I did not wish to intrude." Visiting the baron had never crossed her mind, but courtesy demanded the lie.

"Of course, Your Highness. His Excellency assumed your

business was pressing as you had not announced your visit but wished to offer you rooms suitable to your station."

She had already lost a day by agreeing to stay and help the girls, and she had little desire to guest at the manor house, which would only serve to extend her delay.

"I am honored, but I am afraid that I have work to attend to here," she said as politely as possible. "If I might defer Lord Halthon's generous offer until next time?"

Whatever his own feelings about the matter might have been, Bolton kept himself carefully neutral. "His Lordship will be disappointed, as we very much enjoy the conversations of our royal family. Might you be willing to join him for dinner this evening?" The steward leaned closer and lowered his voice. "We had hoped that you might bring an explanation of the recent events that have taken place in Merallin. The communications we've received have been… cryptic at times and have caused much uncertainty about the direction of our kingdom."

A formal dinner was little better than accepting the offer of a room, but a refusal was likely to cause difficulties not only for herself in the short term but for her family in the future. Unhappy vassals made for a perilous throne, and there was no doubt that the aborted war with the elves had been a source of confusion.

"If I could be allowed a guest—"

"I have no place at that table," Enna said quickly, raising her hands, "and there is work here that needs to be done."

Shalindra was trapped. "Please inform Baron Halthon that I would be honored to dine with him."

* * *

Isabel and Hannah were practically giddy at the thought of Shalindra dining with the baron, and it caused a continuous series of interruptions to the lessons Enna had attempted to provide them. They even insisted on wiping down Shalindra's armor so it gleamed, though she made certain to hold Shining Moon out so they would not risk brushing against it. As much as she would have preferred that they made the most of their short time with Enna, the gesture was appreciated as she had neither formal attire nor the desire to procure such.

Enna had only rolled her eyes at the spectacle and stomped off. When the carriage arrived that afternoon, she barely acknowledged Shalindra's departure, instead shepherding the girls back inside to resume their lessons.

Such transportation was an unneeded extravagance for so short a distance, and Shalindra would have been just as content to have walked. She smiled at the footman but declined his hand as she climbed inside, already wishing she had been more forceful in her refusal.

When the keep came into view, Shalindra took stock of her surroundings as carefully as if she were entering a battlefield. The outer wall had been recently raised and scaffolding around the squared towers of the gate house foretold that they would extend even higher. The inner bailey was cramped and already in shadow from the high walls, and the carriage was forced to maneuver in a tight circle as it drew to a stop before a line of people awaiting her arrival. Soldiers along the ramparts drew to attention as protocol demanded, but the green and gold flag of Actondel did not fly with the red and yellow of House Halthon above the keep. Apparently, there were limits to how far the baron's courtesy extended.

Baron Halthon was a portly, clean-shaven man with the look of one who had never known toil, yet his greeting was kind and his mannerisms likable. He introduced his wife, a plump woman with a severe hairstyle who looked askance at Shalindra's weapons; his two children, both boys on the cusp of manhood; and the commander of his men-at-arms, Sir Browlan.

With the formalities of the greeting well accommodated, Steward Bolton ushered them inside.

"I was delighted you could join us this evening," Halthon said as they stepped through the outer doors of the donjon and into a fortified foyer. "I confess that we did not expect you to visit our fine city so late in the year."

"It was an unexpected decision, unfortunately, or I would certainly have given more suitable notice. I hope this is no imposition."

Halthon waved the apology aside. "Completely understandable. These are strange times we find ourselves in."

A servant drew open the inner doors, revealing a main hall wide enough to accommodate two long tables that ran almost the length of the room. The guests within, an assortment of local courtiers, merchants, and soldiers, all stood as the baron's procession paused at the threshold to be announced. The Steward then led them to the head table at the far end of the hall.

Baron Halthon took his seat in the middle, inviting Shalindra to sit at his right with excessive formality. His wife and sons occupied seats on his left, while Sir Bolton sat next to Shalindra. Sandwiched between the two men, it would be nearly impossible to excuse herself without causing a scene. That was likely intentional, as the dinner was an excellent excuse for the baron to be seen entertaining a princess. She repressed a sigh and wondered again why she had agreed to this waste of time.

When they were all in their places, the Steward directed the guests to their seats once more and bade them welcome. Halthon gave a mercifully short speech and offered a toast in her honor, which she accepted with a polite but minimum number of words. Entertainment was called for, and a fool began to dance to the tunes of a trio of minstrels.

"Your father sent word of your return," Halthon said to Shalindra, "and I must say that I was pleased that you were able to reconcile with each other. It is always best when families can stay together."

"Family is all we have, in the end," Shalindra agreed, almost amused by the clumsiness of the attempt to draw information from her.

"We were, of course, distressed to learn of your brother's passing so soon after."

"As was I," Shalindra replied, keeping her voice emotionless. He was fishing for a reaction, but she was determined not to give him anything to seize upon.

"And our king's health?" Halthon asked as food was set before them.

"I have not seen my father in some weeks. His recovery is expected, but the attempt on his life will leave scars."

Halthon frowned. "That was troubling news, indeed, but we all hope that His Majesty will emerge from the ordeal unscathed."

Shalindra hoped for that as well, though his recovery had been anything but assured when she and Enna had departed for Ildalarial.

The table was set with an extravagant amount of food, and small talk occupied their time as they dined. The music kept a merry tempo and the fool put on a lively show, but, compared to the continuously celebratory nature of the elves, it felt like a subdued affair. Shalindra put the food in her mouth because it was expected of her but, as with everything she tried to eat, it was without taste and she swallowed only out of habit.

After the meal, the minstrels launched into a lively tune once more and the room faded into a comfortable din of conversations. Halthon waved for his glass of wine to be refilled, and once he had taken a sip, he finally broached the subject she had been told to expect.

"I had hoped that you could provide us with insight on the sudden reversal of direction after a year of planning for the campaign."

"Quite unexpected," Bolton added over her shoulder. "Were it not for the torrential rains throughout the summer, the assault against Ildalarial would have commenced much sooner."

"I am most thankful that it did not," Shalindra said, put off by the disappointment in the knight's voice. "The elves pose no threat to our safety, which cannot be said about others."

"By this you mean the wizards of the Conclave?" The baron's eyebrows knit on his forehead. "Can you provide an explanation for that turnabout as well?"

The underlying suspicion in his words was apparent. Jonrin

was a minor fiefdom but an important deterrent against goblins and other creatures in the wilderness just to the west. She had been too far removed from the court to judge if it remained loyal to the crown, however, and so she chose her words carefully, no matter how much it annoyed her to do so.

"The Conclave had a heavy if hidden hand in the decision to prosecute the attack on the elves, and they did not react well when His Majesty chose not to obey. It was another war that would have served their interests far more than ours."

"Ah, yes. The wizards," Browlan said. "They do seem to cause problems when convenient."

Halthon nodded. "The use of magicians as a scapegoat for all of Actondel's ills is difficult to support. We see them infrequently here, but those that have passed through have never given us trouble."

"And yet the Conclave's influence is easy to see," Shalindra pointed out, still wondering where this was going. "What does that have to do with any magician in our kingdom?"

"You were not aware?" Halthon said in surprise. "Delivered just three days prior and bearing His Majesty's seal was an edict branding all users of magic as traitors and subject to immediate arrest."

Shalindra was somehow not surprised, as her father was always impulsive, but this decision was as shortsighted as it was dangerous. The only silver lining was that, no matter how poorly thought out, his issuing of edicts was a sign that his health had improved.

"I would disagree with the wisdom of such a proclamation. The only wizards who made threats against us were members of the

Conclave, and it seems shortsighted to paint every other practitioner with the same brush.”

“You make a valid point, and one I agree with,” Halton said, nodding. “It is certainly beyond our means to search out every such person. However, there are other versions of those same events that paint a very different picture—one in which your role factors much more prominently.”

There it was then. If he was willing to state the accusation so boldly, was he equally willing to do something about it when his family was close enough to be in jeopardy? She willed her hands to remain above the table and away from her weapons. “I can assure you that such rumors are false. If I desired to advance my own position, I would still be in Merallin. I, quite literally, held my father’s life in my hands.” There was no point in mentioning that she had failed miserably at it.

“I meant no offense, of course,” Halthon said quickly. “I only wished to point out the difficulties we face in ascertaining the truth. We have also heard tales of strange creatures during the war, but such beastly oddities were far away and easy to dismiss.”

“The demons are more than just tales, and I would encourage you to take such threats seriously. Conventional armaments were ineffective against them.”

“You witnessed them firsthand?” Browlan asked, less than believing.

“Many times. Eluria’s might and wizard’s magic have been the only things to slow them down.” And Tormjere. He had been so very good at that.

Halthon shivered. “It is well that we have one of your temples here, then.”

On instinct, she pounced on the opening. “And yet it is unfortunate that a more common form of violence has visited them. It would be a blessing if they were secure enough to provide their services as they wished.”

“The loss of your priestess,” Halthon said quickly. “We identified the criminal responsible, of course, but he fled the city before he could be apprehended. It’s something we should keep a closer watch on.”

“Most unsettling,” Browlan added. “The need to send our men away for the war with the elves has hampered His Lordship’s efforts to keep his lands free of brigands.”

“It has,” Halthon said, then waved aside the thought. “But enough talk of all this unhappiness. We should allow Her Highness to enjoy her evening with us.” He stood and raised his glass. “To His Majesty, the King!”

“The King!” the crowd responded.

The evening passed far too slowly for Shalindra’s liking, and it was well past sunset when the gathering finally drew to a close.

“Are you certain you would not care to guest with us tonight?” Halthon asked as she was led towards the waiting carriage. The question was as polite as it should have been, but she doubted that anyone in his household was enthusiastic about that possibility.

“Your offer is gracious, but I must decline so that I may prepare for the remainder of my journey and see to the safety of my Sisters.”

“A most considerate gesture. Should you require anything during your stay, please do not hesitate to impose.”

“I shall,” she promised. “When next I visit, I hope that I may enjoy more time in your company."

Shalindra boarded the carriage, relieved when the door closed and she could drop the false pleasantries. She missed none of it and was not meant for such a life anymore. She had the impression that Halthon had not gotten everything he wanted from her, and though she had approached the dinner without any agenda, she somehow felt the same. The idea crossed her mind to collect Enna and head into the woods this night, but she discarded it as rash and considered instead what she had learned that night. It had been useful on some level, but everything the baron had wanted to know could have been conveyed in a much shorter and far less extravagant conversation.

Still, her father would need to be made aware of the problems arising in the fiefdoms, and she wondered if he was indeed recovered from Logian's knife. A sudden longing to see her family came over her, though the desire was tempered by the need to pursue her own destiny. There had been no mention of family in Lithandris' message, and so it was unlikely she would see them any time soon.

Once the carriage had returned her to the temple, she found Enna sitting alone on a bench in the gardens, looking tired.

"Is anything wrong?" Shalindra asked.

Enna shook her head. "No. I sat with Hannah and Isabel all day, giving them every manner of instruction they could handle. They are too young for this responsibility. Hannah has some talent for restorations, I think, but she desperately needs a mentor." Her frustration was clear. "They need to regain people's trust, but in order to do that, they need worshippers attending daily prayers and coming to them for restorations, not soldiers frightening people away. This morning's turnout was an abnormality. Few of the faithful wish to be seen here, and if She continues not to answer, then even they may stop coming."

Shalindra sat beside her. "What of the girls' safety?"

"They are safe only as long as no one cares enough to make them otherwise. A child could climb these walls—our temples are places of worship, not fortresses."

"I asked Halthon to ease the animosity directed at our church. He was not opposed, but neither was it a problem he wished to deal with."

"How was your banquet with His Lordship?" Enna asked, her mood turning frosty once more.

Shalindra stifled a sigh. "Less productive than either of us would have liked, I fear. I am not sure what to take away from it beyond rumors of demons and my father's branding of all wizards as enemies."

"It's no surprise that the wizards continue to cause trouble for everyone," Enna said, redirecting her animosity.

"And one of them is headed towards my family."

Enna's mouth tightened at the reminder of their meeting with Eljorn. "Are you still committed to leaving tomorrow?"

"We could stay here and have Birion and Honarch come to us." It was a small olive branch, but it might help bridge the divide forming between them.

"I thought you were in a hurry to get there."

"It will be the same amount of time regardless of which of us crosses the distance." Shalindra looked at the parts of the garden still lacking attention. "There is work we can accomplish here."

"It would be wonderful to have more time with them," Enna cautiously agreed, "but how will you tell Birion? Would you trust a common messenger?"

"Do you still have the dohedron?"

Enna fished it from within her neck purse. "I didn't know you could operate it."

"I have never done so, but I might remember."

Truthfully, she had never even held the device in her hand, but Tormjere had often been forced to concentrate as he poked away at it to send a message to the one Honarch held. It had been a useful, if crude, way to communicate, but she had heard enough of his thoughts to have unwillingly memorized the more common phrases.

She tapped one of the gems, and the stone pulsed softly. Its twin would do the same, she knew, pulsing with the same hue no matter where it was. Honarch would have to be looking at it to notice, of course, so there was no guarantee her attempt would work now.

They waited for a response, but the device remained dark long enough that Enna began to fidget. Shalindra tapped the gem once more, and waited. Moments later, the entire device lit up in a hasty series of incomprehensible flashes.

She touched an amber gem twice, hopefully to ask for a stop, then tapped at the jewels in sequence, doing her best to convey her desire for Birion and Honarch to continue on and meet them here in Jonrin. There was no specific sequence for the name of the city, and so she settled for tapping out what she hoped the letters were one by one.

When she was done, the gems flickered rapidly once more, but she only caught 'horse' and 'hurry' before the lights ceased. Shalindra repeated her careful series of taps, hoping the repetition would get the point across.

The dohedron was dark for a time, then a series of gems flashed in a slow pattern almost identical to the one she had sent, which she interpreted as, 'Go to Jonrin?'

She tapped the green gem twice in agreement and received the same in response. Satisfied with that answer, she handed the device back to Enna.

"Did it work?" Enna asked, returning it to her neck purse.

"I believe so. Fallhaven is reachable in two days from here, so if they have not arrived by the third then we will continue on towards them."

"I will tell the girls," Enna said as she stood, sounding genuinely happy for the first time in days.

Shalindra smiled at her as she left but felt none of Enna's enthusiasm. There was still no telling where she would need to go after this, and she could be putting herself days behind. She looked at the statue of Eluria, wondering why she could never seem to reach Fallhaven.

Chapter Twelve
Reunion

It was a relief when Shalindra saw Birion and then Honarch approaching the temple two days later. Their horses were tired, and both men were as alert as if they were riding into battle. She rose from where she had been watching by the gate and tried to catch their attention. Her eagerness was not shared by the townspeople, who bestowed glares and half-muttered curses on Honarch as he passed. The length of his reddish beard and deep red robes, snug at the waist but falling only to the knee, marked him as a practitioner of magic. The same resentment would have been directed at her and Enna just weeks earlier, though the edict vilifying wizards seemed to have struck a deeper chord.

The people's attitude was far less surprising than was the third rider arriving with them: Fendrick. The dwarf had exchanged his blacksmith's apron for a cuirass of steel over a mail shirt much like the one Birion wore, but with more intricate edging that was exquisite without being overstated. His ample beard covered whatever symbol might have been engraved on the front, but there was nothing ceremonial about the steel. It was odd to see them wearing their armor here, for the roads of the Kingdom were far safer than those of the forests and mountains around Newlmir. She had the sense that the arrangement of Honarch between them was more than just happenstance. Honarch waved as he caught sight of her and spurred his mount to a trot.

All three men dismounted wearily at the entrance to the temple grounds.

"Your Highness," Birion said with a bow. Whatever cheerfulness he might have had at seeing her faded as he took note of Tormjere's sword at her side, and his jaw set in a grim line. Honarch came to the same observation moments later, and the color drained from his face.

"There is much for us to discuss," Shalindra said, "but here is not the place. Please, join us inside."

They tied off their horses and followed her to a secluded part of the garden with benches near a bubbling fountain. It was a cool evening, but Shalindra felt suddenly hot. There was no way to soften the blow.

"Tormjere is... no longer with us."

Birion, a knight who was no stranger to death, accepted it with stoic compassion. "I am very sorry, Your Highness. He and I had our differences, but he was a good man."

"I can't believe it," Honarch said, his head moving slowly side to side in shocked disbelief. "I wondered if something was wrong after the exchange on the dohedron, but..."

Fendrick's reaction was the most surprising. His time with Tormjere had been the briefest of all, but the dwarf slumped onto a bench like a deer who had just been poleaxed.

"Are you alone?" Birion asked, his soldier's instincts focused on the immediate practicalities.

"Enna is with me," Shalindra said. "Inside, teaching our Sisters."

"I'll find the three of us a place to stay, and then we can talk. We've a lot to catch up on."

* * *

It was a subdued group that huddled together in the kitchen behind the temple that evening, the only room other than the sanctuary large enough for the five of them to occupy at once.

Shalindra described the journey to Ildalarial, their efforts to stop the war, and her father's near death. Her Ascension she glossed over in a few sentences. It was, perhaps, unfair to minimize Tormjere's actions in that way, but she could not yet trust her ability to constrain her emotions.

"In the end, he gave himself for me, so that I could achieve what I was meant to."

"He would have been satisfied no other way," Birion said. "No matter the demons he faced, there was never a doubt where his loyalties lay."

"I still can't believe it," Honarch said. "Out of all of us, he should have been the last one standing."

The retelling had at least given Shalindra some clarity of the events, as talking through a thing so often could. It, or the renewed company of these men, had served to briefly quiet the debates the various *hers* were engaged in and even managed to diminish the roar of voices in her head.

106

"What of yourselves?" she asked. "Did the elves reach Silvalaria?"

"They did," Birion answered, "though the road was not without its troubles. We encountered no wizards, but there were other groups seeking to prevent our passing."

"The mean little, green-skinned kind," Honarch said. "The Woodswardens with us considered the goblins' numbers and locations unusual, but predictable enough for those prepared to look."

Birion agreed. "I think that with the threat now identified, efforts will be made by both nations to keep the road between them open."

"Thank you," Enna said, the first words she had spoken since Shalindra had begun her narrative.

Birion accepted her thanks politely. "We guested with the elves only a short time before continuing back to Newlmir but made ready to leave again almost as soon as we arrived."

"Tormjere kept me aware of what was happening with the dohedron," Honarch said, "at least in general terms. We were probably closing in on Kirchmont about the time you returned to Ildalarial."

"Just the three of you?"

"Closer to forty," Birion said. "Vestus came with us to try and establish more reliable trade routes, and he returned with both merchants and men."

"We had already resolved to come find you," Honarch said, "and it's not like we could march around the Kingdom with a company of soldiers and not attract notice, though I seem to have garnered all the wrong types of attention already."

Shalindra winced. "My father, no doubt due to the attempts on his life, has apparently branded all users of magic as traitors."

"That… explains a lot."

"What are your plans now?" Birion asked.

"That remains a bit of a question," Shalindra said. "The direction I was given was more vague than I wished for it to be, but it was made clear that I was to learn more of my predecessors, and that it would be accomplished with the help of others."

"I am at a loss for how we can aid your quest," Birion said, "but I will do the best I am able."

"Treven would be the most reliable source of information," Honarch said. "But he wasn't in Kirchmont. No one would say where he went, but he wasn't expected back until next year."

"Anywhere would be better than sitting here," Shalindra said. "Already I feel the pressure of time. Something has changed in the world, and it is not for the better. I need to find answers, and I dare not seek Eluria for them. It is upon me to seek the wisdom of the fallen, but I do not know where to begin."

"What does that even mean?" Birion asked.

Enna answered. "Every Guardian has sought to build upon the knowledge gained by their predecessors. Though each has faced their own trials, it is thought that there is an underlying purpose of which we are simply unaware."

"Would that not be 'wisdom of the dead?'" Honarch asked.

"If you wish to translate it that way. Every Guardian died in pursuit of her goal, so it would not be inaccurate."

"One of them didn't."

Heads turned in surprise at the hoarse statement. Fendrick had been so quiet and still throughout their discussions that Shalindra had almost forgotten he was there.

He raised his eyes to hers with resignation before dropping them once more. "I know whom you seek, my lady."

"I am not looking for someone specific but for the wisdom they left behind. I cannot speak to the dead."

Fendrick took a deep breath, as if mustering the courage to make the words come. "One of them didn't die."

Enna shook her head adamantly. "You are mistaken. Every Guardian's body lies in Ildalarial."

"Aye, all their bodies are there. But one of them never returned."

The color drained from Enna's face, and Honarch sat up a little straighter. "What you speak of…"

"It's not possible," Enna almost whispered. "No Guardian would allow such evil to be done to her."

"What are you talking about?" Shalindra asked.

Honarch's brow furrowed. "There are ways to keep the spirit tied to this world long after death, but it requires the darkest arts, ones that even the Conclave shuns. It's a horrible thing to inflict upon someone."

Shalindra was thankful that she had not mentioned that she held everything that had been Tormjere inside her, or her friends would surely have labeled her a monster for doing so. It opened a new, disturbing possibility that she might be doing harm to his focus simply by possessing it.

"Why not tell us sooner?" Enna almost shouted, leaping to her feet. "If you knew of—"

"She wasn't a Guardian," Fendrick shot back, stabbing a finger at Shalindra. "How many people would you want disturbing your peace?"

"And so you just show up now with the information we need?" Enna challenged, refusing to back down. "The last Guardian was betrayed by a dwarf. Do you seek to erase the stain on your race or repeat that triumph?"

"You've been listening to your mother too much. She wasn't… Never mind. I'll not debate your distortions of history, for it serves little good." He met Shalindra's eyes fully this time. "I'll take you to see her, should you wish to go."

"Where?" Shalindra asked.

"Ask me again when we reach Highfall."

Chapter Thirteen

A Familiar Road

Shalindra watched from her saddle as the golden leaf drifted through the air, following its erratic flight as it floated ever closer until it settled gently on her outstretched palm. Such an improbable set of circumstances were required for the intersection of those seemingly unrelated objects that it could legitimately be considered random. And yet, this coincidence could be traced back through every action and choice which had influenced it and, if relived in the same sequence, would produce an identical result. Indeed, no matter how improbable, the events would not be capable of producing any other outcome. The same might be said of the situation she currently found herself in, though the leaf was undoubtedly more cheerful about its own predicament.

She allowed it to slip from her fingers as she guided her horse off the road and around a downed tree, following Birion's mount as the former knight picked his way through the uneven terrain. The sturdy oak blocking their path had been healthy and strong and should have stood for decades, but the ground had become too soggy to support it during last night's storm. Whether the tree's demise was a fitting allegory for the present situation or a bad omen of what was to come, she could not tell. Her mind toyed with both, using each like a lens to peer into her own future.

It was a thought that went nowhere, as so many of them did now. Or rather, it went somewhere she was simply unable to follow. The true question was whether she needed to be aware of what lay beyond her understanding or if it was simply irrelevant information.

This was a time when she would have welcomed conversation with someone other than herself, but those around her were uninterested in the concept. It was difficult to imagine a more dispirited group on the road today. Honarch had seemed almost indifferent to their chosen direction, his spirits crushed by the loss of what was likely the best friend he had ever known. Enna, whose cheerfulness had been slowly restored while helping the young Sisters in Jonrin, had retreated to sullen unhappiness, certain that her objections were again being ignored. Shalindra glanced over her shoulder and saw Fendrick still bringing up the rear. The normally taciturn dwarf had become even more tight-lipped about their destination since making his proclamation.

Enna caught her look and frowned, though her displeasure could have been directed at either of them, or both. She had already made her distrust of the dwarf known—both publicly and privately—and would likely do so again. But, in spite of the tenuous explanation Fendrick had supplied, they had nothing else to go on. If there was even a glimmer of truth in the dwarf's words, it would be worth it.

Surprisingly, the various *hers* who had made their opinions known were in general agreement that this was the correct path to take, and they had settled into relative silence once the decision had been made. Not that they were idle, they were simply being less noisy about it. There was no pattern to what they might dispute or condone, and Shalindra was beginning to tire of trying to make sense of herself, even if the condition was becoming moderately easier to cope with.

Regardless of the wisdom of this endeavor, Shalindra was ambivalent about retracing her road south and travelling on through Merallin, a necessity for securing passage by boat to the dwarvish city of Highfall. While it would provide an excuse to see her family once more, she worried that she would be dragged deeper into the politics of the Kingdom. Her dinner with Baron Halthon had served as an ungentle reminder that while she might consider herself apart from the affairs of the Kingdom, many others still regarded her as a member of the royal family. It was a responsibility she had no desire to take on and one that would only further complicate her sacred task. She already had enough to worry about.

They passed the site of the demon attack on the company of soldiers without pausing. It had changed dramatically in the few days since she and Enna had first seen it. A large, blackened scar marked the site of an immense fire, and the remnants of a charred boot spoke to the flames' intent. Anything of value looked to have been carried away, though some warped and damaged metal remained. She was glad that someone had been able to do more for them than she and Enna could have.

The day was drawing to a close when they came within sight of the small village, marking them only a few hours north of Merrywood.

"Do we stop here or continue?" Birion asked.

"Merrywood is not much farther, but we will not reach it before sunset," she said. "This will have to do."

There was no inn, nor even a proper tavern, in the tiny village, but one building was filled with light and laughter and was as good a place as any to check. Fendrick and Enna held the horses—Fendrick because it was a chore he had generally taken upon himself, and Enna likely so she could keep an eye on him. Shalindra and Birion were almost to the door when they were stopped by a familiar voice.

"I wouldn't do that if I were you."

Heads turned as Weeby emerged from the shadows, a knowing grin on his small face and a sack slung over a shoulder. "That's not a good place to stay with a wizard."

The halfling drew close, and Birion shifted, interposing himself between Shalindra and the smaller man. Weeby stopped, bemused by the knight's action.

"I would not expect those problems here," Shalindra said guardedly.

"I'd expect it everywhere now if I were you, unfortunately," Weeby said.

"What became of your message to the king?" Shalindra asked, wondering where the wizard was. "I would have thought you to have reached Merallin by now."

Weeby shrugged. "There's always something to slow us down.

We tried to ask for rooms here, but in case you haven't heard, and for reasons known only to himself, your king has taken a disliking to wizards and has put a price on their heads. *All* their heads, including Master Honarch's, no matter his current affiliation."

Honarch's eyes narrowed suspiciously, which Shalindra took to mean that he had never met the halfling before now.

"It is an unfortunate decision," she said, "no matter how unsurprising."

Weeby gestured down the road. "We've a nice place to rest just outside of town. It's a bit below my normal standards, you understand, but one goes where he must. I wanted to push through to Merrywood, but Hammett insisted we stop. I can't decide if he's cracked or brilliant."

"And you are still eager for our company?" Shalindra asked, surprised.

"I fear our difficulties will only increase the further south we travel, and Verelli needs to reach Merallin soon." He glanced at each face in turn, lingering on Honarch longer than the rest. "Still no Tormjere?"

There was a surprising amount of hope in his voice, but his eyes said he already knew the answer.

"He will not be joining us," she said.

"That's too bad," Weeby said softly, then shook his head. "Our camp's not far. Follow me."

* * *

Shalindra read the wary distrust in Verelli's stance long before they drew close enough to speak. The encampment they had established was in a clearing just off the road, with thick branches overhead to shield them from any rain that might appear and a small fire crackling in the middle. Hammett looked up with a smile as if he had been expecting them, but there was no sign of Eljorn.

"Look who I found wandering about," Weeby said, plopping down beside the wizard and pulling food from his sack.

"Ah," Hammett said with a smile, "your path seems to have turned in a new direction, and with more friends, yet without them all. Most unfortunate."

"You have not made it very far since our last meeting," Shalindra said to Verelli, changing the subject.

"We were delayed by the remnants of the battle up the road," Verelli said with a sardonic frown. "The one you obviously rode right past without doing anything."

Shalindra flushed at the rebuke, for they had indeed left the soldiers with little more than a short prayer.

"But you are correct," Verelli continued. "We have been delayed long enough, and I intend to make every effort to speed our way to Merallin. Can I assume that is your destination as well?"

"It is." She certainly was not going to tell him where they were headed beyond that.

"Then I might propose we do so together, to stave off the predations of the uninformed."

Shalindra glanced at Hammett, but the monk was poking at the fire as if nothing was amiss.

"It should be obvious by now that I am not here to cause you harm," Verelli added.

"That would be a first," Enna scoffed.

"The damage we cause is often unintentional," Shalindra said.

"Do you have a demon necklace?"

"A demon…? Do you refer to a summoning focus?" Verelli asked with the bemused superiority of a professional entertaining a layman. "No. It is a branch of magic into which I have never delved, so if that is what you fear you may rest easy."

"He's actually telling the truth," Weeby said in response to her suspicious look. "It's something of a running joke amongst the Conclave."

Shalindra found it difficult to take either of them at their word, but Verelli's offer touched off a tempest of debate within her head. Some of the *hers* argued on his behalf, for differing reasons, while others vocally demanded they leave immediately, and at least one recommended doing away with him on the spot. The argument was unlikely to produce a consensus any time soon, but the people physically standing around her were waiting on her answer.

"We will travel alongside you," Shalindra said to Verelli, "but only as far as Merallin. The success of your venture is not my concern."

"Fair enough," Verelli said.

Their conversation was interrupted by Eljorn appearing from the forest, his arms full of wood.

"Hello again," he said cheerfully, depositing the branches by the fire.

Enna gave her a meaningful poke in the back, but the encouragement was not needed. Shalindra had no intention of allowing the news to reach him from anyone else's lips.

Shalindra addressed the younger monk. "May I speak to you for a moment?"

Eljorn nodded in surprise and followed her a short distance away.

"You travelled with my brother," he said.

"From the day he saved my life," Shalindra replied. "He kept me safe from so many…" She paused, a sudden lump in her throat. No matter how many people she told, it never got any easier.

Eljorn's soft voice drew her back. "I assume that you do not bring good news."

Shalindra shook her head. "Tormjere gave his life for me, not three weeks ago. I am sorry. Every day I struggle to realize that he is no longer here."

Bemused indifference was a hallmark of the monks of Toush, but cracks formed in Eljorn's calm demeanor. "I can see that his loss was difficult for you," he said, his voice thick with emotion, "but I would like to know what happened, if you would be willing to share."

The request was neither morbid nor mopey. Shalindra intended to avoid going into detail, but once she began, the words flowed. She spoke of their battles with the demons, and of how he had helped prevent a war. The rising sliver of the moon had shifted across the sky by the time she told of her Ascension and Tormjere's sacrifice for her. When she was done, she wiped the wetness from her cheeks. Why could she not just say it without falling apart?

"I fear that in my own grief, I have overlooked a great many things, and it was in selfishness that I did not tell you when we first met. Forgive me."

Though his eyes were rimmed in red, Eljorn's smile was as placid as a lake without a breeze. "Every path leads to where it must," he quoted, "and arrives when it should. My brother walked his more assuredly than many who spend their lives trying, and I will find my comfort in that."

* * *

The day had barely begun as the now larger group approached Merrywood, but they made no plans to stop. They had plenty of provisions and a long way to go, and everyone was eager to reach the capital, though for vastly different reasons. Shalindra pondered her own as she rode. Her nighttime musings had been filled with questions about the Guardian who did not die, and she desperately wanted to find someone who would understand what was happening to her. No one else could, no matter how vivid their imagination or how sincere their attempt.

As wonderful as it was to have Hammett nearby once more, she was already questioning the wisdom of travelling with Verelli and Weeby. She intended to be rid of them the moment they reached Merallin, but until then she would caution the group to keep any mention of their true objective a secret. There was no telling what damage the wizard could do should he discover what they intended.

The tavern she and Enna had stayed at almost looked deserted as there were few people out and about this morning. There was nothing unusual about that, but something else felt… odd.

She slowed her horse as her eyes wandered around the area, her thoughts pulled back to the present by the unknown discrepancy. The small collection of buildings clustered around Conygate's Tavern marked a waypoint for travelers, but the town proper followed the elvish custom of situating itself off the road. The low hills between it and her were heavily wooded, with only hints of structures and a narrow wagon track winding into the trees to mark its location. The town was doubtless as beautiful as any elvish one, where trees outnumbered dwellings and there was a positivity in the inhabitants, but it was not the possibility of such a serene appearance that held her interest now.

Nothing amiss was visible, but there was a sharp odor of sulfur and smoke that left an aftertaste in the back of her throat. Her horse eased itself to a halt, sensing her disinterest in continuing forward. The others slowed as well.

Birion began to question the pause, but he was preempted by the sharp crack of splintering wood, accompanied by an all too familiar roar mixed with screams of terror.

Shalindra set heels to her horse, galloping towards the town. Branches whipped past her in a blur of greens and browns, then she was through the forest, bursting into a scene of chaos. Bodies littered the curving street, and a pair of buildings had been gutted. She raced ahead until the street became blocked by the hulking, humanoid form of a goat demon. Its grey fur was torn and matted by dark blood, but it showed no signs of weakness as it savaged the few brave souls who stood against it.

Its elongated head swiveled towards her the moment she came within sight. Tossing aside one of its victims, it leapt towards her.

Shalindra's horse balked, kicking clumps of damp earth into the air as it skidded to a frantic stop, but she vaulted from the saddle and hit the ground at a sprint, Shining Moon already filling her left arm with its radiant warmth. Cold rage gripped her as she sought to take Eluria's symbol with her right, but her fingers had already found their home, wrapped tightly around the hilt of her sword. She yanked it free as the goat demon spread its thick arms wide.

The demon's rush to meet her was clumsy, and slower than expected. She deftly spun beneath its grasping claws and slashed low. The creature stumbled, and Shalindra allowed the swing of Shining Moon to pull her around as it streaked in a blur of slivery blue that impacted the demon's elongated head like a thunderclap. The beast was driven abruptly into the ground, and did not move again.

Even before her hair had settled once more about her shoulders, Shalindra allowed her vision to shift, revealing a reddish haze around the demon. It coalesced into shimmering sparks drifting up from the corpse like embers riding currents of heat above a fire. With eagerness she drew a deep breath, pulling the sparks towards herself, relishing the tingling burn as they—

Shalindra gasped and took a halting step back, shaking her head to clear it. What was she doing?

Taking what you're going to need.

Was she? What possible use could she have for the life energies—or powers, or whatever they were—of so foul a creature? And why was she standing here talking to herself like this?

The multiple *hers* were practically screaming in their attempts to divert her attention, but the impetus of their pleas faded before the warm temptation of those burning embers hanging in the air before her, tantalizingly close. She had only to—

"Guardian?"

She forced her head to twist away from the demon and towards

Enna's hesitant approach. Behind her, Birion stood beside his horse with mouth open, his spear still half in its lashings. Fendrick was lowering a strangely curved metal bow, easing an iron bolt from the string without ever letting the first one fly. Honarch extinguished the flame burning in his palm with a flick of his wrist, and even Verelli regarded her with surprise.

Shalindra's eyes returned to the demon, the air above it now blessedly devoid of what she had thought to consume, and only then did she realize what they were staring at. The creature's massive thigh, as thick as Birion's shoulders were broad, was laid open to the bone, while its bovid head was caved in, the right side crushed into the left like an apple trod upon by a horse.

She cleared her throat and hurriedly wiped her sword on the demon's coarse fur before returning both weapons to her belt, embarrassed. "We should see if there are any more."

Birion was the first to recover his poise. "I will investigate, my lady."

Honarch remained slack jawed at the display, but Weeby just chuckled as he looked up at Verelli. "And you wondered why street thugs never slowed them down."

A muted cheer rose from the villagers, one tempered by the trail of splintered buildings and broken lives the beast had wrought.

Her part in the battle had been short, but the aftermath of the assault was as terrible as any Shalindra had been forced to behold. Merrywood was a town of wood and trees, not a castle with stout walls. The bodies left behind were those of farmers and shopkeeps clad in wool and linen, not soldiers in leather and steel.

Enna set herself to healing those that she could. Shalindra went to join her, hoping that restoring their wounds would settle the unease building within her, but was stopped by a voice from behind.

"Revered Guardian?"

She recognized the speaker as Dorven, the elf from the tavern she and Enna had visited, and she beckoned him closer.

"Eluria preserve us for your arrival," he said, out of breath.

"There are many injured," she replied. "We need to get them to the temple."

"I'm sorry, Guardian," Doren stammered. "Eluria's temple was torn apart by that monstrosity."

Shalindra's blood ran cold. "Show me."

Enna had heard as well, and she rushed her restoration to catch up to them. Shalindra hurried after Dorven, only vaguely aware that most of her group followed.

The temple here was as much wood as marble, but neither material had withstood the demon's wrath. The once beautiful columns had been knocked to the ground and its gardens trampled, and bodies in the white of Eluria could be seen in the rubble.

"They died praying for salvation that never came," Enna said through clenched teeth, choking on the words. Her body shook, and before Shalindra could respond, Enna spun, her eyes locking on Verelli. "Where is its master?"

"I have no idea—"

"Don't lie to me!" Enna screamed, grabbing his tunic and yanking him forward. "I am sick of seeing my Sisters slaughtered for your amusement! Is it yours?"

Birion and Shalindra rushed to pull her away.

Verelli stepped back, straightening his clothes. "I will forgive you that assault as you are understandably distraught, but do not ever think to lay hands on me again."

"Her accusation is valid," Birion said, still holding Enna tightly. "And you should take care with your threats."

Verelli made no attempt to mask his disgust with all of them. "Then I suggest you apply logic rather than emotion to the situation." He began ticking points off on his fingers. "It has been conveyed that uncontrolled demons are the reason I am here. We have further established that I do not possess the required summoning focus nor the desire to use it. And, lastly, I am not the least bit interested in wasting time tearing down this insignificant village when I should have been in Merallin weeks ago."

Enna seethed with barely contained anger, but she shook herself free of Birion's grasp and went to help those retrieving bodies from the temple.

Shalindra felt a similar burn of anger, but it was oddly constrained for its potency. "This village is not insignificant to those who live here."

"There are *thousands* of people dying in Ceringion who think otherwise," Verelli said. "Now, if you'll excuse me, I intend to examine the remains of the creature so that this day is not a complete waste of my time."

"I'll keep an eye on him," Honarch said quietly, hurrying after him.

Shalindra looked around for Eljorn or Hammett, but she was left standing alone with Birion. "I had hoped we were done with demons, but I fear that there will be no avoiding them no matter what we decide."

"You will do what is best, Your Highness. You always have."

Shalindra clenched her hands helplessly. The incarnations of herself arguing in her head could not agree on that sentiment either.

* * *

Shalindra slipped away as the ceremony drew to a close, needing to remove herself from the field which now embraced the dead. Enna's invocation had been eloquent, delivered with a comforting calmness that offered hope to those who had suffered such terrible and unexpected loss. But the departed could not be brought back to life, no matter how unjust the circumstances or how fervent the prayer.

The sounds of crickets overrode the lingering sobs of grief as Shalindra entered the trees, and their song continued as she returned to the winding, wooded roads of the town. The streets were peaceful and empty, save for the debris left from the demon's rampage. It was a horrible thing to have happened to this beautifully unique place. Eluria's temple was so ravaged that it would need to be rebuilt from the ground up. The sight of it angered her even now, but the emotion evaporated as a soft humming reached her ears. She followed the sound and discovered Hammett removing broken stones from the garden in front of a cottage. The old monk paused at her approach.

"Has Sister Enna completed her service?" he asked.

"She has. I am sure the townspeople will be returning soon."

"Good. There is so much to do, and many hands make for light work. Setting order to the chaos can be soothing."

"We are leaving in the morning." The words came faster than they should have and sounded more like a rejection than she would have wished. She was not unsympathetic to what had happened here, but rebuilding a town was not her purpose. Still, Hammett judged her kindly.

"As you should, for there are other places you need to be. My path has brought me here, and here I will remain for a time."

"I wish you did not have to, but their need is far greater than mine."

Hammett rolled a piece of wall stone from the bed and straightened a flower it had bent. "Eljorn's path will continue to coincide with yours, for a time."

"I am grateful for that, but how can you be certain? Can you read my future as clearly?"

"Would you want to know it if I could?"

Shalindra glanced back at the ruined temple. "If I could alter such tragedies as this, then yes. But if I was unable to prevent them… I do not know."

Hammett's face split into a wide grin. "A path cannot be known until it is walked, and a path already known cannot be changed. To know the future is to lose your ability to alter it."

"You seem to know where you are going more than the rest of us."

His eyes twinkled. "That is because I look where I'm going. You should try it sometime. But first, make sure that you know where you are."

* * *

Shalindra closed the door to her room—the same one she and

126

Enna had occupied in their earlier stay at Conygate's Tavern—wishing she was anywhere but here. Weariness gripped her, but it was neither from overexertion nor a soreness of the muscles signaling a solid day's work. It was a numbness that drifted through her mind like a morning fog in the forest. She needed to sleep, to allow herself to find peace in the dreams and darkness that occupied the time between one day and the next, and which could restore her faith and purpose in ways that nothing else could.

But she would not sleep tonight, the same as every other night since her Ascension, and she despaired that she would ever know such tranquility again. Such pleasures seemed destined to elude her, and so she turned her thoughts back to the events of the day. She was finding such introspection to be a calming ritual, as the reality of those recent memories was more certain than those of the other *hers* she was forced to experience.

As Hammett had said, however, she needed to look towards where she was going rather than the past. The manner in which she had defeated the demon was already being celebrated and retold as a display of righteous strength by those who had witnessed it. But it did not feel impressive to her. In fact, it felt like barely any effort at all. There had been no need to invoke Eluria. She had not even been winded, having expended no more energy than one might do to shoo a fly from their food. The specifics of what she had done were already growing fuzzy in her mind, while the shocked expressions on the faces of her friends remained crystal clear.

She sat on the floor and placed Shining Moon on the warped planks before her, then lay the sword alongside it. The hammer was shorter and the slightest bit heavier. The sword stretched two hands longer, its blade broad and perfectly balanced, designed for cutting and slashing rather than stabbing. They complemented each other, both simple weapons made for a specific purpose and employed in perfect harmony with each other.

Before today, she had held a naked blade only once in her entire life, on the smoke-filled streets of Jonrin as her bodyguards were slain before her. Her knowledge of swordplay was no greater now than then, yet she had employed it in her off hand with the precision and strength of one trained to it. And again, she had been driven by anger.

It was not a blind rage that had sent her vaulting from her horse, nor had it been the raw anger that had driven Enna to assault Verelli. It had been a simmering rejection of the unwarranted destruction being done against those who could not defend themselves. And there had been satisfaction in her victory as she had never felt before.

The answer to why was as simple as it was disturbing: she was dangerous. Not only to her enemies but to her friends. Things were happening to her which were well beyond her control, and she possessed incredible power, yet without the knowledge of its proper employment. The people of Merrywood might now be safe from the predations of the demon, but if she succumbed to her anger, if it should blossom into rage as it had in Ildalarial, who would be safe from her?

The door opened on creaking hinges as Enna entered the room, only to stop when she saw the weapons on the floor. "Trying to decide who you are?" she asked, turning to withdraw. "I'll leave you to your thoughts."

"Please do not," Shalindra begged. "I spend too much time with my own and would much rather hear yours."

Enna took another step away, then made an unpleasant sound as she spun to face Shalindra.

"I do not trust the wizard or Fendrick," she declared, stabbing a finger in the general direction of their rooms, "and I have no idea why you would presume to do so either. The Conclave has done nothing but seek our deaths, and the last Guardian was betrayed by a dwarf. On this the histories are clear."

Shalindra returned sword and hammer to where they belonged as she stood. "But could what Fendrick says be true? Could one of the Guardians still exist somehow?"

Enna's shoulders eased. "Such feats are indeed possible, as Honarch said. But it is a crime against nature to cause one's soul to linger beyond death, and only the darkest of arts could make it so. If we find truth in his claims, it will raise far more questions than it might answer."

Shalindra suppressed a shudder. "What you describe is, indeed, a terrible thing to contemplate, but the chance to speak directly to a past Guardian cannot be ignored, no matter how slim."

"And if he seeks to lure you into a trap?" Enna pressed. "We will be far from help in the dwarflands."

"I still have difficulty believing that Fendrick means us harm. Not only did he make the sword I now carry but he arrived with Treven, and I have met no finer judge of character than Amalthee's Legitarso."

"But why would a simple blacksmith journey all the way to the valley and then all the way here seeking you?"

"Because he had something he wanted to tell Tormjere, but never did. I am not blinded by his appearance of a simple profession. This blade is unique and imbued with qualities no average smith could achieve. He was waiting for us to come back, and it follows that he must have been planning to tell us all along."

"But isn't it suspicious—"

The sound of someone clearing their throat drew their attention to where Honarch stood at the open door.

"Sorry to cut you off," Honarch said.

Enna's eyes flashed at the interruption, but Shalindra waved him in. He pointedly closed the door before speaking and kept his voice calm.

"I haven't been able to ask without making a scene, but has Verelli told you who he is?"

"He has not, beyond stating that he is working for the Imaretii. I presume he is a wizard of some standing since he intends to speak to my father. Our conversations have been brief, by choice."

"Premis Verelli is the second most powerful mage in the entire Conclave, working at the right hand of Master Fellaxus. He's probably the most dangerous man you will ever encounter."

Enna made an exasperated noise and rolled her eyes.

"You also feel we should not be travelling with him then?" Shalindra asked.

Honarch shrugged. "You seem to surround yourself with dangerous people all the time, so I'm sure you can handle him, but never forget who he is."

"Can he be trusted?"

The words sounded foolish the moment she said them, and Honarch's frown conveyed his thoughts clearly. "He was well regarded within the highest circles, at least when I was there. I knew him by reputation only, but I would suggest paying more attention to what he *doesn't* promise than what he does."

It was sound advice, but clearly not the only thing on his mind. "Is there anything else about him that troubles you?"

"The fact that he's here. The Conclave is comprised of hundreds of wizards, many of them far more accomplished than me. They have allies in every city and royal house in Ceringion. For him to come this far seeking help implies that whatever has taken place, it's something that all of those wizards have been unable to deal with. I'm not suggesting that you trust him, but it might be wise to listen to what he has to say."

"I will. Thank you for sharing this with us."

"Good night, then," he said, turning for the door.

"Honarch?"

He stopped.

"How are you feeling?"

"I'm fine," he said, closing the door behind himself as he left.

Shalindra knew it for the lie it was, because it was the same one she had been telling herself.

Chapter Fourteen

Uncertain Futures

It was a relief when the squared towers of Adair came into view above the steeply rolling hills. Though they became hidden once more as the road wound over and around the undulating terrain, the simple fact that they were close lifted everyone's spirits. Not only would their arrival in the city mark them only one long day's ride from Merallin but they would all be able to get away from each other before serious injury was inflicted.

They had attracted less attention once Honarch had exchanged his robes for a more common tunic and leggings, but the past four days had been some of the most unenjoyable in Shalindra's recent memory, which was saying something, given all she had been forced to endure. During their short journey, Verelli had drifted between surly silence and thinly veiled superiority, while Weeby had done his best to act as peacemaker between the wizard and the rest of the group, but in an unwholesomely clever kind of way. Fendrick kept to himself at the back and barely spoke at all, and Enna was simply unhappy with everyone. Birion, ever practical, had gone about the business and logistics of moving their group with every semblance of order, though even he was growing tired of Verelli's smugness.

Eljorn's presence was likely the only thing preventing bloodshed. Shalindra was thankful that the monk had remained with them, as he seemed able to redirect them towards more optimistic subjects whenever animosity flared.

"Well, at least there's not an army here anymore," Weeby observed, doing his part to remain chipper.

It was, indeed, the most readily apparent difference in the city Shalindra had visited just weeks before. Gone were the armies that had encamped on the steep hills outside the walls. No signs remained of the tent where her brother had attempted to kill her father, and in turn died as a result. The skies were still grey and the fields still trampled and muddy, but it was a city preparing for winter rather than war.

The gates were guarded but open. Enna received only a distrustful look as they walked their horses through, so at least that attitude was improving.

"We should visit our temple," Enna said to Shalindra, "and see how badly it has suffered."

Verelli ignored the accusatory glance she shot him, keeping his attention focused on something in the city Shalindra could not see.

"Given what has befallen the others we have been to, that would be wise," Shalindra said, "but they will not be able or willing to provide rooms for all of us."

"There's a nice tavern a couple of streets uphill from it," Weeby said. "You can even see the gardens from there."

They all turned to look at him.

"What?" Weeby asked in response. "I can't be the only one who's been here before."

Eljorn gave one of his bemused grins. "A path is always easier the second time it is walked." His demeanor was as calming as any follower of Toush should be, but his words carried a dry humor in the same way Tormjere's always had. "I have often wondered what the gardens of Eluria's temples were like. If it is not an imposition, would I be allowed inside?"

"I don't see why not," Enna said, apparently pleased at his interest.

Shalindra was more thankful for the brevity of the route Weeby chose, as she continued to draw stares and whispers even though she was doing nothing more interesting than walking her horse down the street. Birion moved protectively close to her, and Fendrick took it upon himself to keep close to Enna. Neither supervision was necessary, but she appreciated their concern.

"I confess that I don't like being the center of attention when I travel," Weeby said. "You must be used to it by now."

"Not exactly," Shalindra said.

The temple was situated halfway up the hill on the eastern side of the river and, as Weeby had promised, there was an inn just a short walk uphill. It was to the latter destination they arrived first.

Birion entered to secure rooms, returning moments later with confirmation.

"Does he know what we are?" Honarch asked.

"I neglected to supply any details," Birion said, "but you and Verelli would be wise to appear normal, should you venture anywhere."

"I *was* normal until we came here," Honarch pointed out.

"My purpose does not involve wandering the streets," Verelli said. "I intend to remain here."

"I'll do the same," Honarch agreed.

"We've all got somewhere to be that isn't here," Fendrick reminded them, "and an early day tomorrow."

Weeby handed the reins of his horse to Verelli. "I'm for stretching my legs a bit. I'll be back by nightfall. Try to stay out of trouble until then."

"Where's he off to?" Enna asked suspiciously.

Verelli gave her a withering look. "As he did not say, I have no idea. He is an acquaintance, not a servant."

Shalindra wondered where as well, and no sooner had the thought struck her than her body produced an ethereal copy, which detached itself from her with a sensation not unlike that of pulling apart a loaf of bread. Her ghostly outline followed the halfling out the door while her physical self remained stationary. Her vision shifted in parallax, and from both perspectives she witnessed Weeby's corporal form follow a side street while his ghostly doppelganger, perhaps aware it was being followed by hers, took a turn in the opposite direction.

Both projections disappeared as a wave of nausea swept over her, and she shook her head to clear it. It was interesting that the halfling would have chosen a different street had she been watching, but she would rather learn how to prevent or at least control such foretellings. Having not been visited by them since their dash from Ildalarial, she had begun to believe that she had succeeded in banishing them. Why they had chosen now to return was a mystery.

"Are you alright, my lady?" Birion asked.

"I am fine," she lied, something which she had been doing far too often of late.

She turned to Enna. "Shall we?"

* * *

The temple of Eluria was an elegantly magnificent structure, rising to a white marble peak four stories high and stretching for over a block, with walled terraces of lush greenery spreading down the hillside below. Across the front, six large columns supported a triangular marble face, carved with scenes of sacrifice and compassion, divine restoration, and indomitable conviction. It was a fair summary of the order's history, but what drew Shalindra's eye the most were the figures of the Guardian in battle. Dragons, withered husks, and other monsters all lay vanquished beneath the feet of Eluria's chosen.

Shalindra's current life felt nothing like the exploits depicted in those stone figures. Had any of them wandered blindly as she now did, searching for what they were supposed to achieve?

"It is a beautiful structure," Eljorn commented.

Enna agreed. "The tranquility of our gardens has served as my refuge in more than one human city."

Although the manicured paths were empty of people, the trio's approach did not go unnoticed. The doors of the temple were open and attended by a single, white-robed Sister. She disappeared suddenly before returning to her station moments later, where she stood nervously awaiting their approach, her eyes never leaving

Shalindra.

"Welcome Guardian, Sister," she said as they ascended the broad, flat steps that stretched across the entire front of the building. "How may I assist you?" Her words came out in a nervous tumble, and Shalindra smiled gently to put her at ease.

"We are seeking only a break from our travels, and a few moments of peace."

The Sister began to speak but was interrupted by a middle-aged woman arriving beside her.

"We are blessed by your presence, Guardian," the older woman said calmly. "I am Lillia, Sister Superior of this temple. Welcome to Adair. It is wonderful to see one of our Sisters from Ildalarial as well." She bowed her head to Enna.

"I'm relieved to be here," Enna said.

Lillia smiled at Eljorn. "We are rarely visited by those walking their path, but I pray that our hospitality might repay even a fraction of the kindness so often shown to us by your brothers. Please, be welcome."

"Thank you," Eljorn said. "If it's no trouble, I think I shall wander these magnificent gardens while you attend to business. Every path requires contemplation."

"It does, indeed. I might suggest the far corner on the downhill side as the best suited for that purpose."

Eljorn bowed politely and headed in that direction.

"I, too, could use the time to contemplate things," Enna said suddenly. "If you do not mind."

Shalindra did not want to be left as the center of attention but was hardly surprised. "Take as much time as you need."

Enna bowed politely and followed in the general direction Eljorn had gone.

"Our road has been difficult," Shalindra said in response to Lillia's questioning look, "and if any of us deserve an escape from worry, it is Enna."

"There has been enough worry to go around," Lillia admitted, inviting her inside with a sweep of her arm.

The worship chamber was large, with a vaulted ceiling tall enough to accommodate the large sculpture of Eluria at the far end. A circular pool of water lay at the statue's feet, its edges inscribed with the phases of the moon.

"We only heard of your Ascension a few days ago," Lillia said as they walked slowly towards the statue. "I confess to a certain amount of pride at your selection, though it is not proper. To see a human woman as Her chosen is something generations of the faithful have prayed for."

"If not me, another would have stepped forward," Shalindra said. "It was only a short time ago that our order was unfairly targeted by those seeking harm to Ildalarial. How did you fare here with the armies so close outside the city?"

Sorrow was written on Lillia's face. "We have been fortunate to escape the worst of the persecution. We count several daughters of the nobility within our sisterhood, and their families saw that those of us here were kept safe. The faithful outside the walls faced different hardships and our other temples were abandoned, though one has recently reopened."

Other clerics were entering the sanctuary in twos and threes, and though they maintained a respectful distance, excited whispers began to fill the room. Lillia shooed them away.

"I doubt that you have chosen to visit our temple only to raise our spirits, though you have already done so. All our Sisters will certainly wish to meet you, but would you prefer some time to yourself first?"

"I sorely need it, but duty presses upon me. Enna and I are bound for Merallin, and Eljorn is but one of the five uninitiated who travel with us."

"Is it safe to assume none are women? We are not chaste, but neither could we accommodate so many men here at one time."

Shalindra had always been thankful her order did not suffer from that restriction, but appearances did need to be maintained. "Nor would I impose so greatly on you. They have secured rooms just up the hill from here."

"It would be such an honor for you and Sister Enna to stay here, of course," Lillia said. "I will make sure all is ready. Please, allow yourself at least a short time to gather your thoughts, and may Her Light guide you."

Shalindra had not planned to remain here but saw no way to refuse. "I will, thank you."

Lillia excused herself, and Shalindra stood alone in the sanctuary. It was not what she wanted to be doing, but her Sisters expected their Guardian to be the paragon of piety and devotion, and so she knelt by the pool. She remained that way for as long as she could bear to be alone with the conflicting thoughts of the other *hers*, then rose and walked from the room.

Lillia was waiting for her just outside, staring up at a globe of light floating gently above the door.

"Your visit is a blessing in more ways than one," Lillia said, attempting to remain calm as a Sister Superior must, but there was excitement in her words. "We forget what a miracle Her blessings are until they are denied us."

"It is precious, indeed," Shalindra said.

"I know that your time with us is short, but I can only believe it is your presence that allows us to receive Her gifts once more. We have many here who are in need of restoration, and if you could accompany me to see the injured in our care it would allow us to help so many."

There seemed no reason for her to affect their prayers in such a way, but if her physical presence aided her Sisters then it was a delay she would willingly endure.

* * *

The evening was cool but pleasant as Shalindra and Lillia emerged. She spotted Enna and Eljorn meandering along one of the paths, talking softly to each other, and they turned to join them.

"Did you enjoy our gardens?" Sister Lillia asked Eljorn.

"They are as tranquil as any place I have visited," he answered.

"Thank you for all you have done, Guardian," Sister Lillia said. "I will bid you all a safe evening, and may Her light continue to guide you."

"I'm for bed as well," Enna said quickly. "I'll see you back at the inn." She avoided Shalindra's eyes as she hurried inside, but this time it was not from anger—the wetness on her cheeks glistened in the moonlight.

"She was very close to Tormjere," Eljorn said. "Her path of

healing will take a long time."

"The three of us shared many a hardship," Shalindra answered, wondering how long it would be before she felt better about any of it.

"I believe she cares for you just as much, though, I admit, she has an interesting way of showing it."

Shalindra tried to chuckle, but it came out more of a sigh. "We frustrate each other like siblings."

"We each achieve our balance in different ways and at different times. Grief is a manifestation of our love for something left behind which cannot be retrieved, and we each accommodate it in our own way."

"You are handling this far better than I," Shalindra observed.

Eljorn's smile was one of pleasant memories rather than humor. "Perhaps I only view it from a different perspective. Did he ever tell you about the troll?"

The memory must have been strong, for Tormjere's focus shifted suddenly, pressing against the bounds of what held it together. She clamped down on it and shook her head, determined to hear this from his brother.

"I'm not surprised," Eljorn said. "He was never one to talk about himself in that way. It happened a few years before I began walking my path. Several of us were playing at the edge of town, as children without chores are wont to do, when a troll came crashing from the trees without warning. It was a terrible brute, and impossibly huge to my youthful eyes, and it came straight for us. Amber screamed. William ran. I stood petrified with fear, certain that we were all going to die.

"Then a stone struck it in the head, followed by another. I thought soldiers had come, but there was only my brother. The troll turned on him in anger, but he somehow dodged away. He did not yell or scream. He was not scared. There was an intensity to him that I had never seen, and he forced its attention onto himself and away from the two of us."

Shalindra's breath came fast. How many times had Tormjere done exactly the same for her?

"I cannot say how long that game of cat and mouse continued, for time stretches in unusual ways when one is under stress. Whether it was moments or minutes, soldiers eventually arrived and attacked. It clubbed one of them to death, and his spear fell to the grass. Tormjere was going for it when our mother came rushing in and dragged him away. I believe that had he reached it, he would have won, no matter how improbable that may seem.

"The troll was killed by the soldiers, but at a high cost. I will never forget that day. Tormjere could have fled and saved himself. It was his willingness to put others before himself that inspired me to follow Toush." Eljorn paused, and when he looked at her his eyes were red. "You wonder, perhaps, if his actions surprised me? I would have been more surprised had he done anything different. He never shied away from what needed to be done."

That was such a perfect summation of Tormjere. He always knew what needed to be done, and he always did it. "Would that I had such a clarity of purpose."

"The Way is always in front of us," Eljorn said. "We must only possess the courage to walk it."

His words conveyed different levels of meaning, and she

realized that she knew very little about this man who was Tormjere's younger brother. He filled the role of a tranquil monk so well that he often faded into the background, yet it seemed a mask disguising a much deeper purpose.

But she trusted him because there was sincerity in every word he spoke—the kind that cannot be feigned. It was easy talking with him, almost as much as with Tormjere, though without that unique connection they had shared.

"We are going to Highfall," she said before she could stop herself. "It is part of the task given to me, and… you would be welcome to come with us. I feel you are a boost to us all simply by being here."

"I shall remain with you as long as my path allows, but now I should return to the inn and make use of the bed you have so kindly arranged for me. Sleep well tonight, and may your dreams illuminate the road ahead."

His words followed her like a shadow all the way to her room. Was that what she lacked: The courage to face what lay before her? To do what needed to be done? If only she had the clarity of purpose both brothers seemed to possess.

I love you.

Such a simple statement should not continue to haunt her as it did, but it simmered at the edge of her thoughts whenever her mind was quiet. Those words had not been a lie. She could never accept that. The fierceness of his loyalty knew no bounds, and she would believe him an agent of their enemy before she would consider him a liar. There had to be something.

She was halfway inside his focus before she realized it, like a thief stealing her way into places she should not have been, yet she lacked the willpower to withdraw.

She slipped once more into the jumbled mess of his memories, not wanting to but desperate to find some truth to latch onto. Perhaps she needed to be more specific with what she sought to recall. There were many people Tormjere had loved—his parents, his uncle, his brother—but she wanted, *needed*, to find that emotion anchored to herself and so justify what had happened. It must have been a strong emotion, some realization that left an indelible image stamped into his memories. The past teased her, hovering just out of reach. There was something… They were in the farmer's hut, the one where she had shed her royal trappings and donned her disguise, taking her first step away from who and what she had been.

The scene solidified clearly, her own memories overlapping with his to weave a vision of such depth that it became more real than the present. He handed peasants clothes to the younger version of herself which were taken reluctantly. She turned away with him to look out the doorway, just as he had been told by the frightened princess who wanted only a return to her prior life yet had already begun to believe it would never happen. She felt his wariness as he watched for goblins but could still see her younger self from the corner of his eye as she stripped off her dress. He tried, but it was impossible to keep his attention outside. His furtive glance took in the smoothness of the skin across her back, the way her ribs showed as she bent to retrieve the peasant's robe, and flicked past the tender curve of her breast before hastily returning outside.

He *had* looked.

Shalindra did not know if she should laugh or cry, but she found herself doing both.

Still, a boy's lust was not enough to cause a man to sacrifice his life. She withdrew her thoughts from his focus, gently replacing the bands that held it together. There had to be more, but she would look for it another time.

Chapter Fifteen

Royal Reunion

They followed the road down the final hill and onto the sloping plain that marked the outskirts of Merallin, ancestral home of the Actondel family and capital of their kingdom. The river still ran high from the summer rains as it rushed to join the ocean, its wide mouth flowing past the plateau of bedrock that raised the castle and half the city above the surrounding lands. The skies were grey, and a fine mist was falling, leaving the normally festive pennants atop the spires of the castle hanging limp.

The weather had not altered the business of the many people moving along the road, but Shalindra's appearance did. She felt their eyes linger on her as she rode past, and many openly gawked at her passage. Thus, it was a man who passed her by without the barest glance that caught her attention. He was tall and strong, almost of a size with Birion, and had the look of someone who spent his days away from civilization. Something about him struck her as familiar, but she could not put her finger on it, and he was past before she could glimpse his face. Eljorn did make eye contact with the man, however, and his head cocked to the side inquisitively. There was a hint of acknowledgement in that reaction, but it was so fleeting that she questioned her assessment almost immediately. When nothing changed, she shrugged it off as meaningless.

Her thoughts had settled solidly back around what arguments she would make to her father to get him to rescind his anti-wizard decree when Eljorn unexpectedly pulled his horse to a stop.

"Your feet are on your path," the monk said, sliding from the saddle, "and here is where mine must turn in a different direction."

The group came to a halt on the side of the road with him.

"I had looked forward to your continued company," she said, caught off guard, "but we all have our path to follow."

"There are many ways to reach the same destination," he quoted.

"Where will you go?"

"First, to our monastery," Eljorn said with a pleasant smile, as if this was exactly what they had all planned. "Beyond that, only Toush knows."

"You don't want to keep your horse?" Enna asked, sounding equally surprised by the abrupt change.

"'A slower pace leads to a quicker mind,'" Eljorn quoted, "and you will have more need of it than I. But thank you."

"Allow me to return one favor, at least," Shalindra insisted, retrieving a loaf of bread from her saddle bags and handing it to him. "If you should see Hammett, please thank him again, for everything."

"I shall. May your paths always lead you to where you belong."

His statement encompassed the entire group, though he was looking at Enna when he said it. With that, he set off towards the forest where the monastery lay, whistling a cheerful tune.

Shalindra's heart was heavy as she watched him go, but that aching sense of loss was fleeting, more a memory of what had happened before rather than a reaction to the present.

Fendrick secured Eljorn's horse to his, and Birion led the group into the city. They passed through the outskirts, following the road as it drifted away from the river and towards the more reputable parts of town. The city was bustling with activity as it should have been, but the furtive and unwelcoming glances directed at them were surprising in their intensity. Birion noticed as well.

"They seem less than accommodating toward strangers," he said to her.

"Their hostility has been directed many places of late," she replied. "Eventually, that makes them distrustful of everyone."

"Could they be searching for clerics again?" Enna asked.

Shalindra's brow wrinkled. "I would not expect so given that the war was aborted, but that was barely more than a month ago."

As they drew closer to one of the five gates in the battlements dividing the old city from the new, traffic slowed, forming a long queue at least half a mile long. This same gate had proven a difficult barrier for Shalindra and Enna on their last visit, and the unusually long delay left her with a sense of unease.

Weeby hopped from his horse. "I'll go find out what the problem is," he said, tossing the reins to Fendrick.

The dwarf frowned, but Weeby had already disappeared into the crowds before he could complain.

The queue seemed to advance only when someone ahead of them abandoned their attempt to enter the city, and the halfling returned before they had made it more than a block, a worried look on his face.

"They're searching for wizards, and they're not being overly picky about who they harass. A beard and a robe seem enough to indicate guilt. There's a group working the queue outside the gates, and I saw them accost one of Amalthee's clerics just for walking around with some books. If we get much closer, we're sure to draw their attention."

"What about elves?" Enna asked.

"Hard to say as none are about, but I wouldn't expect a warm greeting either. They don't seem to like anyone right now."

"Our current manner of dress will pass casual scrutiny," Verelli said, "but both Honarch and I carry implements of our trade that will be obvious to anyone searching."

"I could try to demand entry," Shalindra said, "but without banners, a retinue, or anything but my word to go on, I doubt we will simply be allowed through. The best we could hope for would be to have someone summoned from the castle."

"It's more likely we'd be thrown in a cell for our efforts," Birion said. "This level of zealotry is not the kingdom I remember."

"Best to choose a different door then," Weeby said. "I think we'll find the river gate more accommodating."

Birion glanced at Shalindra, who shrugged. "We were fine once inside the walls last time, so one way is as good as another."

Weeby turned them sharply west, and they followed a meandering route towards the river. The quality of the roads slid steadily downward, as did the buildings along them. The noxious odors of tanning and dead fish seemed to blanket everything even more than the dirt and grime, and the streets became a warren of tunnels rather than proper thoroughfares. Even on the brightest day, this part of the city would remain a dingy and depressing place. After a series of sharp turns, Shalindra was thoroughly lost. From the increase in seabirds and the muted sounds of water lapping against the shore, she knew they were close to the riverside wharfs.

The looks they received from those forced to step aside for the horses were almost accusatory. Shalindra felt as out of place here as a beggar in the palace, but there was nothing to do but trust that Weeby knew where he was going.

"You'd both be less remarkable wearing something else," Weeby pointed out, stopping the group just inside a dead-end alley and sliding from his horse.

"No," Shalindra said, dismounting as well. "I have spent too long hiding, and it has caused more problems than it ever solved. The time for disguising myself is past."

Weeby looked around for support, but no one seemed willing to contradict her. "The horses are drawing a lot of attention as well. Most people in the poor quarter don't have any."

"I'll not sell ours," Shalindra said. "They are a gift, and I intend to see them returned to Ildalarial."

Weeby tapped his foot impatiently, then grinned. "Well, I do enjoy being creative. Let's have you and Enna go through with all of them. That will draw all the attention and make it easier for the rest of us to just mix with anyone else going in. Just keep your heads down and shuffle along miserably."

"Won't be hard to do," Fendrick grumbled, dismounting.

"Wait here," Weeby said before disappearing again.

Birion stationed himself at the entrance of the alley to discourage any visitors, but as they waited, they could feel eyes upon them from every direction. Weeby returned after some time, weaving his way back through the crowds.

"Stop standing there at attention like a palace guard," Weeby chastised. "You may as well hang a sign out saying you've got something to steal."

Birion scowled. "We should be done with this and get the ladies back to where they should be."

Weeby ignored him and addressed Shalindra and Enna. "You two go first with the horses as we planned. When the guards ask what you're doing, which hopefully they'll do before trying to steal any of the animals, tell them they're being returned to Mullison."

"Who's that?" Enna asked.

"Biggest fishmonger on the river side of the city."

"I have never heard of him," Shalindra said.

Weeby laughed. "I'd be surprised if you had. He's not the kind of company a lady such as yourself would keep."

"And if this doesn't work?" Fendrick asked.

"Run fast?" Weeby said with a shrug. "If you're stopped, you can argue all you want, but bare steel in front of the watch and there won't be much I can do for you."

"Let us get this over with," Shalindra said.

The horses were tied together in two groups of four and led from the alley. The arrangement was a bit ungainly in the busy streets, but the animals were well-behaved. Under the pretext of checking her charges, Shalindra glanced back to see the rest of the group following at an inconspicuous distance. The flow of people around her slowed as she and Enna neared the gate, becoming a shuffling knot as they waited to be passed through by a pair of soldiers. 'Soldiers' might have been too charitable a moniker, for as she drew close Shalindra could see that their spears needed cleaning and their tabards were ill fitting.

Their attention was on her almost immediately and remained there until she reached them. In fact, everyone seemed to be looking at her.

"Where are you ladies going with all those horses?" one of the guards asked, stepping in front of them and reaching for the bridle.

"These were loaned to us by Mullison," Shalindra said, tugging the horse away just enough that his outstretched hand missed its target.

The man scowled. "Never seen a cleric in such fancy armor, neither."

"Horses are valuable, so care must be taken."

"Moon followers with swords ain't that impressive. How's about you leave the horses here with us and we'll make sure they get to where they need to be."

"Mullison is expecting me to return with all of them, and though I am certain that they would arrive safely in your care, I would hate for any to go missing. Someone in the business of gutting fish is not someone I would wish to disappoint."

The second guard elbowed the first, and they both stepped back, suddenly nervous. "Well go on then. Don't keep him waiting."

Shalindra and Enna continued through and did not pause until they were well out of sight of the gate.

"Dishonorable rogues," Birion said when the rest of the group caught up to them.

"That was quite devious," Weeby said, impressed. "I'd no idea you could be so intimidating."

"It is only the first challenge we faced," Shalindra said, "and I am more interested in what lies ahead than behind." Being devious and intimidating did not seem like the proper characteristics for a Guardian, and it was disturbing to think that she might be good at it.

"And I suppose you now can pass us into His Lordship's castle just as easily?" Fendrick asked Weeby.

"That, I'm afraid, is a bit out of my reach." Weeby chuckled. "Fortunately, his daughter should be able to handle that task."

"Entry to the castle for myself is not an issue but given what happened last time a wizard was within the walls, it might be best if Enna and I go first."

"Why me?" Enna asked, surprised.

"You are known to my family, and there will almost certainly be questions about how Ildalarial is treating this peace. I think your opinions would be valuable, should any issues arise."

Verelli agreed to the delay a little too quickly for her liking, given that he had been the one in such a hurry to get here. They remounted, and Shalindra took the lead. She was not remotely familiar with this part of the city, and after Weeby was forced to offer several course corrections, he reassumed the duty. She might have appreciated the use of the future projections that had guided her escape from Ildalarial, but such premonitions lay beyond her ability to produce. Any assistance proved unnecessary, however, as Weeby was guiding them through the streets and alleys as if born there. His sense of direction did not diminish as the streets became wider, cleaner, and less cluttered, finally stopping at a well-appointed but not extravagant inn near the castle.

As soon as Birion had secured a trio of rooms and the group was safely inside, Shalindra and Enna set out for the front gate of the castle.

It was a surprise to see four members of the Legion standing post at the entrance instead of men in the green and gold of the royal guard. While the war with Ildalarial might have been called off, all four were prepared for battle. Their breastplates were of blackened steel, with matching shoulder pauldrons formed of segmented bands evocative of an earlier era. The two in the rear held spears, while their companions stood with flanged maces in hand. They came alert at her approach, and hooded eyes regarded her warily from inside open-faced helmets.

One of the men stepped in front of her and crossed his arms.

"I am Princess Shalindra," she said.

"You're not the first to claim so," he said brusquely, neither impressed nor amused, "so you'll understand if I choose not to believe you."

"Any member of my family will vouch for me."

"I don't see a need to go disturbing Their Highnesses for everyone who comes knocking." He uncrossed his arms and tightened his grip on his mace. "Why don't you run along before the watch decides they'd like a chat with you and the elf."

"My brother is expecting me," Shalindra said, not moving.

"He didn't tell us." The soldier signaled over his shoulder, and the other three men slowly encircled her and Enna. "Maybe you do need to be dragged off to the watch after all."

Ghostly premonitions began detaching themselves from within her, offering glimpses of possible courses of action that all ended in an explosion of combat, but she was determined not to let it come to that.

Shalindra fixed him with her eyes, doing her best to keep her growing anger in check. "I stood shoulder to shoulder with your brothers on the fields east of Tiridon as they fought to avenge Marshal Brouchard. I restored bodies shattered by demons as we battled our way to Tythir with Lord Deurmark. I do not seek confrontation with my father's most ardent protectors, but I will not leave without seeing my family."

For a moment, no one moved. She held her breath, willing herself not to flinch.

The soldier looked away but did not lower his weapon.

"Find someone who can verify," he barked to a subordinate. He motioned them off to the side towards a small door, which another guard opened for him. "If you wouldn't mind waiting in here."

"Your caution is to be commended," Shalindra said.

Five more soldiers were seated inside, and they all came on guard at the unexpected intrusion. One of the soldiers from the gate entered with them and directed them towards a bench along the wall. He was relieved moments later by a more senior officer who looked both women over but made no comment. No one spoke, and so Shalindra watched the sky through the solitary small window in the stone wall.

Eventually, a knock sounded, and when the door was opened a smartly dressed attendant entered the room. His eyes swept over Shalindra once, then he bowed.

"Chevier, at your service, Your Highness. I am employed by Master Eugeron." He turned to the Legion commander. "It is quite alright, Captain. Thank you for your diligence and discretion in this matter."

"Her weapons?" was all the officer said.

"Family was excluded from that order, if you recall, and as her companion is unarmed, all is proper."

The officer waved the other soldiers aside, and Chevier escorted the ladies from the room, chatting pleasantly. "You must excuse this delay, Your Highness. There is much unpleasantness afoot, and precautions must be taken."

"As I was not known to them, I cannot object. I would see this place well defended rather than not."

"Where do you wish to go, Your Highness?"

"To see my mother, but I can find the way on my own, thank you."

Chevier continued smiling pleasantly but continued walking with them. "Of course, Your Highness. You likely know these halls better than I do. However, given recent events, you may find far less difficulty should I remain with you for a time."

Shalindra grudgingly agreed, purely for the sake of courtesy, but they had not made it far before she was forced to admit that he was correct. There were more guards inside the castle walls than last time, and every one of them were Legion rather than the usual house guard. It was an ominous change that defied tradition and left her doubting for the safety of her family. Each of the soldiers fixed her with an untrusting look as she passed, and she was thankful that Chevier had insisted on staying with them.

They ascended a curving stairway to the second floor and were heading towards the next when the sound of hurried footsteps descended towards them. Her brother Kentrick emerged from the stairway and rushed to greet her.

"Kataria!" he said. "I mean… Shalindra. I'll get it right eventually. We've been worried about you."

He did indeed look worried, despite his youthful complexion and sandy hair. It was not even a month and half since she had seen him last, and yet he had aged. The change saddened her.

"I have been fine," she said. "What cause was there to worry?"

Chevier excused himself. "Should either of Your Highnesses need anything further, please let us know."

"Thank you," Shalindra said.

"Lots of reasons." Kentrick glanced up and down the hall, then he ushered them into the closest state room. "You look… striking, but it suits you. Every time you come back, you've changed."

Shalindra almost laughed, though she would have taken more comfort had she been told that her weapons and armor appeared ill-fitting. "I suppose I do."

"Sister Enna," Kentrick said, taking her hand and brushing his lips on her knuckles. "I never had the opportunity to thank you for saving my father's life. Our family owes you a great debt."

"It is no debt, Your Highness," Enna said. "Any follower of our Mistress would have done the same."

Shalindra suppressed a smile as Enna discreetly wiped the back of her hand on her robes.

"I fear things are even more of a mess than when you left us," Kentrick said to Shalindra, not noticing. "From what we can tell, something big is happening in Ceringion. Every foreign lord and commander has begun the march home, and not because the war was called off. We just don't know why."

Shalindra shared a concerned look with Enna. "We might be able to shed some light on that. We have been told that Tythir is overrun with demons and that they now enter our world unchecked."

Kentrick paled. "How do you know?"

"It is a long story, but I intend to do something about it. I arrived here with a member of the Conclave."

"One of the same wizards that tried to kill us and overthrow our father? Gods, you do keep strange company."

"I would consider myself blessed were he the strangest part of my life now."

"I've half a mind to see him hung at the first opportunity, just like the others we've caught. We have enough enemies in this city right now—we don't need another."

"His intentions are undeniably selfish, but I do not believe them to be hostile. He claims to bring a message from the Conclave."

"Father will never allow a wizard into the castle no matter what his intentions, and should he realize one is here, he will likely order him killed on the spot."

Shalindra had never known a magician until meeting Honarch, but she had difficulty imagining Verelli or any member of the Conclave simply submitting to such a fate. "What does the Lordshouse think of this order?"

"They're too busy to care," Kentrick said. "News of father's poor health is spreading, and more questions are being asked that we cannot turn aside. Some of the northern fiefdoms skirmish with each other. Should it become known that he's again talking to the same wizards he just threw out…"

"Those loyal to our family will surely remain so. Our king just needs to command it."

Kentrick shook his head. "I don't know if he can. I can barely believe that our brother did this to him. Mother blames herself for his upbringing and fears for my safety from every side."

"Should she?"

Kentrick began to make light of it but couldn't. "Probably."

They each grew quiet for a time.

"How is he?" Shalindra finally asked.

"Not well," Kentrick replied. "He seems aware enough at times but tires easily. His speech remains slurred, and he tends to wobble and bump into things when he walks, if he can even muster the strength to stand." He looked at his feet. "He is not the king we need right now."

Shalindra took his hands in hers. "Then you must be."

"He remains our king."

"And you are Heir Apparent. If our father cannot be the public face of our house, then you must take up that mantle. Many followed Logian because he was decisive, no matter his destructive tendencies.”

“You aren’t the first to say so, yet there are many who question my legitimacy right now, no matter what the order of things are. I’m no good at these intrigues, and even if I were, no one listens to a prince. Are you going to stay this time?” he asked, brightening at the possibility.

“I would do so were I able. I am Eluria’s Guardian now, and there are other battles which must be fought. I am trying to reach Highfall, though I am not sure what will come after that.”

Kentrick did not hide his disappointment. “First the elves and now the dwarves. I wish your calling kept you closer to us. When are you leaving?”

“Tomorrow, if possible.”

“That fast? Well, at least I can contribute something this time instead of just watching you leave.” Kentrick stuck his head out the door and signaled a nearby page. “Tell Admiral Cossilton to ready his fastest ship for the morning tide. Passengers only, two weeks’ stores. I’ll send additional instructions later.”

The boy ran off as instructed, and Kentrick closed the door once more. Her brother might still have been young for the responsibilities being thrust upon him, but he understood the business of sailing better than anyone. While Logian had spent his youth in training and tournaments, Kentrick had been drawn to the sea even more than Shalindra.

“Thank you,” Shalindra said. “What do you want me to do about the wizard?”

Kentrick wrinkled his nose. “Take him with you and toss him

in the ocean?" he asked, only half in jest. "Let's talk to Eugeron about it." He motioned them to follow him out the door. "You haven't told anyone else about this, have you?"

"Only you."

Kentrick led them down the wide hallway and up two levels towards the senior advisor's chancery. Shalindra and Enna continued to receive inquisitive looks along the way, the bright purity of their attire a stark contrast to the more subdued fall colors composing everyone else's garments. Most who passed them looked surprised, several suspicious, and more than one was openly hostile.

Upon arriving at the room, Kentrick knocked but did not wait for an answer before entering. They followed him inside.

The chamber was efficiently organized around a mahogany desk that dominated the center of the small space. Maps rather than portraits adorned the walls, and a library's worth of books packed every available shelf. Eugeron, her childhood teacher and now advisor to the king, sat working at the desk. The papers held in his thin fingers looked recently written, but the books he referenced beside them were ancient and worn. Peering over his shoulder was Sir Redivers, Marshal of Actondel's armies. Both men looked up at their entrance.

"Your Highness," Eugeron said as he rose, then smiled more broadly as he caught sight of Shalindra.

"Master Eugeron, it is good to see you again," she said.

"A joy it is. I see that reports of your advancement were not incorrect. You appear quite formidable. And Lady Ennathalerial," he said, bowing to Enna. "It is an honor once more."

"Indeed," Kentrick added. "I fear that in my eagerness to speak to my sister I have overlooked my courtesies. Enna has done so much to safeguard our family that I confess to feeling more at ease from her presence alone."

Color came to Enna's cheeks, and she mumbled a thank you.

"Lord Redivers," Kentrick said, "it's good that you are here. Your opinion will be important in this matter."

"How may we assist Your Highnesses today?" Eugeron asked, smoothing his short beard.

"My sister has brought us a bit of a quandary, but I'll allow her to explain it."

Shalindra did so, relaying in general terms what had happened since her return to the Kingdom. The three men remained silent throughout, and it was to Eugeron that all eyes turned when she was finished.

"This is both informative and problematic on several levels," he said, stroking his chin. "Prince Logian, as you recall, was Duke of Ordry's End, one of the crown's estates outside Liseria. After the failed attack on His Majesty, Logian's cohort retreated there. The moment Adair was settled and Merallin judged secure, a contingent was sent to apprehend them and ensure our claim."

"Near to three thousand men," Redivers added. "Logian had direct responsibility for no more than a thousand, but there were many more who served under his command. It was uncertain what we would find."

"They encountered no resistance," Eugeron continued, "and reported that the manor was looted and Logian's men had fled."

Shalindra raised an eyebrow. "So you have a small army

wandering the Kingdom right now? There are a limited number of places so many could go without notice."

"That is precisely what concerns us," Eugeron said. "Prince Logian was able to stir the passions of many with his youth and military prowess. We are still trying to determine how many lords are or were in his camp and deduce who is sheltering these rebels."

"We've caught a few of his men poking around," Redivers said, "and from the confessions we've been able to extract, we believe the prince's attack was impulsive, but he clearly had designs on the throne and plans had already been set in motion."

Shalindra could not be surprised at that. Logian had never been one for patience, preferring his conquests to be quick and public. His ambition had been the equal of his temper, traits overlooked for one of his standing.

"Not all of this is materially relevant, yet," Eugeron said, "but I wished for you to understand the broader implications of what we may decide here today. Now, to the matter of this wizard you've brought."

"To be clear, our association was not entirely by choice," Shalindra said. "Fate threw us together, but I am not his ally."

"We assumed nothing else," Eugeron said kindly. "Who is he?"

"Premis Verelli. I have been told that he was the second most powerful wizard in the Conclave."

Kentrick and Redivers shrugged blankly, but Eugeron nodded. "I'm familiar with the name, if not the person."

"He has stated that he seeks our help and claims that demons have overrun Tythir. He also believes that King Gymerius and his entire family have been killed."

Kentrick spoke first. "I'm uncertain what we could do about that even should we wish to become involved. I can guarantee that the king will not agree to help those who stole half his kingdom."

"Your Highness," Eugeron said to Kentrick. "If this magister desires an audience, I believe that we should listen to what he has to say, if for no other reason than to discover more of the events unfolding around us."

"My father is in no condition to speak to him," Kentrick said. "And even if he was, he would just order him executed."

"Ah," Eugeron said delicately. "I would also caution against informing His Majesty that Master Verelli is here. You should be the one to meet with him."

"Me?" Kentrick asked in surprise. "There is no way to have a secret meeting without my father learning of it eventually."

"I do not propose that anything be done in secret," Eugeron said. "People seek an audience with His Majesty every day. There is nothing untoward with us vetting their access, especially in this circumstance."

"There is truth to that," Kentrick conceded.

"We must consider appearances," Redivers cut in. "If it's to be done within these walls, we carry considerable risk."

"Yet we must show strength," Eugeron said. "If this wizard is who he claims to be, this meeting is only a step removed from entertaining a visiting monarch. We cannot do that in a closet."

"I was thinking something more informal," Kentrick countered, gazing up at one of the maps. "What about one of our estates outside the city? Bruckhalter maybe?"

He looked lost, reminding Shalindra that despite achieving his manhood, her brother was not entirely prepared for all that was being asked of him. It bothered her that his advisors, good men both, were making this decision almost without his input, but she could not object to their rationale.

"Eugeron is correct, Your Highness," Redivers said. "His Majesty's audience chamber is the proper location for receiving such visitors, and it can be reached discreetly. It is also easy for us to secure."

Eugeron nodded. "We could further reduce awareness of his presence by holding the audience early in the day, when the king is still abed."

"He usually drifts in and out of sleep for most of the morning," Kentrick told Shalindra. "That would also allow us to keep most of the staff unaware of his presence."

"I agree," Redivers said. "Beyond the potential threat to your person, it's dangerous having him here. Should word leak out…"

"As we have resolved, we can mitigate that," Eugeron said. "I can distribute conflicting rumors as to our visitor's origin, and we can have a carriage bring him here. Should he arrive through one of the side gates, few will notice."

"It seems a good plan," Kentrick said, perhaps not entirely convinced.

"I think Lord Redivers and I have enough information to prepare for this," Eugeron said, "but our time is short. If Your Highnesses will excuse us so we can make ready?"

"Of course," Kentrick said. "My ladies, if you would follow me, we'll leave them to their schemes."

"Are you certain you want to do this?" Shalindra asked once

they had exited the room.

"I don't like any of it," her brother confided. "Were it not for…" He trailed off as rapid footsteps approached, accompanied by the swish of fabric, and their mother turned a corner in front of them. Queen Eleanor came to a sudden stop at the sight of them, and her hand flew to her mouth.

Kentrick extended his arm to Enna. "Sister Enna, would you be so kind as to indulge my curiosity of elvish architecture? There is a painting in our gallery that I've always admired, and I would love for you to tell me if the portrayal is accurate."

"I would be happy to do so, my lord," Enna said, though she gave Shalindra a sideways glance that said she would hear about this sacrifice later.

Eleanor smiled her appreciation at them both, but her eyes never left her daughter. She took a half step closer, stopped, then touched her fingers against the bare skin of Shalindra's upper arm, avoiding the silver metal of her armor. "You've changed."

"I am still your daughter."

"And I will always stand proud of what you have accomplished, though I wish it different."

Shalindra was beyond the point of wishing the past were different, but she found it equally difficult to consider all of it an accomplishment. "I can only hope it was for a reason."

"So much has happened so rapidly," Eleanor said. "I've been told things, but I struggle to believe the truth even when the evidence can be beheld with my own eyes. I would hear your description of these terrible events."

They began to walk, her mother steering them through a

doorway and onto a balcony garden. The rain had stopped, though the clouds robbed any cheer from the normally bright space. Shalindra conveyed all that she had been through since the last time they were together, beginning with Logian's attack and ending with their still uncertain plan for Kentrick and Verelli to meet. Her mother listened to it all, tears filling her eyes at the description of Logian's death.

"I hear the doubts in your voice and see your reluctance, but you have the gift of leadership. Eugeron and Redivers listen to you, not because you are a princess but because they respect you. They regard you as their equal in ways they rarely do with others, even Fabrian."

"My decisions are not always the best," Shalindra said. "There are so many things I wish I could change."

"There always are." Eleanor looked down at her hands. "With Logian... I was young, and away from everything that was familiar to me. In my inexperience, I allowed others far too much leeway over his upbringing. Later, with you and even more so with Kentrick, I devoted so much more of myself to your care."

"No one bears responsibility for Logian's actions other than himself."

The queen smiled sadly. "And yet we are all blamed for that outcome one way or another, even if we had no influence on the events. The things that are said about this family behind our backs, and sometimes to our face... I trust almost no one."

"I saw that the Legion has replaced the household guard inside the walls. If any in this city could be called—"

"Members of the Legion were purged as well. Whether they

were under Logian's wayward influence or that of some wizard, it makes little difference. Loyalty is in short supply." Her mother plucked nervously at the frills on her sleeve. "And the king is making it worse. Have you seen him yet?"

Shalindra shook her head.

"It might be best, for all of us, if you did not."

"Is he that bad?" Shalindra asked, shocked.

Her mother glanced away before answering. "His physical health is as good as it will ever be, but his mind… He lashes out like a child. Every affront, real or imagined, is cause for drastic measures. He fears almost everyone is out to take his throne from him. We restrict his visitors, but his affliction is tearing this kingdom apart."

Shalindra gazed up at the tufts of clouds floating across the blue sky, unsure of how to respond. She bore some element of blame for her father's condition, no matter what anyone else might say to her in kindness, and so it should also fall to her to carry some of the weight of her family's struggles. She may have wished to distance herself from the troubles of the Kingdom, but it was impossible to remain unaffected by the desperation in her mother's voice. And yet, she could not set aside her purpose.

"I must travel to Highfall. There is opportunity there to learn more of what drives so much of this upheaval, and I do not know when such a chance will come again. But as soon as I return, I will do what I can to help."

Her mother forced a smile onto her face, brightening Shalindra's mood like the sun after a storm, but her eyes labelled it a false happiness. "We can only hope what we do will be enough."

Chapter Sixteen

A Wizard's Bargain

The carriage rolled to a stop, and Shalindra pulled the curtain aside just enough to reveal a sliver of the outside world. It was almost as dark outside as in, with stars still visible against the palest colors of dawn. The door was opened from the outside, and in the light of flickering torches a dozen men in the blackened armor of the Legion formed a funnel from the carriage to a small, arched doorway. Within the darkened recess of the open portal, Eugeron awaited them in his finest attire, a finely patterned blue tunic with gold buttons and half-sleeves below the elbow.

From the seat across from her, Verelli gave her an amused smirk.

"It is as much for your protection as theirs," she reminded him, though if Honarch was to be believed—and she did—such a small contingent would be no protection from Verelli at all.

Verelli smoothed his robes as he exited, as relaxed as if he arrived at the stronghold of his enemies in such a manner all the time.

Only when they were all safely inside and the door closed behind them did Eugeron speak.

"Master Verelli, it is a pleasure to finally meet you in person. Allow me to welcome you to Merallin. I trust your journey went smoothly."

Verelli was obviously no stranger to court behavior, as his response was remarkably polite and devoid of the arrogance that had infused so many of his earlier remarks. "It was an unusual excursion, but I have known worse."

"Of that I have no doubts," Eugeron said as they began walking. "I hope that you will excuse this modest amount of subterfuge, but these are delicate times, and we wish only to ensure your comfort and security while you are our guest."

"I find your consideration most appropriate. Some negotiations are best held outside the public eye."

The hallway they turned down was empty of anyone save a handful of Legion guards standing at attention, a fact not lost on Verelli. The way he took note of every door and person, even while chatting amicably, reminded her of no one so much as Tormjere.

"Here we are," Eugeron said, indicating an ornately carved pair of polished oak doors embossed with depictions of ships edged in gold leaf. "Prince Kentrick is most eager to meet you."

In spite of the gravity of the situation, Shalindra almost laughed. Unless her brother had been kidnapped and replaced by someone else, there was no way to consider his attitude towards this encounter as 'eager.'

The audience chamber they now entered had been foreign to her as a child, with Logian her only sibling to regularly sit with her father during the sessions. It was opulent without extravagance, with tapestries and richly colored curtains adorning the walls, and patterned marble tiles for the floor. The chamber was empty of the dozens of courtiers and diplomats who would normally be in attendance for such an event, lending a hollow echo to their footsteps. At the far end, Kentrick sat stiffly on the edge of the throne. His deep green jacket befitted the occasion, adding breadth to his shoulders. As a prince, he wore no crown, but the gold trim and cuffs set a regal appearance. Redivers stood to his left, with the ceremonial breastplate and sword appropriate to his rank as commander of House Actondel's forces. His tunic was the same green as Kentrick's but edged in black to match his pants and boots, signifying his association with the Legion.

Eugeron had done everything he could to lend majesty to the setting, but there was no disguising Kentrick's youthfulness, or the lack of the nobles and merchants whose presence would have affirmed the power of the man seated on the throne. Shalindra wondered at what she had gotten her brother into, but it was too late to alter course.

It was difficult to tell what Verelli thought of it all, but he appeared at ease though his bearing was formal. They came to a stop before the throne, and Eugeron made the introduction.

"His Royal Highness, Heir Apparent Prince Kentrick of Actondel. Your Highness, may I present Premis Verelli, Master Magician and Elder of the Conclave of Imaretii."

Where Eugeron had been able to learn his title was beyond her, but she could only assume it was accurate as Verelli made no correction.

"Your Highness," the wizard said with a bow. "Thank you for granting me an audience on such short notice."

"You have come a long way for a most important purpose, and we would not seek to waste your time with needless ceremony. What do you wish of Actondel?"

It was delivered well, though Shalindra was certain that Eugeron had coached Kentrick through at least the opening exchanges.

"I believe that we are all aware of what has brought me here, but allow me to provide some additional detail. The creatures known as demons were employed against your kingdom during its most recent conflict with the Ceringion Reginum, which saw Actondel lose almost a quarter of its holdings." Kentrick and Redivers both stiffened, but Verelli continued in a dispassionately instructional tone. "The effectiveness of that strategy is a subject of debate, but their catastrophic impact is not."

Shalindra repressed a shiver at the memory of just how damaging those encounters had been. A few of the *hers* layered recollections of their own battles atop hers, but she forced them aside to concentrate on what was happening now.

"In each of these cases," Verelli said, "you faced creatures that were operating under some level of control, and which could be dispelled when they were no longer of use."

"We're well aware of their masters' thirst for Actondel blood," Kentrick snapped, far more forcefully than he should have. "Did you come to gloat?"

Eugeron shifted uncomfortably and tried to give Kentrick a subtle motion meant to calm him. If he could not keep his passions under control, this meeting would resolve nothing.

Verelli tapped his foot impatiently but continued in an even tone. "I merely seek to establish a common frame of reference. The problem confronting us now is far more dangerous. Demons were released unchecked in the city of Tythir roughly two months ago. The size of the breach is not accurately known, but in that time, the entire city and much of the surrounding lands have been rendered uninhabitable."

"And how does this affect Actondel?" Kentrick asked. "Tythir is a long way from here."

Verelli's sigh was almost audible. "You have probably been made aware that the Ceringion contribution to your expedition against Ildalarial is now streaming back to their homes. Anyone and everything they can scrape together is being sent east in hopes of containing this threat."

"If they are so hard-pressed, why have we not heard from King Gymerius himself?"

"A question for which the answer is self-evident. But if you choose not to believe me, you are free to inquire of him yourself. You do still maintain the means to contact your peer?"

"We do," Kentrick said, "but it will take time."

"Of course it will, and whether you send a single pigeon or a hundred, you will grow old and die long before any of them return."

Kentrick gripped the edges of the chair and leaned forward, his face red. "I do not care to be lectured by you."

"That was a statement of fact. A lecture would require far more explanation than either of us have time for." He glanced over his shoulder at Shalindra. "There are others here who have faced demons. Perhaps you could ask what standing before one or two of them felt like. I will repeat: there were *hundreds* of them rampaging through Tythir when I fled."

There was an edge to Verelli's words that Shalindra had not heard before and likely would have missed had she not spoken to him so frequently. He was frightened. Despite her distrust of the man, that gave her more cause for alarm than anything he had ever said to her. She wanted to add her warning to his and calm her brother's growing anger, but Kentrick plowed ahead, not picking up on the implications.

"I'm well aware of what they are capable of."

"It is a dire situation," Eugeron agreed. "Do we know if your order has seen any success in repelling them?"

"I have not seen any of them since I began making my way here, but all were told to lend their efforts to that task."

"Then they are doing a poor job," Kentrick scoffed, "as these demons are also appearing within our own borders. Were you aware of that? I fail to see why it would be in our interest to help you when our own people are at risk."

"The greatest threat originates in Tythir, and that is where our defenses must ultimately be made."

"I'm sure we all know the source of this mistake. It seems fitting that your order should be the first to suffer for the destruction they have caused."

"If I may, Your Highness," Eugeron interrupted. "What Master Verelli attempts to point out is that this threat may escalate beyond the ability of Ceringion to control. This is a valid concern, and one that His Majesty will wish to consider."

It was an acknowledgement of the threat Verelli had brought to light, but the damage of Kentrick's outburst had already been done.

Verelli's eyes flashed as he addressed the prince. "If you choose to be blinded by your petty hatreds, you will sacrifice what may be our only opportunity to stop this. Ignore it at your peril, because when they are finished with Ceringion, they will not ignore you."

Eugeron caught Kentrick's attention, allowing the hand hidden from Verelli's view to give the prince a silent yet frantic signal.

Kentrick sat back in his chair and returned to words that had been rehearsed. "We may sound unsympathetic to your cause, but our caution is not without reason. I will take your request under advisement but can make no guarantees that His Majesty will be willing to relinquish any of our forces to aid you at this time. Return to your inn, and we will be in contact when we have an answer."

Verelli glared at Eugeron, as if blaming him for the prince's poor showing. "I should hope the answer comes quickly, before anyone seeks to make me another victim of Actondel 'justice.'"

Verelli offered Kentrick the barest of nods, then turned on his heel and strode from the room.

Eugeron raised a hand to halt Kentrick or Redivers from doing anything to stop him, and Shalindra gave all three a worried look as she hurried after the wizard.

Verelli kept his jaw clamped firmly shut as they retraced their route to the waiting carriage, but once inside he jerked the door closed in disgust. "Your brother's show of authority was as unnecessary as it was pointless, but I hope it made him feel good."

"They are making do with what they have available," Shalindra said defensively. "Given the recent wars and reversals, it would be almost impossible to order a sizable force into Ceringion—my family does not rule with an iron fist."

Verelli gave her a withering look. "Your father ruled with a wet noodle, which is why your armies fell so quickly. A few bands of goblins nearly gutted your western territory, and if not for the mistakes of a few, you likely would have joined them in defeat."

His criticism set her teeth on edge, but his assessment was accurate enough and she did not want to make the situation any worse than it already was. "In that, we should both count ourselves fortunate."

"It was a long shot coming here to seek help, but my conscience is clear. Your king has been warned of the threat, and whether he chooses to do anything about it or not, it will soon become your problem. You know it as well as I. Demons dislike the cold and will likely stay where they are for the winter, but without a unified front, nothing will stop them in the spring. I only hope I'm still alive to watch your kingdom burn with all the others."

* * *

Honarch repressed a sigh as he rose from the table. The eating room of Sea Feather's Commonhouse, like those of most inns in such a large city, did not cater to the public, and so it was all but unoccupied. In fact, the inn itself was almost completely empty, though that would not have been unusual in the colder months. To be honest, it was probably because no one wanted to go anywhere, which was anything but normal. Today was the fall equinox, and while the date was of minor note to most people, it was typically greeted with some level of festivity. He had seen no preparations for such as they had travelled through the city. The constant fighting of consecutive wars—or attempted wars—and the infighting of their aftermath was grinding the people down.

Not that he was feeling any better.

There were only two men he considered as true friends, and one of them was gone. He would have to find a way to tell Treven, but he could not bring himself to simply pen a message. Such news was best delivered in person.

He nodded his thanks to the young woman who came to clear away the remnants of his early dinner. She gave him a furtive smile in return before quickly averting her eyes. He wished he knew her name, but even if he did, she would not speak to him anyway. No matter how he dressed, he was still recognized as a wizard. Maybe it was the beard.

Honarch wandered down the hall towards his room. The inn was constructed in an antiquated style that reminded him of those along the eastern coast of Ceringion, with two levels of rooms arranged in a rectangle around an open courtyard. Tempted by the fresh air of the inner plaza, he paused to gaze up at the open sky. It would have been nice to wander the streets of a large city again, but thanks to that idiot of a king it was far too great a risk. Other than Verelli, no one else was under such restriction, and they had all departed towards a variety of tasks.

Weeby had headed out alone, likely collecting whatever information he could find. Honarch was under no illusions of how dangerous the halfling was. The enchantments carried about his small person—Honarch had checked for them when they began travelling together—were not only powerful but subtle in their radiance, a sign of masterwork-level craftsmanship. He also considered it no accident that the halfling was matched with such a senior member of the Conclave. That mystery had kept him travelling with the group more than any loyalty to a cause. Something of great import was happening, something Tormjere had believed in very strongly, and he could not simply abandon Shalindra to her fate.

That meant taking ship to Highfall in search of a dead Guardian. What would come after was still open to debate. Shalindra would probably continue to need his help, as she had a terrible habit of running into unpleasant creatures.

He continued from the courtyard, returning to the room he shared with Verelli and Weeby. When he opened the door, he found the senior wizard sitting at the nightstand and staring out the window in thought, his pen poised over an open book. Verelli shifted in surprise and closed the book.

"I didn't mean to interrupt," Honarch apologized.

"My thoughts wander, and I was getting nowhere," Verelli said.

"You've heard nothing else?" Honarch asked, spying the darkened dohedron resting beside the book. Like his own, the device was capable of sending messages over hundreds of miles, though he suspected that the one Verelli possessed was somehow linked to more than one other. Verelli had checked it constantly on their journey to Merallin, but Honarch had seen it flicker with light only once.

"Not for days." Verelli returned the device to an inner pocket. "I am told that you crafted your own dohedron."

"An experiment," Honarch said, aware of his own limitations when it came to crafting devices.

"Even imperfect results can yield revelations, and when my mind is blocked, I find it useful to consider other, less weighty subjects. May I see it?"

Honarch had not looked at it since reuniting with Shalindra and learning that it had been she who was communicating with him instead of Tormjere. He swallowed past the sudden lump in his throat then retrieved it from his travelling bag. It was a pale imitation of the artistry and craftsmanship of the smaller device that Verelli had.

The senior wizard accepted it like a teacher evaluating a pupil. "What was your basis for the design?"

"Anything that could be learned from my somewhat limited library, and what I could copy from the others I had seen." And which he hoped Verelli would not inquire about, as they had all come as bounty from Tormjere's dispatching of other wizards.

"It's range?"

Honarch considered. "Merallin to Kirchmont, at a minimum."

Verelli's eyebrows twitched upwards in surprise. "Exemplary for a first attempt. The construction is functional if limiting, but the delicacies of the metalworking and gem cutting are best left to specialists. When done properly, both will enhance the pairing. Shalindra carries its twin?"

"Yes."

"My experience with our warrior-princess is somewhat limited, and perhaps colored by unsound thinking. How would you evaluate her?"

"She's a good person," Honarch said, now on his guard. "Life has been unkind to her in many ways."

Their conversations up to now had been brief and few, and always with others around to hear what was said. Without knowing Verelli's ultimate purpose in coming here, Honarch was not about to divulge any secrets.

"The fates are cruel to many of us, and for varying reasons," Verelli said. "But she is undeniably different. You've examined the artifacts she carries?"

Honarch had—from a distance—though purely out of curiosity. "She is strongly equipped."

"Strong is an understatement. Her weapons and armor radiate might. She does not eat, she does not sleep, and yet she is never tired. She dispatched a lesser demon as a knight would swat aside a fly. So much power concentrated in a single individual can, and has, led to calamity."

"I don't subscribe to her holy quests any more than all the others I've seen foretold, but she means to do right."

"But will she? When the time comes for her to apply her strengths, will she choose what is best for those around her or only what is most attractive for herself?"

"We all face such decisions," Honarch said. "I'm sure she will make the right ones."

"Right and wrong is often a matter of degree." Verelli regarded the dohedron still held in his hand. "I have no doubt whose books you consulted in this construction. The style and arrangement echo that of your former master, lost under questionable circumstances." Verelli's eyes drilled into him, scrutinizing everything in uncomfortable detail. "Was it right, or was it wrong?"

Honarch's heart skipped a beat. He knew. Somehow, he was aware of Honarch's role in Felzig's death and his subsequent theft of the bookshelf, which had supplied him with a treasure trove of knowledge he might never have been given. It was not his proudest moment, but those trials had given him the closest friends he had ever known, and he would not dishonor them for anything.

"Sometimes, things are neither. They're simply necessary."

Verelli almost appeared impressed by the answer but did not relent. "If so, why did you not return to us when Felzig was lost?"

"I enjoyed living."

"We do not kill people for failing."

"The thugs you sent after me in Kirchmont indicated otherwise."

Verelli's mouth set in a thin line. "There were reasons."

Honarch retrieved his dohedron from Verelli's hand, eager to be done with this conversation. "There always are."

* * *

"Do you really mean to go through with this?" Enna demanded, shoving open the door to their room and storming inside, almost wishing that some assailant was waiting for them so she would have an outlet for her ire. She wasn't sure who she should be most angry with, but as everyone was making horrible decisions it hardly mattered.

Shalindra followed her in at a more respectable pace. "I am still not sure why I would not. It is what I was meant to do."

By Her light, she was starting to sound like she believed the adulations of that mob of worshippers at the temple. They should have just stayed here and never gone. Guardians did not arise to squander their gifts on personal problems.

"Demons are popping up all over the place, Ceringion is overrun, and your kingdom is coming apart at the seams. Now might not be the best time to follow a dwarf you barely know into the mountains where your predecessor was betrayed and murdered."

Shalindra did not hide her sigh, which only served to be more infuriating. "Yet we know the importance of it. Lithandris himself delivered the message to me."

"I'll admit the dwarf's claim is convenient, but every time you leave and come back, the world becomes more unstable. We'll be gone a week and a half, possibly longer, and I fully expect to return to see this city in flames and a new king on the throne."

It was an unkind blow, and Enna saw the fear register in Shalindra's eyes as she turned away. Enna took a deep breath, but whatever apology she might have considered was preempted by a voice behind her.

"Pardon the interruption," Verelli said from the doorway. "As your friend has pointed out, the dwarf's trustworthiness is subject to debate."

Enna's eyes narrowed. "Eavesdropping now?"

"The door was open, and your voices carried perhaps further than you intended." He entered the room and closed the door. "I only wished to point out that Highfall is considerably out of the way and offer my opinion on this topic."

"The road to Tythir is even longer," Enna snapped, in no mood for the wizard's meddling, "and far more perilous. Why not just say you're here for yourself and be done with the charade?"

Verelli's eyes turned cold. "Of course I have my own interests at heart. I did not travel this far for yours, save for where they intersect. Regardless of why any of us have arrived here, the threat we now face is the same, and it will not be mitigated from within the Ironspike Mountains."

"You are both correct," Shalindra said, forestalling further argument, "and I am more than aware of the horrors demons may visit upon us all, but how effective would I be fighting my way across the countryside?"

"More so than those battling with nothing but arrows and spears," Verelli said. "You have abilities that no one else has attained, and they will be critical in the days ahead."

"Why do you care what she does?" Enna demanded. "You owe us no debts and are free to return to Tythir and aid your friends if you desire."

Verelli shook his head. "No, I am not. Your king's laughable decree that all wizards are to be apprehended is not only depriving you of your best defense against the creatures, but it also leaves my odds of departing this city in peace far smaller than anyone thinks. Were I to strike out for Ceringion on my own, I would likely leave a trail of bodies in every city between here and the border. My fate is tied to yours, at least for now."

"I do not think that we will need the services of another wizard," Shalindra said, "and while you have thus far been an exception, the Conclave has done much to bring me harm." At least she had the sense not to accept him at his word.

"I'll not deny it, but wizardry is an art with many specialties. There are sorcerers who focus on curing disease or on increasing the efficiency of a harvest. Some devote their lives to imbuing ordinary objects with defensive and preventative powers, and they would be incapable of harming anyone with magic even if they wished to. Judging an entire population based on the actions of a few is pointless."

"But often indicative of an underlying truth. I can name the places and describe the demons employed against me, if it helps."

"As I could enumerate the wizards you killed along with what their purpose actually was, but it would do little good. As I said, we are stuck working towards the same ends—on the same path, as our monkish friends would have said. If you wish to rid the world of demons, your road will take you to Tythir, whether you want it to or not. The sooner we get there, the more will be left to save."

"What do you propose?" Shalindra asked.

"If you truly mean to go to Highfall, I will accompany you and do whatever I can to speed your travels. All I ask is that, at the soonest opportunity, we turn for Tythir and seek to put an end to this."

"That seems a fair bargain."

"*If* you follow through with it," Enna said to Verelli, not believing a word he had said.

"How, then, can we consecrate this agreement to your satisfaction?" Verelli challenged with a sardonic smirk. "Shall we simply shake hands, or should we cut our palms first and share our blood, or sacrifice a goat in each other's honor? We can perform any other childish ritual that will make you feel better. In the end, it comes down to my word, and yours."

"Your word is acceptable," Shalindra said.

Absolutely nothing about any of it was acceptable, but all Enna could do was bite her tongue to keep from screaming at them both.

Chapter Seventeen

To the Edge of the Sky

Shalindra stood at the bow, feet planted wide to balance against the pitch of the vessel as it surged through the choppy seas. Fendrick had taken station beside her, as silent and stoic as the mountains that loomed before them. Enna, far less comfortable than either of them, maintained a white-knuckled grip on the rail with one hand while the other clutched just as tightly to her silver disc of Eluria.

Shalindra offered her a sympathetic smile, but any response was obscured as the wind whipped Enna's white hair across her face. It had to be difficult for her to maintain equilibrium without the horizon line, still lost in the grey clouds somewhere off to the west. The winter winds driving those storms closer had been blowing since they left Merallin, and four days at sea had done Enna no kindness. At least they would be back on land today.

The jagged, perpetually snow-capped peaks towering miles above the water rose before the ship in silhouette, edged in radiance by the hidden sunrise as it cast infinite streaks of shadows across the sky. The entire western face of the Ironspike Mountains was as dark as the waters surrounding their ship. Large swells sloshed against the near vertical rock face, but there were no breakers or shoals marking shallow water that might interfere with their travel. Only a small collection of lights tucked into the base of a deep, jagged cleft torn into the near vertical rock face broke the darkness.

A trio of double-masted ships, similar to their own but constructed in the more squared style of the southern kingdoms, floated a short distance away, their lanterns dim specks of light bobbing up and down on the darkened sea.

"Reef sails!"

Men scurried to obey the captain's command. Deprived of the force of the wind, the ship's momentum rapidly bled off, and the pounding of the waves became a gentle rolling as the hull settled in the water.

The captain made his way from the quarter deck to where they were. Coming beside her, he pointed towards the lights of the city. "There it is, Your Highness: Dwarfport."

Fendrick scowled over his shoulder, and the captain immediately bowed his head. "Apologies, friend dwarf. 'Tis a convenient moniker, nothing more. I meant no disrespect."

Fendrick mumbled something under his breath but returned to staring at the city. There was a certain resignation in his gaze, an air of inevitability at what was to come, that had increased every day.

"I can see why those who live here would prefer 'Highfall,'" Shalindra said in his defense, noting the many-tiered cascade that carved its way down plateaus of rock as it descended through the town. "The waterfall is beautiful."

The captain shook his head. "Your eyes are far better than mine, Your Highness. I can see naught but darkness and the lights of the city."

Fendrick and Enna exchanged a glance Shalindra was not meant to see. Was their vision equally obscured by the shadows? If so, what other things had she taken note of that they might have missed?

"Why are we stopping here?" she asked, not wishing to dwell on it now.

"The tide's out and the currents near the mouth of the bay swirl dangerously, Your Highness. We'll lay offshore a bit before making the approach." He gestured to the other ships doing the same. "Smart captains wait for high tide, only daring ones will attempt low."

"And unlucky fools try to ride the middle," Fendrick added. "They wind up smashed against the rocks as often as not. It's not a pleasant swim."

"We aren't going to drop anchor?" Enna asked as she joined the conversation. Though an anchor would do nothing but hold them in place, she was probably desperate for anything that might stabilize the constant rocking motion imparted by the large swells.

The captain shook his head. "We could let ours full out and not come close to the bottom. No one knows the depths of the waters here, and no one has yet made a rope long enough to find out." He glanced at the sky. "We'll be near midday before we've enough light to head in. By some miracle, we're going to see the sun today, for the mountains are near to always shrouded in clouds this time of year. I'd advise you to make yourself comfortable."

The captain withdrew with a polite bow, and the three of them stood in silence. Shalindra had never been to Highfall or to any other dwarvish city, and while the peaks of the Ironspike Mountains were tall enough to be seen from the towers of Merallin on a clear day, she had never beheld them up close. She almost asked Fendrick where they would go once ashore, but, close though they were, they had yet to set foot in Highfall, and she had a feeling the taciturn dwarf would stick to the exact letter of his promise.

Apparently through with the conversation or having seen all he wished, Fendrick stumped off, leaving her alone with Enna, who continued to look queasy. Shalindra sighed, resigning herself to talking to the voices in her head.

Unlike everyone else aboard, she had nothing to prepare before stepping ashore. She had remained in her armor throughout the voyage, just as she had every day since donning it. Her militant attire had earned her more than a few odd looks from the sailors, given that it would have proved deadly had she fallen overboard.

Or not.

For all she knew, it might grant her the power to swim through the waves like a fish. The incarnations of herself floating around inside her head voiced their own opinions, even though such an outlandish thought did not require a response. Their reactions ranged from amusement to derision, with at least one of the more adventuresome ones encouraging her to leap from the ship just to see what would happen.

She put a hand to her forehead and tried to ignore the ongoing debate as she waited for the sun to rise and the tides to become favorable. It was distracting when the *hers* decided to maintain differing opinions, and even more annoying when they decided to be vocal about it.

From time to time, the crew would partially unfurl a sail to keep them away from the rocks, but there was no other activity as the sky slowly brightened. Eventually, the currents drifted them within shouting distance of another of the waiting ships, and jovial insults and challenges were hurled between the two crews. One of the sailors on the other vessel called a warning, then hurled a small bag towards them.

The missile's trajectory was high and a little short, setting off a mad scramble as the deckhands rushed to catch it. One of the men on her own vessel stretched precariously far over the rail and plucked it from the air as his friends grabbed him by the legs to keep him from going over. After being dragged back on deck, he held the bag aloft triumphantly.

A rousing cheer rose from the other vessel.

The bag was opened and passed around, with each man withdrawing an object from inside without looking. Dice, beads, feathers, and whittled figures emerged.

When the bag was emptied, it was passed around once more, and the crew dropped their own trinkets and mementos into it. After tying it securely shut, the sailor who had originally caught it took a running start and lobbed it back towards the other ship. This one flew true, landing square in the middeck. The sailors on both vessels cheered.

"Had they brought that bag near me, I would have thrown up in it," Enna said, finally taking a few steps away from the railing to join Shalindra.

"It would have been an apt memento of your journey, though our fellow sailors may not have found it agreeable," Shalindra said with a chuckle. "Would you like something to eat?"

"Asks the person who hasn't touched food in weeks." Enna shook her head. "Not until I'm standing on something that doesn't move, and then I'll eat more than Tormjere after…"

Enna's voice caught in her throat. With an apologetic half-smile, she turned away to stare at the ocean once more. Shalindra began to reach for her but stopped. There were no words to be said that would make it better for either of them—she missed him, too.

Seeking to dispel that unhappy thought, she cast her gaze away from the dim face of the mountains and towards the fading line of the mountains' shadow on the water as it drew steadily closer. Beyond its edge, the ocean danced and shimmered with the sparkle of the sun across a thousand waves, but their ship still rested in the half-light of a prolonged dawn.

Turning back towards the harbor, she spied a group of small boats being rowed towards the waiting ships. When one drew alongside their ship, a rope ladder was lowered, and a dwarvish pilot climbed aboard. He was as stocky as Fendrick but shorter, clad in cheerfully colored breeches and a loose shirt, and made his way to the helm on bare feet.

Eventually the sun, already approaching its zenith, cleared the towering peaks and blazed down with light and warmth. Enormous bonfires flared on either side of the harbor entrance at almost the same time. At that signal, the large ships queued in the order of their arrival. The captain called for sails, and the wind's tug sent the ship slowly forward behind the other vessels.

Under the pilot's expert guidance, they passed through the uncomfortably narrow opening between the twin massive, squared towers guarding the entrance to the bay. The top face of each tower was broken by a checkerboard of openings, and large siege engines were visible on all of the levels. The harbor they were entering was as close to impenetrable as Shalindra could imagine, but there were marks on the outer walls—scratches and scrapes larger than the ship on which she stood—that said the defenses were far from ceremonial. She might have dismissed her feelings of dread had the crew not been visibly nervous.

"Not every monster lives on the land," Fendrick said, rejoining her. His manner was so practical as to be considered brusque, but there was something oddly reassuring about that. A bulky leather bag was tied across his back, atop which was stowed his metal bow and quiver of steel bolts. A utilitarian knife and axe rounded out his appearance. Birion joined them on deck as well, but the wizards and Weeby remained inside.

The pilot barked orders in a voice that easily carried above the hollow echo of waves pounding against the sides of the gorge, and the sailors hurried to obey. Seabirds filled the air with the sounds of their calls, searching for their next meal above the bottomless waters of the small bay. Shalindra shuddered to think of what would befall any of those aboard should the ship founder against the rocks.

Their pilot kept a steady hand, holding a slow approach until finally ordering the sails secured, then making an expertly sharp turn to starboard which allowed the currents to ease the ship into position at the dock. Only when the ship was secure in its berth did anyone relax, and the sailors slipped into the routine of tending to their vessel and unloading the small amount of cargo they had brought.

Enna rushed ashore the moment the gangplanks were run out, while the rest of their companions and the captain followed at a more relaxed pace.

"Are you certain you don't wish us to wait for you, Your Highness?" the captain asked her.

Shalindra looked at Fendrick, but the dwarf shook his head, unwilling to speak in the open.

"If we are not back aboard in five days, you may return home and inform the queen we are well, and we shall secure passage back on our own."

The captain ran a good ship and likely could have put back to sea the next day if there had been reason, but five days would allow ample time to restock and even permit shore leave for the crew. It was the least she could do for them.

"As you wish, Your Highness," the captain said with a bow before excusing himself.

She let the sweep of her gaze take in the city. The docks bustled with sailors and laborers trying to finish their tasks before the rain arrived. Shalindra, like the handful of humans around her, rose head and shoulders above the dwarves. She had never felt so tall in her life. Only Weeby was small enough to get lost in the crowd.

The towering waterfall that had cut this gorge fell from so high in the mountains that it appeared to come directly from the clouds, which obscured the peaks far above. It fell in a series of long steps, each one taller than the one below it. The city was stacked around it in terraced levels, its buildings climbing both sides of the steep-walled gorge like vines, and with bridges of carved stone spanning the divide. Broad stairways were as common as the streets they connected, and many dwellings looked to have been carved from the rock itself. The place was angular and orderly and as durable as the mountains themselves, with the buildings differentiated more by the color of their stone than their design.

"Interesting place to live," Weeby said cheerfully.

"It's only a couple of miles to the top of the city," Fendrick said, ignoring him, "but we'll walk at least three times as far to get there. Let's not stand here gawking like a bunch of fools."

He settled his bag more comfortably on his shoulder and set off. Shalindra followed a step behind, still enjoying the newness of the place.

Fendrick led them to the end of the docks, where he paused abruptly and looked in both directions.

"Are we lost already?" Verelli asked.

"It's been a while. Trying to figure out where to get you some warmer clothes."

"We're plenty warm enough," Enna said, still looking a little wobbly.

"Do you think we're going to find what we're looking for down here?" Fendrick asked.

Enna gave Shalindra one of her I-told-you-so looks, but Shalindra would have been surprised if the journey had ended in the city.

"Really?" Weeby asked as no one made a move. "I'm the only

one who's been here too? There's a clothier of good repute that deals in your sizes two stairs and a street over. Come on."

* * *

As Fendrick had predicted, it took them the entirety of the day to reach the top of the town. He shouldn't have expected them to get there any faster, but it annoyed him nonetheless.

The last group he had led through the city had covered the distance much faster, and their composition had been so similar that the two could have been one and the same set of people. It was those similarities more than the differences that helped to keep his mind from wallowing in the past. On that prior visit, his group had been faced with an undetermined direction and even more uncertain destination. Both mysteries were known to him this time, but he was unsure if such knowledge made things better or worse.

He placed a hand against his vest. The angular shape of the tiny box could still be felt through the leather and fur, held fast inside a pocket sewn shut. Only a few more days.

They came to an intersection that was unfamiliar to him, and he turned in what he hoped was the right direction before the halfling could chime in with his opinion again. Fendrick still had no idea what the little man did, but Weeby knew too much about far too many things to be trusted. Fendrick would have been much happier were he able to leave them all behind and take only Shalindra, but no one would have agreed to that. He worried about the consequences of taking so many, but it was a risk he had to accept.

It was colder than he remembered, but his last visit had been during the height of summer. There had been fewer clouds, and sunlight had streamed over the sea and through the break in the mountains like fire through a half-shuttered lantern, illuminating the city until the last hint of it had slipped beneath the waves.

This evening's sun was too far south and too low in the sky to have the same effect, and so the city grew dark with shadows. Oil lamps glowed from above shop doors and at every street corner, allowing normal commerce to continue well into the dusk. The deep shadows had never given him pause before, but now the twisting, unfamiliar streets left him turned around as often as not, and increasingly frustrated.

There it was then. He was annoyed with himself, and he knew it. It was unreasonable to have expected the city to remain unchanged after so many years, and it was on his own shoulders for waiting so long to return. It would be unfair for him to blame Shalindra for not becoming Guardian sooner, or the gods for not accounting for his suffering when choosing to work so slowly.

He glanced over his shoulder, ostensibly to check on those who followed him. Shalindra looked and acted every bit like the Guardian she was and by all accounts deserved to be. Her casual disposal of the demon had been awesome to behold, and she remained unaffected by the emotions that rose and fell in those around her. By Hyrim's forge, he prayed she was the one. But her build was too stocky and her eyes far too blue to match his memories of what this woman should be, and the sword she carried—the one painstakingly crafted by his own hands—was as out of place on a cleric of Eluria as a ship in the desert.

The recollections of the past threatened to overwhelm him, and he forced them aside and concentrated on speeding their climb. It was already growing colder, the air made almost frigid by both altitude and mists. Most in the group had donned cloaks even before the sun's shadow had crept up the lowest waterfall, but Shalindra remained in her armor alone.

The buildings increased in size and stature the higher up the valley they travelled, as the wealthy congregated in the places that afforded the longest amount of sunlight and the most pleasing views.

That is, except for the highest terrace, an area known appropriately as Questor's Folly. Continuous walls of decoratively arranged stonework stood as a barrier between the pinnacles of society and the dilapidated structures and discarded equipment which lay beyond. The few buildings there were rough and weathered, having more in common with the docks than the elegant dwellings of the terrace they stood above. It was a place where the desperate and the foolish mingled at the edge of the civilized world before risking everything on the unforgiving mountains beyond. For all its distress, it felt more like home than any other part of the city.

The Frozen Foot was still here at least, standing like a marker of the city's upper boundary. Whether legend or inhospitable terrain had kept the city in check was irrelevant, but the squat, sharply roofed long hall remained the final stopping point before civilization abruptly changed to wilderness. Walls of mismatched stone supported a thickly shingled roof that had been patched so many times that there was not a straight row left on it.

Two sets of doors had to be passed through to gain entry, like gates in a castle wall. Here, however, the layered defenses served only to protect against the cold, and Fendrick made sure the outer doors were closed before opening the inner portal and leading the group inside.

Twin fires burned in pits near either end of the hall, both well stoked against the chill sliding down the mountainside. Smoke gathered in the rafters before making a sluggish escape through slit chimneys that no longer vented as they should. The near end held a collection of tables and a door to the kitchen, while the other two-thirds of the building was simply open space where guests could make whatever comfort they could find on the uneven planks of the floor. The building could have accommodated sixty people or more, and often did during the warmer months when adventurous fools embarked on their quests seeking fame and fortune. A far smaller crowd was cloistered at the tables this evening, and heads turned towards the newcomers with curiosity. They would draw less attention if Shalindra would at least cover herself with a cloak, but he understood why she chose not to—none of the others ever had, either.

The proprietor, a dwarf as gnarled and wrinkled as the building, was perched atop a sturdy stool leaned up against the wall, right where he was supposed to be. He, too, was different than Fendrick remembered, though he looked old enough to have been here through all the intervening years. Fendrick directed Shalindra and the rest to the first open table and circled the firepit to meet him.

He sized Fendrick up from beneath bushy grey eyebrows as he approached, then stood and held his forearm vertical beneath a clenched fist. "Tolith Shortstaff," he announced in a deep, gravelly voice. "Make yourself here in my home, named and known as the Frozen Foot."

Fendrick raised his arm in the same manner. "Fendrick Hammerstrike, your cousin beneath this roof."

They knocked their forearms together in the traditional high mountain greeting. Depending on the mood of the participants, the gesture could often be hard enough to leave bruises, but it was generally no worse than a firm nudge.

Tolith stepped back and stroked his tangled grey beard as he studied Fendrick's face. "Haven't seen you through here before."

"It's been a few years."

Tolith barked a sharp laugh. "Must've been more 'en a few, as I've had my command of the place for eighty-two winters now, and you're half my age if you're a day, but no matter. We've plenty of space for that sorry gaggle of tall folk you dragged in."

"Warmth for the night and food for the morning, then we'll be on our way."

"Are you really meaning to take those lowlanders up the Obahn Fayd?" Tolith asked, turning a skeptical eye on them. "Hope you've given them fair warning of what they're in for. Elves and halflings usually freeze—not enough meat on their bones."

"They know the risks."

Tolith made an uncomplimentary noise in his throat. "No, they don't, or they wouldn't be going. That was the last bit o' sun we'll be seeing for weeks, and it'll be an early snow this year. But I don't care what they've a mind to do so long as they stay nice and settled tonight."

Fendrick made a face. "The walk up that little hill wiped them out enough that they'll sleep sound and cause no issues."

"Need anything else to take with you? Weapons? Cloaks? Charcloth?"

"We need spears and shovels."

"I've a fair assortment of both in the shed outside. No cost for the shovels if you bring 'em back. Pair of Cronin each for the spears, take any two you like." He glanced over at the table where the rest of the party sat. "Or maybe three. The warrior woman looks competent enough for it."

"Two's plenty. All I've got is Kingdom Ships."

Tolith frowned but held out a hand. "Three silvers each, then, and another seven for your board. You should know better'n to deal with those things up here. Next time, change 'em out down by the docks."

"I'll do that," Fendrick promised, offering a silent prayer to Hyrim that he would never be forced to lead anyone else up these heartless mountains.

"Breakfast will be hot and ready when you wake. If you're needing anything else let me know."

Fendrick thanked him and returned to the group.

"He wasn't happy with Kingdom coins, was he?" Weeby asked, casually, cleaning a fingernail with the smaller of his two knives.

Fendrick considered punching him for being so smug, but he stifled the urge. "They prefer local currency this far from the harbor, but he was accommodating enough."

The halfling made a point of not smiling.

"We've got our space here and two meals, and there's spears

we'll collect tomorrow for Birion and me."

"No rooms?" Verelli asked.

"You're free to sleep outside if this isn't to your liking."

"How long will it take us to get where we are going?" Shalindra asked.

Fendrick shrugged. "If all goes well and no one dies, three days."

"Is death likely?" Honarch asked.

"It has been for most who've made the attempt."

Weeby elbowed the wizard. "Maybe you were right to leave the Conclave. Had I known you had such fun, I would have joined you years ago."

* * *

The next day, they climbed. The rocky trail that meandered away from the Frozen Foot took them steadily up, switching back and forth through a thick forest of massive spruce and fir trees. Shalindra could only wonder at the towering majesty of the mountains that might be revealed should the sun ever emerge, but the sky was an ever-changing mass of whites and greys that seemed unlikely to clear. There was nothing different to be seen looking down either, as the moisture from the sea turned to clouds in visible waves that rushed upwards. It was only from one brief vantage point that she was able to look down upon the still sleeping city, where ships bobbed like toys in the harbor far below.

Fendrick led the way, the steady plod of his feet and the tap of his spear shaft—now serving as a walking stick—driving them more east than north, though direction was difficult to judge without a clear view of the sun.

From the rear of the line Birion's spear tapped a similar cadence. Talking happened infrequently, as if conversation was an unnecessary disturbance to the perpetual song of the wind, or perhaps because everyone was gasping for breath in the thin air as they struggled beneath the weight of their bulky cloaks and thick bedrolls.

By midday, snow began to dust the trees, and was soon accumulating in patches on the ground. The cloaks Fendrick had chosen for them—oiled leather lined with thick furs—were stiff and uncomfortable, but surprisingly warm and dry.

Evening came sooner than it should have, and shivering fingers worked to establish a camp. Fendrick chopped logs into roughly equal lengths and stacked them at a slant atop each other against the fire, such that as the lower one burned, the others would then slide down and invigorate the fire without intervention. The logs were damp, but Honarch's method of igniting it with magic was more expeditious than flint and steel. Fendrick demonstrated making a wall of snow and branches, and everyone joined in to create one sufficiently high to shield themselves from the incessant wind. Once complete, they hunkered down behind it for the night.

"Two people on watch at a time," Fendrick insisted. "Makes it less likely one of you will fall asleep and freeze to death in the night."

They were miserable, wolfing down their dinner and hurriedly wrapping themselves head to toe in every bit of clothing and blankets they had, but not a one offered any protest. Not even Verelli, who had the least reason to be there out of all of them. The guilt Shalindra felt for leading them here was universally shared by the *hers* who rendered their opinions. Yet she had no power over the elements and could not make the fire warmer any more than she could blow the snow from their path. Enna tucked herself into a tight ball, buried within her blankets and furs so deeply that only her nose was visible. Shalindra leaned close against her as the others not on watch bedded down behind the protective wall.

Shalindra sat in silence, one part of her watching for signs of trouble while all the rest of her wondered what they might find if they did meet the former Guardian. It surprised her that almost all of the *hers* accepted that another Guardian was still here and able to communicate, but there was considerable disagreement on the usefulness of whatever she might convey. Each of them provided their own suggestion of what their ultimate purpose should be, but all of the options seemed just as nebulous as anything she might choose for herself. Shalindra just wanted to discover *something*. Anything that would give her a strong sense of purpose and direction. It was almost certain that—

Her eyes snapped to the darkened trees as the scuff of footsteps carried above the wind. Birion heard it too and kicked the others awake as he brought his spear to the ready and peeked over the wall. Shalindra did the same.

Tiny glints of light revealed first one pair of yellow eyes and then another, both low to the ground like a creature ready to pounce. The steady clump of slow movements in the snow could be heard, and soon there were dozens of eyes staring at them.

"Bolin," Fendrick said, relaxing.

"What?" Enna asked.

"Grass-eaters. You'll be fine."

One of the animals wandered into the light. Its curved horns and legs resembled those of a goat, but it was built more like a miniature cow and covered with a long, shaggy coat. The thick fur above its eyes gave it the appearance of perpetually scowling, while the directness of its gaze was unnerving.

"They don't look terribly friendly," Birion said.

Fendrick dismissed the idea with a wave of his arm. "They're harmless enough unless you bother them. The shaggy coat keeps 'em warm, so they give milk far longer into the winter months than a cow, if you can keep them in one place long enough. They're also dumber than a rock and prone to following each other off a cliff."

Weeby snickered. "Are falling cows that much of a problem here?"

"Their turds weigh more than you do," Fendrick said crossly. "Care to have half a herd dropped on your head?"

"An ignominious way to die," Honarch said, masking his grin behind a raised hand, and even Verelli seemed amused by the concept.

The herd wandered off once it had determined that there was no food to be had, and the group resumed their slumber.

* * *

The next day brought more of the same. It was a landscape of ice and cold, of sheer cliffs that never stopped growing, of frigid streams and lakes so pure they could see through them like glass. They slipped their way across fields of ice and snow that were disarmingly smooth from a distance yet became precipitously steep once upon them.

And still they climbed.

Vegetation grew sparse, confined to scrub and short trees strong enough to drive their roots deep into the rocky ground. In the open expanses where there was dirt to be found, it was covered in short grasses and thin bushes that stayed close to the ground. It was a coldly beautiful place, one of sharp ridges and flowing winds.

At one point they caught sight of another group of eight people—probably dwarves—descending the mountains, but they were miles away and their path would bring them nowhere close. They would have been greeted as family if they had, for in such an uninhabitable expanse as they travelled, everyone who struggled against it was a friend.

The cold grew so absolute that it permeated their heavy clothing, and even with the constant exertion it left fingers and toes numb. They were forced to stop frequently and boil water for warm drinks to stave off the effects. Shalindra watched Enna's deteriorating condition with concern.

"I'm fine," Enna said through chattering teeth, catching her look. "But I'll be glad when we get there." She said it with a brave face, but she shook as she drank her tea.

Shalindra cast about for some way to make any of this better and received her answer as one of the *hers* rather bluntly pointed out that Enna needed Shalindra's cloak far more than she did. It was nonsensical, for Shalindra had only her armor beneath, but this particular *her* was insistent that she had already done so much earlier and suffered no ill effects. Shalindra hesitated, then unlaced her cloak and wrapped it around Enna.

"You'll freeze!" Enna protested, almost spilling her drink as she tried to push it away.

Shalindra forced it around her shoulders, holding firm. "I am warm enough."

She should not be. If the air alone was not frigid enough to freeze skin, the ice covering the ground surely was. She felt the coldness of the air against the bare parts of her arms, and the wind swirled beneath her armor and around her exposed thighs. Her skin took on a touch of pink, but beyond that the weather did not bother her. She was warm because she wanted to be, and if that helped someone else, she would not question it.

Everyone else did question it, however, with glances if not with words. What must her friends be thinking about her now that she was the warrior who could stave off the cold with her will, see in the dark, and vanquish demons without effort? How much more different from them could she become before their admiration turned to fear and their commitment faded to reluctance? What if she lost control of it all and struck out at them the way she had in Ildalarial?

You don't sound very grateful for all you've been given.

I deserve it no more than they do. Why must I be set so far above them?

Someone's got to do it.

She grumbled at that answer, no matter how obvious a statement it might be, even as she wondered at its source. The voice was distinctive from any thought or impression offered by one of the *hers*, and as familiar to her as her own thoughts, for indeed it was her own.

Probably.

It was disturbing to think that one of the *hers* might be

developing the ability to communicate on a more direct level. None of it made any sense. In what hidden verse of the prophecy was it written that the Guardian should be constantly arguing with different versions of herself?

A reminder of how dangerous the cold could be came not an hour later, as they were traversed a long slope. Rocks jutted through the snow and ice, speckling the whiteness with dots of dark grey. As they drew close to one such grey shape, Shalindra spied an arm and then a shoulder protruding from the ground. Fendrick continued past, but Shalindra stopped and brushed away the snow. Beneath it lay a pair of elves huddled together, their skin blackened and mummified by the cold. The frozen tatters of their clothes were of an unfamiliar style, one that evoked fashion not seen in an age.

"How long have they been here?" Shalindra asked no one in particular.

"Who knows?" Fendrick answered. "Up this far, they might have been fortunate to have the cold kill them, but unless you'd care to sit down and join them, we'd best keep moving."

Enna said a prayer as they passed, and the group walked on.

It grew somehow colder that night. They were above the tree line now, and suitable wood for a fire became difficult to find.

Fendrick and Birion set out down the slope in search of something they could burn while Verelli and Honarch boiled snow with their magic. Enna and Weeby both gulped down the warm liquid without anything to flavor it, desperate for anything to thaw themselves out. The cold had reached the point of silencing even Weeby's cheerful banter.

The rest of them set about making snow walls once more. Honarch, never the fastest with a shovel, began experimenting with ways he could use magic to accomplish the same result. After several failed attempts, one of which sent a mass of snow exploding into the air, Verelli offered a suggestion and joined the efforts. More false starts came, but eventually they succeeded in forming a mound that at least looked intentional. Through repetition, they expanded enough of the barrier to be effective.

"Water is an odd material to shape," Verelli said as they sat behind it and began melting snow again. "It is far easier to guide its motion than to place it as you might clay or stone."

"It's progress, though," Honarch said. "With practice, I think we could even form it into a full dome and put a roof over our heads, so long as it stayed frozen while it was moved around."

"There is no way I'm sitting beneath a snow roof," Enna protested. "We'd all freeze when it collapsed on us."

"Not if we can figure out the correct level of binding," Honarch said, passing her a cup of hot water. "All things are possible with magic."

"Like keeping someone alive after death?" Shalindra asked.

The question added a chill to the already cold air, but she wanted to know. Honarch looked to Verelli, willing to let the senior mage answer.

"Death is the natural opposite of life," Verelli began, "and while there are many who seek to extend their existence and avoid their inevitable end, the majority use methods no more unsavory than your order." His look was piercing. "No matter how it is attempted, it never succeeds. Those who make a study of necromancy, however, are aware of ways in which the spirit may be bound outside the body and kept 'alive.' It's not really life, but the concept holds true for the purposes of this conversation. None of the methods are pleasant."

"It takes another death," Enna said, disgusted. "A sacrifice. A slaughter for your own evil purpose."

Verelli spread his hands, then quickly thought better of it and wrapped them around himself once more. "This is not my field of study, but good and evil are moral terms and tend to fall apart upon inspection. But I believe you are correct that such spells require an exchange of some sort."

"And speaking to these not-dead spirits?" Shalindra asked. "Is that actually possible?"

Enna answered. "Our lore tells that something must entice the spirit to you. Gifts of what they desired during life, oaths taken, those types of offerings."

Shalindra shook her head. "I have difficulty believing we have been lured up here for some cult ritual."

"So you may choose," Verelli said. "Our guide knows exactly where we are going and what we will find when we arrive, but he won't tell you. Were I a suspicious type, I would question how a simple blacksmith gained such knowledge." He glanced at the snow-shrouded peaks jutting up around them. "And what it will cost us to find out."

* * *

The next day saw a return of the heavy snow that had plagued them ever since leaving Highfall. The cold had become so bitter that the snow froze almost as it fell, and each step resisted for an instant before the crust collapsed and their feet sank into the softer snow beneath.

"I'd give an awful lot just to see the sun again," Honarch commented as they trudged up a steeply sloped snowfield.

"The Ironspike Mountains are so high that they block all the moisture that sweeps up from the ocean," Fendrick said. "Were we to cross the divide, the weather would turn sunny and dry at the snap of your fingers, and you'd wish for clouds as you descended to the desert that lies beyond."

Weeby perked up at the thought. "Will we reach that desert and finally be warm?"

"No."

"More's the pity," Weeby said with a sigh muffled by the covering on his face.

Enna came to a stop and threw her pack to the ground in disgust. "Then perhaps you could tell us how much farther we're going?"

The rest of the group stopped with her.

"Until we get there," Fendrick said, turning to face them.

"Her request is not unreasonable," Verelli pointed out, "though a bit melodramatic. If you're unwilling to divulge our destination, perhaps you could tell us the mechanism you intend to employ when summoning this shade? I'm familiar with the principles."

"You would be," Enna said with a cross look, even though the pair were nominally on the same side in this dispute.

Unwilling allies or not, Verelli did not allow her implied accusation to go unanswered. "Mages of my standing are required to be familiar with all the disciplines of magic, regardless of whether one practices them or not. For an order devoted to healing, the two of you seem remarkably acquainted with killing people."

Enna flushed at the rebuke. "We kill demons, not people."

"I'm no wizard," Fendrick said, answering Verelli's original question.

Verelli shifted his attention back to the dwarf. "Nor do you appear to be a cleric."

"I said I would take you to her, not tell you how to get there yourself."

"Trust is a river that flows both ways," Shalindra said, agreeing that Enna's demand was not unreasonable, given what they were being forced to endure. "We have followed you on faith up to now, but we will go no farther unless you tell us where we are going."

Fendrick's scowl could have flayed skin. "Fine. We're going to walk up, over snow and stone. We'll turn at a specific rock that's not much different than all the others lying about and double back the direction we came. Another turn will place us on a ledge that leads to a river with no bridge. If you don't fall off or freeze to death after getting wet, we'll go up and around more rocks until we're close, and from there the Guardian and I will continue alone. Happy?"

The dwarf stumped off without waiting for an answer. "You can keep up or go back. I don't care."

He had taken no more than three steps when the snow exploded around him, obscuring him in a white haze. A cry of pain was torn from him as his body went flying through the air. A sleek and powerful shape, white flecked with grey so similar to the snow and ice it was almost translucent, roared as it shot from the mists, bounding past Shalindra before her sword could clear its scabbard.

Enna's silvery blue shield snapped in front of Birion as the great cat's jaws plunged towards his throat. The beast rebounded from her barrier with a violent twisting motion that took it farther away from Shalindra, landing deftly on all four paws. Honarch stumbled away from it, frantically doffing his gloves, but before he could call forth his magic, the cat was on Birion again.

The knight was ready this time, and as Enna's shield turned the cat away once more, his spear caught it in the shoulder. It dodged sideways with a hissing snarl and swatted the polearm aside.

Shalindra joined the fray, but her attack faltered as she sought to strike with Shining Moon only to discover that she held her sword instead, and her swing missed. Claws longer than her fingers raked across her back. The scales of her armor held, but the force of the impact knocked her sideways. Sensing weakness, the cat leapt atop her.

Instinct overrode indecision, and Shalindra thrust her blade into its gaping maw, allowing the cat's momentum to do the work. Its weight crashed down onto her, impaling the animal on her blade. Her knees buckled, but she shoved the limp animal to the side and stepped back, at last taking Shining Moon in hand. The beast lay still in the snow, her sword still lodged in its throat and protruding from the back of its head. Birion thrust his spear through its lungs for good measure, then hastily retreated.

"Circle up and be wary of more," he commanded, breathing

heavily.

"I will get Fendrick," Shalindra called, rushing to where the dwarf lay dazed on the snow. He had to live, or they would be stuck atop this icy mountain with no idea of where they needed to go. His hood was shredded, and blood ran down the side of his head. Globs of flesh had been torn loose where the cat's claws had found their mark, but, incredibly, he had regained his knees and was pushing his torn skin back together.

"I'll be fine," he said.

"You will be in a moment," she said as she knelt beside him, seeking his eyes. "Hold still."

He turned his head and pushed her away. "Don't waste your time. It's not needed."

"But—"

He grasped at his chest, and she feared that he was having a seizure, but his hand came to a rest and he sighed in relief.

"Just help me up and don't let them ask any more questions." His eyes met hers. "You'll understand soon enough."

Shalindra was struck by the amount of sadness in that plea. It might not have made sense, but she had trusted him this far, and at this point she had no other alternative. She gently wiped the blood from his face, amazed that the deep wounds had stopped bleeding and were already beginning to heal. She helped him to his feet.

"Should we expect more?" Birion called as Fendrick wobbled over to collect his pack and spear.

Fendrick shook his head, though the motion caused him pain and he kept his face averted as he answered. "Were it a pack of silver wolves that caught us by surprise, we'd have been finished, but the snow cats wander alone. I just gave him too good a target." He sounded disgusted with himself. He pushed a handful of snow against his damaged head, and in quiet tones he said to Shalindra: "Give me a moment and we'll get moving again."

She had no idea how he planned to continue after receiving such a blow to the head, but witnessing such rapid improvement, she was willing to allow him the time to sort himself out.

"We will regroup before continuing," she said, moving to retrieve her sword. She wiped it clean on the cat's surprisingly soft fur before returning it to its scabbard.

Honarch was already examining the animal. Verelli, after a long, calculating stare at Fendrick, did the same. Birion's attention was directed outward, alert for any additional threats.

Honarch pressed one of the cat's claws all the way out and gave a low whistle. "Look at that."

"I'd rather not," Weeby said.

For Shalindra, it was all she could look at. The sleek predator was longer than Birion was tall and several times his weight. Its short, dense fur was exquisite in its softness, stained only by the bright blood that flowed from its wounds and was already beginning to freeze. Large eyes, beautifully patterned in metallic hues, stared unseeing at the sky.

Suddenly angry, Shalindra spun on her heel and walked away before she started screaming at it. Nothing about that conflict was right. Why had it attacked them? Was it driven by desperation or hunger, or had it acted in defense of its territory? In the end, it did not matter. It was dead and they were not. But Enna was the one who had protected the group, not her. Why? Why was killing the only thing she could do now?

Enna's hand on her shoulder pulled her from her reverie. "Are you well?"

"No." Shalindra shook her head vigorously but kept her voice low enough that no one else would overhear. "No, I am not. I chose to follow Eluria so that I could heal, not leave a trail of corpses in my wake. What noble purpose did this serve?"

"It wasn't your choice to fight."

"But it was my choice which placed us here and could have seen one of you killed, a decision you argued against more than once."

"And I would argue it still, but it was your decision to make, not mine, and certainly not Verelli's. We accept the road you lead us down, even when we don't agree with it."

Shalindra would have been just as happy if such choices could be made by someone else, or if she could at least have someone with whom to confer about the merits and perils. They were far too trusting in her to make the correct choices, and she questioned those decisions so frequently that she could find little to trust in herself. Enna was waiting expectantly, her eyes full of understanding. It was something that had been missing between them for too long.

"Enna, I…"

"Come on then," Fendrick called, waving them all forward. "If we stand here long enough, something a lot meaner is going to find us."

Shalindra sighed as they rejoined the group, wondering how

much worse this could get.

* * *

"That's... a long way down," Weeby said with dramatic understatement, edging closer to the precipice.

"Then don't fall off," Fendrick admonished, setting his pack down. "We're fortunate the wind's blown it dry. It's not fun to cross when frozen."

Shalindra could only imagine how impossible the obstacle facing them would be were the stones slick with ice. It was a small consolation that the narrow ledge was exactly where Fendrick had declared it would be, and just as deadly as he had promised. Though proving that he was headed somewhere specific, it did nothing to ease their crossing. The shelf was barely the width of her shoulders at its widest point and irregular in its composition, curving to the right around the face of the mountain and out of sight. If she chose to look over the edge far enough, she might be able to see the ground below, but the distance would be measured in miles. The mountain continued sharply upward just as far, or at least until it disappeared in the clouds. The faintest whisper of flowing water carried above the swirl of the wind, which was blessedly blowing upslope instead of down.

"There's really no way around?" Honarch asked.

Fendrick, meticulously tightening every strap and buckle he had, did not pause his work. "You're welcome to try digging a tunnel."

Honarch glanced up at the sheer face of the mountain towering above them, giving serious consideration to the option.

"If there's another way," Fendrick continued, "it's at least two days' to the east. That's why we picked it."

"Why who picked this?" Enna asked.

Fendrick did not answer as he shouldered his pack once more. "Just go slow and don't look down."

"What if we tied ourselves together?" Birion suggested.

Fendrick gave a curt shake of his head. "There's nothing for the rest to grab hold of. Should one person go over the edge, they'd likely take all of us with them."

Fendrick moved to the ledge and steeled himself, but she doubted that it was the height which bothered him. Since their encounter with the snow cat that morning, Shalindra had watched his steps grow steadily slower and his comments less frequent, as if an immense weight had settled around his shoulders, and he seemed a man walking towards some inevitable doom. He pressed himself against the stone face as tightly as possible and stepped onto the ledge.

"Face the cliff, move only one limb at a time, and pray we don't run into any bolin coming the other way. Make sure of every step before you make it, and if you're not certain then crawl."

One by one, the remainder of the group followed.

Shalindra regretted the decision before she was ten steps out. Every shift of the wind seemed like an angry hand that meant to push her off. She kept herself flattened against the wall so closely that she could feel the texture of the rock on her cheek and taste the metals trapped within the stone. At her back was nothing. Not a gap or a void or a distance, simply *nothing*. Nothing between her and the horizon. To stand at the edge of such a vast emptiness was a sensation without compare, exhilarating in its uniqueness. She kept her movements slow enough that Enna remained within arm's reach behind her, though if either of them slipped, she doubted that the other could react fast enough to alter their fate.

The ledge spanned a length of no more than fifty or sixty paces, but it felt like a day before they succeeded in edging their way across it. By the time they reached wider ground they were shaking from more than the cold.

"I think I'm going to throw up," Weeby said.

"If we have to do that again, I'm going to crawl," Honarch agreed, his hands still trembling from the effort.

The area beyond the ledge broadened to a more comfortable width, and, though exhausted from the ordeal, no one wished to linger. A game trail led up a slight grade and away from the edge, and as they followed it the sound of rushing water grew steadily louder.

Shalindra placed her hand against a rocky protuberance to steady herself but came to a halt as a pattern too regular to be natural caught her eye. A trio of notches were cut into the stone in matching lines, resembling nothing so much as giant claw marks. They were old, worn almost smooth by rain and weather, but the strength required to cut through solid rock—and the angle at which they were made—put her in mind of a much larger creature. She might have passed it off as her imagination were it not for an identical set of scrapes just ahead.

She glanced over her shoulder to seek another opinion, but Enna's grim nod said that she had seen it as well and come to the same conclusion: a demon had been here.

Enna gave a meaningful toss of her head towards Fendrick, but

Shalindra just shrugged. The marks were troubling, but she still doubted that he meant them any harm.

A light snow was drifting down when they came to a fast-moving river at least forty feet across. There was a flat area along the rocky wall on the opposite side, but the crossing was barely a stone's throw from the edge of a roaring waterfall that plummeted into the bottomless chasm they had skirted once already today.

Fendrick's entire body trembled as he stared at the water plummeting over the edge, and he seemed unable to move. Then, taking a shuddering breath, he bent and began to remove his boots.

"Take yours off as well," he called back. "It'll give you better footing."

"Are you insane?" Verelli questioned.

"Your toes'll freeze whether they're covered or not, but having something dry when you get out is all that will keep them from turning black and falling off."

No one rushed to believe him, but by the time Fendrick had his second boot off, it became clear that it was not a jest. Weeby seemed willing to take Fendrick at his word and had already worked a boot off. He dipped a toe in the water and hastily withdrew it. "That's cold enough it hurts. Can either of our wizards get us across?"

"I am capable of slowing your rate of descent," Verelli said, "but I cannot make you lighter than air."

Honarch also shook his head.

"Some good wizards are," the halfling muttered, only half under his breath. "Even if we don't freeze, some of us won't be able to stand against that current."

"He's got a point," Birion said. "The water will sweep us over the edge."

"Then hold tight to each other, or you'll return to Highfall far faster than you care to," Fendrick answered. "This is—"

He never finished his thought, as Shalindra grabbed him by the back of his coat and lifted him off his feet with one hand. It was time she put her gifts towards protecting those with her instead of dragging them further into danger, and if she could drive a sword clean through a demon's leg, she should be able to lift a pair of men easily.

"What...?" he sputtered as she hoisted Weeby in a similar manner.

"You might want to hold still," Weeby said, dangling like a cat held by the scruff of its neck. "I'd prefer not to be dropped."

Shalindra waded into the river before anyone could object, or before she could entertain her own second thoughts. The water was so cold that it burned, threatening her self-enforced feeling of warmth. By the time she was knee deep, the cold was so severe that she began to wonder if she was actually as warm as she felt or if her body was freezing and she was only convincing herself otherwise. Either way, she needed to hurry. With every step, she jammed her feet into the rocks to keep herself upright against the current, sloshing her way across as quickly as she could. The water fought against her, threatening to sweep her off her feet with the slightest misstep. She deposited the two men unceremoniously on the far side and slogged back through the current for the others.

"Wizards next," she said.

Verelli held up a hand. "Might I request that I not be hoisted like a sack of potatoes?"

She extended her arms to either side. "You may hold on yourself, if you find it more agreeable."

It would be easier for her to balance the two of them in that manner anyway. Neither man appeared eager to accept, but Honarch rather gingerly pulled himself onto one arm, and Verelli followed a moment later.

Though the weight was more evenly distributed, the crossing was made more difficult by the squirming of both men. Honarch slipped as they were reaching the deepest part, and she feared he might fall into the water. The mage righted himself and clung to her arm more tightly, and Shalindra forged across the remaining distance as fast as she could manage. Now soaked from the waist down, she returned for Birion.

"I'm heavier than the magicians," the knight said.

"So was Fendrick."

He shook his head in protest. "This is a burden that—"

"I am happy to bear," she finished for him. "Obligations of friendship are not burdens at all. Secure yourself on my shoulders."

Birion took a deep breath then did, as delicately as possible. It was more of an effort to hold him up, and her back was beginning to feel the strain of her repeated trips across the river. The weight at least provided added resistance to the current.

The moment they had reached dry land, Birion eased himself from her back and bowed with as much dignity as was possible. "Thank you, my lady."

Shalindra turned and made her way back one last time for Enna. The elf's eyes were moist from more than the biting wind, and her fingers drifted across her symbol of Eluria as Shalindra drew close. Shalindra took Enna's hand in her own and drew her close, cradling the smaller woman in both arms.

This final crossing was less of a struggle as Shalindra's feet found familiar rocks and currents, but it was the hardest for her to accomplish. The look of eager surrender in Enna's eyes was uncomfortable in its adulation.

She's idolized you for a long time.

I do not want to be worshipped. I want her to remain my friend.

You're doing it the wrong way then.

What other way was there? How could she have walked herself across without harm only to stand idle and risk watching one of them plummet to their death over the edge of the waterfall, or lose toes or feet to the cold?

Shalindra was thankful when she reached the far bank and eased Enna to the ground. Her legs were chilled, and her boots soaked through, but neither inconvenience would deter her. The knowledge that she had helped instead of hurt was enough to rekindle the warmth flowing through her, overriding any discomfort.

Fendrick cleared his throat and scratched at the pink lines of the almost healed cuts on his face. "Ah, we're not far now. Tonight's camp will be our last."

'Not far' had them walking until sunset, though they had not seen the sun since leaving Highfall and could only tell by how the light began to fade. They followed no path or markings, instead scrambling over slick stone and icy snow. The mountains showed the effects of water and time, with deep crags and numerous streams cutting grooves into the granite.

When Fendrick called a halt, it was in such a nondescript location that Shalindra almost thought it a random decision.

"It's just down here a bit," Fendrick said. "We'll make a shelter here, then Shalindra and I will go in."

"You really mean to leave us exposed and freezing up here?" Verelli asked. "The snow is—"

"I said you'll go no further!" Fendrick roared. The whites of his eyes were wide and crazed enough that even the normally assured wizard took a step back.

Shalindra placed a hand on his shoulder, and Fendrick regained his composure.

"Fendrick and I will continue," Shalindra said. "The resting place of the dead should suffer the smallest interruption possible. If it is safe, we will return for you."

Enna and Birion both looked as if they would argue the point, though more for her safety than their own comfort.

"We will be fine," she promised them. Shalindra had nothing but her beliefs to prove that statement was correct, but she was well beyond the point of doubting Fendrick's intentions.

Now that they were here, she could only hope that whatever she discovered would justify the danger she had put her friends through.

Chapter Eighteen

A Sacrifice Unforgotten

The draw Shalindra followed Fendrick down was unremarkable, a fissure in the rock no different than the countless others all around them, with steep walls of dark grey granite alternately fractured and smoothed by eons of ice and water. The footing was treacherous as they picked their way over crumbled rock made slippery from patches of ice and snow. The twisting crevasse soon hid the campsite from view and eventually swallowed the sounds of the wind as well. The air moved calmly, as if the canyon itself was breathing, and the ensuing silence left Shalindra with the irrational feeling that they were entering a tomb.

At last, the ground levelled off and the tiny canyon grew wider at the base than at its top. Upon turning the next bend, they were confronted by a dead-end. The hollowed-out space in the mountain was perhaps twenty or thirty paces across and open to the sky. Spread across almost the entire floor was a pool of water so still that the reflection it provided seemed more real than the world itself, giving it the illusion of a much larger space. Only the narrowest strip of dry land hugged the right-hand wall, forming a shelf not a handspan above the surface of the water.

Fendrick stopped at the edge of the pool and intoned what must have been a prayer, but it was in a language thick with accents and inflections she had never heard. The tingle of magic filled the air, leaving goosebumps on her arms. Shalindra waited in silence, half expecting the former Guardian to appear. Fendrick waited as well, as would a man standing before an open door, struggling to find the courage to proceed.

With reluctance, he placed a foot on the shelf and began to edge his way around the pool. Shalindra could see no destination, but upon reaching the end he disappeared into a shaded alcove of rock. When he did not immediately return, she followed.

Poking her head into the darkened recess that appeared to have swallowed him, she discovered that the shadows obscured an entrance to a cave. The opening was wide but low, such that even Fendrick would have had to duck to enter. Shalindra bent nearly in half as she squeezed her way in, and was thankful when the tunnel grew into a cave large enough for her to stand upright.

Fendrick waited there in silence, his back to her. As her eyes adjusted to the dim light, she beheld hundreds of figures and symbols painted in ocher on the walls. The images were almost crude in their simplicity, drawn with the unrefined smudges of fingers rather than the delicate strokes of a brush, yet there was a vibrance to their shapes and arrangement that gave life to the art.

"Who made these?" she wondered aloud.

"Only the gods know."

Fendrick struck flint to steel, and she winced at the sudden brightness as the torch sprang to life. He held the brand aloft and led the way deeper into the cave. The floor had been levelled in the distant past, perhaps by those who had made the paintings, but small stalagmites and crumbled stone now marred their efforts.

Shalindra studied the paintings as she followed, pausing when she spied one that was an oddly familiar depiction of a pair of clay tablets held together. "What is this symbol?"

"The mark of Vanirus, the Lost God," Fendrick answered. "It was Amalthee who took up His book when He was slain, assuming dominion over both wealth and knowledge."

She had never heard of a lost god, nor could she recall any mention of Amalthee's Book ever being anyone's other than her own. Was it even possible for a god to die?

Fendrick came to a halt at a break in the floor. Kneeling, he thrust his torch into it, causing the hole to glow in the now darkened tunnel. Flattening himself on the damp floor, he followed it with his head. He withdrew both after a moment and handed her the torch.

"I'll climb down, and you can drop it to me."

He wriggled feet first into the hole, slipping and muttering as he descended a near vertical drop. The bottom was a good twenty feet down, and upon reaching it he waved for the torch. Shalindra dropped it into his waiting hands, then slipped down the damp rock after him.

Fendrick started moving the moment her feet were level with his, but their pace was now slower. The tunnel—more of a crack in the rock than a proper passage—narrowed and split as it burrowed deeper into the mountain, and they were forced to twist sideways to squeeze through. Both walls and floor were slick with moisture, and the occasional drip of water was the only sound other than their own footsteps that broke the silence. Though still cold, the air warmed gradually the further they went, even as it became more stagnant.

Fendrick paused several times to whisper words at certain places before proceeding. As she recognized the pattern of it, Shalindra allowed her vision to subtly shift, and was surprised to see the sparkling dissolution of protective wards at every juncture. He had claimed that he was no wizard, and Shalindra believed him, but he was also not a cleric, or at least not in the traditional sense. What that made him was as much a mystery as was how he had come to know this place, but she suspected that knowledge had been gained firsthand.

At last, they arrived at a small cave where all the dripping water along their route coalesced into a wide puddle before falling a short distance into a larger pool. The pool was large enough to be deemed a small lake, with a shore of smoothed stones and pebbles deposited untold ages earlier. Now its mirrored surface was broken only by the occasional ripple triggered by a drip from the ceiling above. Luminescent fungi clung in patches on the walls, giving the cavern a dim bluish-green glow. Crystalline formations scattered throughout the cave reflected the light, giving it a sense of life.

Fendrick hesitated again, then indicated the way down. Shalindra descended the short wall and heard him do the same behind her. His footsteps grew wooden and clunky as he trailed further behind, but Shalindra no longer needed his direction. She stopped at the water's edge, aware of a presence within. It was faint, an added coolness in air still cold enough to make visible her breath.

The presence, whatever it happened to be, was as aware of her as she was of it. They each waited on the other in silence, neither moving.

Shalindra was about to ask Fendrick what she was expected to do when the surface of the water exploded upwards in a billowing cloud of mist. The vapor solidified into the glowing, translucent figure of a female elf draped in flowing robes which had been cut and slashed. Anger and hatred twisted her mottled face into an appalling visage as she flew forward with hands outstretched. The protective nimbus of Shalindra's shield snapped into place just in time to keep the shade's hands from her neck.

"Where is it?" the ghostly elf shrieked, an action which caused her jaw to move further open than was natural.

Was she requesting an offering of some sort? "I do not know what—"

"How did you find it? Do you think to torment me with it? I will never do your bidding!" The tattered remnants of the elf's robes swirled into a frenzy around her, lashing at Shalindra and sending sparks dancing across her divine shield.

The shade flew back to regroup, then flung herself at Shalindra once more. Her rant continued, switching from common to elvish and back, though Shalindra understood it all.

"Do not seek to trick me, fiend!" the shade screamed. "You may shift your form, but I feel the taint of death wrapped around your soul, and I know you for what you truly are!" She struck impotently at Shalindra once more. "I am cursed for eternity to reside here, but an eternity more will pass before I supply aid to your conquest!"

Shalindra willed herself to remain still, using the minimum force possible to protect herself. She tried repeatedly to speak, but no matter how calm she remained, the shade showed no signs of attenuating her attacks. The tormented elf would never speak to her in this condition, and Shalindra would not seek to force her. But Shalindra was not the only one in the cavern, and she could not help but think that this behavior was what Fendrick had feared the entire way here.

Without taking her eyes from the shade, she spoke to him over her shoulder. "Speak her name."

Fendrick sucked in a deep breath in surprise. She could tell from the echoes of his rapid breathing that he did not raise his head, and when at last he spoke, she barley recognized the hoarse croak of his voice.

"Alharania."

The shade's spinning ceased abruptly, her tattered robes swirling to a sudden stop. Still floating above the water, she eased herself to the side and looked past Shalindra.

"Fendrick," Alharania whispered, a lifetime's worth of emotion tangled in every syllable of his name. She hovered uncertainly, then seemed to shrink as she wrapped her arms around herself like a fearful child. Eyes wide and clear, she regarded Shalindra as if seeing her for the first time. "You are the Guardian, then?"

"I am."

Alharania drifted closer, inspecting everything about her. "You are clad in Elurithlia's armor and carry Alta Suralia as I once did, but you are… different, inside."

"My Ascension was unconventional."

Worry creased Alharania's translucent forehead. "Are you a demon?"

"No, though I carry some of that essence within." There was no way to fully explain the mark Tormjere had left on her, or describe how so much of what he had been now resided inside her.

Alharania withdrew but did not turn away. "That may be for the best, or at least not for the worst."

"I have come—"

"For the wisdom of the fallen. Yes, that is my role to fulfill, and why I have endured this torment for so long. Yet first must I ask: have you discovered what it is which must be done?"

"No," Shalindra said with a frustrated shake of her head. "Demons flood into our world, and Eluria lies weakened. It was her will that sent me in search of answers, though I had no idea my road would lead to you."

"Then I shall do my best to convey all that I can remember and hope that it is enough. But where to begin? You must have been told each of the Guardian's additions to the Prophecy?"

"I have," Shalindra answered. "Though they are a bit obtuse."

"It has always been thus, though I do not understand why. I…" Alharania paused, and traces of fear found their way into her voice. "What is written beneath my statue?"

The question was surprising, but Shalindra would have been filled with the same morbid curiosity were their roles reversed. "The pedestal is noticeably bare, though your effigy is full of beauty and vigor."

The shade mulled that over. "That is unfortunate. Yet, as I am still here, perhaps it is not unexpected." She winced at some passing discomfort, then continued. "Alta Suralia is key to what we… what you must do. Take heed of what it tells you and learn from what it does not. I assumed, once, that I had at last deduced its secrets. I was more wrong than I could have ever imagined, for Her weapon contains a power more suited to a less noble purpose, one which does not align to our nature. Even with that realization, still I believed that I was capable of doing what was required, for it is in darkness that our light may shine the brightest. Again, I was mistaken, and the cost of my poor judgement was more than I could bear." Her eyes fell sadly on Fendrick, who had yet to lift his head to look at her.

"The entirety of my tale cannot be told. Every appearance I make in this world takes its toll on my spirit. Our Sister Erithrial was correct in declaring demons to be our ultimate enemy, but our victory is not to be achieved in the lands of elf or dwarf or man. This was not a realization that came quickly or without trial, but once made we ventured into the demonic realm, seeking to prevent them from achieving entry into our own. It seemed a straightforward proposition. Such fiends have long sought access to our world, after all, and every incursion has a leader who can be coerced or discouraged. But the hordes we found were vast, and they came at us in numbers without measure."

Alharania's voice was rising, taking on an edge of hysteria, and she swayed back and forth as she became caught up in her own tale.

"We were naïve in our decision to seek them out, for we could have slain thousands and still changed nothing. Their world is unlike ours in every way. A place without grass or trees, where birds and livestock cannot exist, utterly devoid of any sustenance that might pass our lips. It is a land without water or light, only death and shadows. Every creature that walks or crawls or flies, every sentient being, whether capable of speech or not, will know you as its enemy. There is no disguising your purpose or hiding behind a veil. There is nothing there but death."

"Then why go?" Shalindra asked, fighting to quell her rising sense of helplessness.

A spasm of pain robbed Alharania of words, but she gritted her teeth and continued. "Because it is there the Guardian's road will end. Someone—or something—wants into our world, and if it succeeds then all we know will be destroyed. Not out of anger or cruelty but simple necessity. To support their way of life would lead to the utter dissolution of all that we know and a reordering of the natural laws to better fit their nature. And within that puzzle is what we are meant to do: put an end to whatever force drives this assault on our world. Who or what it is was not fated for us to discover, but it is there. Upon realizing the impossible magnitude of what we faced, we fled…" Her voice caught in her throat. "But not soon enough."

"How did you perish?" Shalindra asked gently.

The question hung still in the air for long moments. Alharania tried but failed to keep her eyes from Fendrick before looking down, and her words were so soft they were barely audible. "By my choice."

She drifted in silence once more before composing herself. "The price of being Guardian is steep. One last warning will I give you: be wary of Alta Suralia. It awakened unwholesome cravings inside me that I could barely control. I do not know if it was afflicted or was I, but the urges that took hold of me once in that realm of devastation were horrid in ways that I can never forget. Be true to who we are, and do not succumb should they visit you as well." She winced again. "I regret that this is all I may give you. I must go."

There were so many questions Shalindra wished to ask, but to hold Alharania here in such obvious pain would be the height of selfishness. She had been given enough.

"You have helped more than I could have hoped. Know that your sacrifice will be celebrated, and never will our Sisters forget how much you have given. May Eluria continue to bless you, always."

"May you reach the end I could never achieve," Alharania said.

Shalindra turned to leave but paused beside Fendrick. "We will wait for you."

Fendrick barely heard her. His eyes remained fixed on the pebbles at the water's edge as Shalindra's footsteps receded up the tunnel. He could not look up. Could not bear to see what Alharania had become. He tried to speak but was blocked by the wall of emotion that robbed him of his voice and left his throat sandy. When at last he succeeded in dragging the words forth, they emerged as a hoarse croak.

"I know what I should have given. I know because another did what I could not. I faltered when you needed me most. Forgive me."

The effort of that desperate plea robbed him of strength, and his trembling legs gave out, dropping him helplessly to his knees. He prayed to be struck down where he was, to have an end to the shame he had carried for so long, even knowing that death would never provide the release he so desperately wanted.

"Fendrick, look at me."

Her voice was hollow, lacking the melodic tones that had once danced in his ears, but it had lost none of its tenderness. It was a comfort he did not deserve, but she had always overlooked his failings.

With effort, he raised his face to hers. It burned at his soul to see her delicate features sallow and torn, ravaged by the undeath to which she was consigned. But he forced himself to meet her gaze, to suffer the penance of her blame that he so rightly deserved.

And, as always, she allowed him only kindness.

"You must help her."

Fendrick shook his head. "How can I, when I wasn't even able to—"

"She has strength unlike anything I ever possessed. You can see it in her eyes, feel it in the air when she speaks. I thought once, as you did, that failure was our curse. But we have done more than any who have gone before me ever did." She slid forward, and placed a hand to his head, though her fingers left no feeling and disturbed nothing as they passed through his hair. "We have given her the key! She will find a way where we could not. She must."

Alharania shivered in pain, and Fendrick knew he could not linger. This time, at least, he could supply her with some measure of joy by returning a part of what had been torn from her. He reached into his vest and, after freeing the pocket he had sewn shut, withdrew the small, ornate box given to him in payment by the priests of Amalthee. This he presented to her like an offering held with trembling hands. "I ran from my promise, hid from it for decades, and despaired that I would fail at that as I had failed at so many things for you. But I never forgot."

Alharania's eyes brightened, released from pain for one unfairly brief moment. But she made no move to accept it.

"I would have it remain with you," she said. "Allow me to be your strength when you need it most, and to fuel your will when you succumb to doubt. Return with all that I was, and I will truly believe that I am no longer needed. Then we may both rest."

A Tangled Path

The afternoon sun was bright and graciously warm in the skies above Merallin, and the frigid wastes of the mountains an unpleasant memory, when Shalindra slipped quietly into her father's darkened chambers. Heavy curtains were drawn tight across the tall windows, leaving the sumptuously decorated room lit only by a handful of lanterns. She had not passed through those doors since sneaking into the castle… Had it really only been two months ago? That desperate attempt to prevent the outbreak of war with the elves, daunting though it had been, paled in comparison with the seemingly impossible one which now loomed before her.

On this day, it was her mother who looked up from behind a desk piled high with orderly arrangements of papers. The queen's eyes lit up as she rushed on tiptoe to embrace her daughter.

"You look tired," her mother whispered.

I can't imagine why.

"I have had much to do and even more to think about," Shalindra said in equally soft tones, "as it appears you have as well."

Eleanor glanced back at the piles of paper on the desk. "The king is incapable of evaluating every request and proclamation that he should, and so we predispose of the uncontentious issues."

"At least you are here to do so. So many duties never wait for a convenient time."

"It must be done, but should it become known just how much our decisions govern the Kingdom instead of his…" Eleanor shook her head. "We are distrusted enough as is."

"How is he?"

Her mother began to speak, then looked away and waved her towards the adjoining bedroom.

Shalindra moved silently across the rugs—new ones, unstained by blood—and cracked open the door to the bedchamber. Her father lay asleep, tucked beneath thick blankets in spite of the warmth radiating from the nearby fireplace. His mouth hung open, allowing his pale cheeks to droop beneath his chin. Only the slightest rise and fall of the covers gave any indication that he was alive. An attendant waited beside the bed, but he did not look up to acknowledge her presence. Saddened to see him this way, Shalindra closed the door softly and returned to her mother.

"How much does he sleep?"

"Practically all day. He has spoken about you at random times, but never with compliments. Whatever thoughts occupy him now cause him to blame you for much of the ill that has befallen us."

For all that she had risked saving his life, that admission stung. But his wound had been severe and not something to recover from in a day. Shalindra tried to be encouraging. "It cannot remain this way forever. In time, he will—"

"He will never get better."

Resignation drove the finality of that statement. It hurt to see her mother so sad, and Shalindra wondered what part of their future was still within her power to change.

"You should go find Kentrick," her mother said, trying to lighten the mood. "I believe he's down at the kennels. He has some idea in his head, and… Well, I will let him explain it. I would like to hear your opinion on it this evening."

Shalindra wondered if this idea was related to her father. That there was some scheme afoot was hardly unusual, but she would remain apart. She finally had a direction of her own to follow, and while she did not know where her road would lead, it would not be found here. If it eased her mother's mind, however, she would certainly listen.

"Of course I will," she said.

They said a quiet goodbye, and Shalindra made her way down to the kennels. Her family, like most of the nobility, had kept dogs for years, and while their pens were not a place she had frequented as a child, she remembered well enough how to get there.

Everyone bowed to her as she passed, but she quickly grew tired of the need to respond. It was far easier to move about when no one cared who you were.

It was a relief when she exited to the rear of the building, where there were almost no people. The lawn was neatly manicured, though the grass was beginning to fade with the coming of winter. Paths of crushed stone led in different directions, one of which she followed towards the sounds of barking dogs, where she spied her brother leaning against a rail, watching the animals play.

"Ah, you are here," Kentrick said as he caught sight of her, a smile pushing aside the frown on his face. "When did you arrive? And where is Sister Enna?"

"We disembarked not two hours past," Shalindra answered, coming to stand beside him. "I am afraid that the seas were unkind to Enna, and she is in bed recovering from our voyage."

"No surprise this time of year," Kentrick said, before suddenly turning suspicious. "What happened to your wizard?"

"He returned with me as well. We were able to secure rooms at the same inn, but I came straight here."

"It would be best if he kept out of sight. Too many people learned of our meeting, and we cannot chance a repeat visit. Have you spoken to anyone else yet?"

"Just mother," Shalindra answered, dropping her hand inside the pen so it could be licked by a sturdy shepherd. "She was buried beneath piles of paper, doing the king's work."

"As do we all. He spends more time asleep than awake."

"There has truly been no improvement to his condition?"

Her brother paused and looked around before answering. "None. I don't mean this to be harsh, but it would have been a kinder fate for all of us had he fallen to Logian's knife rather than lingering in this state."

Shalindra understood why he would say that, no matter how cruel it might sound. With a bedridden king and an unexpected heir, the kingdom faced more strife at a time when they desperately needed unity.

Kentrick attempted to wave away the gloomy mood as he turned from the dogs and began to stroll down the gravel path.

"Other than the rough seas, how went your foray to Dwarfport? Did you accomplish what you set out to?"

"Things went as smoothly as they could have."

In truth, her recollection of their journey down from the mountains was like walking through someone else's memory. The perilous return to Highfall, securing a ship, sailing north back to Merallin—all of it had passed like a dream. Since meeting Alharania, the multitude of *hers* had been debating their interpretations of every word with a vocalness that bordered on incivility. As evidence, they argued not only with logic but with images—memories and impressions that spanned forests and mountains and deserts—pulled from the lives she could have lived and still arrived here. She possessed more concrete visions of other places and other events than those she had participated in, and it bothered her that she had no recollection of what she had told her friends of the meeting.

"Well, I'm glad that you accomplished something, whatever it was. It feels like we've done nothing since you left but sit and worry."

"Mother said that you had plans."

Kentrick nodded and turned them towards an entrance. "We do, but it's not something to be discussed in the open."

They reentered the palace and mounted a stairway up several levels, heading back in the direction from whence Shalindra had come.

"We've a bit of a problem," Kentrick said as they climbed.

He's only got one? That must be nice.

Reaching the top, they turned down a wide hallway, and

Kentrick lowered his voice. "It's not something I'd—"

"You!"

Scorn laced the voice that interrupted their conversation.

Kentrick's shoulders sagged a little as he turned around and forced a smile onto his face. "Father, it is good to see you on your feet today."

It was a respectful lie. Their father, Fabrian, remained upright only with the assistance of two of his strongest servants. The left side of his face drooped as lifelessly as the arm beneath it, and the corners of his mouth were wet with spittle. He had never been an athletic man even before age had added girth to his stomach, and his body slid loosely about, as if the muscles had been removed. His appearance should have triggered sorrow within her, but what Shalindra felt now was more akin to pity.

"Father," she greeted him. "Are you well?"

"Yoow brought thems here?" the king slurred. He forced one foot forward, his servants doing the work of moving him closer. "Elvsh and wizurds in my castle?" His face grew red and splotchy. "You're here for my throwen."

"The elves agreed to your peace," Kentrick reminded him gently. "Sister Enna was instrumental in saving your life, and Master Verelli arrived of his own accord, to—"

"You killed my ssson!" Fabrian screamed at Shalindra, as if his words could reach out and strangle her as his arms could not.

Shalindra felt the blood drain from her face as a knot of emotions constricted her throat. As much as she wished to, she had no defense from the accusation. Tormjere might have carried out the act, but it was she who had passed the sentence.

"Father, please," Kentrick said. "None of us wish to relive that day of betrayal. I beg you to sit and offer us your guidance to the kingdom. We have a matter of the utmost importance that requires your attention."

Fabrian blinked and wobbled unsteadily. His eyes wandered to the decorations hanging on the wall, and he waved his acceptance.

Kentrick motioned for the servants supporting the king to take him into the closest stateroom. He hurriedly shooed away the handful of occupants as Fabrian was deposited as gently as possible into one of the freshly vacated chairs.

Kentrick fetched him a small glass of brandy, which the king drank sloppily.

"Ceringion has been attacked, father. The Conclave has lost control of their demons and now request our aid to rid their lands of the beasts."

Fabrian frowned with half his face.

"We are not concerned with Ceringion's problems, of course, but Lord Redivers recommends that we seize the opportunity to lead an expeditionary force, in your name, and secure Braunton against a possible invasion."

"Againsht the wizards?"

Kentrick paused. "Yes."

Her brother was bending the truth, but Shalindra doubted that a correction would have mattered. She had recognized that he was not a healthy man, but to see him like this…

"Wizards musht be killt."

Shalindra forced herself to remain quiet, to not even move. Sentencing every mage and hedge wizard in the Kingdom for the crimes of a few would only turn more people against her family. But her father seemed to have forgotten she was there, and any words she spoke in their defense—no matter how truthful—would likely inflame him further.

Kentrick winced but remained patient. "That order was sent to all your fiefdoms, as you commanded. Several of our lords reported success in carrying them out. However, we must consider that magic may be useful to us if these demons are running loose."

"My kingdom," Fabrian stated.

"Yes, father. Actondel is still your kingdom, as it should be."

"It muscht be defended," the king said, waving his good arm in the air.

"You are wise to say so. Have I your permission to take the Actondel banner in your name and lead our army against them?"

"Thasht good. Yes, good." His eyes wandered. "I wansht to go outside."

Kentrick beckoned the servants forward and helped them lift the king from his chair, a deliberate action which served to block the king's view of Shalindra as he stood. She did not know if she should be proud of the way her younger brother had handled the situation or ashamed that it had been necessary.

As the king was led away, Kentrick signaled a nearby page.

"Find Master Eugeron and ask that he join me in the Grey Room."

"At once, my lord."

"Come on," Kentrick said to Shalindra.

Most considered the nearby Grey Room drab and unappealing, especially since the windows faced one of the castle walls instead of providing a view of the sea, so it was rarely occupied.

Two men in the dark livery of the Legion stood watch at the entrance. They saluted as the siblings entered, then closed the doors behind them.

The desk which had always resided here had been moved closer to the window, and a coatrack, couch, and refreshments table looked to be recent additions.

"I'm sorry you had to see that," Kentrick said, offering her a seat. "If it's any consolation, he's accused me of murdering Logian several times."

"But you were not even there," Shalindra protested. "I am the one who did it."

"And none of us fault you for it. Redivers was there with you, and he's stated that his only regret was not wringing more information from him first." He stopped. "That sounds like a terrible thing to say about my brother, but neither of us were close to him. What I mean is that you did what had to be done."

It might have been right, but Shalindra doubted that she would ever be able to escape the consequences of that day. "Was that the plan mother spoke about, to lead troops to Braunton?"

"It is, but I don't know if I should be glad he said yes or not."

"He must have thought it a good decision."

"Who can tell what he thinks these days? By tomorrow he may well have forgotten you were even here."

"He will not ever recover, will he?" she asked, finally surrendering to it. Despite all that had happened, she had held out some hope that she had somehow done enough. But the truth had shattered any chance of redemption, and she would never be able to escape her failings that day on the hill outside Adair. She should have recognized the danger of Logian's anger, and, failing that, she should have been stronger in her attempts to restore her father's wounds. So much unhappiness could have been spared if she had done more.

You can't protect everyone.

She wished that such annoyingly accurate things were not constantly being pointed out to her. There was something unbalanced about talking to yourself in such a manner.

Kentrick closed his eyes and took a resigned breath before answering. "The mediturgeons do not believe so and have advised that we see to his comfort and restrict his activities. We all do what we can to make the best of it, but he is still the king, and it is difficult to sway his impulses at times. There are plenty who are willing to plant suggestions in his ear, knowing that he's incapable of evaluating anything fairly. I fear that he creates more problems than he solves."

"What are you going to do?"

"It seems there was truth to your wizard's ill omens." Kentrick retrieved an unrolled missive from the desk and handed it to her. She read it quickly, then looked up.

"This speaks of monsters in Halisford."

Kentrick plopped ungracefully onto the couch and ran a hand over his face. "It's not the only one. There have been numerous reports from all over. We've no idea where the demons are coming from, but they aren't walking all the way from Tythir. When your wizard told his story of doom and gloom, none of us gave—" A knock at the door silenced him, and he waited as Eugeron entered.

"Your Highnesses," the advisor said with a bow. "My lady, I am pleased to see you returned to us again, and not a moment too soon."

"He's right about the timing," Kentrick agreed. "As I was saying, no one believed your wizard's vague warnings, considering them no more than an elaborate ruse. Tythir is weeks away from here, and we should have plenty of time to prepare before anything reaches our borders. It does, however, provide a perfect excuse for a show of force."

"Are the Ceringions still a threat?" she asked.

"Worse, Your Highness," Eugeron answered. He glanced at Kentrick, who nodded. "The loyalty of many vassal families is in question. Some were shaky even before the war with Ceringion, as is not uncommon, but even more have grown reluctant after the recent reversals. We anticipate an increasing amount of unrest in the spring, and perhaps open rebellion. As the prince has indicated, we worried that Master Verelli's warning was simply another ploy meant to push us further off balance, though certainly worthy of investigation. As further corroboration of these otherworldly creatures arrived, we began to accept the truth of it. Without a defined source, however, there is little we could do beyond stationing our armies everywhere and waiting. Such a dilution of strength would be a waste of time and effort, but raising a force in the name of striking at the demons provides us with a remarkably convenient falsehood. As our army tours the cities, it will remind our more recalcitrant lords who still rules."

"But it's a lie no longer," Kentrick said in disgust. "Half the dukes are demanding we send reinforcements to save them from these demons, while the other half accuses me of engineering the attacks as some elaborate plot against their houses."

Shalindra felt her annoyance growing once more. The situation might have been easier to deal with if so many loyal families had not been thrown out of their holdings or killed after her father's capitulation to the Ceringions. "Who is saying such things?"

"We don't know," Eugeron answered. "That is part of what drives the decision to venture out and see for ourselves. Whatever the source of the unrest, it is coordinated enough to point to a larger hand."

As much as she wished nothing but happiness for her family, Shalindra found herself struggling to care about the details of these new problems. She had saved them from a disastrous war once already, only to have that peace descend into infighting. Alharania's warning had to remain her priority, and stabilizing the Kingdom was not something she had time to be sucked into. She cherished her brother and respected Eugeron, but they were so wrapped up in the smallness of their own world that neither could see the larger threat.

And yet she was not about to tell either of them that she had been tasked with traveling to another realm to stop an invasion of demons intent on destroying their entire world. She shook her head. It sounded ridiculous even to herself.

Since when has any of this made sense?

"What is it?" Kentrick asked.

She waved aside the question. "Nothing. I was wondering at the strange paths that have brought us all here. So, now that you have the king's blessing, you intend to head this army?"

Eugeron shot Kentrick a surprised glance, and the young prince shrank. "I just asked him."

"As a passing conversation in the hallway, perhaps?" Eugeron asked, exasperated. "Your Highness, we had meticulously planned the best time and manner in which to broach the subject."

"It just kind of happened."

"These things cannot 'just happen.' You more than anyone should be aware of just how far some of His Majesty's commands have been stretched already. If you mean to secure his permission for something, it must be done with as many witnesses as you can muster."

"I know, and you are correct, of course. I needed his mind off… other things, and it was all I could think to say."

"What did he agree to, exactly?"

"For me to take our banner and lead an army against the wizards."

"The wizards?" Eugeron asked, dismayed.

"And the demons. It still gives us our permission, and I never said what road we would take."

"Redivers can alter the route a bit to make it work," Eugeron agreed. "It can still be used to bring the wayward fiefdoms in line."

"But the demons are the major threat," Shalindra protested. "I can vouch for that, and we know that Verelli was telling the truth."

Her brother looked pained. "No one will rally to our cause on the words of a prophet and a wizard."

"Not that we think you a crazed harbinger of doom," Eugeron hurriedly interjected. "But to those who are trying to topple the throne, that is exactly what they will call you."

"I do not care what names they choose for me," Shalindra said. "Demons mass in Tythir, and that is where my fight lies." She couldn't actually recall when she had reached that decision, but it seemed the most obvious.

"I believe you," Kentrick said, coming to stand before her. "And I do want to slay whatever beasts are attacking our cities. But you must recognize what will happen to us were we to name this as a foray to help our former enemy."

"In either case, the problems within our borders must be dealt with first," Eugeron agreed. "We cannot send our limited forces away for a campaign while ignoring the danger at our doorstep."

"I cannot stay here and fight another war," Shalindra insisted.

"I'll not ask you to," Kentrick said. "We intend to take the Gold Road all the way to the border before turning north. Could you at least ride with me that far? It's the same road you will travel anyway. I'll need your help."

"You have plenty of advisors."

"I will not be going with him," Eugeron said. "The king is too frail and easily manipulated to be left in only your mother's care. Of those we trust, only Redivers will accompany your brother."

Their logic was difficult to fault, and she truly did not want to abandon her brother no matter how much she wished to avoid these problems. "To the Small Sea, and no further," she conceded, wondering how she would explain this decision to her friends.

"By spring we should be in a better position to help," Kentrick said. "Who knows, maybe Ceringion will find their own way to deal with the problem before then."

"We will see," was all Shalindra could say.

Chapter Twenty

Roads of Gold, Roads of Blood

The green and gold banner of House Actondel hung limp in the still air as Kentrick's cold and bedraggled forces marched into Tornton, a week and a day since leaving Merallin. The air was so still that the pennant had been robbed of its desires to flutter and snap smartly in the breeze and was incapable of doing so unless the rider holding it aloft spurred his horse to a full gallop. The royal emblem had nevertheless been recognized, and a company of Lord Ingerhill's lancers had ridden out to escort them into the city.

A few people turned out to view their arrival, as even their paltry contingent of two hundred men-at-arms was noteworthy, but the chill in the air and the dearth of sunlight conspired to keep most inside. Those who had taken to the streets gawked at Shalindra.

"I think they're more interested in you than me," Kentrick said in jest as he rode beside her.

Shalindra felt color come to her cheeks but said nothing. It had been the same in every town they had travelled through, though she did not understand why. A prince surrounded by knights of the Legion, all in mail beneath dark and heavy cloaks and with spears and lances held high like the masts of ships, should have been spectacle enough. She was nobody to these people, save perhaps to those who worshipped Eluria. Her last foray along this road had been that of a child princess, and the years since then had taken her far away from who and what she had been.

She caught Redivers' frown out of the corner of her eye but could not tell if he was dissatisfied with Kentrick or herself. The commander returned his attention outward, watching for threats. His diligence was not for show alone. This part of the Kingdom was largely free of brigands and other unsavory sorts, but the strife within their borders created a very real threat outside the protective walls of Merallin. They had encountered nothing more troubling than the cold fall rain thus far, but the undercurrent of discontent was palpable everywhere they had stopped.

At least the Gold Road was taking her towards where she needed to go, even if she lacked understanding of what would be required of her when she arrived. The well-maintained thoroughfare had climbed slowly from Merallin, winding its way east as it skirted the undulating foothills of the Ironspike Mountains. Were it not for that formidable barrier, the road and the cities along it might never have existed.

She turned to look back down the column, hoping to catch sight of Enna or Birion, but spied neither. Fendrick was too short to see amidst the taller men and had been doing everything in his power to avoid her anyway. Weeby had joined the wizards in a carriage. The arrangement placing them there had taken some doing and left none of the participants happy with the outcome. After several arguments with Kentrick, she had threatened to leave him if Honarch and Verelli were not allowed to accompany her. He had finally relented, but given the danger the king's order posed, they were dressed as dignitaries and kept out of sight as much as possible.

Riding alongside her brother also gave her time to think about what she had been told without having to answer questions. There had been no time for contemplation during the dangerous descent from the mountains, and no place private enough aboard the ship that had returned them to Merallin. Enna, like everyone else, had wanted to know more of what Shalindra and Fendrick had seen after disappearing into the cave.

Fendrick had outright refused to say a single word about the experience, which surprised no one. Shalindra found herself equally reluctant, though for much different reasons. Too many questions and she might let slip that their journey would take them inside that portal instead of just to it. Alharania had taken Fendrick with her, and whatever had occurred in the demonic realm had torn him apart. She could not bear the thought of the same happening to any of her friends.

And so, she had spoken of the need to defeat the demons and drive them from this world while avoiding any mention of where that battle would need to be fought. It was a lie of omission, but she would not burden anyone with that fate until she was certain there was no other way. Her chosen direction was a vindication of what Verelli had asked her to do from the start, but the mage had at least been kind enough not to gloat. No matter the reasoning, her next steps lay to the east, and the decision to ride with her brother seemed to satisfy everyone's needs. For now.

The troop came to a stop at the edge of town, and the logistics of their stay were arranged. Before Shalindra could search for Enna, she and her brother were whisked away to the fortified manor house of Baron Ingerhill. There was no need for a keep or castle here, as the lands had been pacified for such time as to make those defenses unnecessary. Within that elegant estate, there was dinner and entertainment, and talk of the future without mention of wars past or present. Ingerhill was a proper host and a likable man, but Shalindra's thoughts were so far away that the evening disappeared into the memories of one of her selves, and she did not pursue them.

Thus, it was with great relief when she was at last shown a room. As soon as the servants had been sent away and she was alone, she sat heavily on the bed, wondering at how much of a waste the entire affair had been.

"Did you enjoy your dinner?"

Shalindra jumped to her feet, hand on her sword. Leaning against an ornate wardrobe, so still he almost looked a part of it, was Weeby.

"How did you get in here?" she demanded.

The halfling looked so insulted by the question that she wondered if she had actually offended him. "Through the door, like everyone else, though a cat burglar could make an easy entrance of the window if such is your worry." He pushed himself off the wall and came slowly towards her, stopping just short of uncomfortably close.

"Dinner was boring," Shalindra said, releasing her sword but wary of his intent. Her caution was plainly visible, but Weeby seemed more amused than put off by it.

"Such a pity. His Lordship's roast pig is the tastiest in this kingdom. I offer my condolences that you find yourself unable to partake."

"Enna spends enough of her time worrying about my health, I would advise you not to waste yours doing the same."

Weeby steepled his fingers and smiled as he turned away from her. "Lord Ingerhill was a gracious host, of course. Did he fill you with food and wine, dazzle you with entertainment, and put you at ease with his generosity?"

"I believe that is what he was attempting," she said.

Weeby turned back to her without a trace of levity. "Did he bother to tell you that you are riding into a trap, and that your brother will soon be dead?"

The boldness of that statement caught her off guard. "He omitted that bit of information."

"How very loyal of him. Well, that's precisely what's waiting for this little company at Locksall."

"How do you know?" she asked suspiciously.

"A better question would be: how do you not? Locksall has been increasingly resistant to your family's authority for two generations. Surely, no one considers the Tynewarks neutral after they sent such a miniscule force in support of the Kingdom when Ceringion was on its march of conquest? And where did your dear brother's personal army depart to after Tormjere twisted his head off? Twelve hundred men up and vanished after carefully looting his estates? That's not the behavior of a leaderless band of defeated soldiers."

"Are you suggesting Lord Tynewark commands them? That they now flock to his banner?"

Weeby laughed. "That old codger couldn't inspire anyone. All he can do is bludgeon the poor souls into submission. They would only have followed someone they already trusted, and who was close to your brother: Lord Anton."

It took a moment for Shalindra to put a face to that name, so short a time had she known him. Anton had been one of her father's senior advisors and had ridden with his retinue from Merallin to Adair to meet Logian, and there to debate whether to call off the looming war with the elves.

She shook her head. "Lord Anton was lost—"

"Outside Adair during your brother's botched assassination attempt. His body was never found."

"Your narrative is plausible," she said grudgingly, "but you have supplied no evidence."

Besides knowing everything that happened when he wasn't there to see any of it.

"I'm only telling you because if you march this little army into Locksall, you'll probably never leave. You and your brother there at the same time? Even if they aren't actively hunting you down right now, removing you both is simply too good an opportunity to pass up."

"Why are you suddenly concerned about Kentrick's health?" she asked.

"You shouldn't take my word for it," Weeby said, ignoring the question. "The Prince and Sir Redivers will corroborate enough of it, though you may wish to have that discussion outside the city. There are far too many ears listening within these walls."

If being Guardian granted her premonitions of the future, she wished it would somehow apply to the broader world instead of what was immediately in front of her, and it was not even doing that right now. Shalindra glanced about the room, uneasy at the thought of being watched. "And those same listeners heard none of what you just told me?"

Weeby strolled towards the door and let himself out, but gave her a smile that was unsettlingly confident. "They did not. Good night, Your Highness."

* * *

Shalindra rode back to the camp outside the city the next day, under the pretense of checking on some of the soldiers who had fallen ill. As a princess, the lie was not required, and it bothered her that she had even felt a need for the misdirection.

Redivers did not await her arrival, riding instead to meet her with a squad of the Legion.

"Your Highness," he greeted her. "Where is Prince Kentrick?"

"He is well," she reassured him. "I felt the need for some fresh air."

"All is acceptable here too," he said, falling in beside her. "We're ready to strike camp and continue our tour when commanded."

"I have heard talk of disloyalty in our eastern fiefdoms, especially so soon after the war. How does the road ahead look?"

"There are always rumors of discontent, Your Highness. We

should encounter no problems along the Gold Road, especially given the size of our contingent."

"Yet some of the cities are ruled by those of questionable intent—Locksall, for example. Is there some possibility that our missing troops are not as leaderless as—"

Redivers stiffened in his saddle and motioned her to silence with a short chop of his hand. His sharp reaction was completely unexpected and confirmed Weeby's information more than words ever could have.

Neither spoke for the remainder of the ride, and as soon as they reached the camp, he led her into the command tent.

"How did you learn of that?" he asked in a piercing whisper. "Did one of the wizards tell you?"

"Neither Honarch nor Verelli supplied the information," she said, annoyed that he still refused to call them by their names. "I assume, then, that it is true? Lord Anton is alive?"

"It's something we've worried about," he admitted, "but we had no idea he would go there, or that he had retained so many of Logian's men."

"If Locksall has joined him in casting its lot against my family…"

"We would be outnumbered more than fifteen to one." Redivers shook his head. "I told Eugeron to come with us. Locksall is where we most needed to go. Reaffirming their loyalty would have gone a long way towards quelling this unrest, but to venture there now would be folly. If we turn north for Kendenhall and Halisford it will weaken our position, but will also give us time to gather more of the lords firmly to our cause. Then we can visit them in strength."

"While this information may sound sensible, I have not seen any of this with my own eyes," she cautioned.

"Duly noted. I'll send our Rangers to see if those missing troops are indeed there—they'll not be needed should we turn north. This is ill news, Your Highness, but as you may have saved our lives, I thank you for it."

Shalindra took her leave of him, somewhat vexed by their discussion. She did not know if she was angry at being mired once more in another family conflict or mad at herself for secretly welcoming it.

She debated the wisdom of this change in direction as she went in search of Enna. A turn north towards Halisford would be a costly delay. The oftentimes narrow and unpaved road would slow and frustrate so large a troop, and navigating the forests, bridges, and water crossings might bottle them up for hours at a time. To leave her brother now and continue straight for the Small Sea would save time, but that would take her directly through Locksall. If Weeby was correct, however, and an army was there plotting against her family… She did not want to be forced into a confrontation with the people she was trying to save.

Like it or not, her road would continue to follow her brother's. Perhaps Kendenhall and Halisford would reaffirm their loyalty, and in so doing serve to speed their passage.

Spying Enna's white robes at one of the campfires, she turned towards her. The entire group was there. Honarch and Verelli were in quiet conversation on one side, while Enna and Birion sat silently on the other. Fendrick sat apart from them all, staring deep into the flames.

"What's wrong?" Enna asked, catching sight of her.

"It seems likely that we will need to abandon the Gold Road and turn north, which will lengthen our journey."

Enna's eyes narrowed. "By how much?"

Shalindra looked to Birion for that answer, as he was the most experienced with troop movements. "At the rate this command moves, at least a week and a half."

"Then why continue with them?" Enna asked incredulously. "How is it helping anything?"

It was a question Shalindra had already posed to herself. "We think it likely that some of our lords are plotting rebellion. If so, they would be just as likely to strike at me." She sought Weeby for confirmation, only to notice that he was not there. "It seems the safest way for all of us."

It was both truthful and a weak argument at the same time. No one seemed willing to raise additional objections, but it was difficult to tell if Enna or Verelli was most annoyed by it. Were they accepting her decision because of who she was, or had they just given up on her making good ones?

Either attitude was depressing, and she excused herself to return to the castle. She was reaching to pull herself onto her horse when Verelli's soft voice stopped her from behind.

"How much longer are you going to let your brother make all the decisions?"

Shalindra turned to face him, annoyed at his tone but somehow grateful that he at least would confront her. "They are his decisions to make, and I am his sister, not his queen."

"Title does not convey capability, and, even if it did, I doubt that you would accept such responsibility."

"You say that as if it were a bad thing."

"On the contrary. I find your humility refreshing, if a bit naïve."

"I am glad you have discovered some amusement in all of this," Shalindra said.

"Amusement is often our only defense against hopelessness."

"Are you that worried about what we will find in Tythir?"

For the first time since she had met him, Verelli's face betrayed uncertainty, which was more unnerving than any threat he could have made. "I'm worried we'll find much less than when I left, and at the pace things move perhaps nothing at all. This is a token force at best, and history has never been kind to armies led by boy-kings or prophets."

"Yet that is what you came here looking for, is it not? If you wish Actondel's help, you will never get it from my father."

"It is presumptive on your part to believe that the king's aid was what I came to find. He lacks the fortitude that this situation demands, but there are others with the power to mobilize what is needed. I think it clear that both you and your brother have come recently into yours, despite your lineage. And neither of you have learned how to wield it."

"I am not a despot, and I choose to use such 'power,' as you call it, only when I must."

"Which is why you continue to struggle. Those around you recognize your strength. They hold back, expecting you to use your gifts as you should. Your dilemma is easy to recognize because it is a condition with which I am familiar."

"You have an interesting assumption of your own superiority."

"I know I'm superior," Verelli said. He directed her attention to the camp around them. "Pluck any peasant or soldier from the streets and place them in charge, and what would you have? Disaster. Their needs and wants are shaped by and limited to their own experiences. Oh, you might find a rare gem capable of instantly comprehending the politics and logistics of ruling and defending a kingdom, but by and large, they would destroy the very thing they wished to make better, regardless of their intentions."

"I have no desire to rule anyone, if that is what you are suggesting." She was certain it was the truth, yet the words rang hollow in her own ears the moment she said them.

"A noble sentiment. But sooner or later, you will be expected to act like the leader everyone assumes you to be. I have been around power all my life. Power over things, power over people…" Multicolored flames shimmered and danced between his fingers. "…and power over the natural order of the world. You have that same power but are afraid to use it, and thus doom all those who depend on you. You cannot squander your talents forever."

"What do you propose?" Shalindra asked, nettled at being lectured by someone whose hand in recent events had caused so much destruction. "Shall we charge down a road you yourself avoided, slaying everything in our tracks as we carve a bloody trail to Tythir?"

Verelli looked disappointed, if not surprised. "Your mind is already set, and I'll not waste more of my time attempting to alter it. We will see what decision you reach when there are no choices left to be made."

* * *

They resumed their slow caravan a day later. Kentrick had indeed turned them towards Kendenhall as soon as he learned of the threat posed by the Tynewarks' rumored duplicity, and with Redivers had immediately begun planning how they might swing through the troubled eastern fiefdoms on the way back to Merallin. Both men remained unconcerned at the potential threat posed by the demons in Tythir, and their indifference to the declared purpose of this excursion annoyed Shalindra yet again.

It was for that offense that she chose to ride with her friends, though the gesture was meaninglessly symbolic and did nothing to make her feel better. She doubted anything would until she was able to balance her destiny with what she was capable of achieving.

It would be easier if she could get the *hers* to work with each other on a single question, but the almost universal agreement they had settled into while seeking Alharania had fractured into an assortment of incompatible threads. A few supported a slow extermination of each and every demon between here and the gate, even if it took a lifetime or two. A greater number were in favor of proceeding to Tythir, though the specific manner in which to accomplish that journey had no consensus.

There was even one, a small idea among the multitude, that insisted on her going beyond the barrier of protection she had erected around her reality, to revisit that raging chaos that swirled around her. That one, at least, was easy to deal with—Shalindra would find no answers by driving herself insane.

"Pondering the fate of the world again?" Enna asked, sliding her horse closer. "It might be less of a burden if you shared your worries with us."

Shalindra shrugged. How could they help if she could not even explain what was happening inside her head? "Here does not seem the best place for that discussion."

"Then when we stop?" Enna offered, not giving in this time. "You've never been so silent before. We can all tell that whatever you learned is eating at you, and it has nothing to do with your brother."

The road they were following dipped down, snaking its way lower towards a broad and rocky river. Shalindra watched Kentrick as he crossed the low wooden bridge over the swift waters. Her thoughts were like that river: an obstacle to moving forward. Maybe Enna and Honarch, and perhaps even Verelli, could be her way out of these self-erected walls that kept her trapped within her own mind.

"It is not that I fear being overheard; it is simply difficult to know what to discuss."

Enna appeared unsatisfied with that answer, and her eyes narrowed. "If you're unsure of—"

Her words were cut off by a gargled scream from one of the Legion soldiers as an arrow struck his throat. Chaos descended on them as more arrows rained down from every direction. The column surged forward, trying to escape the ambush, but the soldiers were bottlenecked at the narrow bridge. Across the water, armored men exploded from the trees on either side of the road. With spears and swords, they charged inwards, attempting to seize the crossing and divide the column in two. Her brother and Redivers were quickly cut off with only a small group of men, and Shalindra caught a flash of steel as Kentrick drew his sword to strike at someone.

The defense on the far bank solidified, allowing the column to lurch forward and Shalindra to reach the bridge. Blocked by the clog of men still on it, she could only watch helplessly as Redivers rallied those around her brother. The frantic swirl of men and horses obscured her view of Kentrick, and she regained it just in time to see him knocked backwards from his horse.

"No!" she shouted. She leapt from her horse and off the bridge, landing with a splash in the knee-deep water. The current almost knocked her from the slippery rocks, but she regained her balance and scrambled up the bank, sword in hand. As she entered the fray, thousands of ghostly premonitions overlaid themselves in a disorienting blur akin to a heavy fog. She struck down the first man to meet her, even while desperately trying to separate the future from the now.

Sharing the same sense of self-preservation, the *hers* joined the effort, evaluating the thousands of choices before her and removing those that proved fatal. The sum of their resolutions manifested as an expanded field of vision, allowing her to see not only everything and everyone around her but even herself from a different point of view. Such awareness was thrilling in its omnipotence, even as their frantic warnings sent her twisting away from spear thrusts and ducking beneath blades that should have ended her life. Her divine shield flashed and shimmered, turning away anything she could not avoid, while her sword carved through metal and flesh with equal ease.

Two men fell to her assault, then another. Her shield simultaneously snapped the head off an arrow and deflected an axe, and her answering strike savaged a trio of attackers. She was butchering her way through a battle that had already been won; she just needed everyone else to realize it.

Then the enemy was running. Three more died before she could stop herself, their terrified flight not fast enough to escape her wrath.

"Cowards!" someone screamed at the retreating enemy in a voice that was disturbingly similar to her own.

That drew a rousing cheer from the defenders, but Shalindra felt sick to her stomach. The all-seeing awareness that had enabled her victory shrank as suddenly as it had expanded, returning to its normal scope. Her eyes remained on the trees, wary of another attack but also unwilling to look back at the trail of mangled bodies she had left behind her. She knelt and wiped clean her sword on the body of an enemy soldier out of habit, trying to avoid the grisly evidence of what she had done, but his severed head stared accusingly at her from several feet away.

She stood and made her way from the trees as calmly as she could, fighting the urge to flee before she hurt anyone else. The soldiers who saw her gave her space and respectful nods, but the whispers started almost immediately. Men were barking commands, and order was rapidly restored. Quiet settled over the forest once more.

Enna's voice pulled Shalindra from her daze.

"Place him on the ground here," she directed a pair of soldiers carrying a wounded comrade.

She cast a concerned glance at Shalindra, then covered the soldier's wounded face with one hand as she took the symbol of her faith in the other and prayed.

It was what Shalindra should be doing: saving lives to atone for those she had taken. She was moving to help when she felt an insistent tingle deep within, a tugging sensation in the direction of the sky. She directed her perceptions upwards, looking beyond the sky as something streaked down from the raging void of noise from which she had protected herself, passing through the barrier to make contact with her. It was gone before she could identify it, returned to that place outside her awareness.

She froze as she sought to bolster her mental defenses, terrified that some part of her had been taken. She returned her awareness to the physical world just as Enna's hand pressed against the broken leg of the next man. As the melodic words of Enna's elvish prayer slid from her lips, Shalindra felt another tingle press against the barrier.

She looked to the heavens again and allowed the globe of her defenses to shrink. The chaotic, swirling soup seeped through the sky as if the entire world was upside down and being dipped into a pool of liquid. She stopped its descent just above the treetops, studying the hazy border separating it from herself. She identified that one insistent tingle, loosening the weave of the barrier to allow it free entry. It flashed downwards like sunlight off a mirror, a flicker of light that streaked into her and then bounced upward so quickly that she barely caught a glimpse before it passed back through her barrier, undeniably larger than it had been on its arrival.

Beside her, Enna rose to her feet, wearing the satisfied expression she always had when healing people: a sense of self-assurance and purpose mixed with belief.

Shalindra turned away from her quickly, terrified that Enna would see the thoughts written on her face. Was that what those sounds were in that realm of noise and motion she had forced away? Thousands of pleas and supplications meant not for her ears but for Eluria's?

She realized, with a growing sense of despair, that this was exactly what she had just witnessed. Aghast, she forced the globe of her barrier outward until the sky resumed its expected appearance.

The implications of her apparent intrusion were staggering in scope. If she indeed stood between Eluria and her followers, could it mean that prayers to the moon were failing not because the goddess was weakened but because she herself was actively preventing it? And if she were to allow all those prayers in, to accept them into herself as a proxy for the goddess, would those requests devour her piece by piece until there was nothing left to take?

She was shaken from her daze as Redivers hurried past.

"Sister Enna?" he said. "The prince is wounded and requests your attention."

"Of course." Enna glanced at Shalindra in surprise as she hurried after him towards the front of the line.

I no longer exist to save. Now, I only destroy.

Shalindra could have collapsed in the middle of the road and wept, so great was her sorrow at what she had become. Instead, she forced one foot in front of the other and followed Enna to where her brother sat, propped up against a tree and surrounded by two ranks of Legion guards standing shoulder to shoulder. They parted at her approach.

"It's not bad," Kentrick said in response to her look, though he winced and clutched at his shoulder. "It's just hard to be knocked from your horse gracefully."

"He was struck by both arrow and spear," Redivers said.

"The armor took most of the blow," Kentrick said.

"Well, it's in the way now," Enna said. "Please remove it."

"Is that necessary?' Redivers asked. "We remain vulnerable to another attack here."

"I don't tell you how to kill people," Enna countered. "Kindly do not instruct me on how to restore them."

Kentrick motioned to a nearby squire, who helped the injured prince unbuckle and remove his breastplate and mail coat. Though done with the utmost care, his face was white with pain.

Shalindra could have restored her brother without the hassle, but she stood rooted in place, a spectator to the proceedings. Kentrick clenched his teeth in pain as Enna placed her hands on his arm and shoulder.

"You've definitely broken something," she said. "Hold still."

Enna's prayer was calm and controlled, perfectly balanced between the need for divine assistance and her own gift to the recipient.

And Shalindra felt every word.

With her shifted sight, she saw its approach as the request streaked through the turbulent and terrifying place beyond her defenses, passed through the barrier without pause to receive what was given, and returned to the place from which it had arrived, flying away until disappearing in the distance. The entire cycle could have been repeated a thousand times and still have passed in the blink of an eye. In the physical world, she saw the silvery blue aura slide down Enna's arms and into her brother.

"You should be gentle with it for two days," Enna instructed when she was finished, "to allow time for it to completely set."

"I'll do my best not to chance death again anytime soon," Kentrick said, flexing his arm gingerly. "Thank you." His eyes were alight as he stood, despite his wounds, and his voice flushed with emotion. It was a look that terrified Shalindra, for it was the same way Logian had always appeared after a martial victory. Thankfully, Kentrick's eagerness faded rapidly as he viewed the aftermath of the battle, and he shook his head at some thought.

"You must be seen healthy and whole," Redivers said, pulling the prince towards a horse. "Those were Logian's men, and they likely watch to see if they were successful. Ride the line with me now."

Kentrick hurriedly donned his armor and mounted his horse. As he galloped off, Shalindra searched for some way in which to put the impossibilities of this day into words.

"Enna?"

Enna turned towards her, face alight with anticipation.

"I… am glad that your prayers are still being answered. I would not wish to do this alone."

"She will always be there for me."

Shalindra forced a smile onto her face, but she had never been less certain that it was true.

Chapter Twenty-One

Differing Directions

By the time they had buried their dead and resumed the trek north, the various *hers* within Shalindra had returned to explaining how they planned on solving all the unknowns confronting her. The number of voices seemed to have diminished, but their impassioned arguments had only grown louder. Their efforts would have been helpful were it not that they tackled every possible issue at once, a condition that left her with a headache.

How she would reach the demon realm seemed a straightforward proposition, as the location of a doorway in Tythir was known. What she might find there, however, remained a mystery. Alharania had lost her life venturing there unprepared, and Shalindra had no desire to meet the same fate. What she needed was information, yet she remained reluctant to share her worries. Going to that other realm might still be an act of final desperation, or it could even be avoidable.

But it *was* possible. Tormjere had done so, though not by choice. Alharania had managed it somehow, centuries ago.

Countless demons had bridged the divide between the worlds. But even were she able to manage it, she had no idea what needed to be done there.

Enna poked her arm. "We're here."

Shalindra pulled herself from her musings and saw that 'here' was an open field.

"We won't make the next town before nightfall," Enna said, being far more accommodating than usual. "There's a full moon tonight. I'm hoping the clouds blow away so we can see it."

They dismounted and turned over their mounts to a soldier charged with their care. Shalindra looked about for the rest of her friends, spying Birion as he guided the carriage to a stop on the far side of the camp. After the loss of so many in the ambush, Redivers had been forced to shift duties, and Birion had assumed the role of carriage driver. His shrewd decision made it less likely that anyone would be around the wizards long enough to suspect who they were. Fendrick was probably close by, though she could not see him.

Enna followed her gaze. "Would you like—"

"Alharania told me something else," Shalindra blurted. It escaped almost before she realized it, but with it came a wave of relief.

Enna instantly turned serious and pulled Shalindra away from those setting up camp. "What?"

"She believed that some force drives the demons to enter our world, and she attempted to enter their realm and identify it, so certain was she of its existence."

"She actually went there? Our histories contain nothing about that.”

“Then I would judge them incomplete, rather than wrong. She was willing to risk her life to find out, and I want to know if what she sought is real or only imagined.”

Enna crossed her arms. “I thought we were going to close this portal to their realm, not go into it.”

“That is still what I intend,” Shalindra said, “but if Alharania’s suspicions were correct, it could mean that closing the portal would not be enough to end the threat. We might never know without discovering what she could not.”

“How can you prepare yourself for that?” Enna demanded. “And don’t say by asking Verelli.”

“No, I do not believe that his order has the information I need. Tormjere would have been the best to consult, but I need to find someone with more knowledge of the demon’s world than we have, and that person is Fendrick.”

Enna frowned. “I will grant that he led us to her as promised, but how does knowing where to find a Guardian convey knowledge of where demons live?”

“Because I believe he went there with her.”

Enna rejected the idea with a chop of her hand. “For that to be true, he should have been dead a century and a half ago, at best.”

“Nevertheless, he may be my only link. I have been reluctant to inquire before now, for it is clearly painful to him, but I have no other options.”

Enna shrugged. “I don’t see how you could be right about this, but if you wish me to go with you and ask him, now is the perfect time. He usually takes his meals alone.”

"I do," Shalindra said, already headed in the right direction.

They found him sitting apart from everyone by a stand of trees.

"I know what you want," he said before she could ask, "and I can't give it to you."

"You knew Alharania when she was alive," Shalindra said.

Fendrick's eyes remained focused on something he alone could see. "Yes."

"Impossible," Enna said. "That would make you more than two hundred years old. A rare elf may live such a long life, but none of the other races are so blessed."

Fendrick ignored the observation.

Shalindra knelt in front of him. "You went with her."

"I did, and it is not a memory I care to relive."

"You could tell us—"

"I can tell you nothing!" Fendrick cried in anguish. "Everything we thought we knew was a lie. If you wish to go there, you should find someone else who can keep you alive. I obviously couldn't."

Enna began to ask another question, but Shalindra warned her to silence with the barest shake of her head.

"What you consider a failing, others would name your greatest accomplishment," she said as she stood. "Should you change your mind, I would value anything you have to say."

Fendrick returned to staring at nothing in silence, his jaw clenched so tightly his cheeks quivered.

Both women retreated, but Enna pulled Shalindra off to the side rather than seek to join their friends.

"Do you really think he knows something?" Enna asked.

"He believes that what he might say would do more harm than good, and I must respect that. Alharania admitted that she was unprepared for the attempt, and I am certain he blames himself for that."

"Are you sure this is necessary then?"

She was, but she remained reluctant to say why. She accepted Alharania's words on faith, because of the lengths she had gone to in order to provide that knowledge. Yet Alharania could have misinterpreted something. After all the intervening years, she might even be wrong.

Or I am. Or we both are.

She's right about Shining Moon.

That is possible, as she is the only one to have possessed it in the demon realm.

But they aren't the only ones who've been there. There's somewhere else you can look.

Shalindra pushed the thought aside but it refused to yield and continued to dance stubbornly around the edges of her mind.

It's a wealth of knowledge, just waiting to be opened.

He is not a treasure to be plundered.

But you want to see.

Before she could prevent it, a memory that was not hers leapt into her mind. A mountainous pillar of dark stone stood upon a shattered plain. Angry clouds of grey and fiery red swirled above it, and blanketing its craggy surface were thousands upon thousands of demons, their faces upturned in—

Shalindra tore herself away from the scene, refusing to yield to such dark desires. She redoubled the constraints that held

Tormjere's focus in place. It had been a mistake to have ever sought answers within, and it lingered now as a constant temptation. What kind of abomination would she become should she consume him fully?

Enna was still looking at her, waiting for an answer, but Shalindra's thought were moving too fast to explain.

If Fendrick could not tell her what she needed to know and she refused to pillage Tormjere's memories, there was only one other who might divulge what she so desperately sought to learn. But one was all that was needed.

And he's such a dear friend.

Chapter Twenty-Two

A Change of Plans

"You want to do what?" Birion asked incredulously.

"I need to go to the demon realm," Shalindra repeated. "Before we reach the portal in Tythir." The mute silence greeting her proclamation was so profound that everyone around her could have become statues. "I realize that may seem unwise, but I have good reason."

Weeby broke them from their shocked paralysis with a laugh. "It sounds more like you need a drink and time to reconsider."

"I don't think that would be any better," Enna said, throwing the halfling a withering look.

"I must at least acknowledge his sentiment if not the method," Birion said.

Honarch agreed. "From what little Tormjere told us, it's a miserable place."

"Why?" Verelli's question brought the group to silence once more.

Shalindra would have preferred if no one had asked her that. It was not a question that could be avoided, but she did not choose to answer it fully. "Because I wish to be prepared for what we will face. Alharania was not, and it cost her everything."

"What do you seek to gain, then?" Verelli pressed. "It is a dangerous proposition under the best of circumstances, and the advantages it might convey are nebulous."

He was being far too rational about this decision. "Even if we close the gate in Tythir and find a way to banish them forever, we know almost nothing of how they live, what they do, or what motivates them. If your estimates are accurate, we do not have the numbers to simply drive them back, so anything that might gain us an advantage would be worth the risk."

Verelli looked unsatisfied with her answer but did not question further.

Birion looked to Enna. "Can you not talk her out of this foolishness?"

Shalindra found herself growing annoyed at their reluctance even as she appreciated their concern. At some point, she needed to stop asking questions and do something. "Regardless of the danger, I feel it needs to be done. Can it?"

Verelli nodded slowly. "It is, in theory, possible with a summoning focus." Before she could ask how or when, he held up a hand to forestall further questions. "But only with the proper components, which we have already established that I do not have."

"Well," Enna jumped in, apparently pleased that it was out of reach. "Then it can't be done unless we can find someone who has everything we need."

"All the necessities can be obtained," Verelli said, earning him an unkind look. "I should point out that, even should we be able to create the required artifact, the process will not be pleasant."

"I do not care about pleasant," Shalindra said.

"Indeed? You will probably care a good deal about how we go about it." Verelli steepled his fingers. "And you will care even more about what must be given in order to create one. Let us assume, for a moment, that we manage to craft the requisite pendant. Passages from this world to Urtratu—or the 'demon realm' as you choose to colloquially name it—cannot simply be waved into existence. They require an anchor at both ends. We accomplish this by knowing the bound creature's name on the one hand, and by use of the summoning focus on the other. The difficulty increases when the bound creature is already here, but the concepts are the same."

"Why not use two names?"

"The binding of names is a method which allows one being some manner of control over another. Given that, I would not risk sharing mine with such creatures."

Shalindra's eyes narrowed. "So I would have to cede some control of myself over to you, in order to accomplish this bit of magic?"

"That is how it has always worked."

"And why would she do that?" Enna demanded, jumping up. "Why can't you just open it, as with any door?"

Verelli swallowed whatever retort had first come to mind. "Portals are keyed to specific beings. If we were to simply open a door as you suggest, it would allow anything and anyone to pass through it."

"I've seen it done before," Fendrick said, surprising everyone as he joined the group.

"And how well did that turn out?" Verelli almost sneered. "There's one such unattenuated opening in Tythir right now. I believe everyone here can comprehend the consequences of *that* mistake."

Shalindra cut them off before the argument could spiral further out of control. "So, we need a name and a demon necklace, or summoning focus. Where are we to find them?"

"Ordinarily, we would be able to request a focus from the armory at Solor-Majalis."

"What about Master Arsalan in Kendenhall?" Weeby offered.

Verelli nodded thoughtfully. "He is an experienced summoner. However, his focus would have already been keyed to a specific creature and would not suit our needs. We would still need to create a new one."

"The stones used for them were given out at one time, I believe," Honarch said. "Could any of those be available?"

"Indeed. Your former mentor, Felzig, had one, which disappeared along with many other items of value when he failed to return." He looked pointedly at Honarch. "After that debacle, all such gems were locked away, as were those capable of making them."

Enna looked appalled.

"Forgive me," Verelli added. "I did not mean to imply that those capable of creating the stones were physically restricted in any way."

"Of course," Enna said, seeming less than convinced.

"I used some of the gems when we made the dohedrons," Honarch said. "What did it look like, the one that Felzig had?"

"It would have been large, at least the size of a thumbnail and generally oblong and crystalline in cut. It could have been any type, though it likely would have been azurite or dark quartz."

Honarch shook his head. "I'm certain that nothing matching that description was with the ones I kept, but Tormjere and I split them. There is no telling what he did with his share."

"I never… *he* never spent them," Shalindra said as the memory of those precious stones wormed itself into her mind. Aghast that things were leaking out with increasing frequency, she sealed the boundaries of Tormjere's focus once more. She had to find a better way to contain them, no matter how useful they could be.

Verelli considered. "They can remain unbound for centuries, so it could serve our purposes, should you discover where it is."

"It could have ended up anywhere," Enna said, "and it might be impossible to locate. I still say we should direct our energy to closing portals, not opening new ones."

"Here, here," Weeby said.

Shalindra felt the memory she needed pushing against the edges of Tormjere's focus, and in her desperation to find a way forward, her resolve wavered just enough for it to escape. There was a specific rock beneath the tree with an intertwined double trunk. She could still feel the dirt between her fingers as she dug the hole and then hid the bag beneath that rock. "I know exactly where the gems are."

Enna spun to face her. "How can you—?"

"Kenzing. A small village not far from Fallhaven."

"That will take weeks from here," Birion said, "even on horseback."

"But can it be done?" Shalindra pressed. "The only other way to it may be in Tythir, and by then we will be fighting our way in. If I can retrieve the stone, what other components do we need?"

"The other materials are fairly common—any jeweler of sufficient status would have them. I am aware of how to fashion a pendant and bind the gem, but there is no way for me to enchant the stone itself."

Shalindra looked at Honarch, who shook his head.

"I can't do any of it, sorry. I was still years away from learning such things, if ever."

"Do you really mean to leave now?" Birion asked.

"I am convinced this course of action is needed, but you are correct that I cannot abandon my brother."

"I'm going," Enna said, in tones that brooked no argument.

"I'll go as well," Fendrick said.

"I dislike being cooped up in that carriage all day," Verelli said, "but it's preferable to the treatment I'll receive anywhere else. I will stay."

Shalindra held up her hand to forestall further volunteers. "I feel no need to do this by myself, but Enna and I should be fine."

"It would be good for you to have three," Birion said. "Honarch and I can handle things here."

Shalindra caught the double meaning of that statement and silently gave thanks for Birion's astute appraisal of the situation. What he meant was that he and Honarch could keep an eye on

Verelli and Weeby.

She gave her agreement. "Very well. The three of us will leave tomorrow and look to reunite in Kendenhall."

"And if your brother continues on before you return?" Birion asked.

Shalindra hesitated, but Kentrick's battles were not theirs to fight. "Do what you feel is best."

* * *

Dawn had just touched the tips of the trees when Shalindra, Enna, and Fendrick took their leave, heading generally northwest in an attempt to locate the road to Gyland, a major duchy at the edge of the largest lake in Actondel. The interior of the kingdom was sparsely populated, its countryside given over to wide pastures and airy forests. It would have been pleasant to allow the horses to wander their way to Kenzing, if time had allowed it.

That requirement to accomplish this task quickly weighed heavy on her as they pushed the horses to a faster pace. Neither Kentrick nor the demons would sit idle for her, just as neither of them were doing anything to ease her burdens. Once more, her hand was being forced by the cascade of complications stemming from the wizard's attempt to kill her father in his own chambers. If not for Tormjere's timely appearance... Her eyes flicked to Enna. He had brought Enna into the castle from miles away with a portal of his own creation.

Mist gate. A portal is only a door.

Why does it matter what I wish to call them?

They're easier to find when you call them the right thing.

The memory came suddenly, and with enough force to

overwhelm her objections. She plummeted from her horse onto a broken plain of rock and sand. Her success hung in the air before her—a twisting vortex of black smoke laced with dark reds and deep purples. A thrill of satisfaction ran through her as its twin appeared atop the nearby outcropping jutting from wind-scoured sands. Through the mist gate she ran, aware of the textures and stability of the magic which had created it. She held it in place through force of will, emerging from the other side…

…onto her horse. She jerked at the suddenness of the shift from desolation to forest, and her involuntary jerk of the reins brought her mount to a stop. Enna and Fendrick were already past her before they could do the same.

"What is it?" Enna asked.

"I think I can create mist gates," Shalindra said.

"Create what?"

"Those swirly portals Tormjere used to jump from one place to another."

"When did you learn that, and why?"

"I— He thought I would need to know. But if I can, they could be used to speed our travel," she said quickly, hoping to avoid the questions that lie would prompt.

Enna crossed her arms and shook her head vehemently. "No. Absolutely not. I was dragged through one of those against my will and wish to never experience that again."

"Unpleasant or not, if I can make them, it could cut days off our journey."

Fendrick grunted his disapproval. "Those sorts of things tend to attract unwanted attention, even when they do work, and every time I've heard of their use, it was a mage that did it."

"Are you certain you know how to do it?" Enna asked.

Shalindra nodded, convinced that she did.

"Why didn't you say anything earlier?" Fendrick asked.

"I forgot. And I did not wish for Verelli to know, because I do not trust him." Another lie.

"Well, that makes two of us," he said. "But that's neither here nor there. When were you planning on conjuring one?"

"I was thinking I would try now."

"You've never done it before?" Fendrick asked incredulously.

"Ah… no."

The dwarf put a hand to his forehead and muttered something indecipherable but uncomplimentary.

"I have to try," Shalindra implored. "We cannot spend the entire winter traipsing back and forth. At some point we have to take risks."

"Go on and try then," Fendrick huffed. "The worst that could happen is we die a horrible death trapped in some lifeless void."

They were not the encouraging words she needed, but she slid from her horse, determined to make the attempt. The skill was one of a million things Tormjere should never have known, and she had stolen it from him like a thief in the night. She was losing control of herself, taking his focus apart piece by piece, all the while denying the damage she was surely inflicting.

She had never felt so ashamed in her life, but Enna and Fendrick were waiting expectantly, so she pushed her feelings aside and concentrated. The destination needed to be some place close, someplace she could see in order to gauge the location properly.

Shalindra extended her arm, though the gesture did not seem necessary, and with her mind found a seam in the reality in front of her. Had she not been shown what to look for, she never would have noticed it. Stretching the seam apart, she exposed what lay beneath: a billowing vortex of mist that twisted along an unseen corridor. It exited atop another hill some forty paces away. The mist gate fought against her desires, like channeled water seeking a more natural path than the one she had forced it into, and collapsed almost immediately.

She forged ahead to create another before anyone could object.

This one opened just as easily as the first. Holding it in that state was like balancing on a plank atop a barrel. It wobbled unsteadily, but both ends remained in place. There was no time for amazement, for it would fade quickly. She stepped towards it but was stopped by Fendrick's hand.

"I'll go through first," he said. There was nothing but terror written on his face, but he swallowed resolutely and cast himself into it without waiting for any discussion, emerging from the other end an instant later. Enna took a deep breath before doing the same, then Shalindra stepped inside.

It was a place both familiar and foreign, a swaying bridge suspended above a dark nothingness. Her feet pressed against something solid, but she suspected that to stray left or right would have met with terrible consequences. The entire construct wobbled with every step, and she hurried forward to emerge beside the other two. Both gates winked from existence with a barely audible pop behind her.

"Wasn't so bad," Fendrick said, sounding as if he was trying to convince himself more than anyone else.

"We didn't go very far," Enna pointed out.

Shalindra conceded the point. "I think I still need to see where it is going, so that is a limitation. But even so, it could save us days if we hop from one place to another."

"Can you make another so soon?" Enna asked.

"I feel no ill effects, though we must assume that at some point I will tire from the effort."

"We'll have to leave the horses," Fendrick said. "They won't fit."

"We can take what we need and release them. They will find their way home."

When the essentials had been retrieved, Shalindra fixed her gaze on a hill a fair distance away, willing the mist gate into existence once more. "Let us get ourselves to Kenzing."

Chapter Twenty-Three

Hidden Treasure

Fendrick landed face first in the grass, letting out a small "oof" as Enna tumbled from the swirling mists onto his back. Shalindra came down solidly astride them both and quickly hopped aside so they could remove themselves from the damp ground.

"That might be a good sign we should stop for the night," Fendrick grumbled, picking himself up.

"I am sorry," Shalindra apologized. "The haze obscured the details and affected my aim." It was mostly true, though she had no difficulty in seeing through the twilight.

Fendrick muttered something under his breath about pushing their luck but said nothing else as he set about making camp.

"You're doing incredibly well," Enna said, "even though the horses would have been less stressful. How far do you think we travelled?"

Shalindra peered into the gathering dusk. What she assumed to be the Merallin River lay a morning's walk to the west, its still-high waters churning south towards the capital city of the same name. That meant the road that paralleled its path was nearby, but she saw no sign of any towns. The hilly terrain to the east, where they had come from, was covered in forests, and there was no sign of the mountains to the north.

"We have crossed no rivers, so I would say we are somewhere north of Merrywood but south of Jonrin."

"That's easily three days' ride on horseback," Enna said. "Amazing."

It was an unbelievable feat. She wondered why Tormjere had not used his ability more when they had covered so much ground to reach her father and prevent the war with Ildalarial. It would have saved so much effort and perhaps a significant amount of trouble. Was it from a lack of confidence in his ability to control it or were there consequences of which she was unaware?

Fendrick had assembled the beginnings of a fire, but before he even reached for flint and steel, flames sprang up in the wood. He jumped back and glanced in alarm at Enna, who gave an uncertain shrug.

Fendrick returned to his task, adding more wood to the tinder and setting water to boil for tea.

Their silent exchange drew Shalindra's attention, and she realized with some embarrassment that she must have been the one to create the flames. Was her mind so divided now that she could affect the world around her yet remain unaware of her actions? She supposed that was the case. After all, she had been able to make fire that way for so long now that… Wait, *he* had been able to do that, not her.

It's not that difficult.

She frowned, trying to remember how he had learned the skill. Was it another of his innate talents, like communicating with her without speaking? That did not seem correct, even though he had been able to control flame at least since they met.

No, he had learned it much earlier. Honarch had taught him, on those nights in the wilderness when they travelled with Gelid and Treven. Felzig had been angry about that, but she remembered how satisfying it had felt in Evermen's Forge when she had first—

She realized what was happening, and where such thoughts had taken her. She was inside his focus again, reliving a past that was not hers. The memories sloshed around her in her haste to withdraw, spilling from the vessel she had so carefully crafted and drifting into her own consciousness.

She tried to recapture what had escaped. But they were gone, indistinguishable now amidst the countless thoughts that swirled in her head. No matter how much she tried, she kept coming back to take more, steadily consuming him as he had done to countless demons. There was a wrongness to it, no matter the benefits.

"Guardian?"

Shalindra looked up at Enna's worried face.

"Are you well?"

"An unpleasant memory," Shalindra lied, something else she was becoming far too good at. "I am fine, thank you."

Enna appeared unconvinced but returned to preparing the meal. Shalindra forced herself to consume the offered food when it was ready, though she had no appetite. The trio ate in awkward silence, each lost to their own thoughts.

When she had forced down enough to satisfy Enna's

reproachful glances, Shalindra drew her sword for its nightly inspection, angling the blade to allow moonlight to slide up one edge and down the other. There was no sign of wear, of course. The weapon was as perfect and sharp as the day she had received it from Fendrick, though it had no right to be so. The thought put her in mind of the last conversation—argument really—she'd had with him at the forge in Newlmir.

Her eyes flicked suddenly to the dwarf. "I know the difference between a blessing and an enchantment."

Fendrick choked on his tea, then frowned to mask his uncertainty as he set it aside. "I would expect that you do."

"What else were you going to tell me?"

Tell you?

I mean… tell him. It does not matter right now.

If having arguments like this with herself was a side effect of slowly becoming a god, it was not something she cared to spend eternity doing.

Fendrick cleared his throat uncomfortably. "That sword was not given as a reward for helping me."

"Who then? The priests?"

"Aye, the priests. It was no small feat him taking the old man all the way to the valley and bringing Treven back with Amalthee's Book, but unless Father Nathan knew the results in advance, it would be irrelevant. I was forging the sword before I met him, yet he knew it was special the moment he laid eyes on it."

"It's an exceptional weapon," Shalindra said. "But what gives it such uniqueness?"

"It carries the blessings of two gods."

"That's not possible," Enna said.

"So I thought, as well," Fendrick agreed. "But they are there: Hyrim and Amalthee. When Nathan brought me the block of steel, I could tell it had already been blessed."

"How?" Enna asked.

Fendrick continued without acknowledging the question. "I set to working it, certain that it would fail."

"*You* put the second blessing on it?" Shalindra asked.

"It's never been done," Enna said before he could answer. "Not that it's never been tried, especially with the pantheons that have some alignment in their teachings. But it always fails. The gods don't like sharing."

"Who knows how the gods work?" Fendrick said, stirring the fire with a stick. "They often do a poor job of telling us."

He lapsed back into silence, ending his part in the conversation.

Enna stared at the sword as if it might come alive in Shalindra's hand.

Shalindra returned it to its scabbard, certain that there was importance in what Fendrick had revealed but at a loss for what it could mean. Being entangled in the destiny of Eluria was bad enough. If two of the gods were indeed working in concert, even for an instant, how much deeper could this mystery go?

* * *

The sun was just past its zenith when they arrived at the valley of Kenzing. Rather than two days of walking, Shalindra's use of the mist gates had required only the balance of the morning to cover the distance. A short climb had brought them to the ridge, and they now stood looking down into the valley. Closing her eyes, Shalindra savored the familiar smells of ash and pine and fir as they mixed with those of damp earth and decaying wood. Her senses chased those smells, flowing through the forest like fingertips along stone and wood, allowing her to ascertain what her eyes could not see. It felt good to be back.

She opened her eyes, knowing that she was experiencing someone else's feelings for a place she had visited only once. That brief stay had come when accompanying her father on his tour of the Kingdom in search of a politically beneficial suitor for her hand. The journey had not ended the way either of them had intended, but she had met Tormjere and that was the only thing that mattered. She examined the valley anew through both of their eyes, aware that she was not the only thing to have changed during the intervening years.

Baron Cheldiff's manor had been completed, a squat building of imported stone with a single crenelated tower with a modest wall encompassing a stable and barracks. There were a few more buildings clustered in the center of town now, but the biggest difference was the forest.

The dark needles of evergreens and bare branches of seasonal trees that covered the sweep of the mountains were marred by large swaths of blackened and bare trunks. The golds and reds of the leaves now on the ground mirrored the inferno which had ravaged the valley and chased her and Tormjere away, forcing them to turn east as they sought sanctuary from the goblins chasing her. Grasses and ferns had rushed to reclaim the newly exposed forest floor, feeding on the sunlight allowed in by a diminished canopy.

Though Tormjere was not here to feel sadness at the destruction of his cherished woods, Shalindra swallowed past the lump in her throat.

"Cozy little place," Fendrick said.

Enna shivered from the chill of the breeze. "Are you sure we shouldn't just walk down the road?"

Shalindra shook her head. "I wish to retrieve the gems without drawing unwelcome attention to his family, and should a princess wander into town, it will invite too many questions."

"Then let's get on with it," Fendrick said. "You're certain of their location?"

"I am." Shalindra pointed down to the foot of the mountain. "Along that road is where the house is."

"That guard tower looks to be new construction," Fendrick said, looking west along the ridgeline. "With so many trees down, we'll need to be cautious of it."

"I know a way around, though we will cross the trail that leads to it."

Of course she knew. She remembered every wrinkle and bend in the slopes ringing the valley as if she was the one who grew up here. She led them down at a diagonal, into a specific crease that would mask their passage, following game trails that were familiar and new at the same time. The dilapidated road that led up to the tower had been cleared into a proper trail, and they cut across it cautiously. The trees still standing bore marks from the fire. Many were down, slowing their pace as they climbed over and around them. Shalindra was gripped with a sudden panic that what she expected would no longer be there. What if his parents had left or the land been cleared for some other purpose? It was a relief when the sound of barking dogs reached her ears, and at least one fear was assuaged.

Fendrick brought them to a stop. "I'll keep watch here while you two retrieve the gems. No need giving the animals an easy scent to track."

Enna set her pack down, then followed Shalindra as they crept closer. Shalindra slowed even more as she began to make out the familiar outlines of the house she had grown up in.

She shook her head. Where *he* had lived. No matter what it felt like to her now, this was not her home. The trees surrounding the dwelling had escaped the fires, and the gentle murmur of the creek carried through the air.

A man's voice called out the back door, and Shalindra and Enna ducked behind a tree. Moments later, two young boys emerged with sacks over their shoulders, and the dogs began jumping and barking in anticipation.

The voice called out again, exhorting the boys in their efforts to feed the excited animals. Tormjere's father, Byron, emerged, followed by a black dog hobbling along gamely behind him. Shalindra's heart leapt into her throat, relieved to see Blackwolf still healthy. Though the dog's once midnight-colored coat was now flecked with grey, his tail wagged as enthusiastically as ever.

Blackwolf's head turned sharply in their direction, ears up and sniffing at the air. Shalindra felt a sudden tug on her arm.

"Guardian!" Enna whispered frantically, pulling her back behind the tree.

Shalindra flushed, realizing that she had risen from their hiding place and was headed towards the animal. Embarrassed at the lapse, she settled back into her hiding place.

When the dogs were fed and the pens cleaned, Byron gave each of the boys a coin, which they promptly pocketed before running off down the road. He retreated into the house with Blackwolf, limping almost as much as the old dog.

"Wait here," Shalindra whispered.

She rose and hurried down the hill. It took only moments to locate the tree with the double trunk and the clump of river stones at its base. Keeping one eye on the house, she rolled the top stone off, then dug out the one beneath with her hands. The pouch was still there, exactly where she… where *he* had left it. With a gentle tug, the drawstring parted, and she emptied the contents into her palm. Instantly recognizing the one she sought, she plucked it from the pile of sparkling stones with thumb and forefinger and held it up for inspection. The small, almost rectangular crystal was a deep green and seemed to be wrapped in a dark haze. What Tormjere had once considered an interesting trick of the light she now knew as a tinge of demonic influence.

Shalindra began to drop them all back in, then changed her mind and tucked the special one inside another pouch on her belt. She tipped the rest into the bag, pulled it closed, and returned it to its hiding place once more. Then she carefully replaced the river stones and arranged the moss and leaves above to conceal it once more. Wind and rain and falling leaves would render the hiding place indistinguishable from any other piece of the forest floor within a short time.

Before leaving, she took a final look at the house. His parents deserved to know, to be given the opportunity to grieve his loss and celebrate his sacrifice. But she could not simply appear on their doorstep now, not with so many mysteries left unanswered. She would return when this was over and make certain that everyone knew what he had given in the end.

She retraced her route towards Enna but stopped again as doubt crept into her thoughts. She looked back over her shoulder. Her mistake of not telling Eljorn had been forgiven, but would she ever have another opportunity to speak to his parents?

"What were you doing?" Enna asked, pulling her away. "I thought you didn't want to visit."

"I just… wanted to see him again."

"The man? Was that Tormjere's father?"

"No. I mean, yes, Byron is his father. Blackwolf was the dog with him. I… wanted to pet him."

Enna looked at her dubiously, and Shalindra hoped she asked no further questions lest she have to explain what had triggered such an emotional reaction. Thankfully, Enna remained silent, and the pair hurried back to where Fendrick waited.

"Do you have them?" he asked.

"I have the one we need," Shalindra answered, showing them both.

"It looks as the wizard described," he said. "Are you certain you'd not want to bring them all, just in case?"

"They are not mine," Shalindra said. "And while Tormjere would be the last to question our use for this one, added wealth is not our objective. We have what was requested. Now we will see if it is truly the key Verelli claims it to be."

Chapter Twenty-Four

A Broken Trust

Two days later, they emerged from a mist gate far from Kenzing. The famed white tower of Kendenhall stood tall above the treetops ahead, marking their destination. Long the ancestral home of the Deurmark family—of which Shalindra's cousin Edward was the last survivor—the three stacked cylinders of the citadel stretched some fifteen stories into the sky, commanding both attention and countryside for miles around. It was with fondness that Shalindra remembered her younger self standing atop that tower, reveling in the grand view it provided, even as it left her dizzy from the height. As then, the city surrounding it was modestly sized and surprisingly compact, nothing more than a convenient stopping point at the intersection of roads that led to Halisford in the north, Locksall and the Gold Road to the southeast, and Lisiria and on to Merallin in the southwest.

Yet the wrong banner now flew above the battlements: one belonging to a Ceringion house that had been awarded the fiefdom after the Deurmark family had been brutally cast aside. That injustice still burned at her as they made their way towards the tower. It would be a long walk over cold and wet fields, but there were far too many people on the roads—and too many devoting too much attention to her—to use a mist gate to speed their travel. It had been easier to move through the Kingdom when no one knew who she was. Now everyone seemed to recognize her.

The road emerged from trees into fields, and they spied Kentrick's command bivouacked in the fields south of town. It was a relief that her brother was still here.

"Where do you think they'll be?" Enna asked.

"Either city or camp is possible," Shalindra said, "but I think the camp more likely."

They altered course towards Kentrick's banner but had covered less than half the distance when they were hailed by a pair of approaching riders. Both men wore tunics and leggings of muted earthen colors and rode with longbows strapped to their backs. The first was clean-shaven while the second possessed a dark beard, and both looked to have spent more nights sleeping outside than in. Shalindra recognized the Rangers as Loren and Drex, more from Tormjere's memory than her own.

"Your Highness," Loren said with a bow as he dismounted. "It's a relief to see you healthy."

"And you as well. How did you find us?"

"We discovered your horses wandering several days ago. This was cause for concern, as you might imagine. It took some time given how far apart they were, but after locating your campsites I concluded that your method of travel had become… unusual. I would dearly like to know how it was achieved."

"My brother sent you?" Shalindra asked, avoiding his question.

Loren affirmed her guess. "I followed long enough to gauge your speed and direction and estimated when you might return. His Highness was concerned for your safety."

Everyone was, of late. "I will see that his fears are assuaged. May I ask what details of your investigation were shared with him?"

"Your horses were returned to our care without notice. I have not personally seen His Highness in several days, and so my message to him was, of necessity, a generalization. It was presumed that you were simply more comfortable walking."

"Thank you for your discretion," Shalindra said, genuinely relieved. There were already enough tales about her floating around; the last thing she needed was one detailing magical abilities she had only just discovered in herself.

Loren's eyes flicked to her sword. He began to speak, then stopped. Swallowing whatever he had meant to say, he pointed towards the city. "Prince Kentrick guests with Lord Balewan in the tower. If I may be so bold, His Highness would likely welcome your involvement in the… negotiations taking place."

She could only wonder at what trouble was happening now, but Loren was a perceptive man, and his suggestion was not made idly.

"Thank you for letting me know. I will seek him out as soon as I locate the rest of my friends."

"They are also in the city," Loren said. "Though I do not know what their business was about." He offered the reins of his horse to her. "You should take our horses, of course, though I regret that there are only two."

"Enna and I can double easily enough. Thank you."

Both Rangers bowed as they surrendered their mounts, and the trio resumed their journey.

The horses covered the remaining distance quickly, and once inside the outer wall, their altered vantage point revealed a second tower rising above the city. This one was slender, composed of a darker stone with gently tapered walls in a shape that evoked memories of Honarch's tower. Or at least it would have, were it complete. The top third of the tower was missing, and the jagged edges implied that it had been ungracefully removed.

Intrigued, Shalindra guided their course through the winding streets so that they would pass closer to it. The missing section now lay in a pile of rubble at its base, though the entrance looked to have been cleared. A wall encircling the spire served to hold back the city and block the view within. The soldiers standing guard at the gate and outside the perimeter wore tabards adorned with brown and grey chevrons in the style of the current lord, but their attention was focused inward rather than out.

"What happened?" Fendrick wondered aloud.

"Maybe a demon appeared here also," Enna said.

"The foulest of creatures walk among us!" a woman screeched nearby, casting her voice farther than it was meant to go. Her podium was an empty crate further around the tower, and she stood with her back to Shalindra, gesticulating wildly as she sought the attention of a small crowd of onlookers. She waved a cheap medallion like a holy symbol, but her brightly mismatched assortment of robes aligned with no pantheon Shalindra recognized. "Our homes are gone! All that we know will be destroyed! Weep for us! Weep for all we have known!"

Many on the streets passed her by, but those who stopped to listen carried a hollow look of loss and desperation about them, no matter their class.

"Do they believe that nonsense?" Fendrick scoffed.

"Anything is believable in the absence of truth," Enna said. "The soldiers listen as much as the people."

Several in the crowd took note of their approach, and soon they were pointing to Shalindra.

The woman tossed her unkempt hair to the side to view the interruption, and her eyes widened as they fell on Shalindra.

"The Guardian! The Guardian is come!" she cried, pointing to Shalindra. "She will protect us from this evil!"

Shalindra's mouth dropped open in surprise. She was given no time to deny it as the crowd surged towards her in a desperate jumble, shouting questions.

"Will you save us?"

"Can you stop the wizards?"

"Why don't you heal us anymore?"

Arms stretched upwards to touch her, grasping at her legs. Enna pulled her feet up, scrunching tight against Shalindra's back.

"Please, make way!" Shalindra shouted, but no one responded to her pleas.

Fendrick used his horse to bluster his way forward, trying to force a path through the growing mob that Shalindra and Enna could follow. Shalindra resisted the urge to kick her horse to a gallop, unwilling to trample those before her.

"We are trying to help!" she called. "Please allow us through!"

Her pleas seemed only to inflame their passions rather than quell them. The strange prophet woman just stared at her in self-righteous vindication, as if Shalindra's existence was proof of whatever claims she had made. Hands which had been outstretched for attention became rough as they grasped at her legs. Enna's arms tightened around her waist suddenly as she was pulled down. Shalindra's hand shot back reflexively, knocking Enna's assailant aside. The mob paused as if taking a breath, their momentary hesitation opening a sliver of a path through them. With a kick, she sent her horse surging forward. Fendrick was less delicate in extricating himself, bursting from the crowd right behind them.

The mob briefly followed, still shouting at her, but failed to keep pace. Once they were well clear, Shalindra forced her grip on the reins to loosen, shaken by the encounter. She had done nothing to encourage such behavior, but the desperate had still looked to her for salvation. How was she supposed to save everyone?

* * *

The interior of the castle was far more serene than the streets of the city. Their horses were taken by waiting groomsmen, and they were shown to a small parlor. Shalindra was informed that the duke would see her immediately. Servants wiped away the dust of the road from her armor, then escorted her away. Neither Enna nor Fendrick objected to the slight, but Shalindra was growing tired of being removed from her friends.

She tried to refocus her thoughts on the needs of her brother as she followed a servant through the halls, but the unfamiliar décor did nothing to improve her mood. Gone were the paintings of the

Deurmark family, replaced by colorful tapestries depicting conquests of a different house. The banners were grey and brown rather than blue and white, and several of the interior doors had been replaced recently, perhaps because the ones that had originally hung there had been forced open.

They at last reached their destination, and the servant opened the door and announced her. "Her Royal Highness, Princess Shalindra of Actondel."

She entered the sitting room, one incongruously decorated with low cushions instead of chairs, and long drapes of silks in bright colors hanging from walls and windows in place of the traditional curtains.

Kentrick and the duke both rose from cushioned divans.

"Your Highness," the duke said with a bow. "Thaddaeus Ptolney, at your service. Such an unexpected but welcome surprise that you could join us."

His name and rich accent would have identified him as Ceringion even had she not been aware of the history of this fiefdom. Age had turned Thaddaeus' muscles soft without robbing the color from his hair, but there was a shrewdness to his gaze that reinforced her caution despite the sincerity of his welcome.

Shalindra smiled, as was appropriate. "I was able to attend to business more quickly than expected, thank you."

"Please, sit with us," Thaddaeus said, offering her a seat. "As I told the prince earlier, I find this arrangement more comfortable than stiff wooden chairs. I travelled extensively in the deserts of Namarin during my youth and took a liking to their comforts."

"They are quite comfortable," Shalindra agreed, sinking into a plush cushion. "I hope I did not disturb your conversation."

"Not at all, not at all. Your brother and I were speaking of the perils of his journey."

"Our greatest adversary was this early cold snap, thankfully," Kentrick said.

"Indeed. But the foul business that befell you is an indication that you are well served to travel so heavily armed. I understand that you, Princess, have become quite daunting on the battlefield, and your appearance confirms it."

"When the need arises," was all she said. Even strangers knew her as a killer.

You're walking around in full armor with a pair of magic weapons and they're lounging in court fashion. What do you expect them to think?

Thaddaeus turned back to Kentrick. "Do you have any idea why this vile attack happened?"

"None," Kentrick answered. "All those left alive fled, but it was probably a group of deserters turned rogue."

"Forgive me, Your Highness. I'm not certain if you really think that or you simply wish to allay my worries. Brigands do not attack a column of horsemen on a whim. I think it more likely that someone is displeased with your recent actions."

"It is possible that our intentions were misinterpreted," Kentrick said.

He seemed to include her in that statement, but they were his intentions, not hers, that had brought them here. Shalindra wished he would stop dragging her into every conversation.

Thaddaeus sipped his drink. "From afar, it does appear that

your direction and that of Our Majesty are in disagreement. There is nothing untoward about this—so much more can be conveyed in person than from words on a piece of paper. Forgive my plain speech, but your arrival does place me in a delicate position."

"Clarity of purpose is what His Majesty and I hoped to achieve," Kentrick said. "We have a duty to our subjects that must be upheld, and the security of our realm is our primary concern."

The line was well delivered. Kentrick's diplomacy was already improving, but the duke was not won over.

"An honorable sentiment. Allow me to tell you this thing: I was the one who engineered the taking of Braunton, a feat of some accomplishment, if I do say so myself. This outpost in the middle of nowhere is not how I expected to be rewarded, no matter how impressive the tower. I had nothing to do with the fortunes of its former owners and so cannot even view it as a valid conquest. Nevertheless, when the King called for men and materials to conquer the elves, I sent over a thousand of my best. Less than nine hundred returned, the rest being lost to disease, injury, and desertion. All without the first coin in plunder, and nothing but incoherent mumblings at the reason. You will understand why I would be reluctant to commit them again for something so vague."

"Your position is quite understandable," Kentrick said. "And I can assure you the situation is far different now. The reversal came about suddenly, after the discovery of a plot by the wizards of the Conclave against His Majesty."

"And yet it is curious that you arrive with two members of that same order, the one that our king so vehemently denounced just weeks ago."

Kentrick stiffened. "Our goals are similar, for a short time. But they are not my wizards, nor do I solicit their advice."

"And do those goals include performing conjurations inside the tower of my former minder? I was not the least bit sorry at his demise, but the manner in which it occurred caused considerable damage. It is widely reported that there were strange lights within the tower last night. Coincidence, perhaps. But if the sorcerers you've brought attempt any trouble…"

"I can assure you there will be none," Shalindra said. It had to be Verelli poking about in there, and if so, she did not want his work to be interrupted. "They are researching the demon attacks for me, and it would be only natural to investigate the site. Had my arrival not been delayed, I would have informed you of our plans in advance, of course."

It was falsehood, but close enough to the actual truth that it did not feel like a lie. Were Verelli looking for components for the summoning focus, another wizard's tower would be the perfect place to start.

The duke's eyes drifted over the symbol of Eluria worked into the patterns on her armor. "I know that you follow the moon, despite your warlike appearance. Your collusion with members of the Conclave is an even more unusual pairing, given that the Imaretii sought to have your entire order wiped out."

Shalindra started in surprise. "What?"

He shook his head. "Did your wizard not tell you? There was a bounty on any of your sisterhood that could be killed, though it wasn't something talked about or even openly acknowledged. Your goddess is not widely worshipped in Ceringion, as we prefer the sciences over superstition, but neither are Her followers persecuted. Most of the older houses, mine included, ignored the request, but there were several of the smaller ones that took the chance."

Shalindra fought to keep her anger at the notion in check. "There are a number of prior mistakes we are attempting to rectify."

"Such as the demon they unleashed upon my city?"

"Is that what happened?" Shalindra asked. "I saw the remains of the tower…"

"A large chunk of the merchant quarter has been reduced to the same state. By the time we dispatched the fiend, I'd lost close to sixty men and near as many townsfolk. Were the wizard not dead from his own sorcery, I would have fulfilled His Majesty's edict and had him hung from the highest tower."

"What of the other wizards here?" Shalindra asked.

"I'm told that there were only a handful," the duke replied, affecting an indifferent pose. "It was made known to them what their fate would be, but there are many demands on my time and they all managed to flee before there was a need for trouble."

"That was very kind of you," she said.

"As long as they and their foul creatures are gone, I consider my duty to our king to be fulfilled."

"As do I," Kentrick said. "But where we travel may take me closer to those same threats."

"I'm aware of the rumors in the east and want no part in it. We are through with demons, Your Highness."

"You faced only one," Shalindra interjected. "There may be hundreds loose in Ceringion."

"Let them tear the Reginum apart," Thaddaeus said, his loyalties to his former nation apparently open to discussion. "It would do some good to clean out the peerage."

"Where do you think they will go when they are through with Ceringion?" Shalindra asked.

"Hopefully, somewhere else. If you're here to drum up support for the defense of the Reginum, Your Highness, I must say that you're going about it in an incredibly circumspect manner. Are Kingdom politics always so unclear?"

"Of late, they seem to be," Kentrick admitted.

"Then please humor me with directness. What are you asking for?"

"Reinforcements to travel with us along the eastern border and see to its security."

"How many?"

"Ideally, five thousand."

"It won't happen," Thaddaeus said bluntly. "No one is going to rearm and send their men away with winter fast approaching. Not after most of those same men were gone the entire summer preparing for an invasion that never happened."

"I appreciate your candor," Kentrick said stiffly.

"We'll see if you mean that." Thaddaeus considered for a moment. "I'll provide you with one hundred men and see to their provisioning for a week's time. They will ride under the Kingdom banner, but if you seek to do anything with them other than keep these demons at bay, they'll abandon you no matter what predicament you might be in."

"The crown thanks you for your support," Kentrick said, not

sounding thankful.

Thaddaeus stood. "They will be ready in two days. And do make certain your wizards leave with you."

Her brother seethed at the dismissal but rose to his feet as well. "Allow me to convey His Majesty's thanks, and I bid you good day."

Shalindra followed him from the room but waited until they were out of earshot of the guards to speak. "He seemed quite suspicious of your motives."

"He isn't the only one," Kentrick said snippishly. "What *are* you doing with the wizards?"

"It is best if you do not know," Shalindra said.

He turned to her in surprise. "Secrets, from me?"

"It is nothing that relates to the problems within the Kingdom, and so I would spare you the added concern. There are enough burdens on your mind already."

He grinned ruefully. "There is truth to that. Will you at least tell me if I should be worried?"

"Probably not."

Kentrick frowned. "You've become far too cryptic."

I think it's more to do with lack of sleep.

"I am tired," she said, though such a feeling was as foreign to her now as hunger.

"Get some rest then. It doesn't appear that anyone will be getting enough of that in the coming days."

Shalindra's hand covered the pouch that held the demonic gemstone. Sleep was the last thing on her mind now. It was time to find Verelli.

Their return to the wizard's tower was accomplished more cleanly than their earlier escape, owing to the escort Thaddaeus provided to her. Shalindra would have preferred a more subdued arrival but accepted it without complaint. The half-dozen or so *hers* currently debating what she was about to attempt had commanded her attentions anyway, as they were divided evenly on the wisdom of this attempt. Several maintained that they had made the same choice, while others urged a delay until more could be learned. Shalindra forced them aside when their group came to a stop.

The soldiers guarding the gate rushed to take their horses as others formed a cordon between them and the crowd. The strange prophet was no longer there, but a cluster of townspeople continued to mill about. Upon seeing her, they grew more vocal and pressed closer.

"Your Highness," one of the soldiers greeted her, raising his voice to be heard above the fray. "Sergeant Burhomm, at your service."

"Has anything happened here today?" she asked.

"We've seen naught since the lights last night coming from that window there."

Shalindra followed his pointed finger up to a narrow window near the top of the shortened tower. There was no guarantee that Verelli and the others were inside, but it seemed a logical connection. Neither the soldiers nor the crowd needed to know that, however. "We will see if we can put a stop to them for you."

"You're going in there?" Burhomm asked incredulously, then stood tall. "Should you require our services, we stand ready to assist.”

He offered because her station demanded it, but his face was almost green at the prospect of entering a wizard’s lair.

“I expect this to go peacefully,” she replied, hiding her smile, “but thank you for your dedication.”

The trio picked their way through the debris towards the door, all the while being bombarded by the shouts of the crowd.

“Free us from the evil!”

“Kill the wizards!”

Their thirst for blood was understandable given the damage to the city, but she was not here to be their vengeance.

The door of the tower opened at their approach, and a hand beckoned them to enter quickly.

“That was fast,” Honarch said by way of greeting as he pushed the door shut and dropped the bar the instant they were inside.

The floor was open and airy but dimly lit by a series of small windows. A central column wrapped with tightly curving stairs provided access to the upper floors, and chairs, benches, and wardrobes were arranged around the walls.

“Welcome back, Your Highness,” Birion said as he rose from his seat, tired but clearly relieved.

“It is good to see you both,” Shalindra greeted them. “I had worried that everyone would have moved on by now.”

“Kind of stuck at the moment,” Honarch said, “but we’ve been busy. Were you able to find them?”

Shalindra withdrew the demon gem and handed it to him.

Honarch made a motion over it with his hand, then grinned. “This is it. I can’t believe I missed it before, but then I didn’t really know what to look for. We've been working as well, as long as we were here. It made for a nice break from bouncing around in that carriage. The container is almost prepared. Let's take this to Verelli," he said, leading them towards the stairs.

"I'll keep watch on the door," Birion said.

"Same for me," Fendrick added. "I've had enough magic for a while."

"He did nothing nefarious while we were gone?" Enna asked Honarch as they ascended.

"I don't think so. The spells share some similarities with those used to create dohedrons, in that they provide linkages via projections across—"

"Speak plainly, please," Enna cut him off. "I'm more concerned with *if* this will work rather than *how*."

Honarch blinked, then continued up the steps. "It's fine. But when this is over, I'll want to spend some time studying how it actually functions."

"You do not know that already?" Shalindra asked in surprise.

"No one does. Summoning is one of the arts that was all but lost during the collapse of the final Great Empire. We can make it work, but understanding it is another matter."

"No wonder the world's a disaster," Enna muttered, sounding like Fendrick.

The steps ended at what was the fourth or fifth level, depositing them into an open landing occupying a quarter of the floor. Shalindra could taste a freshness in the air, likely indicating that they were close to the upper limits of the shortened tower. Steps along the outer wall continued upwards, but it was towards a closed door that Honarch ushered them. He knocked softly, then proceeded inside.

The room they entered was cozy and comfortable, a master craftsman's workshop and library rolled together. The curving outer wall was lined with shelves stacked full of books, flasks, and souvenirs from countless explorations. Tall windows with the curtains thrown wide allowed light to fill the room, and it was at a desk beneath one such window that Verelli worked. He was alone in the room, hunched over a delicately shaped metal cage which he viewed through a magnifying glass. It was beautifully constructed, but knowing the purpose it would be used for lent the polished metal a sinister air.

Honarch passed the gem to the older wizard, who sized it against the tiny cage.

"Perfect," Verelli said.

"How long before it will be ready?" Shalindra asked.

"Only a few moments. All that remains is the final binding."

"Is that enough time?" Enna asked.

He stood to face them. "Great magic is not measured by the amount of time it takes, but by what it achieves in the time it is given. I would, however, suggest that it be done immediately before the attempt to open the portal to minimize potential side effects."

"What side effects?" Enna demanded.

"I am ready now," Shalindra said, contradicting the butterflies in her stomach. "But should we do this outside the city?"

"That would be foolish. The summoning chamber in this tower remains intact, a fact which leads me to believe that the demon was called here outside of its protections for some reason."

"Maybe he was angry at someone," Enna said. "That seems to be the usual reason."

"Or desperate," Honarch pointed out. "There's not much use for them in daily life."

"Either way," Verelli said, "the summoning chamber would be the safest place. To reconstruct one outside of a controlled environment would invite failure." He waved towards the stairs. "It is already prepared, so if you are indeed ready, we will begin."

Enna shot her a worried look, but Shalindra was eager to get this over with before she allowed doubts to change her mind. She nodded to Verelli. "We can start now."

Verelli turned to Enna. "Would you bring our companions up to join us while I complete the assembly? I would only caution against wandering into any of the other rooms. There are things here that would be dangerous to disturb."

"Wonderful place to live," Enna sniped, but wasted no time in descending the stairs.

Verelli turned back to the desk and slipped the gem into the pendant. Soft words and a delicate movement of his fingers above the device sent the metal wire inside twisting around the stone to lock it in place. He turned and extended his hand towards her, the pendant dangling from his fingers. His eyes met hers, seeking confirmation to continue.

She gave a curt nod, not trusting herself to speak without calling the whole thing off. Her need for this had seemed so clear, but now that the moment had arrived, she found herself filled with doubt.

Verelli locked his intense gaze on the pendant as he began the spell, his words spoken in an arcane language that was clipped and precise. It was unlike any spell she had heard before, save for the one word she recognized clearly: Shalindra.

With the speaking of her name, the center of the gemstone began to move, swirling with dark mists that clung to it like morning fog above the water. No longer a simple adornment, the necklace was now a thing alive. She felt an awareness of it, as it, in turn, was aware of her.

Verelli's spell ended, and he inspected the pendant with a critical eye before making a satisfied sound. Shalindra heard a small gasp behind her and turned to see Enna standing in the doorway, her face pale as she stared at it.

"The chamber is directly above us," Verelli said. "Follow."

Those on the landing stepped aside as Shalindra followed him from the room, and they fell in behind. She ran her fingers over Shining Moon as they made their way up the steps, seeking reassurance. What would she learn from that place where Tormjere himself had struggled to survive? The various *hers* had considered little else, but even they had failed to reach any consensus beyond the probability of her dying in the same way Alharania had.

They continued up the stairs for not even half a turn of the tower. Fresh air descended from above, and Shalindra could see patches of the night sky where the next level of the tower should have been.

Verelli paused at a door leading to the interior of the tower. "Keep to the walls," he cautioned, "and do not disturb the markings on the floor. And touch nothing." With that admonishment, he led them inside.

Shalindra had never been inside a summoning chamber, though the space felt eerily familiar. It was circular, occupying almost the entire width of the tower, with a high, vaulted ceiling. The floor was devoid of furnishings or rugs, its smooth stones marred only by a wide circle of five concentric rings. The powdered substances used for each ring were unknown to her, but the colors lent a prismatic effect to the arcane symbols contained within each circle.

"Nothing here to touch," Fendrick muttered, but he stood with his back pressed tight against the wall next to Enna. Honarch guided Birion to a position across the room from them.

Verelli motioned Shalindra closer. "You may enter the summoning circle here, but take care not to disturb the glyphs. I will raise the protections around you and then attempt to open the gate in the center."

"Wait," Enna interrupted. "I thought we were all going. How are we to help if something goes wrong?"

I can get out easily enough.

"The wards are a reasonable precaution," Shalindra said. "We cannot risk further devastation to the city."

"What about devastation to you?" Enna demanded. "Let one of us go first."

Shalindra glanced to each face in the room. Any of them would take her place. Birion out of duty, Fendrick for atonement, Honarch for the discovery, and Enna because she was Enna and cared more than anyone. But Shalindra wanted none of her friends to take this risk for her. She was stronger and quicker than all of them, and if there were problems, she could be back through the mist gate faster than they would even realize the need. No, it would be her and her alone this time.

"I think it safer if I go," Shalindra said. "I will step through and immediately return, and we can decide then how to proceed."

"But—" Enna began.

"I will remind you all," Verelli cut in, "that the summoning focus is associated with Shalindra. Should we encounter issues and the portal closes unexpectedly, there is some probability we will be able to reestablish it at her location. For anyone else, there is not."

"Shouldn't you have more control over this?" Enna asked.

"Few sane people are willing to follow demons to their own world, and, sane or not, none have ever returned."

"What does that make me?" Shalindra asked.

"Hopefully, unique. We should stop wasting time."

Verelli waved her forward as everyone readied their weapons, anxiously preparing for anything that might happen. Shalindra stepped into the circle, careful not to disturb any of the symbols or rings. She felt the protective wards materialize around her at Verelli's command, and looked through their shimmering translucence to her companions. Every one of them was frightened for her, though they all tried to hide it. It was heartwarming and terrifying at the same time. Enna's mouth opened, perhaps for some final encouragement, but she was preempted as Verelli began the spell.

The words he spoke were a surprisingly brief series of phrases constructed with deliberate cadence and meticulous inflection. Shalindra took a deep breath and steeled herself for the creation of the gate.

Nothing happened.

Verelli frowned and repeated himself, making subtle adjustments to his words and motions, but again nothing materialized. She glanced at him, but her eyes were drawn instead to the pendant around his neck. The gem swirled, wrapped in tendrils of black mists. On a sudden impulse, she allowed her vision to shift, and instead of empty air, she saw a slender filament of mist stretching out from the pendant. It was like a line that passed through air and earth to trail into nothingness, never seeming to end. It moved almost imperceptibly, like sap dripping down a tree, as if whatever tethered it on the other end was in motion.

Follow it.

Trusting her instincts, Shalindra called forth a mist gate of her own and sent it tunneling through space and time along that slender filament. She felt it latch into place, anchoring itself to some distant endpoint she could not perceive. Without waiting to question the decision, she plunged into it.

The dot of reddish light marking the end of the dark tunnel grew exponentially larger as she raced forwards. Even before reaching it, she realized that something had gone terribly wrong.

But by then it was too late.

Chapter Twenty-Five

Between Friends

Mataasrhu reclaimed the final remnants of his once mighty opponent, savoring his victory as the burning sting of a hundred wounds healing coated him like a soothing balm. The scars and notches left in their wake crisscrossed in dark streaks across the texture of his bare, reddish-brown skin, each one adding another entry to his litany of triumphs. Sore but satiated, he stretched his dark wings and used the rock wall to rub the molt from between his shoulder blades. It was a risk putting so much energy into those appendages so soon, but they were now of sufficient size as to no longer limit his flight, and the status they conveyed was unmistakable.

He furled his wings, pleased that his broad, muscular torso was no longer wide enough to hide them. A quick inspection of both arms and his taloned fingers—two of which had just regrown after having been bitten off during the contest—confirmed that he was again whole. His thick legs were both in similar condition, and his wide hooves were once again dark and smooth. His red eyes glowed with an inner light as they surveyed the cave where the other demons of his *wharra* picked and fought over the remains of the vanquished den. The air sparkled and danced with *marhu*—the Fires of Reclamation—as it drifted up from the bodies of the slain to be consumed by the strong, or the daring. The scent of those fires mixed with that of the black blood pooling on the floor, producing an intoxicating scent of victory that put him in mind of the subtle flavors of otherworldly metals. It was a taste of a different realm that he had sampled only briefly, but it was one to be relished and never forgotten.

The cavern his wharra had conquered was long and narrow, carved in a deliberate manner from the rock of the canyon. The single, snaking entrance blocked any view of the interior from the outside, preventing others from knowing exactly who or what lay inside without first daring to enter—a dangerous proposition. Near to fifty demons could reside in the shallowed-out depressions that dotted the striated walls within. Along the back of the cavern where Mataasrhu stood, there was only one nesting hole, a large and perfectly hemispherical space that he would line with the hides of his enemies to ensure his warmth and comfort. A suitable place for one such as he, who commanded the bargains of so many. It would make a good home.

Zaralzur approached him with the proper amount of deference and dipped his bulbous head, causing the fleshy appendages drooping from his skull to slide over his hunched shoulders. The tentacles, each writhing with a mind of its own, marked him as one of the Attuned, those who could interpret the clouds and glean from them the will of Mergolatrhu, Mistress of Torments and Goddess of All, and so enforce Her will.

"Another victory, mighty Mataasrhu," the Attuned said. "It is a sign of Her favor that you have achieved so much, and with such unprecedented speed."

A rumble of frustration formed in Mataasrhu's throat, but there it stayed. One did not challenge the words of the Attuned. "A costly triumph."

Zaralzur plucked a handful of embers from above a nearby corpse, one being torn open by another demon. The demon whirled, ready to contest the theft, but upon spying the lidless black eyes of the Attuned, he quickly turned his back in submission. None would deny Zaralzur his share of their spoils and, even if they had tried, their attempt would have been impotent. The Attuned were not without their defenses.

Such imaginary squabbles only served to distract Mataasrhu's thoughts from the source of his unhappiness. The raid had been daring, yes, but his wharra now numbered half of what it had been when they forced their way into the cave. Should it become known how depleted they were, he would have to defend his conquest from other assaults. He scowled as he again regarded the entrance to the cave.

"It will need defending," Zaralzur affirmed, following his stare. "Who should attend to the duty?"

"Have the goats see to it."

The strands of flesh running down the back of Zaralzur's head writhed in annoyance. "The hadraal do not appreciate being called that and would continue to serve you best if their efforts were met by your approvals."

Mataasrhu did not care what they thought. He had never encountered the creatures known as goats in the human world, but he liked the sound of their name. It was a short, ugly word that was fitting for short, brutal thralls. Ones whose coarse, grey fur marked them as lesser creatures when compared to his own textured but bare skin. Mataasrhu, like Zaralzur, was a product of this world. The goats were simply animals that lived upon it. "That is why I use such language with you, so that you may translate with the most appropriate manner."

The Attuned might be the most powerful—and only—conduits to the goddess, but they had their place, and Mataasrhu had his.

Another demon came forward with his head down. "We have squeezed fourteen barrels from the remnants."

A satisfied grin split Mataasrhu's broad face. "Light four barrels. There will be no cold after such a victory."

"Your might knows no bounds," the demon said, turning his back.

That large a harvest would be good. The cycle was drawing to a close, and the air would soon cool. There were few things more despised in all the world than the cold. It slowed muscles and dulled minds, and times without warmth could cause a wharra to collapse into infighting. It was an extravagant risk to burn that much so early, but the light would serve as a display of might that would give pause to any who sought to take it from him. And he had plans to add to the reserves long before they ran out.

When his wharra had gorged on the bodies of the conquered,

the husks were dragged outside and spread to dry. Once they became as hard as the rocks they lay on they would be ground into a powder that could be combined with blood and used to heal wounds more rapidly.

All his immediate needs satisfied, Mataasrhu returned to his examination of the cave, this time studying the striations of the rock walls. The layers were predominately of dark grey zhora and brown uhvama, both hard enough to give the stone-eaters difficulty and provide suitable defense against a burrowing attack. He would need to bargain with some of the more agreeable stone-eaters to raise the height of the cavern's ceiling eventually, but it would serve his wharra well for some time. Those he commanded were already organizing themselves, staking claim to their burrows. The weakest settled near the entrance while the strongest congregated towards the rear, closer to where Mataasrhu stood. Snarls and roars filled the chamber as the choicest locations were contested. More than a few demons were already sequestered inside those spaces, and those who were capable had established their protective wards, sealing themselves inside to rest.

A scraping noise outside the cave drew the attention of every demon inside, and as one they faced the entrance, ready to fight for their lives. Mataasrhu was about to order the goats to investigate when a series of three sharp clacks echoed through the entrance: Nameless ones. Newly arisen demons who wandered without the protection of a wharra and fought each other for prominence.

The one who led them was either bold or foolish to come seeking acceptance so soon after a battle. Mataasrhu hoped it was the former, and that they would be fit, so he would not be forced to compromise. Unless they were crippled, however, he would welcome the reinforcements. It would be a long cycle before the next birthing.

He motioned his wharra back against both walls and called out in a booming voice, "Enter, Nameless ones."

Five demons, the largest of whom was driving the others forward from the rear, slunk cautiously into the cave.

Mataasrhu considered it a divine blessing for so many to arrive at once, but he evaluated each as they approached. None would measure to the height of his waist, but it was a good group.

One was a serpent, with hairless but sickly greenish skin. Those could be dangerous when grown but rarely fared well in their youth. Two of the others walked on four legs more than two and would never develop into anything beyond fodder. And, of course, there was another goat. He had to be cautious with the goat. The wharra already had three of the brutish beasts. Should he allow the balance to tip too far in their favor they might try to take the wharra from him. At the back was a vorl, a dark-haired beast as savage as the goats but with a jaw full of fangs and a reputation for cunning and viciousness. This one stood head and shoulders taller than the other four, and his claws already showed signs of recent use. It was a good mark that he had managed to corral them and bend them to his cause.

"Mighty Mataasrhu," the vorl said, bowing his head as the others crouched low, their timidity as evident as the stench of fear they carried with them. "We have heard of the strength of your wharra, and its victories bring glory to your name. It is because of this that we would offer our bargains to you."

Mataasrhu raised himself to his full height. Muscles rippled as he planted either hoof upon the platform in a broad stance and clenched his fists at his side. His wings stretched out behind him like a dark shadow, adding height and width to his already sizable bulk. He could have propelled himself into the air, a rare feat, but refrained from doing so, as the display of might had already had its desired effect. All five of the Nameless ones turned their backs in submission.

"I will accept only the best," Mataasrhu stated. "What makes you think you are worthy?"

The Nameless ones began to stomp about and display their strength, pounding the ground and occasionally each other, as the rest of the wharra shouted jeers of encouragement. It was a frenetic show of immature muscles and—

Mataasrhu.

He whirled, teeth bared and fists clenched, prepared to strike at whoever dared to stand behind him. Yet there was nothing but a rock wall facing him.

The display of the Nameless ones ceased abruptly, and many eyes regarded him with wary disbelief.

"Why do you stop?" he bellowed at them. "Are you so easily distracted as to fall for such an obvious ploy? Continue, or I shall cast you all out."

The Nameless ones resumed their antics, redoubling their efforts to impress him. Mataasrhu scowled and nodded, giving every appearance of judging them shrewdly, but his attention now lay elsewhere.

The mocking inflections of the voice gave name to who it was that called—there could be little doubt. Was Mataasrhu himself now the one being hunted? No. However taunting the caller was, it had been an invitation, not a threat. Mataasrhu found himself oddly tempted by the possibilities, yet there was great risk in pursuing such futures at this pivotal time. The odds of a counterattack from a rival wharra were significant, and should he not be here when it occurred, he risked losing not just the cave but every bargain within. But the potential rewards…

He began walking towards the Nameless ones. "My wharra is the strongest and most daring of all in this canyon. We have won every battle, advanced our station with every conquest. I bargain that you will have my protection, and you shall serve at my whim. You will not betray me or any other under my protection, and in exchange I will accept the four of you into my wharra."

The growing relief on their faces turned to confusion.

"It is bargained, mighty Mataasrhu," the vorl said, seemingly aware of where this was headed. His compatriots were slower to catch on, but that would be their problem. It was expected to reward accepted Nameless ones with gifts of reclamation, but so soon after a battle, there was none to spare. As he did not find the reptile worthy, the solution was obvious. With a single swipe, Mataasrhu tore the reptile's head off, then hurled the body at the Nameless ones' feet.

"A bounty, to celebrate your bargain!"

His wharra hooted and shrieked in glee as the four new members eagerly descended on the corpse.

Mataasrhu waved Zaralzur closer. "Put them near the entrance where they belong but separate them from one another."

Zaralzur's lidless eyes narrowed. "Are you going somewhere?"

"I am. I shall let our enemies see me in flight, and that will remind them what will happen should any dare attack us."

"Bold, mighty Mataasrhu."

"Keep everyone inside until I return."

The other demons turned their backs to him as he strode through the cavern.

Once outside, he unfurled his massive wings in display for any who might be watching. With muscle and magic, he launched himself into the sky, circling upwards from the depths of the canyon.

It was a long ascent to the rim. Despite his stated intent of striking fear into his enemies, a solo display such as this was so dangerous as to be considered foolhardy. So close to the edge of their territory, he risked an attack of opportunity.

The walls of the canyon were stacked in layers of reds and browns, with an occasional streak of black. It had been carved by sand and wind, or perhaps even water at some point in the ancient past, if the musings of the Attuned were to be believed. How the canyons had come to be mattered little to Mataasrhu beyond an awareness of which protrusions were most likely to crumble and fall, or which types of stone would resist digging efforts and thus make the best caves.

His newly strengthened wings propelled him ever higher, and he leveled out just beneath the tops of the canyon walls, cautious not to rise above them. He was not strong enough to contest another for the right to soar above the plains, and so he kept his place. For now.

A storm of ash and lightning loomed large ahead of him, filling the horizon from the ground to the perpetual clouds of the Lathgaz, the Shield of Mergolatrhu. No demon of any breed, no matter how powerful, ever ventured into those clouds. He judged that the storm would arrive late that cycle, and he would do well to be back inside when it did.

The call had come from an unusual direction. All demons were capable of producing such telekinetic signals, though most never achieved anything more than a simple announcement of their location no more precise than a shout. Most of the higher species, such as himself, could convey some simple phrases and even a modicum of emotion, but only the Attuned were adept at sending their thoughts and impressions across a distance. Mataasrhu had encountered only one exception to that rule, and it was that singular variance which now pushed him to risk all in pursuit of this meeting.

His flight brought him even with a craggy notch cut at a nearly perpendicular angle from the path of the canyon, and he banked into it. Skimming along the jagged slope within, he emerged onto the windswept plains of the surface. This was a shortcut to the next canyon, one which he would never have been aware of had he not once been among those bound to a human wizard.

That indignity still burned, but he cast such distracting thoughts aside and remained vigilant. Like all such forays into the swirling sands of the overworld, the venture was measured not in time or distance but in risk of destruction. There were few beings here with which he could hope to compete, demon or otherwise, and so it was with annoyed relief that he dropped into the relative safety of the canyon he sought. The time would come when he would be strong enough to stand in the overworld without fear.

Fortune continued to be with him as he managed to avoid both rivals and watchers, and he soon grew near the source of the call. The canyon here was wide, open, and sparsely populated, as close to unclaimed ground as could be found in any direction. Only one cave was cut into the walls here, its entrance so low it practically rested on the valley floor. It was marked by the construction of two immense columns of rock resembling the stone fortifications that humans built, which was appropriate, given its purpose.

Mataasrhu circled cautiously. There was no activity to be seen, but that was not a surprise. What was unexpected was the smell of death that carried to his sensitive nostrils, even this far above the entrance. Had the thralls finally tired of being kept as slaves, or had Zarglarhu grown lax in his defenses? Would anyone actually risk violation of the Edict by bringing war to a place where even the mildest slight was forbidden?

Though demons now warred openly in the human world, the Edict of Servitude had not been disbanded, nor had he himself explicitly been released from its confining requirements, despite the convenient death of his wizard and subsequent rise in his standing. Sulfaxrhu could take his horde there and pillage all he wished, but there was nothing for Mataasrhu to gain from travelling to the human's world again.

Mataasrhu circled once more, his instincts overruling any sense of eagerness and reminding him it was folly to enter a rival's lair uninvited. He had no standing here and could just as easily be met with an attack as a greeting, no matter his past. For a moment, he wavered, almost following his urge to depart.

But his curiosity got the better of him. There could be only one man willing to call him from this location, and his lust for those bound to the wizards was legendary.

Mataasrhu dove, gliding into the open maw of the cave and through the bent tunnel, towards the gathering arena inside. The tunnel narrowed rapidly and turned back on itself, and his wings filled the width of the space as he beat them furiously to bring himself to a stop. Such a defensive measure was not unexpected, as it forced any flying creatures to land. It would place more powerful attackers on even footing, as all of those inside should have lacked the ability to leave the ground. A pair of smaller tunnels branched off to either side, another oddity of this place, but he passed them and continued on, claws ready.

As he edged forward, another scent tingled in his nostrils: that of expiring energies left unclaimed. To allow the Fires to disperse unclaimed was an unmistakable sign of dominance by one strong enough to let a death go to waste. Mataasrhu again hesitated, but he was too far committed to turn back now.

At the final turn, the body of a demon lay crumpled on the floor. Mataasrhu was no stranger to death—no demon was. It was a part of who they were, as surely as the sands that scoured the earth bare. Yet his pace slowed involuntarily at the violence done to it. Or at least, what was done to the half of it he could see. It bore the thicker skin granted to all who served under the Edict and were forced to the human world, though the added defense had not altered its fate. Only the faintest of fires rose from the ruined body—a fresh kill.

Mataasrhu drew them to himself. To waste a reclamation was unwise, but its ready availability again caused him to question his choice. What had happened here? Turning the corner, he followed the messy trail the creature's torso had taken as it rolled.

The scene which was revealed caused him to question his desire.

Mangled bodies were strewn across every segment of the floor, and thick, dark blood dripped in messy splatters from the walls. Many of the demons had died trying to submit or flee, their backs turned towards the center of the chamber. Both of the Attuned who had watched over this gathering chamber had been slain—an act as dangerous as it was wasteful. Their tentacles still slithered about in a futile attempt to stave off death, but they were the only thing that moved. Some of the dead had been crushed by thunderous blows, others bore the cleanly precise cuts of a blade. Demons had no use for metal weapons and no ability to forge them. There was only one sword that could have delivered those wounds, but its owner was not the one who stood before him.

In the center of the carnage, like a beacon amidst the dark blood and reddish-brown tones of the surrounding walls, stood a solitary figure. The elf—no, human—woman was clad in an unearthly white, and the silver scales of her armor blazed in the light of the burning oils. But it was her eyes, cold and blue, that disturbed him the most.

"You are not he," Mataasrhu stated, making no effort to hide his displeasure. "Shieldmaiden."

The woman raised a mocking eyebrow. "Certain of that, are you?"

Mataasrhu was not, but uncertainty gave rise to weakness, and weakness equaled death. She had called in *his* voice and carried *his* sword, while the hammer she held opposite that fearsome weapon radiated an unholy energy that was uncomfortable even to observe.

"You have done well for yourself," the woman said conversationally. "I like the wings."

Mataasrhu scowled at her, resisting the urge to display them. *He* had never been intimidated by such displays—no matter how grand—and it was unlikely his shieldmaiden would be either. If that was who she was. He pondered squashing the girl and being done with it. The rewards for her death would be great and would propel his status to unimaginable heights. Yet there had to be a purpose to her arrival here, and he wished to know what it was. Only then could he evaluate which choice would be most advantageous.

A knowing smile lifted the corners of the woman's mouth, as if she could hear the thoughts running through his mind. "Your rate of conquest has slowed, has it not?"

Mataasrhu snorted. She was correct, and she obviously knew why. Losing his favored assassin had forced him to exert more effort with every victory.

He stalked in a circle around her, using the motion to place a wall at his back instead of the openness of the entryway. The familiar squish of blood beneath his hooves was calming, though the reassurance it provided was destroyed by the knowledge that he was not the one who had claimed the victory.

The woman made no effort to move yet always remained facing him, refusing to show her back. *He* had always done that, as well.

"And why, exactly, do you care?" Mataasrhu asked. "Are you come to offer yourself into service, as did he?"

She laughed, a sound of merriment that was nauseating in its sincerity and frightening in its implied superiority. "Of course not. But that does not mean I am unwilling to help an old friend when I am able."

That word set his teeth on edge. Mataasrhu had hated being called that every time *he* had used it.

"Here there are masters and servants, nothing more." Mataasrhu stopped circling. "What do you want?"

"An ally."

"For what purpose? If you are not here to serve, then you have nothing which I desire. Do you know the rewards I would be given, the bounties which would be heaped upon me, for your head?"

"I can only imagine," she replied, unfazed. "But I can offer you something greater."

"If you desire a bargain, then state it and let it be out. I do not have time for games."

Her blue eyes gained a sudden intensity, and he struggled against the urge to bend before the weight of that gaze. "To kill the one you answer to."

So she—or whatever it was—was here to kill demons once more. Targeting the rulers of the hapdrhu to which his wharra was bargained would solve nothing and betrayed her ignorance of this world. No doubt she wished to save her own somehow, though Sulfaxrhu's arrival there was something that could never be undone. Her world would fall, one way or another. Yet her attempts might play to his advantage. If he could turn her efforts towards those who stood in his way…

He made a show of shaking his head and sought to draw out more information. "I fail to see how the demise of any above me would suit any purpose of mine. Tell me, do you seek revenge for some slight, or did one of us succeed in bringing about *his* death?"

The slightest wavering of her gaze gave him his answer. It was a surprising vindication of the prophecy, yet not unexpected. But if vengeance was what she sought, that could most assuredly be turned to his advantage.

"Revenge is not what I seek," she said. "I want to know why demons invade my world."

"Because we wish to."

"Food? Wealth? Power? There must be something that drives your desire beyond simple conquest."

It was amusing how naïve she was, and he toyed with her as he answered.

"There are many reasons for us to venture into your domain, but it is our Mistress of Torments, Mergolatrhu, that drives us in that purpose. Did *he* not tell you?"

The question left her face as white as the flimsy clothing she covered herself with, but Mataasrhu did not relent. "I wonder how many other secrets he kept from you. Do you think that knowing this will spare you, then? Your efforts will stop nothing, and we will continue to ravage your world as we please."

Her jaw tightened, and Mataasrhu drew in his breath with a hiss of satisfaction. She had no idea what she wanted. There were many possible offers she could now make, but he had already won this contest, and in the end, she offered everything at the cost of almost nothing.

"For now," she said, "I want only your agreement to help me reach my goals, as I shall help you achieve yours."

"When?"

"The next time you see me."

Mataasrhu almost laughed at her ineptitude. Such a request for help was so ill-defined that it could be twisted into anything he desired, and distort it he would. "It is bargained, You-Who-Are-Not-He. We shall see if you can hold up your end of this agreement as well as *he* did." Mataasrhu backed towards the exit, but not without making sure he had the last word. "Because if you fail, I will not offer you salvation again."

His view of the chamber disappeared as he entered the tunnel, and with a flap of his black wings, he shot from the cave and raced for the safety of his own, already plotting the ways in which this bargain could be put to his advantage.

Alone in the lifeless cavern, Shalindra looked in dismay at the carnage around her and shuddered at how wrong this experiment had gone. "If I fail, there will not be anything left of me to save."

Chapter Twenty-Six

Lost Magics

The mist gate snapped shut behind Shalindra the moment she reappeared inside the summoning circle in the wizard's tower, but her thoughts remained in the world she had just left behind.

Mergolath.

To rid her world of demons, she needed to stop a *god.* Mataasrhu had given her the one thing she needed without ever realizing it, but she almost wished he had not.

Enna rushed towards her, only to smack uncomfortably into the invisible barrier of the summoning circle.

"I told you I didn't do it," Verelli snapped, pushing himself away from Fendrick and raising a warning hand.

"Did not do what?" Shalindra asked, stepping over the markings on the floor and out of the circle. "Fendrick, allow him to speak."

"Abandon you in Urtratu," Verelli said, keeping a wary eye on Fendrick. He gestured, dropping the enchanted wards even as he fixed her with a curious eye for passing through them so easily.

"You left it shut too long!" Fendrick growled, fists clenched at his side.

"The portal closed after you went through," Enna explained, inspecting every inch of Shalindra for damage.

Mist gate. Mist. Gate. Why is this so difficult?

Be quiet.

"That is because I closed it," Shalindra told them.

The conversation continued, but her mind struggled to grasp the magnitude of what must be done, and she was left reeling from the sheer impossibility of it.

"How?" Verelli asked. "It is not a door which can be kicked shut. The portal establishes a bond between two locations…"

"…which was never yours to control."

Verelli came up short. "What?"

"You were not the one who opened the mist gate to begin with, though you unknowingly guided where it went. It came out exactly where it should have, but that, too, was not where you intended."

Mergolath.

What hope for her was there? She had expected to discover some demon lord or faction, perhaps even some alliance or breakaway cult within their society, but instead her adversary had been revealed as the one true god of their existence.

"I warned you that the location could be anywhere," Verelli reminded her. "These are normally used in conjunction with a name, drawing the demon to the summoner."

"The demon goes to the summoner," Shalindra corrected. "Not by choice, perhaps, but also not by your command."

Verelli shook his head. "That contradicts hundreds of years of evidence."

Honarch looked as concerned as Enna, though slightly less confused. "You said it was your gate, but if so, why did it not take you where you wanted?"

"When the spell was cast, I saw a line appear from the pendant, like a rope tossed into a well. I used it to guide the direction of my own gate, though where it led, I could not see. I emerged into a large cave, a kind of gathering place, occupied by dozens of demons. They were less than pleased at my arrival, and I closed the mist gate to prevent them from coming here."

"I knew I should've gone first," Fendrick muttered.

"How did you return?" Enna asked.

"In the same manner I found my way there: the necklace."

"I was attempting to summon you back," Verelli said with a sideways glare at Fendrick. "Despite the interruptions."

Shalindra shrugged. "I heard you every time you called, and simply ignored you. I did not need you to find my way back to the summoning focus—I could see it the entire time."

Honarch leaned forward excitedly. "You are the only one who has been tied to its location. The binding isn't about control; it's about sharing information!"

Verelli brushed the thought aside. "Demons who are here operate under our direction. They can relay limited types of information and obey our commands."

"Not at the moment," Fendrick pointed out.

"This line of thinking remains conjecture on your part. There could be other forces of which you were unaware. If this is an open beacon, why are demons not appearing around us?"

"Who says they aren't?" Enna asked. "They seem to be running loose all over the place right now."

Verelli appeared unsettled by that thought and did not refute it.

Shalindra drew his attention. "You said before that wizards would carry the prepared gem with them before it was made into the necklace. Why?"

"There was a certain amount of prestige involved," Verelli answered, "but it also made the attunement easier, just as it did with you."

"That might explain one half but not the other. How did you get the demons' names?"

"I don't know."

"You're lying," Fendrick scoffed.

Verelli looked at him in disdain and waved at Honarch. "Ask him if you don't believe me. Demons are dangerous, and there has always been rigor around the selection process. The knowledge of how to retrieve a name and the ability to summon were never granted to the same wizard."

"He's correct," Honarch said. "Many disciplines are governed by rules and safeguards. In this case, to give a single person the knowledge of both tasks would allow them to summon their own personal horde."

"This is also why no summoner was permitted more than one name," Verelli finished. "Contrary to your opinion of us, we were rigorous in preventing such misuses of power."

Enna broke in. "Almost everyone here has seen a demon open a portal of its own accord. If nothing was actually preventing them from doing so…"

Verelli gritted his teeth. "One can assume that, given enough willpower, the controlled creature is capable of…"

"There is no control," Shalindra said more forcefully, jabbing a finger at the talisman still in Verelli's hand. "That provides a path between the realms, nothing more. If you doubt it, try giving me a command and see if I obey." She held out her hand. "The necklace, please."

Verelli hesitated, then handed it to her. It had to be destroyed, but smashing the others with Shining Moon had released an evil energy. The memory of Mataasrhu destroying one reminded her that there were other ways. She clenched her fist around it. The device felt oddly pliable between her fingers and resisted only a moment before the stone within shattered, leaking black mist from between her fingers.

"That took days of effort!" Verelli cried. "The stone was irreplaceable!"

"It was a door that swings both ways."

"A hypothesis as yet unverified. It could have been studied!"

"Or misused. Or we could have awoken one morning to find ourselves overrun with demons, as did the master of this tower."

Verelli lapsed into sullen silence.

"What of the others?" Honarch asked. "Every summoner was in possession of such a device. If you are correct—and I'm willing to take you at your word, for now—that means that every summoning stone is an open door to our world."

"The ones in the valley!" Enna shouted, her eyes wide in sudden fright.

Birion looked alarmed as well. "Should even one demon appear in Newlmir with you both absent…"

"We may be protected," Honarch said. "All of the summoning stones are locked away in my tower, and given how they reacted to Treven's presence, they were all sealed and warded to the best of my abilities."

"Edward must be warned, regardless," Shalindra said, "as should everyone who has one." She stepped closer to Verelli. "How many wizards had these?"

Verelli hesitated at revealing what must have been a secret, then relented. "Less than a hundred, in total."

Birion cursed. "If that's the case, then an amazing amount of effort was devoted to preventing Shalindra's success during the war."

"Where were they?" Shalindra asked, trying to retain focus on the path forward.

Verelli hesitated again, then shook his head. "I do not know the specifics. We could assume at least one in every major city in Actondel. Many more would have been scattered about Ceringion, but most are clustered around Tythir. A handful would have been… elsewhere."

"And my people?" Enna challenged. "How many did you send into the forests around Ildalarial?"

"I was aware of the broad strategies but not the individual plans," Verelli said with indifference. "I would expect three to five."

I know a few of them that won't be bothering us anymore.

Now is not the time to remind Verelli that I killed his friends.

I don't think he has friends.

"I need to tell this to my brother so he can get the warning out," Shalindra said. "And I will see that word is sent to Ildalarial as well." She looked at Verelli. "You should do the same through any channels you possess. Unproven or not, care must be taken. Kentrick will likely march to Halisford within the next day or so."

"And you intend to remain with him?" Verelli asked.

"We have to go there anyway, regardless of when we choose to depart, or who we are with."

"Ah, speaking of leaving," Honarch said. "What are we supposed to do about that angry mob outside the walls?"

"They were not angry to us," Enna said.

Fendrick shot her a disbelieving look.

"Though they were a bit forceful with their affections," she admitted.

"They also don't incorrectly blame you for the destruction of the city," Verelli said.

"Is there a bolt hole or side gate?" Shalindra asked. "Any way other than out the front?"

Verelli shook his head. "The tunnel was blocked when the tower collapsed."

"I say we just walk out," Fendrick said. "It's past midnight, everyone's tired by now, and if we don't do anything rash they'll hardly notice."

"I've no objection," Honarch said. "I'm eager to be elsewhere."

They all turned to Verelli.

"Give me a few moments to gather my things," the wizard said before hurrying down the steps.

"I'll help speed things along," Honarch said, following him from the room.

Enna glanced at her in concern, but Shalindra doubted that anything was afoot. If the tower had remained undisturbed since its owner's death, it was certain to contain items of value to the two wizards.

The rest of them made their way down the spiral steps to the ground level. Both wizards joined them shortly, each with a travelling bag slung over his shoulder.

"Are we doing as suggested, and just walking out?" Birion asked, peering through the peek-hole in the door.

"At least to the gate," Shalindra said. "We have only two horses."

"We've none," the knight said. "Seemed easier to keep a lower profile coming in."

"Shalindra and Enna should ride," Fendrick said, "in case anything goes sour."

Birion nodded. "A good idea. You and I can keep Verelli and Honarch between us and stay behind the horses, which might shield them from the crowd."

Shalindra looked around for objections but saw none. "We will attempt that."

Birion opened the door and took the lead once more. Shalindra and Enna came next, followed by Honarch and Verelli. Fendrick brought up the rear, as usual. It was dark, probably near dawn judging from the stars, but not as tranquil as she would have liked.

The guards at the gate stirred, and one said something to someone beyond the wall.

"Your Highness," a sleepy Sergeant Burhomm greeted her as they reached the gate, casting a distrustful eye towards Verelli and Honarch. "May I ask where they are going?"

"I am escorting these men from the city, as I promised Lord Ptolney," Shalindra said. "There should be no more cause for concern."

"Should I fetch some irons for you?"

"That will not be necessary," Shalindra said, aware that the crowd was slowly stirring. "We have things well in hand, though if you could point us to the nearest exit from the city, it would be appreciated."

"Fiddler's Gate would be best," he said pointing down the street. "Right at the fountain and then bear left when the road forks. If you'd care to wait, I can have one of the city watch come and show you there."

"She returns!" someone yelled.

Murmured voices began to rise from the crowd as it edged closer to them.

"Thank you for the offer, but I believe all will be happier if we leave as soon as possible."

Burhomm saluted, and Shalindra and Enna mounted as nonchalantly as possible and nudged their horses into motion. Birion and Fendrick flanked both magicians and kept to the side of the horses away from the crowd.

"So we're your prisoners now?" Verelli asked, his voice dripping with scorn.

"Be glad it's working," Birion said under his breath. "Just keep up, and let's get out of here."

The crowd's disquiet swelled quickly as they realized there would be no public humiliation.

"Make them pay!" someone shouted.

"Hang them!"

Shalindra did her best to ignore their protests and increased the pace. For a moment, it seemed the crowd would fall behind, but the jeers and insults being hurled at them were soon replaced by food and rocks.

"Faster," Fendrick growled, pushing those in front of him into a jog.

Enna's shield flashed, deflecting the makeshift missiles, but that seemed only to enrage the crowd further.

"They're using sorcery!"

Shalindra thought to place herself in front of the mob, to give them a target that would allow her friends to escape. Just as she went to turn around, she spied a small hand waving at them from an alley, and did a double take when Weeby stepped out, gesturing frantically. She wheeled towards him, sharply enough that the others had to scramble to catch up. More projectiles rained down as they ducked between the buildings. Weeby was there, holding two bridled but unsaddled horses.

"It's all I could find," he said throwing the reins at them. "I'll meet you at camp."

"What about—?" Shalindra called out, but the halfling had already disappeared through a door.

Honarch and Verelli scrambled onto a mount, and Birion vaulted up behind Fendrick on another.

"Go!" Fendrick shouted as the mob surged into the alley

behind them.

Shalindra kicked her horse to a gallop, and they raced from the city.

Chapter Twenty-Seven

Uncertain Loyalties

Shalindra hoped that their arrival in Halisford, one of the most dependable and loyal fiefdoms in the kingdom, would provide a more welcoming environment for the tired troop. Though the march from Kendenhall had been free of conflict, the constant need to guard against another attack had worn on everyone. Two days out, things had become worse as the road grew thick with people fleeing south. They brought with them tales of destruction and chaos caused by monsters within the city, and Kentrick had dispatched scouts to confirm the claims. Seeing the deeply serious expression on Loren's face as he now galloped towards them, Shalindra could only brace herself for what lay ahead.

"Your Highness," Loren said, coming to stop before Kentrick.

"What news, Ranger?"

"We confirmed the reports of demons within the city. They're still there, as far as we can tell."

Redivers frowned. "You didn't enter to verify?"

"We were refused entry, my lord."

"For what reason?" Kentrick demanded.

"It's difficult to say, Your Highness. They may have discovered who our travelling companions are. There are almost twenty bodies hanging from the walls, all supposedly convicted of practicing magic."

It saddened Shalindra to think that anyone had carried out her father's command. How many of them were Conclave, she wondered, and how many were just unfortunate innocents?

Redivers grew even more worried. "Could it be that even Gyldenholt has turned against us?"

"We'll see about that," Kentrick said. Turning to Shalindra, he added: "Looks like we'll get to deal with some of your demons after all."

He was filled with the bravado and confidence a leader should have, but to Shalindra, who had confronted them more times than she cared to count, it came across as childish. "I would prefer them elsewhere, but if they are within the city, they must be dealt with."

Though they soon spied the massive ramparts of Gyldenholt castle in the distance, it took them several hours to reach the fields beneath its watchful gaze. The walled city was spread along the southern edge of the shallow canyon carved by the Yarrowonli River. An old settlement that predated her family's rise to power by centuries, its bridges were the only way to cross the river for miles in either direction, and the docks along that waterway were the last civilized stop for anyone travelling upriver.

"Set camp here," Kentrick ordered, pointing towards a farmer's field that had already seen the scythe. "We'll take a contingent to the gates and see if they refuse *me* entry."

Redivers assembled the honor guard quickly, calling together almost twenty men from the Legion. Shalindra, uneasy at the haste of it, joined Kentrick as he departed with them. If there were open hostilities, he might need the protection she could provide.

Shouldn't he be taking care of himself by now?

He should be, and he was entirely capable at this point. She should no longer feel obligated to protect him, but it was too late to turn back. The commoners on the road shuffled aside before the banner of Actondel, but the city gate was manned by a complement of house soldiers beneath the red and black standard of Gyldenholt rather than the city watch, and they moved to obstruct the entryway.

"Make way for Prince Kentrick!" Redivers called out, loud enough to be heard by anyone close by.

"Lord Gyldenholt declares that you and your wizards are not welcome here," the captain of the guard shouted back.

"You would stand against the royal house?" Redivers demanded.

"My orders are quite specific on how to treat the usurper," the captain replied. "We don't need you or your wizards."

There was motion along the crenelated wall above them, and Shalindra glanced up. A group of bowmen had taken station along the barrier.

"We can help!" Kentrick yell back in frustration.

"The Duke doesn't want your kind of help, so leave, before you're made to!"

Kentrick just sat there, fuming. "What game do these idiots play at?"

Redivers forced his horse against Kentrick's, turning the mount away. "My Lord, you need to withdraw beyond range of their bows."

Kentrick looked for a moment as if he would not, then yanked the reins around and rode away at a deliberately slow trot.

"This is dangerous country to be trapped in, my lord," Redivers pointed out, staying close beside him. "With the city denied to us, we will find no support for at least two days in any direction. Attaining passage downriver for all of us will be all but impossible."

"Halisford has always been one of the most loyal vassals," Kentrick complained. "I cannot believe this. We will remain here, within sight of his walls, for as long as it takes for him to acknowledge us."

"That can only last a short time, and Gyldenholt knows it," Redivers countered. "The weather grows colder by the day, and we'll have early snows before long. We cannot seize stores from our own people."

Kentrick clenched his fists in frustration. "Where is your wizard?" he asked Shalindra.

"He is no more mine than yours," she reminded him. "I assume that he is where he's supposed to be."

"See if he knows anything about this," Kentrick said.

"I think it improbable, given the time he has been with us, but I will ask."

She agreed to it as much to separate herself from them as to find an answer. Had there been any indication that every city they went to would be this much of a mess, she would never have agreed to travel with him. But she was here, and her memories of the gutted remnants of their temple in Merrywood were strong. Waiting outside the walls now might lead to a similar fate for those inside.

It did not take long to find her friends occupying their usual spot at the edge of the camp. Shalindra dismounted before them. "Lord Gyldenholt has—"

"I can see the bodies from here," Verelli said, his voice cold. "Your lordling made sure they were hung high enough to be visible for miles."

"He was doing as he was told," Shalindra said, though she had given up guessing at anyone's motives. "Some are more willing to take the king at his word."

Birion shook his head. "It pains me to say it, but this begins to resemble the fractured lands of Westholm more than the Kingdom I remember."

"They've gone off a cliff," Fendrick agreed. "Is there no one still sane in this miserable kingdom?"

Verelli directed an accusatory frown at Weeby. "Fine," the halfling said, folding his arms across his chest. "Maybe I left things a bit messier than I should have."

"You had a hand in all this?" Shalindra asked incredulously.

"Here and there. Oh, don't look at me like that. It takes surprisingly little effort to push people in the direction they're already leaning."

Shalindra shook her head. "It is something we can address at a later time. My brother's hands may be tied, but mine are not. Can you get me into the city?"

Weeby considered. "It would have been a lot easier if we hadn't arrived with a small army. I probably can, depending on how tight they're buttoned up. Are you sure they're worth saving?"

"This is not a village in the middle of nowhere. There are thousands of lives at stake, and I will not turn my back on them."

"Well, as I can't get all three hundred of us inside, who goes then?"

After what she had faced in Urtratu, the demon or demons inside would cause her no problems. "I should be able to—"

"No," Enna said, faster than anyone else could. "You're not doing this alone."

"She's right, my lady," Birion chimed in. "You place too much of this burden on yourself, and no matter what your gifts, you will be better off with our help."

"Not Honarch or Verelli," she said. "Given their animosity towards wizards here, I would not risk your lives."

"You will have no objection from me," Verelli said. "They can suffer for all I care."

Honarch's tone was more even, but his demeanor was equally hostile. "It's hard to care about people who do things like this. I, too, have no interest in helping."

"There is no honor in these hangings," Birion agreed, "but Shalindra is right not to blame the population. We saw much the same treatment directed at us in Tythir, years ago."

Honarch's voice softened. "I know you did, but I'll not lift a finger for any lord that orders my death without ever having met me."

This was a worrisome turn, but Shalindra could hardly blame him. Not for the first time, she wished that Eljorn was still with them to smooth such disputes. But they had not seen him or any other monk of Toush since... since they had left Merallin. That was odd enough to be noteworthy, but she had to deal with this problem now.

"The four of us then," Birion said. "Her Highness, Lady Enna, myself and Fendrick."

That was still almost everyone, but Shalindra acquiesced. Despite her fear of endangering them yet again, she was glad that they were coming. She just wished that it did not feel like the wrong thing to do.

* * *

Shalindra jumped, dropping the apple she had just pulled from the merchant's cart, as Weeby appeared out of nowhere behind her.

"That was fun," the halfling said, trying to catch his breath. "I haven't gotten to do that in years."

Enna frowned disapprovingly at him as a trio of the city watch ran through the crowded market, looking for someone. He ducked to retrieve the apple at Shalindra's feet at just the right time to avoid the guards' search. He plucked another from the vendor's cart as he straightened and passed a coin to the man.

"You know," Weeby said, handing one of the apples to Enna, "you two have a lot of trouble getting into your own cities."

"They were never my cities," Shalindra said, almost to herself. "Where are Birion and Fendrick?"

Weeby inclined his head to where the two men approached. Both carried spears and had donned mail and cuirass, a configuration that drew untrusting looks from nearly everyone. Not that the attention she was receiving was any more

353

complimentary. Shalindra doubted that any of them would have been allowed into the city even on a normal day, given how heavily armed and armored they were. She did not know how Weeby had managed to distract *all* the guards at the gate and suspected that she did not want to, but it had made their entry easier.

"Let's go find these beasts," Fendrick said, "before someone else comes looking for us."

"Oh, that part's easy," Weeby declared. "Just follow the smoke."

It was, indeed, that simple. They traversed the city quickly, moving from the southern extent to the east, and drawing closer to the river. A surreal mix of people bustled by, some going about their day as normal while others had everything they owned packed atop wagons as they fled.

The crowds thinned the closer they drew to the columns of smoke rising into the sky. Barricades had been set across the street, and soldiers stood nervously behind the makeshift wall. A hasty platform had been erected and a scorpion mounted atop it, loaded and ready. Every soldier in the city seemed to be there, with some standing atop buildings as lookouts. A sergeant took note of their approach and stepped towards them.

"No more wannabe heroes," the sergeant said, holding up his hands and waving them back.

Shalindra came to a stop. "What do the demons look like?"

"Big and ugly. Now go back to your homes."

"We have faced demons many times and are here to help," she said.

"Look, miss—"

"Princess," she corrected, having no further reason to hide it.

"Ah…"

"Surely you have been informed that His Majesty sent us here for the specific purpose of clearing away wizards and demons." She looked over his shoulder and beyond the barrier. "Do you know where they are now?"

"They, um, haven't moved around much for a couple of days," the sergeant said. "Your Highness."

Shalindra glanced back at Birion. "We'll have to go find them."

"You're going to get yourself killed," the soldier protested.

"Then there is no point to standing in my way," Shalindra said as she drew sword and hammer and began walking.

The sergeant stepped aside.

"Are you joining us?" Fendrick asked Weeby.

"As I've got nothing more intimidating than a brace of knives and my keen wit, I think I'll watch along with everyone else."

Shalindra led them over the barricade and down the empty thoroughfare, stopping at the first cross street. Fendrick and Enna flanked her on either side, and Birion put his back to them and watched the rear.

"Try not to get squished!" Weeby called cheerfully. Fendrick turned to voice some objection, but the halfling had already disappeared into the crowd.

It was good, if unhelpful, advice. Shalindra had no fear for herself from only two demons. But she would have to keep the others safe.

The fenced cliff at the river's edge lay only a short distance ahead, and the damage there was minimal. She turned down a street, and the group followed. It was eerily quiet after the noise outside, and the air was filled with a dank, sulfurous odor that was as unmistakable as it was unpleasant. Everyone listened, searching for any indication of the demons' location. They heard nothing, but signs of the creatures' passing were everywhere: damaged buildings, broken carts, and claw marks that showed their patterns of movement like game trails in the forest.

Every collapsed wall and dark alleyway loomed as a potential ambush, and they moved cautiously past each. She would have welcomed a return of her premonitions, but no ghostly projection emerged from her body to investigate any of the hiding places. Clouds drifted across the late afternoon sun, deepening the shadows.

The sound of shifting stone caused them all to freeze. The thump of heavy footfalls receded into the distance.

"Split up?" Birion asked quietly as silence returned.

"We would be safer together," Shalindra said.

"They've been here longer and can play cat and mouse with us all day," Fendrick pointed out. "I don't care to be walking these streets after dark."

Shalindra relented. "Fendrick and I will continue this direction. Circle back around and move east with us from the next street over. Yell if you see anything."

Birion and Enna turned back the way they had come and disappeared down another street. Shalindra watched them go with a dark sense of foreboding, then turned and continued ahead.

The demons had to be close, but it bothered her that the creatures had chosen to hunker down inside the city. She had never known them to do anything but attack and move on, and this new behavior of seizing territory was troubling.

Birion's warning shout came suddenly, accompanied by a beastly roar. Shalindra spun without hesitation and sprinted towards the sounds of combat. Fendrick lagged behind, his short legs no match for her long strides, but she did not slow. She cut through a narrow walkway, bursting from the far end to find one of the goat-like demons facing down Birion. The demon's grey bulk blocked most of the street, and it towered over the knight. Were it not for Enna's skilled use of her divine defenses, he would surely have been crushed.

Seeing Shalindra's approach, the goat demon turned to flee, but Birion rushed to stab it with his heavy spear. The steel tip drew blood, forcing the demon to pause and drive him back. The knight ducked away from the raking claws even as Enna denied the creature's attack with her shield. The demon spun to retreat, but the delay had been enough.

Shalindra hurtled past Birion and slammed Shining Moon into the demon's back. The metal head cracked bone and pulped muscle, sending the demon to its stomach with an agonized roar. It twisted away with its legs flopping limp, swinging blindly at her with one long arm while the other hurled chunks of stone and wood back at her.

Her shield blocked the missiles with a thought, but behind her, Birion cursed as he was struck by the debris. Shalindra drove her hammer into the closest leg of the demon as it tried to crawl away, and her sword severed the hand reaching for her. The creature's slit-pupiled eyes were wide with fear as she brought Shining Moon crashing into its skull. It shuddered once, then lay still.

Shalindra quickly turned away from it, avoiding any temptation to consume what its death offered.

Enna hurried to Birion, who was wiping blood from his face, but he waved her away. "It stings but is nothing serious," he said.

Before they could ponder their next move, the wall of a nearby building exploded, and a wolf-like creature emerged to make a dash for freedom. Fendrick was ready and sent a steel bolt whistling through the air to thunk solidly into its back with the force of a ballista. The demon stumbled but dove around the corner and onto the main street.

By the time Shalindra reached the road, the demon was barreling towards the crowd behind the barricade.

Shalindra invoked her shield and sent it streaking outward, striking the demon a glancing blow that sent it careening sideways into a house. Masonry went flying as it scrambled onto four legs and launched itself away from her and towards the frightened onlookers. The commander of the guard shouted orders, and his men brought polearms to the ready. The crowd fell back in a panic, suddenly realizing that they had become participants rather than spectators, but could never outrun its charge.

Shalindra caught it first.

Shining Moon carved a silvery arc through the air, striking the demon in the side and sending it to the ground. She was atop it before it could rise, plunging her blade through the thick skull from behind.

The burning scent of its death danced in her nostrils as it flew upwards, awakening an unnatural hunger once more. She stood immersed in it, fighting to suppress the overwhelming urge. She clamped her jaw tightly shut, distracting herself by letting her gaze sweep the silent crowd.

"The Guardian has saved us!"

Shalindra did not see the woman whose voice echoed down the street, but her shout spurred the crowd to action. Soon they were shouting her name, exuberant in their relief.

Shalindra withdrew her sword from the demon's back, wiping it clean out of habit.

I am death. It is all I can do now.

Everyone's good at something.

She climbed off the corpse as Fendrick and Birion joined her.

"Where is Enna?" she asked, a sudden hollow fear gripping her.

"Here," Enna called, emerging from a side street. "I wanted to make sure there wasn't a third."

Something rang false with that explanation, but Shalindra could not focus her thoughts on why. The *hers* were feeling mixed reactions to the victory as well, and an upswelling of conflicting emotions flooded through her. Shalindra turned to her friends but found could not bring herself to meet their eyes.

One day, I will be too slow, and they will die because of my failure.

She waited, but no answer came to contradict her.

"The people rejoice for what you've done," Enna said, sensing her distress. "They can rebuild instead of cowering in fear."

"We should go," Shalindra said, eager to be away from the temptations of the demon's corpse. "I want to get out of the city."

She almost expected Weeby to be waiting for them, but the halfling was nowhere to be seen. The crowd was now chanting her name with such vigor that it was almost impossible to hear anything else.

Birion took the lead as they pushed past the soldiers, who simply stood aside, awestruck. The crowd swarmed around them in a stifling embrace, pressing close as they sought to congratulate or touch Shalindra. She held Shining Moon tight against her stomach, hoping that no one would touch it and unwillingly feel the sting of its displeasure. Her other hand she pressed against Birion's back to keep pace. Enna squeeze tightly against her back, but Shalindra could only hope that Fendrick was still behind them.

Birion tried to take them out the way they had come, but the crowd was too dense, and it was as futile as pushing against a mountain. Shalindra looked about, trying to find a side street or some other way out. The only thing she could focus on through the waving arms was the white-peaked apex of Eluria's temple.

"The temple!" she shouted to Birion, hoping her voice would carry above the noise.

The knight altered course as best he could, forcing his way forward. The refuge they sought could not have been more than a handful of blocks away, but it seemed to take hours to reach it.

The low temple wall was ungated, opening directly onto a broad and welcoming path straight through the gardens. Obstructing that gap was a row of women in white, as what had to be every Sister in the temple stood shoulder to shoulder to form a barrier that the crowd refused to assault. The elderly matriarch of the church stood two steps in front of them, the sternness of her gaze strong enough to repel any who thought to come close.

The Sisters waited, unmoving, as Shalindra's group drew near, then parted just enough to allow them through. The youngest in line was literally a girl, but she stood as resolute as those three times her age. It was a courageous act, and it shamed her to hide behind them. Enna gave her no options, however, continuing to push her with both hands through the garden and up the stairs until the doors of the temple closed solidly behind them.

* * *

Shalindra sat with her head in her hands, alone in the sanctuary. The large room was cool and dark, lit with a soft glow by floating orbs of Enna's creation. A large statue of Eluria watched over the empty room, and the small, circular fountain at its feet provided a pleasing tone. It was as contemplative a space as could be asked for, but despite the pleasant trickle of the fountain and the thickness of the stone walls around her, she could still hear the sounds of the crowd outside.

The various *hers* within her mind took the quiet opportunity to engage in a spirited debate. She paid attention to them in an attempt to distract herself from the misery of her own thoughts, with only moderate success. There were fewer of them now—perhaps only three or four—and each advanced a different claim of how they had arrived here and where they might go next. One was certain they should sneak out of the city and rejoin her brother's forces, while another argued for using her position to demand men and material from Lord Gyldenholt. The loudest, the one who sounded most like herself, insisted that now was the time to sail downriver and leave it all behind.

A commotion came from just outside the room, and the doors cracked open.

"Guardian?"

Shalindra rose and turned to face Enna.

"There are soldiers here who want to take you to see the duke. A lot of soldiers. They claim that your brother is already within the castle."

Before Shalindra could respond, an armored soldier pushed his way into the room over the protests of the elderly Sister Superior, Denella.

"Princess Kataria?" the soldier demanded, ignoring Denella's objections.

Shalindra's anger rose hot at the intrusion. "By what right do you force yourself into this sacred chamber?"

"In the name of Lord Gyldenholt, I—"

"This is my domain," Shalindra cut him off, advancing towards him with hand upon her sword. "You and your master are nothing here, and if you do not leave willingly, I will send you out in pieces." Her threat was delivered with such vitriol that even Enna took a step back.

The soldier raised a hand in protest. "You should not—"

Shalindra's sword was halfway from its scabbard, and she almost wished that he would stand and confront her. This temple was old enough to remember a time when offerings to the moon were made with more than prayers. It had seen blood before.

The soldier began backing away at the same rate of her advance. She stopped the moment his feet were on the steps outside and stood glaring down at him. "You were saying?"

The soldier swallowed. "Lord Gyldenholt requests your presence at his keep. I am here to see that you arrive, ah… safely, given the mob in the streets. His Highness, the Prince, is already on his way."

Shalindra fought to bring her anger under control. Never in her life had she been provoked so easily or responded so aggressively. With deliberate slowness to mask her shaking hand, she forced her sword back where it belonged.

"I think it would be well if His Lordship and I were to meet. If you will allow me a few moments to prepare."

The soldier bowed. "We will await you outside the walls, then." He turned on his heel and retreated, and the soldiers with him followed.

When they were gone, Shalindra turned to Sister Superior Denella. "I am sorry to have forced you to endure these intrusions."

"The acts of a fool are their burden alone," Denella said. "No matter what you choose, Guardian, we will stand by your decision."

Shalindra remembered the young girl included in that commitment. The last thing she wanted was to bring further conflict to this place of peace and risk the lives of those who worshiped here.

"The duke was a reasonable man once and was counted as my father's closest ally," she said. "I cannot believe that he would attempt to harm me in any way, but his recent actions indicate that he might do so to those around me."

"Stay strong in Her light," Denella said. "We will pray for you."

She smiled her thanks, and the old woman took her leave of them.

Shalindra turned back to Enna. "I will be fine," she said, forestalling the argument that was certainly coming, "and so long as no one does anything rash, they will be too."

"I don't care what happens to anyone else," Enna said, a worried expression on her face, "but I care very much what will happen to you."

"Today was trying," Shalindra said. "But you are right, and I promise to be cautious."

Enna did not look convinced. "If you aren't back by sunrise, we're coming to get you."

"A fair bargain," she said. "Keep our Sisters safe, and we will hope that the duke is still a reasonable man."

As Shalindra stepped into the night, she found almost forty horsemen awaiting her. The flickering glow of their torches illuminated both themselves and the still substantial crowd lingering in the streets. It was a less tumultuous gathering than the one that had forced her to shelter here, but her appearance was greeted with enthusiasm.

She mounted a waiting horse, and they rode for the keep with the guardsmen in a tight group around her. After two turns, they were on a wide street that paralleled the river and ran all the way to the castle. They rode through the main gate as expected, but once in the outer bailey, they turned away from the inner gatehouse and made for a secondary entrance likely used for servants and supplies. It was impossible to ignore the similarities to how Verelli had been treated in Merallin, and it did not bode well.

Inside the castle, she was escorted to the main audience hall with the minimum of courtesy.

Lord Gyldenholt stood straight and tall before his mahogany throne, flanked by a complement of soldiers. He was a fit man for his age, his salt and pepper hair and neatly trimmed grey beard enhancing the sternness of his countenance. Kentrick stood in the center of the room a few steps ahead of Redivers and a squad of the Legion. A smattering of advisors and men-at-arms held themselves off to each side. She recognized none among them save the castellan, Lord Imner. The assemblage had the look of armies facing each other on the field, and the tension was thick enough to stifle the air.

Whatever exchange she had interrupted with her entrance had been unpleasant, and both men took a deep breath as they turned to watch her approach.

"I'm relieved you're safe," Kentrick said as she came to stand beside him.

"We all are," Gyldenholt added with much less warmth. "It would have been a shame had I been forced to inform His Majesty that his daughter had been killed by her recklessness."

"And sending a company of riders to accost a temple of unarmed healers was somehow more sensible?" she shot back, in no mood for games.

"As you ignored my orders to remain outside my walls, and then failed to present yourself as courtesy demands, I considered your intentions suspect."

"Why you would challenge our purpose is disturbing," Kentrick said.

"His Majesty's message said you were headed to the border to fight wizards, not to wander through the center of the kingdom and use my city as your private preserve."

"Hunting demons was not our purpose," Shalindra said, "but it is something I am, unfortunately, skilled at doing."

"What you are good at is making His Majesty look like a fool," the duke said, making no effort to hide his disgust. "You stood in this very hall and insulted him before lords and ladies alike, then ran away like a coward rather than face his justice."

And knocked your betrothed's teeth out. Can't forget that.

Shalindra took a deep breath. "An act for which he and I have come to a resolution."

"Of course. Given your attire and the religious zeal you embrace, I almost forgot you were a princess. It's a shame you never learned to act like one."

"We are not here to be chastised by you for perceived wrongs," Kentrick said, bristling at the mocking tones. "You owe at least some courtesy to those who saved your city."

Shalindra noticed that he, intentionally or otherwise, had included himself in that group, and while his meaning was clear, it still bothered her.

"While I might applaud the results of your timely arrival—the coincidence of which I still regard as contrived—I know the true purpose of your incursion. Do not ever expect that I will swear loyalty to either of you."

"It is our king who is owed your allegiance," Kentrick said tersely. "Neither of us wish it to be any different."

"And yet you arrive at my doorstep with not one but two wizards, an elf, and clerics of Eluria, all of which His Majesty demanded we take steps to expel from our holdings. Yes, I know what you truly think to do.”

“What I wish to do is exactly what was stated,” Kentrick said. “Will you refuse us aid and so stand against the crown you swore fealty to?”

The gauntlet was thrown, but it was a risky gambit to publicly force him into such a corner. Gyldenholt was already angry with them, and while Shalindra had no doubt that she could fight her way from the castle, the consequences of that course would be disastrous.

“If I may, my lord,” one of the advisors said, stepping forward from the other side of the chamber. “Might I offer a solution?”

“Sir Jeffrey,” the duke acknowledged him, still glaring at Kentrick.

“It is clear that there is confusion surrounding the Prince’s mission, but his need is apparent, and to turn them away could be misinterpreted as hostility towards the crown at a time when less honorable men speak of rebellion. I was forced to vacate one of my homes due to the appearance of these monsters. As the estate was saved from destruction through their efforts, I would be willing to offer it to Their Highnesses for the time they are here, so long as we have their parole that there will be no magic done.”

It was a deft maneuver, one that provided a way out for both sides. Gyldenholt could refuse to support them without having to publicly turn them away, and Kentrick would be treated with the respect he deserved without having to force the duke into submission.

“You are most kind, Sir Jeffrey,” Kentrick said quickly, recognizing the opportunity, “and we would be pleased to accept your hospitality."

Gyldenholt grudgingly agreed. "As always, Sir Jeffrey, your suggestion is well considered. If Their Highnesses are in agreement, I will not object."

* * *

Jeffrey escorted them personally to his home, though they took a circuitous route to get there as Shalindra insisted on retrieving her friends from the temple first.

Despite the late hour, neither Enna, Birion, nor Fendrick were asleep, though they all were in need of rest. The crowd had almost completely dispersed, much to her relief, and the group's exit from the temple compound was far more sedate than their arrival.

Their destination proved to be a three-story manor on the eastern end of the city. Ivy climbed its way up the brick walls, and numerous balconies promised a pleasant view downriver. The estate was a good distance from the site where the demons had been vanquished, and while it might have been threatened, it showed no signs of ever having been vacated.

"I hope that this will meet your needs," Jeffrey said as they passed through the wrought iron gates.

"It will be the grandest place we have stayed since leaving Merallin," Kentrick complemented him.

"Given that you are travelling with wizards, may I assume that you do not agree with His Majesty's decree that they should be exterminated?"

"I would be the last to support that," Shalindra said. "While more than one has sought my life, others have risked theirs to defend it."

Jeffrey's relief was apparent. "It is good to hear you say such things, and, in truth, it is good that you have come here. We had begun to wonder if the king's attentions were too far afield to send help."

"His Majesty cares for all his subjects," Kentrick said.

"I've always found magic to be fascinating, though I've absolutely no talent for it," Jeffrey said as they dismounted in front of the house. "One of my closest friends is hanging from a yardarm outside the walls right now. Our dear duke may have blindly obeyed your father in ordering their executions, but he made enemies in the process. You should know that you have many allies in this city, my lord, should you need them."

He was practically offering to instigate a rebellion in Kentrick's name, but if her brother recognized it, he gave no sign.

"Actondel is always appreciative of our friends," he said, following Jeffrey inside. "Hopefully, we can put such disagreements behind us soon."

"Can you tell us how these demons came to be here?" Shalindra asked.

"There were actually three that appeared. Master Rogan, one of three members of the Conclave who had taken residence here, died trying to keep them at bay. He bought time for at least some of the people around him to escape. He had been sequestered in his tower with another wizard—I do not know his name, unfortunately—since the murders began. They succeeded in killing one of the demons, and the remaining beasts drove everyone away. Both devils seemed content to stay put after that, and no one here had the courage to displace them."

"The demons made no attempts to escape?" Shalindra asked.

Jeffrey shook his head. "None. They were there for almost two weeks. Just made themselves a little nest and settled in to wait for who knows what. They would wander about every now and again, but they never left the territory they had established."

It was strange behavior, but the mystery was yet another one she could solve later, if ever. Every city and town in which they had stopped had yielded nothing more than intrigues and uncertainty. While dispatching demons could be considered a part of her duty as Guardian, solving the politics of Actondel was most certainly not, and the divide between those two goals was becoming wider by the day.

* * *

Standing on a balcony of Jeffrey's manor, Shalindra's view over the river to the fields and farms of the northern pastures was beautiful beneath the rays of sunlight that blazed through the clouds. Unfortunately, the home was downwind from the carnage of the day before, and the smell was atrocious. Almost as unpleasant was the argument Shalindra was engaged in.

"Why are you still here?" Enna demanded for at least the third time.

It was the question Shalindra had wrestled with all night, and she still could not produce a satisfactory answer. This time, however, Enna would not relent.

"How many more times do you need to save your family's kingdom?"

"You sound like you do not want it saved."

"What I want is for you to achieve what you're meant to," Enna replied, undeterred. "These demons may be your destined enemy, but nothing more than bad luck has placed you against the handful that we've faced."

Shalindra recognized the truth of it, but it remained a bitter pill to swallow. To leave would mean abandoning her brother to the predations of disloyal fiefdoms and a simmering uprising.

You've been fighting this for too long.

I cannot abandon my family.

You've known this was coming, one way or another, and you made your choice a long time ago.

She closed her eyes and swallowed her regrets. Her fear of this day had, indeed, colored many of her decisions. Sooner or later, as everyone kept telling her, she would have to start acting like who she was, not who she wanted to be.

"You are right," she admitted. "Everyone is right. If I am to do something about these demons, it will not be accomplished here in Actondel."

Enna blinked, as if waiting for another excuse to follow that admission. "I don't know if I should be happy that you've come to your senses or scared at where we must go. Do we have to stay with Verelli?"

Shalindra managed a half grin. "So Fendrick is trustworthy now?"

"Mostly, but you're avoiding the question. Honarch is not my closest friend, but he's proved reliable and even honorable over the years. We don't need another wizard."

"I do not know," Shalindra admitted, "but he has remained true to his word, and I shall continue to do the same."

Enna pursed her lips, clearly ready to continue the debate. "Will you tell everyone else?" she asked instead.

"I will," Shalindra answered. "Now, I think, so that it will not drag out any longer than it already has."

It was not difficult to assemble the group, as they were all present at the manor. She brought them together on a downstairs patio, where hopefully none of the staff would overhear.

"I intend to leave for Tythir as soon as possible, without my brother's army," she told them. It was a simple statement that seemed almost anticlimactic once voiced.

"I'm relieved you've reached that decision," Verelli said, "though I am aware of how difficult it must have been."

"None of you must come with me," Shalindra said. "You have all done so much more than was ever required."

It was Birion who answered. "I believe, Your Highness, that we are all coming with you."

Shalindra looked at each of their faces in turn but saw no signs of doubt or disagreement.

"I must thank you, though it seems insufficient. How soon can we leave?"

Everyone turned to Weeby.

"That would be where I come in," the halfling said. "Again. I can certainly get us down the river without all the attention an army attracts. I'll be able to find someone in a day or two, so I'd make yourself ready to go quickly."

"What about your brother?" Enna asked.

"I will tell him now," Shalindra said.

She left them and made her way upstairs to the lord's suite that

Kentrick had been given. As she approached, she was surprised to hear raised voices coming from the other side of the door. They quieted at Shalindra's knock.

"Enter," Kentrick said.

She pushed open the door and was greeted by unhappy expressions from Redivers and her brother.

"What has happened?" she asked.

Kentrick made a face and waved disgustedly at a tiny roll of paper on the desk. "These just arrived from Eugeron. The elves have violated the truce they so desperately wanted."

Shalindra looked to Redivers, who nodded. "They seem to have taken notice of the fact that we've stripped our garrisons in the west and sent everything east once more. It is not outright war, but they have forced a number of villages west of the Merallin River to disband."

She retrieved the missive and scanned quickly. "This says that only a handful of villages have been displaced."

"A handful can become a flood very rapidly," Redivers warned. "It will be impossible to respond this year without stripping Merallin of its defenses. No matter our choice, this will erode our position even more and give further fuel to the fires of rebellion."

"We must act," Kentrick said. "Our family sacrificed heavily to spare them, and now they betray us at the first opportunity. I doubt the ink is fully dried on the treaty. Is there no one with honor left to us? I'm willing to turn everything west, and not stop until their nation is no more."

"Lord Ptolney's troops will leave us," Redivers cautioned. "Switching direction again will cost us the backing of even more."

Shalindra put a hand to her head. Why would they do such a thing, and why now of all times? "We cannot allow a minor transgression to pull us from our task."

"Minor?" Kentrick scoffed. "That's our land they steal! Families driven from their homes on the eve of winter. When father hears of this, he may well try to call up the entire army again, and this time I will support it. I begin to think Logian was right in his assessment of your friends."

Shalindra tried desperately to muster an argument that would not ring hollow. Elothlirial had to be behind this, or at least party to it. She controlled the elvish calontier and the church. But what could be done? Shalindra could not fly back to Ildalarial and attempt to reason with them, and she had no way to send a message fast enough.

Or did she?

"The elves have been doing this for years," she said, "and they have never turned it into a full invasion. Will you at least allow me the chance to nip this in the bud?"

"The only thing that should be cut is our ties with these backstabbers," Kentrick said in disgust, then looked to Redivers. "But I'm angry enough to know I need a second opinion."

"If there is any way to stop this, it might be wise to allow her the chance, Your Highness. Even were His Majesty to command it, there is no way to get ourselves to the western border in less than a month. Should we change course back and forth, we will only be continuing the pattern of uncertain decision making which has gotten us to this point. Reclaiming our lands from demons and traitors is where our efforts are best focused."

Kentrick grudgingly agreed. "I don't know what you hope to accomplish but remember your promise not to use magic. Regardless of your success, I will not forget their betrayal."

* * *

Shalindra retreated to her room and fastened the latch securely once inside. The idea that had come to her was almost impossible, but if there was even the slightest chance of preventing full-scale war between Enna's people and hers, she would take it. Enna's prayers for her brother had established a connection between Enna and herself, if only for the briefest of moments. It had been an involuntary response, a subconscious reaction over which Shalindra had no control. But if she *could* control it…

Timing would be critical. The attempt had to occur during the evening invocations, when Elothlirial was certain to be praying to her goddess, and when there was some hope that Shalindra could locate that specific prayer within the untold multitudes of voices. It was daunting, but the fate of more than one kingdom could ride on her ability to stop this incursion from continuing.

And so, she sat at the edge of her bed, waiting.

As twilight slipped towards night, Shalindra felt it was time. She rose and stepped onto the balcony, directing her eyes away from river and farmland and up towards the sky. The brightest stars were just beginning to appear, but the half moon was hidden somewhere behind the building she occupied.

With a nervous breath, she allowed the protective sphere encircling her to slowly contract. The deep blues of the heavens shifted to a deeper purple, consuming the light of the stars. Streaks of crimson and orange flickered across the dome of the sky as the other reality melted it away, sinking towards her as if she dangled above a pot beginning to boil over. It was unsettling in its vastness, this ocean of visible sound which swirled and churned in a dazzling display. Shalindra's determination wavered as she confronted the chaotic nature of the place she needed to go, but it was the only option left to her.

She brought that other realm down, to the point it began to eat away at first the edges of the horizon and then the trees. A wave of vertigo swept over her as the stability of the real world faded further away. Stretching her hand upwards, she sought to touch it. Her equilibrium lurched uncontrollably, and she stumbled like a drunkard. Unable to right herself, she forced her barrier outwards once more, driving the otherworld away until the real one filled her vision.

Frustrated, she returned to the bed and sat, waiting for her body to readjust. This had to be done, or events might spiral well past the point of no return. If she was unable to bring that realm of prayers to her, she would have to take herself to it.

She closed her eyes and withdrew into herself. Within the bounds of her mind, she stood there whole, anchored to Tormjere's focus. Orbiting around her were the other *hers*, manifested as incorporeal duplicates of what could have been and harbingers of what might yet be. Surrounding them all was the same protective sphere shielding them from the cosmic wind of light and sound careening around in chaotically unpredictable directions.

Using Tormjere's focus as an anchor, she allowed her awareness to drift closer to that boundary. It yielded as she pressed against it, but she hesitated, unsure if she could reach through without rupturing her defenses like a soap bubble.

But it was a risk she would have to take. Steeling herself, she sank into it like a child testing the cold waters of the ocean with her toes.

When nothing untoward happened, she moved deeper, allowing her head and torso to slide through. Immediately, she was deluged by multicolored streaks of tangible light that buffeted her with the speed of their passing. Each one that came close enough to be examined hummed with sound, and some were sufficiently strong enough to become images, visions of what was happening in and around the Sister who had uttered the prayer. There were thousands, perhaps millions of these events, each so brief that Shalindra could not grasp them no matter how hard she tried.

Frustrated by her inability to affect even a single prayer, she attempted to channel the flow around her, like guiding the water in a creek by placing stones for it to run through. This achieved part of what she desired, funneling some of the prayers in a predictable direction. She caught one, though again the physicality of the action seemed more a metaphorical reference for what actually transpired. It penetrated her arm, and she witnessed the need within: a deep cut in a man's arm that gushed blood at a desperate rate. The injured arm and the Sister's hands that held it were rendered in shades of white across Shalindra's vision. Their appendages were all she could see of the two people, but the plea carried commitment and conviction, illuminating the injury in the most intimate detail.

Shalindra allowed her knowledge to flow into the requestor, guiding the woman's efforts as she gave of her own fortitude to close the wound and restore the damage done. Her connection ended with the last words of the prayer, but Shalindra's assumption was validated. Yet there was only one of her for a seemingly infinite number of prayers to answer, and she dared not linger in the instability of this place.

She needed to find a single voice amongst the multitude, one that was familiar as well as disliked: Elothlirial. She had touched that mind, in anger more than compassion, but it had given her a signature as unique as any key.

To the funnel of prayers, she added a new construct: a lock. One which matched the pattern of thoughts specific to the mind she sought. No sooner was it complete that a prayer streamed through—only one.

Shalindra flung herself at it, though such physical reactions were merely a manipulation of the unreality she was creating. Her thoughts wrapped around it with desperate force, and then she was standing beside Elothlirial as the elvish priestess led the evening prayer within the Glade of Worship in Ildalarial. The cavernous clearing and all its congregation was rendered as a backdrop layered in shades of white on white. Elothlirial's eyes snapped open at her mental touch, and Shalindra plunged into them.

~ This assault should never have been allowed ~

Elothlirial lurched to the side midsentence as if struck, staggering into the Sister beside her. Those around her rushed to her aid, but they could do nothing to save her from what she was to endure.

~ See now what you have wrought ~

Shalindra called upon memories of a future that had been

shown to her that night on the mountain so long ago and sent them flowing into the elf. The trees and people around them melted away as all of Ildalarial burned. Into those flames was Elothlirial flung, a witness to the death and destruction enveloping everything she held dear, and at the center of the conflagration rose the hideous visage of a demon.

Elothlirial collapsed to the ground, screaming denials. It was a vision that the elvish matriarch would never forget, but Shalindra could not trust that she would share the message.

So she did it herself.

Shalindra pulled towards her the other prayers that travelled close to Elothlirial's, hoping that their juxtaposition within the funnel of Shalindra's mind equated to physical proximity in the real world. Those pleas sought solace and salvation, mercy and forgiveness, but Shalindra supplied none of it. Her response was formed of images from a life she remembered but which was never hers, scenes of violence and death spread across a hellish landscape blasted by rock and sand. By her will, they felt the pain of claw and lash, the rending of their bodies by torture and torment. Every horror that Tormjere had hidden from her, she forced them to endure, and she did not relent. The elvish clerics had to understand the disaster facing them before they unwillingly ensured the demon's victory.

Throughout the glade, elves crumpled beneath the overwhelming onslaught to their senses. Shalindra reveled in the justice of it, the soothing balm of their terror washing away the pain and hopelessness of her own loss, a pain which she had buried so deeply that it had almost been forgotten.

Amidst the horrified shrieks, one scream cut through loudly enough to cause her distress. It rose above the others in Shalindra's awareness, a sound arriving not as a supplication from far away, but through the ears of her physical being.

Enna.

Something was wrong.

Shalindra abandoned the elvish prayers with harsh abruptness, casting them aside as she flew back into herself. As she rejoined her body, she was already racing into the hall, covering the distance to Enna's room at a full sprint. She took the impact with the door on her shoulder, not slowing as the portal crashed open.

Enna was on the floor, wedged tightly into a corner, every muscle straining as if she could force herself through the solid walls at her back. Violent spasms wracked her small body, and her fingers clawed mindlessly at her face, leaving streaks of scarlet beneath eyes that were wide and white, staring unseeing as her mouth twisted itself around the terrible shrieks that issued from it.

Shalindra slid to her knees and clutched Enna to her breast, pinning her arms so she could do no further damage to herself. "You are fine, Enna. I am here. You are safe. It was only a glimpse of what could be." She stroked Enna's hair as if she was comforting a child, murmuring soothing words.

A surprised gasp came from behind, and she knew without looking that Fendrick and Birion stood at the doorway, sharing a meaningful look at the twisted hinges that left the door hanging askew.

In time, Enna's breathing slowed, and she ran a trembling hand over her face, smearing blood across her pale cheeks. "It… I was dying, over and over."

"A vision, nothing more," Shalindra whispered.

"It was so real. Did you see it as well?"

"Yes," Shalindra lied.

"What… what was it?"

"A warning, I believe—a vision of what could come," Shalindra said, her face burning with guilt.

"We have angered our goddess."

Shalindra held her tighter. "It will be made right. We must believe that."

She shuddered, aghast at what she had done. To manipulate so many so easily… What damage had she just inflicted? Terrified of this thing she was becoming, she leaned her head against Enna's shoulder and wept. She could not continue floundering in the dark, hurting those she cared for the most.

It was time for answers.

Chapter Twenty-Eight

What Was Meant to Be

Shalindra stood once more in the beautifully pure white amphitheater. It was arranged exactly as she had seen it before—the curving, terraced steps, the columns rising into the mist, the marble-edged pool occupying the stage—and it carried an air of familiarity that had been lacking on her first visit. She walked alongside the raised pool, letting her fingers trail along the polished marble rim. This time, its waters were not filled with stars or planets. Now it revealed glimpses of different places, locations she had never visited and never imagined might exist. Forests, deserts, castles, farms, all flickered before her eyes in a constantly shifting parade of motion.

A solitary figure in white awaited her at the end of the pool. Slender and supple, she stood with grace and poise that would have shamed the finest noblewoman. The elongated points of her ears peeked through hair as white as fresh snow and as fine as silk, though they betrayed something other than elvish heritage. Her skin was pale and her robes so light and airy they seemed to float about her rather than hang from her frame. Yet it was her eyes that betrayed her true nature: black as night and filled with just as many stars, and with large irises which revealed the slender white crescent of the waning moon. For all her regality, she appeared tired and lacking the vitality that she should normally have enjoyed.

"Are you well?" Shalindra asked.

Eluria smiled at the question, but there was no mirth to be found in her star-filled eyes. "The same could I ask of you."

The subtle hints of wariness in that answer were surprising. "I continue to do what I must, though not always in the manner in which it should be done."

"You show wisdom in that admission. The rapidity of the change you endured was as unexpected as it was unprecedented, and there is much for which you were unprepared. But you are not speaking in abstractions and refer specifically to your most recent experience."

Shalindra was not surprised that Eluria knew of it, but could not decide if that was worthy of concern. "I worry at what I have done by attempting to communicate with others as you have spoken to me. I fear I have again caused more harm than good."

The corners of Eluria's delicate mouth turned upwards. "And that was an astounding feat. Know that it had the desired effect, even as it affected desires which should have lain undisturbed."

If that was supposed to make her feel any better, it did not. Shalindra doubted she would ever be able to forget the look on Enna's face. "I wanted to be yours, to devote myself to the wonderous art of healing. It was with reluctance that I accepted the idea that I was worthy of being a Guardian, and I assumed that mantle only out of necessity. But I did not want this.”

“Such was not our design either.”

Shalindra cared little for what anyone had wanted. None of that mattered now. “Am I to believe that you did not intend for this to happen? You, whose hand played such a part in its instigation?”

“Beliefs may obscure facts, but they never alter them. The circumstances of your Ascension were unplanned but, once begun, I knew this is what you would become.”

“And what am I becoming?” she demanded. “The same monster you wish me to slay?”

Eluria’s eyes flickered with panic, but her words were calm. “Your future holds many possibilities, but repeating Mergolath’s failings is not one of them.”

“How can you say that with such certainty?” Shalindra asked. “How can you know the future?”

“What is the future but a probability of what has yet to happen?” Eluria replied. She raised her left hand, and an apple materialized in her open palm. With a casual motion, she tossed it into the air above her head. As the fruit reached the apex of its trajectory, it froze, suspended in a stillness that encompassed everything around them, as if they were occupying a single moment in time. “Where will the apple land?”

The answer was obvious, even if Eluria’s purpose was not. “In your hand.”

“You expect this because experience tells you that an object thrown straight up will fall straight down. Your skin tells you there is not enough wind to alter its trajectory, nor enough motion in the floor to alter mine. You suppose that, based upon my demeanor and the way in which I hold my body, I will catch it rather than allow it to strike the ground, yes?"

"Of course."

Time began to flow once more, allowing the apple to drop into her hand.

"Expand your consciousness from this one simple act. Travel beyond what you see with your eyes and hear with your ears, and listen to all of what you are being told."

Eluria's hand passed over the pool, and beneath it the water rippled with hundreds if not thousands of images. The goddess brought herself closer, wrapping her slender fingers around Shalindra's own.

"Close your eyes, and follow."

Shalindra did, falling beside Eluria into her own consciousness. She saw her awareness as the jumbled, poorly ordered place that it was, an inelegant construct where she had sought to bring structure and reason to a mind which was always a moment's doubt away from buckling under the strain of managing far more than it was capable of understanding. Tormjere's focus lay centered in her true self, and it was from here that she and Eluria began. Shalindra wished to linger near its comfort, but their thoughts flowed away after the briefest of acknowledgements, instead travelling out towards the wall separating herself from the chaotic stream of voices and prayers. Shalindra experienced a return of her fear of that place, and of what she had done in it, but Eluria's voice was soothing.

"An admirable defense. I had wondered at how you managed

to remain sane, and much does this explain. Yet a barrier works both ways, and you fear only what you do not understand. Come."

Eluria drew her through the membrane, but this time it was not the chaotic realm it had once been. Eluria plucked passing prayers from the air as they sped by, holding them for inspection. The goddess' grip on her hand remained, yet Eluria was everywhere even as she was nowhere.

"Look more closely."

Shalindra did. The goddess did not catch the prayers so much as choose to exist where they would appear. Eluria went from one to the next so quickly that there seemed to be more than one of her, and indeed there were. And Shalindra understood. She did not need fewer of herself, as she had been trying to accomplish for so long—she needed more.

"Do not resist this change."

Shalindra released her fear, no longer repressing the urge to separate into multiple versions of herself. She felt Eluria's reassuring touch, guiding her as she became two, and then four, and next eight. She continued dividing herself into so many that she stopped counting. It was disconcerting to think about, but it felt… right, like an instrument put into tune.

A pattern began to emerge, rippling energies that ebbed and flowed between her and those voices like waves on the ocean.

Eluria's voice carried softly to her. "What do they ask for?"

"Some wish for health, others aid. Some are in pain, some attempt to remove pain from others. Many offer only thanks."

"Allow them their answer."

Shalindra was puzzled at first, but then she remembered the

moment during Alta Amalia when she had given to the woman praying, and she did the same once more. Again, and again and again she answered, feeling the joy of each Sister as her prayers were answered, and experiencing their relief at the pain they had removed, and the injuries they restored.

Shalindra opened her eyes, returning them both to where they stood in the amphitheater, and looked at Eluria in surprise. "Am I answering them, or are you?"

"Of that I am unsure, but I suspect that we both are. The situation we have placed ourselves in is unique."

"Every prayer cannot be answered, can it?"

"No. Compared to a mortal, our energy appears without end, yet a million scratches can bleed a woman dry, and our powers remain finite."

"Is that what this is, power?"

"In a way. Your language, and indeed your entire method of thinking, lacks the means to describe what you now possess. A wolf can never comprehend the construction of the bridge he walks across, but that does not prevent him from using it to his advantage. As such, you are free to choose whatever word you wish, or even invent a new one. 'Power' is as close a concept as any."

Eluria's explanation made sense, almost as if Shalindra had already known it somehow, but it was mildly vexing not to receive a more impressive answer. She regarded the prayers swirling around them once more.

"Can I grant them other than what they ask for?"

Eluria hesitated. "No, though we are also under no obligation to give them anything. Not every prayer is worth answering. What they receive may be different than what they expected, but not different than what they wanted."

"But we could tell them to do things."

"Perhaps, but not as you attempted. We do not control mortals as one would a puppet on a string. We influence. We suggest. We punish and we reward. These actions manifest as the nuances of the material world, but in the end, your choices are your own, and even we must react accordingly."

Shalindra thought through her past, examining her interactions with Eluria in a new light, and at times from a different perspective. She could not believe that this would have been done to someone so completely unprepared, and those doubts gave voice to the question in her heart.

"I was not your first choice for Guardian."

"Shalindralia was first to call herself my Guardian, and you are aware of those who have ascended before you. In each, I hoped to find no need of another."

It was a half-answer that avoided her question. "I was not your first choice *this time*, was I?"

Eluria's starry eyes seemed to stare deep inside her. "You were not."

That begged another question, one which had burned inside of her for a long time. It was not wise to ask, but she had to know. "Was he?"

Eluria disengaged her hand and regarded the pool. "The role of Valtilaniar is no longer relevant, and you would do well to put such questions aside. Time on the scale that we operate in has a different meaning than upon your world, and what seems a rapid series of events to us has stretched across generations for you. We have all walked many roads to get to where we are, and still there remains a mountain before us."

"What, then, was different about Tormjere?" Shalindra pressed. "You aided him time and again, and yet he never worshiped you."

"No," Eluria smiled, "he worshiped you."

Shalindra raised a skeptical eyebrow. "Thinking of several arguments that we had, I would dispute that."

"And what did you disagree upon? Did he ever protest your intent, or only the manner in which you sought to accomplish it?"

"I cannot judge what, if anything, I have truly accomplished. Tell me, then, what task did you want me to complete as your Guardian? I feel as if I am being asked to finish another's plan without knowing how it should appear once done."

Eluria looked down at the pool once more, and the images within changed, keeping in time with her answer like notes from a song. "The assault upon your world has taken neither the form we had anticipated nor arrived at the location we sought to guide it towards. The gateway which was opened in a capital city has resulted in uncontrolled devastation. We preferred somewhere different. A place far from civilization. A place where I was strong and could better influence events."

"The valley of the Three Sisters."

"Yes. Together with Lithandris, I led our people to these shores so long ago that the legends of those trials have faded from memory. Through their struggles, they cleansed the land of its fouler inhabitants and nurtured the life that existed there. Did you ever wonder why the woods of your kingdom were so free of the fouler beasts which stalk the mountains to the west? Or why the lands that humans occupied were so ready for home and plow?"

The scale and scope of what she described was staggering. "Thousands of years of history, all by your design?"

"Not everything went as desired, but as the time of Mergolath's assault onto this world grew near, the conditions in the place where we wished it to arrive were almost perfect. Rugged, cold lands that would hinder beings more suited to heat, isolated from civilizations that could be enslaved, and free of lesser species that would be subjugated. And around them, no easy escape. In one direction, plains devoid of food to sustain them. In the other, a narrow pass blocked by a fortified city which Amalthee had spent generations establishing, stocked with warriors who followed Hestag's call to battle. Below lay the elves, the most faithful to my cause and whose blades would be blessed with the might I could supply. All that was needed was a Guardian and someone to open the gate."

"The wizards."

"*A* wizard. One who possessed the strength to make the attempt and the weakness to fail. One with a proud and often cruel master, who already possessed both the tools and the desire to use them for his own ends. A man who was willing to kill for what he wanted." Eluria's moon-shaped eyes turned to Shalindra in wonder. "And then he met you."

"You mean Honarch? I did not meet him until…"

Kirchmont. With Father Gelid.

That was not right. She had first met Honarch as they fled back to Tythir after renouncing her title as Princess of Actondel.

Shalindra pushed Tormjere's memory of the earlier meeting back where it belonged within his focus, but Eluria gave her no time to rectify her own confusion.

"And when faced with his choice, your friend's loyalty overrode his desires for self-advancement, and while he took possession of the key, he never learned of the name that his master already knew. Amalthee had sacrificed her most precious artifact to draw them there, and so she was forced to seek another way to pass on that critical information."

"Tormjere."

"He possessed a willingness to do anything for those he cared for, and his gifts were extraordinary. It was thought that the two men would share that secret, as they had shared so many others. But he did not tell Honarch the name, nor was it revealed to any other, and when he used his knowledge to bargain for your freedom, again he did not do as expected. He offered the demon Mataasrhu a choice. One that, inexplicably, was accepted."

"I… He just wanted to save me."

These were all *his* memories, not hers. She was entrusted with them, but no matter how many times she viewed them or how many she was forced to consume, she would never think of them any other way.

Eluria seemed almost bemused at her confusion. "Saving you was all he ever wanted. The only thing he ever asked for. But while knowing how you have arrived here may soothe your sorrows, it does not alter the reality we face. Our fears are realized, for the demons are here, and they are spurred to action by prophecies of their own. They have cast off the yoke that never existed and roam unabated in your world."

"And you are weakened because of what Tormjere took for me during the ceremony."

"You are what I so desperately needed you to be, no matter the path you took to get here."

"And where does it lead? I searched where Alharania bade me go, and it is the demon goddess who drives them to attack my world. Thus, it is she who must be stopped. You want me to kill Mergolath."

"This is unfortunate, but yes. It was she who slew Vanirus, brother of Amalthee and Keeper of All Wisdom. She was forced to take up his mantle and now writes in his book. It is a loss that haunts us to this day."

"I cannot do it," Shalindra said in dismay. "I can barely keep myself together much less confront another god. Every time I have used this… power it has caused as much harm as good. I do not have enough of it to face another god."

"No, you do not."

The confirmation was disheartening, no matter how true it was. Yet there was too much at stake to simply give up. Tormjere never had, and though it could not have been intended, his efforts on her behalf offered another possibility, one that was not entirely dependent on direct conflict.

"What if Mergolath could be weakened in the same way you were?"

Eluria considered before responding. "There is merit to that idea, but it is a gambit fraught with peril. Are you certain you wish to make that choice? To achieve it will require you to go far beyond who you wished to be. Are you willing to do so?"

Every Guardian before her had faced such a challenge, and their answers were immortalized in the statues which stood in Ildalarial. Tormjere had not flinched from his destiny. How could she do any less and remain worthy of their legacies?

"I am."

"Time still exists for you to prepare, for such plans must be constructed piece by piece. Seek first to constrain the demons on your world, or they will continue to wage war on our followers. Mergolath is well aware of who opposes her, and without the faithful, we will wither like a plant without water. What strength you can gather must be preserved."

"I strive towards their gate in Tythir and mean to close it."

"You must move more quickly. We are already within the final battle." Eluria placed a hand on her arm. "I know it was ever your desire for peace, but I must ask you to be the warrior whom all your people require."

"And the prayers of the faithful?" Shalindra asked. "Should I fulfill them?"

"You cannot respond to every plea for aid, for every answer carries a cost. Their praise and their love can restore us as we so desperately need, and so you must give them some hope and become my voice where I cannot speak."

"I will," Shalindra promised.

"Do not seek me here again, for even this exchange is taxing. When you at last stand where you were meant to, I shall come, and together we will seek our victory."

Chapter Twenty-Nine

Never an Easy Road

Shalindra returned to herself, her arms still wrapped around Enna. The room in Jeffery's manor seemed somehow smaller and of less consequence than it had moments before. Everything had been easier with Eluria beside her, guiding her immature flailings and giving direction to her desires. But that level of attention was denied to her once more.

Until I stand where I was meant to.

What damage would they suffer by following her into the demon realm? Could she even risk telling them what lay ahead?

They'll never believe the gods are fighting.

But Enna deserved to know something, if anyone did. Shalindra could not keep secrets from them forever.

She rose, pulling Enna gently to her feet.

"Enna, I know the meaning of the visions we were shown."

Enna put a hand to her cheek, wincing as her fingers brushed over the scratches there.

Shalindra placed her hand tenderly atop those bloody trails.

She had ultimately been the one to inflict them, and it was upon her to see them repaired. Enna's green eyes met hers eagerly, open and accepting. Shalindra travelled through them, seeking out every hurt and restoring every pain with a thought, leaving her friend's cheeks smooth and unblemished. Enna's mind lay open and inviting, almost begging Shalindra to seek anything within that she might desire. She withdrew quickly, unable to face the adoration in Enna's eyes.

"I sought Eluria once more, and this time she answered."

"You spoke to Her?" Enna asked, her words an excited rush.

"Yes. For now, my task is simply to deny the demons' access to our world, and that means continuing to Tythir and closing the gate."

"And after?" Enna asked, never satisfied with half an explanation.

The sound of hurried footsteps preceded Kentrick's rapid entrance. "What happened? Sister Enna, are you unharmed?"

"I am," Enna said, embarrassed by the attention. "Thank you."

Shalindra glanced at the still open door, but Birion was a step ahead of her. He bowed as he and Fendrick withdrew, pulling it shut as best he could.

Shalindra turned to Kentrick. "I believe that the recent misunderstanding with the elves is resolved."

"In only a few hours?" Kentrick asked suspiciously. "What did you do?"

"I did nothing," she said, trying to think of a way to explain it without revealing her role.

"Our Mistress made Her will known," Enna answered. "There

can be no doubt of Her desires in this matter, and I can assure you that all in Ildalarial will take heed of Her warning."

"I'm relieved, I think," Kentrick said, "though it stretches belief. Eugeron should be able to send word in a few days if this… event was successful. If so, we'll continue towards the Small Sea."

Shalindra winced. "Kentrick, I am leaving tomorrow."

Her brother was stunned. "Shalindra, I… If my words earlier were too strong, please forgive me. Nothing that we do seems to alter the slide of our kingdom into the abyss, and I truly fear that our house is on the brink of collapse."

The apology and worry in his voice was heartbreaking, and his assumption of fault rendered him more a man and less her little brother than she had ever realized. "I know, and that is not the reason. I have spoken with my goddess, and my path is clear. I must reach Tythir, and I cannot wait on armies to march there."

"How are we supposed to win against these creatures without you?"

"I want nothing more than to remain with you and drive these demons away, but for every one that we kill, a hundred more may take its place. If we have any hope of truly ending this, it will take a more decisive action." She stepped close to her brother. "Kentrick, you know I would not abandon you unless the need was great."

"Why now?" His question was more suspicious than it should have been.

"Because I have delayed long enough, and it is time to deal with these demons before it is too late, for all of us."

"They've shown up everywhere, including here."

"But the bulk of them are in Tythir. Those which have appeared here arise from the summoning focus carried by individual wizards."

"Maybe your wizard just wants his own kingdom saved instead of ours."

"This is not about kingdoms anymore. An open gate cannot be allowed to stand, and so I must go."

Kentrick shook his head. "It's not like I could stop you, and I should be grateful for what you've done already. What am I to do when we find another of these monsters?"

"You need magic, and that means you need to put a stop to this order to hang every wizard walking about. You heard what Jeffrey said: not every lord agrees with it, and some seem willing to openly oppose it. You would also do well to gain the support of the temples of Eluria. Enna and I are only two people, and we cannot be everywhere."

"I'll do what I can, but it's hard to contradict a king." He sighed. "I envy you, in many ways. I wish that I could run from such responsibilities and learn what freedom really felt like."

"So do I," Shalindra said. "But I am not fleeing from what must be done; I am running towards it."

Chapter Thirty

Across the Small Sea

The wide, cold waters of the Yarrowonli River carried their boat swiftly downriver as it wound its way steadily east. The vessel, a single masted river runner with a shallow draft, had taken Weeby almost an entire day to hire. As Shalindra shifted her feet to avoid breaking through a rotting section of the deck, she wondered if they could have built a sounder boat in the same amount of time.

The captain, a scrawny and weathered man named Cabot, was in only slightly better condition that his ship, and she considered that it would be a minor miracle if any of them survived the trip. Nevertheless, it was large enough to accommodate the entire group and the four sailors reasonably well, and, most importantly, Cabot had been willing to carry the wizards.

While the river had expedited their travel, it had been anything but empty. An almost continuous stream of boats had been slowly travelling the opposite direction, tacking against the wind. It was an unfavorable time of year to do so, which made the situation all the more unusual.

It was a relief to now be within sight of the fortress city of Braunton, three days after leaving her brother. Even more of a relief was that she did not arrive beneath a royal banner or at the head of a column of soldiers. There would be no state dinners, or speeches, or anything else to slow them down this time. The open horizon of the Small Sea beckoned her from the far side of the city, promising an escape from the obligations of family and kingdom.

Rather than standing atop a hill or defensible escarpment, the city had been planted on the lowest ground to be had for miles. It was unique among Kingdom cities for its wall, massive bulwarks that stood sixty feet high and half as wide, and which encircled almost the entire city. Though it lacked a proper castle, every tower and bastion set along the wall could have fulfilled that role. It was a remnant of a different era, when armies numbering in the tens of thousands fought at the frontier of a vast empire. Both that empire and its armies had faded centuries ago, but Braunton still endured.

The ship limped into the docks, which were overrun with a frenzy of activity as unseasonable as the coldness of the air.

Weeby motioned Shalindra closer to the bow, away from captain and crew. "Would you still like me to find another boat?"

"You've asked Cabot's price to cross the Small Sea already, I assume?"

The halfling looked as if he had swallowed something unpleasant. "He asked for sixty silver ships. I could almost buy our own boat for that, if I could find one."

"Do you think you can?" she asked, taking in the activity in the harbor around them.

Weeby began to answer with his typical flair, then seemed to deflate. "No. I've never seen it like this. We should've had our pick from dozens, but there's not an empty vessel in sight, and they're all packed with people instead of goods. I think if we set foot off this floating shipwreck, we'll never be able to get back on it or anything else."

Shalindra fished the coins from her purse. "Here is the price, plus another ten to see if you can fix anything within a day. I would prefer not to sink in the middle of the Small Sea."

"I always enjoy working with royalty," Weeby said with a grin as he accepted the coins. "I'll see what I can do."

"Everyone else can stay," Enna said, joining their conversation, "but I've got to get off this thing before it sinks. Can we visit our temple? I see it just there."

"And risk the ship not being here?" Shalindra asked.

"We could be there and back before nightfall," Enna insisted. "Not everyone has to go."

She made a good point, and Eluria had said that Shalindra would need to be her voice. This might be a good opportunity to do so.

"We could do that, so long as we are quick." She called Birion and Fendrick over to explain what she and Enna were going to do. "Just make sure the boat doesn't leave without us."

"It may leave without the current owner," Birion rumbled, "but I guarantee it will not depart without the two of you on it."

As soon as the boat was moored, she and Enna disembarked. Even without banners, people began to take notice of her almost the moment she set foot on the docks.

"How do they know me?" Shalindra asked.

"Given all that you have done, how could they not?"

"I do not want to run from another mob."

"Then acknowledge them," Enna said. "Accept what they offer and let them see your strength."

Shalindra considered those to be wise words, ones that echoed what she had been taught as a girl-princess so long ago. Confidence and the appearance of purpose could mask many frailties. So she did not shirk from the stares. She smiled to those who stopped and pointed, and she thanked them when they stepped aside. It felt as if she was accumulating just as many followers as in Halisford, but their mood was more curious than angry.

Something else about the situation was out of place, but she had difficulty putting her finger on it. She surveyed the crowds of people, a veritable throng of motion and color as different cultures…

"Have you seen any followers of Toush recently?" she asked.

Enna fixed her with one of her is-this-really-necessary looks, but a more thoughtful expression filtered through as she looked around. "No. I can't say when the last time I saw one of them was."

"Eljorn is the last I can remember."

"It's strange that they are not here helping," Enna admitted, "but we should keep moving so we can make it back to the boat well before sundown."

She was correct as always, so Shalindra set aside the mystery and hurried on to the temple.

The building was constructed in the familiar style, but it opened directly onto the street, set back only by a set of stairs rather than nestled behind serene gardens.

Inside, they found perhaps twenty Sisters in white robes kneeling together in the sanctuary. The Sister Superior, a trim, dark haired woman not much older than Shalindra, was speaking to them on the need for continued faith, but she stopped midsentence as they entered. Every head turned in their direction, then the women rose in excitement and rushed to greet her.

A sharp clap brought their eager chatter to silence, and they parted to allow the Sister Superior through.

"You must forgive us our enthusiasm, Guardian," she said. "Eluria could not have answered our prayers any more clearly. I am Tess, Sister Superior of this temple."

"What did you ask of Eluria?" Shalindra asked.

Nervous whispers arose from the Sisters, but Tess was open with her answer: "Our faith has been greatly tested of late. First, our prayers ceased to produce results. We took this in stride and examined our faith as we were meant to. Then, just days ago, some of us were granted a vision."

"It was terrifying," one of the younger women blurted, then looked down in embarrassment.

"Yes, it was," Shalindra said. "But know that it was a warning of what could come, not what is guaranteed. There is still time to avoid that future."

Tess looked relieved. "We have prayed for guidance as fervently as we might every day since the vision, and I can only view your arrival as the answer we sought."

"Have you seen any success with your restorations?" Shalindra asked, not wishing to remain the center of attention.

"We continue to tend to the injured as best we can, but we are constrained without Her aid. There are many who now turn away from us in favor of more reliable help from Amalthee or a common mediturgeon."

"Not to interrupt," Enna said from the door, "but we have a situation outside."

Shalindra and Tess joined her in looking outside and saw that the small number of people who had followed Shalindra there had grown considerably. The curious had been displaced by the desperate, and the crowd was growing unruly.

"If we were to leave by a different way," Enna began, "perhaps they would—"

"No," Shalindra said. "I will stand in front of our Sisters, not behind."

She walked out the door with her head high and stopped at the top of the steps.

"Why won't you heal us?" someone called out.

"Their god has abandoned them!"

Their voices were agitated, on the verge of anger and recrimination.

Shalindra raised her hands for calm. "Eluria has not left us. I stand here before you as her Guardian. Now is not the time to ask of our goddess what we are capable of doing for ourselves."

"She has forsaken us!" another yelled.

The proclamation was greeted with murmurs of confirmation.

"When the sun is hidden by the clouds, do you fear it is gone forever?" Shalindra asked.

The crowd seemed to deflate as her words resonated.

"It is by the blessings of Eluria that we have enjoyed such ready access to her restorative gifts," Shalindra continued, "but now is a time when we are all threatened. Much of her energy is being spent to keep us safe."

"Wicked devils are destroying the Reginum!" someone shouted. It was a confirmation of her argument, but one that steered the crowd more towards fear than calm.

"Yes," she replied, meeting their fright head on. "There is foul business to the east, and that it where I will make it stay."

A smattering of applause greeted that declaration, but few would be satisfied with words alone. She had a plan, however, and could only hope that it would work as she wished.

"Who among you is truly in need, not with an inconvenience, but with an actual debilitation?"

The crowd quieted, each perhaps concerned at being judged greedy by their peers for asking. Shalindra's gaze swept over them, searching for her volunteer, but none seemed willing to raise their hand.

"Here!" came a shout from the side. "His arm's broke!"

"Come forward," Shalindra said.

After a shove from behind, the man did, cradling one arm with the other. "It's not that bad," he said, clearly embarrassed at being singled out. "I can just rest it for a spell."

Enna moved to attend, but Shalindra motioned her back. They would both be gone tomorrow, and for this to work, it had to be one of the resident Sisters who healed him. Shalindra's eyes fell on the young woman who had spoken out of turn earlier, and she beckoned her closer.

"Have you mended arms before?"

"Yes," the woman whispered, "but I haven't been able to for weeks."

"Have faith that she will answer you today," Shalindra said.

The woman took the injured arm in her hands and inspected it gently. She took a deep breath and spoke her prayer.

Shalindra listened for the request within herself, and allowed it in. Silvery blue light slid across the fractured arm, guiding the restorative gift given by the cleric as she repaired the damage.

"It's healed!" the man exclaimed, holding up his arm.

The crowd reacted far more strongly than Shalindra would have expected. Restorations were not everyday occurrences for the average person but were still common enough to not be unusual.

"Not every wound is grievous enough to require such attention," Shalindra cautioned. "Not every prayer will be answered. Know that we fight for you, and that this struggle may occupy more of our attention than we would prefer. Above all, pray for your goddess. In aiding her, so you will aid yourself. If there are any of you who are truly in need, come forward, and we will tend to you as we are able. May Her light watch over you."

Shalindra turned away from the crowd and reentered the temple. They needed the signal to know that this event was over and that they should return to their lives.

She found Tess already directing the other Sisters on the most orderly way to deal with the anticipated influx of patients.

"I am sorry that I spoke for you," Shalindra said to her.

"Nonsense. Your directions were proper and far more eloquently stated than I could have managed. Thank you for that, Guardian. Will you stay here tonight?"

"I would like nothing more, but our journey requires haste, and we must return to our ship before sunset. We will remain here just long enough to ensure that everything remains orderly."

While Enna helped the Sisters with the injured who were beginning to trickle in, Shalindra removed herself to a side chamber, allowing herself a quiet moment to ponder her problem. She could not lift her Sisters' spirits by granting their restorations now only to dash their hopes when she left, but how would she deal with it when she was no longer here?

She needed to be in two different places, doing two different tasks at the same time. It was something she had accomplished before entirely by accident, but Eluria had shown her that it could be done. Cautiously, Shalindra allowed a fractional piece of her awareness to separate. It was like creating another *her*, but different from the others—one no longer bound to a past which could have been. This one was as real as she was, and her purpose could be commanded in the same manner as Shalindra's own thoughts. To this new her, Shalindra assigned only one purpose: to evaluate incoming prayers for restoration and grant or deny them as appropriate.

She watched it for a time, afraid that it would permit too many, that the Sisters would be allowed to take too much. There proved no reason to worry. She had not created a new being or delegated the task to a hired hand; it was still her making the decisions, simply in a manner which did not require continuous attention from her prime consciousness.

Shalindra returned to herself, brushing against Tormjere's focus to ensure that her awareness was properly centered.

Satisfied that she had indeed accomplished something here, she and Enna took their leave through the rear of the compound, avoiding the modest crowd that still lingered in front of the temple.

They were almost back to the docks when she caught sight of Verelli hovering near a shop, waiting for them.

"A rousing speech," he said as they drew near.

"You would have preferred I told them something different?" Shalindra asked, allowing annoyance to mask her surprise at finding him there. It was bad enough when Weeby showed up unexpectedly.

A smile graced his blocky features, and for once it was not mocking. "Not at all. You quelled a rising panic while at the same time bolstering your own cause. I do not follow your god, but I can understand why you were chosen to be the symbol that you are."

"And the Conclave tried to kill me because of it." It was an unfair, if truthful, jab. He had given her a compliment in his own way, and it was unbecoming for her to be petty with her replies. Surprisingly, he ignored the slight.

"That was kind of you not to blame me directly. In hindsight, that choice seems to have been the wrong decision, though it was made for reasons no less noble than those that drive your actions now. If we manage to live through this, I may even tell you why."

Chapter Thirty-One

Unlikely Friends

Their ship was listing heavily to starboard as it limped into the sprawling port city of Gramaria, situated at the eastern point of the Small Sea. Sunlight blazed across the wet, snowy rooftops, causing them to shine and sparkle in stark contrast to the dark grey of the sky beyond. Everything aboard their ship was just as wet as the city, and ironically made even soggier as the sun melted the snow and ice deposited by the storm. Yet the breeze across the water was biting, leaving all aboard shivering at its touch.

Everyone but Shalindra.

Her armor had already shed every vestige of moisture, and she was no more cold than she had been atop the Ironspike Mountains. She accepted it now as she had then, though she wished she had dry clothing to offer to those less fortunate.

At least it was almost over. The ripped sail flapping impotently in the breeze was hampering their speed, and she almost wondered if she could make better time swimming to shore and dragging the boat behind her.

Footsteps on the soggy planks signaled someone's approach from behind. From the drowned rat smell, she knew it to be Cabot.

"This'll be as a far as we go," he said without preamble.

"You were paid to take us farther downriver," she pointed out.

Cabot spit over the rail, an action that drew an unhappy rumble from Birion. "That was before the gods decided to crack the hull and shred my sail. It's a miracle we're not at the bottom of the sea. I'll spend every copper you've given tryin' to fix up enough to get home before the real snows hit. I'll not be wanting to walk all the way around the Small Sea with the rest of the refugees, no matter how much coin you've got."

Shalindra was willing to dispute the matter, even to the point of commandeering the vessel, but Weeby caught her attention from behind Cabot's back. He waved the captain's argument aside and winked. She had no idea what he might have planned, but it was clear that his designs did not require Cabot or his boat.

"Then we will find more reliable assistance elsewhere," she said. "Weeby will instruct you on where to let us off."

Cabot smirked, until she added: "And how much of our commission is due back to us."

The captain looked ready to argue until Birion folded his arms across his chest and glared sternly down at him. Cabot slunk away, muttering to himself.

When the ship reached the docks, the group disembarked and gathered at the end of the pier. The docks looked and smelled like any other Shalindra had visited, but their scale was enormous.

"Himerius' tower is missing," Weeby observed.

Verelli nodded but said nothing.

"Well, staring at the sky won't get us anywhere," Fendrick said. "Where to first?"

"The home of Master Rydevan," Verelli said, pointing to a tower banded with jade and silver accents. "Assuming he's still here, he will be able to provide us a clear picture of what is happening."

"Best to do so quickly," Birion said, eyeing the groups of people beginning to take notice of Shalindra, "or we'll be wading through crowds again."

Shalindra had hoped to leave that element of their travels behind, but she could not deny that she was the one causing the stir.

Weeby led them away from the water, and they were soon travelling wide thoroughfares that cut jagged paths through the city. Graceful towers and multi-storied mansions rose above the rooftops of the common buildings in numbers too large to enumerate. Shutters were thrown open as the clouds dissipated, and the streets steadily filled with activity despite the chill in the air.

They arrived at a small, gated compound, and Weeby pushed his way inside without hesitation. Inside the walls, a trio of smaller buildings were crammed together. An ornate, tapering spire rose from between them, needle thin at the base with a bulbous segment occupying the top.

The door to that tower opened at their approach, revealing an older man with a long beard and longer robes of bright blues and greens. The silken garments were arranged in diagonal patterns with rich embroidery at the edges, marking him as a man of both wealth and magic. His greeting to Verelli was guarded.

"Which of you is the captive?" he asked.

"We seem to be prisoners of each other, at the moment," Verelli responded.

A disbelieving smile split the wizard's face. "I was first to say it could not be done, and you proved me wrong for the thousandth time. One of these days I shall cease doubting you. Come in, come in."

Weeby entered last, unable to hide his grin. Rydevan frowned, then moved to a cabinet and withdrew a small pouch, which he tossed to the halfling. Weeby caught it with a clink of coins, then glanced at Enna, and his smirk grew wider.

Rydevan rolled his eyes and threw a second pouch, this time at the halfling instead of to him.

"Little swindler," Rydevan complained to Verelli. "I swear, he's worse than you."

Verelli laughed. The display of mirth was so out of character that Shalindra shared a surprised glance with Enna.

"It's good to be back," Verelli said. "I can't tell you how thankful I am that you're still here. How stands the Reginum?"

Rydevan gave an inquiring glance at the group.

"They're all coming with me," Verelli said. "You may speak plainly."

"Then I think we should all sit down," Rydevan said gravely. "I have nothing good to convey."

Servants appeared to take their kit, handling the assortment of weapons and armor as if they dealt with such implements every day. Shalindra politely retained her weapons, then the group followed Rydevan across the base of the tower to a sitting room that must have been in one of the adjoining buildings. It was an opulent but still cozy space, one of darkly polished wood and muted fabrics. Matching campaign chairs that likely dated from the time of the Three Empires flanked the small fireplace, and couches faced each other in front of it. In place of a tapestry, the long wall was hung with shelves, each displaying a bewildering array of implements and devices crafted in metal and glass. Rydevan waved them to the seats but remained standing.

"Things have gone from bad to worse since you left," he said. "Everyone capable of holding a spear or drawing a bow is being conscripted and sent east while the small people flee the opposite direction. A few dozen men on horseback could mount an effective assault on any city west of here, so thinly are they garrisoned." He waved a hand as if throwing sand into the wind. "It's a disorganized mess."

Shalindra doubted that anyone in Actondel was in position to reclaim their lands right now no matter how easily it could be managed, though more than one lord would likely have used such knowledge to expand their holdings.

"Our Conclave?" Verelli asked.

"Decimated," Rydevan said, his shoulders sagging. "Not one member in three is accounted for. Anyone with the requisite talent has joined the containment efforts, the others have been sheltered as possible."

"How contained are the demons?" Weeby asked.

"Reasonably, but they constrain their own activities far more than we do. Avalta is the closest anyone has gotten to Tythir in a

412

month."

"That's fifty miles upriver from the coast," Weeby supplied helpfully to the others.

"I should explain these things better for our guests," Rydevan acknowledged. "That distance holds true in every direction, even from the ocean. No one can get within sight of Tythir."

"Have the demons appeared anywhere else?" Shalindra asked.

"They've appeared everywhere else," Rydevan answered, "but only in twos and threes, thankfully." He looked back to Verelli. "Your missive regarding their connection of these events to the summoning focuses seems to have been validated, and measures were taken to secure any which were yet unaffected. It seems to have helped."

Rydevan paused, as if waiting for Verelli to speak, but he sat quietly, his thoughts far away. "Your decision was the correct one," Rydevan said kindly. "You would not have changed this outcome had you stayed."

"The question is whether it is too late to change it now," Verelli said, shaking off his musings. "How quickly can you get us to Avalta?"

"You know the protocols better than any of us. We have a ship ready to sail on a day's notice, possibly faster, should you wish it."

Verelli turned to Shalindra. "I'd like to take tomorrow to rest and prepare. Given how long it has taken to get this far, another day will not hurt anything."

"We could all put the time to good use," she agreed.

"My home is yours, of course," Rydevan said. "I do not often entertain so many guests, but I will see to your accommodations."

* * *

Shalindra stood on the balcony that evening, watching the moonlight skim across the surface of the Small Sea. It was difficult to imagine a world more upside down than current circumstances made it appear. Her childhood desire to follow Eluria had been a dream of hope and healing, but no matter what choices she had made, it had turned into a journey of death and destruction. As had happened in the cave on the demon's world, it seemed her destiny as Guardian was to be one of revenge more than restoration. And every one of her friends was following her down a path that was only going to become more violent.

She forced her attentions away from such thoughts and turned inward, seeking the comforting reassurance of Tormjere's focus. The edges of it were now blurred like the outlines of trees in the morning mist. Whether it was a good thing or not was still open to debate.

Some things aren't good nor bad, they just are.

I prefer them to be good.

"Still contemplating how to save the world?"

She turned to see Enna entering the room they shared. "I used to stand on a balcony such as this when I was a girl and dream of being Eluria's cleric." She sighed. "There is much I would give to return to those simpler times."

"As would we all," Enna said. "But you were thinking of something more specific, weren't you?"

Shalindra reached for some way to avoid the honest answer, but it escaped anyway. "Yes."

Enna waited expectantly.

"I was thinking about taking the mist gate to the demon realm." It was factual enough, for a misdirection. Thankfully, Enna's attention went to the gate Shalindra had already been through rather than the one which lay ahead.

Enna shivered. "It terrified us when you disappeared. Even Verelli, though I think he feared for his own neck as much as yours."

Shalindra smiled, but it faded quickly as she was reminded of what she had done there. The silence grew long.

"First Tormjere, then Fendrick, and now you," Enna said with a shake of her head. "Why does no one want to talk about that place?"

"There is nothing that I care to remember, even though I must. As dangerous as the creatures who reside there are, I am concerned that I might pose a greater danger to you all."

It felt good to say those words, to admit to her greatest fear, but Enna stood bewildered.

"How could you consider yourself a danger to any of us?"

"How can I not? The things that I am capable of doing..."

Enna came closer. "Tell me what is giving you such doubts. You're keeping far too many things locked inside. You may be our Guardian, but not every burden is yours alone."

Maybe she did need to let some of it out. Tormjere had kept his thoughts and feelings hidden deep inside, never sharing, and she had been doing the same.

But what could she say? What good would it do to describe the demons she had killed, or the bargain she had made?

"To have such power..., it is a double-edged sword, and I

understand why Tormjere tried to put it in his past."

Enna took Shalindra's hands in hers. "I offered to listen when he needed it, and though I would hope you'd never feel you required such encouragement, still I would remind you that I am here."

Enna's touch was comforting, an invitation to surrender just a fraction of the burden she held. Sometimes, that friendly presence was all that was needed.

"When I emerged into the demon realm, I arrived in some type of gathering place for the creatures. They were ready for me, and one attacked even before I had fully emerged from the gate. I killed it, and the two behind it, purely by instinct. I was halfway through the cave before I even realized what I was doing."

"When we are afraid, we react," Enna said. "You did what you needed to in order to survive."

"No, I was not fearful. The demons were, and some sought to flee rather than fight. I made certain that they could not."

Shalindra found her hands trembling and withdrew them from Enna's as she turned away. "It was easy, Enna. There were probably forty demons, as large or larger than we struggled against during the war, but I was not fighting for my life; they were fighting for theirs." Her hands gripped the stone railing of the balcony, squeezing until a fracture snapped across its surface. "I do not want to be the warrior that Tormjere was, and I do not want to be Eluria. I only wish to be me."

"You will always be you," Enna said, but there was a quiver in her voice that contradicted those words, no matter how much she tried to mask it.

It had been a mistake to say anything, for now they both held doubts. She would add nothing further about her bargain with the demon Mataasrhu or what she had been shown by Eluria. They truly were her burdens, for no one else was prepared to deal with such significances. She forced a smile onto her face. "You are right, and I should not worry. There will be plenty of problems for us to deal with without me adding imaginary ones to the pile."

"You are Guardian because you deserved to be," Enna said, embracing her. "No matter how much you struggle, anyone else would be doing far worse."

It was probably true, but it did not make it any better.

Chapter Thirty-Two

An Interrupted Journey

Shalindra watched the sun break the distant horizon, a brief blaze of brilliant reds and oranges slicing between the featurelessly white sky and the snow-covered ground. The brightness and color were gone almost as quickly as they had appeared, fading into the clouds blanketing the world. Their last view of clear skies had been all the way back in Gramaria, a factor that had lent a level of depression to the entire trip.

The boat Rydevan had furnished for them was expertly crewed, speeding them down the Haliestos River without pause. The waterway which spilled from the eastern tip of the Small Sea was wide and deep, and carved a path through the heart of the Ceringion Reginum. The same distance that had taken weeks to traverse from Merallin to Braunton had flown by in a matter of days. The ship had passed so many cities, and often at night, that she had barely had time to take them in.

As they neared Avalta, she studied the city in the half-light of the cloudy dawn. It was old, an early outpost of an expanding empire and one founded hundreds of years before the discovery of the route now known as the Gold Road. Its architecture was carried from a different land, eschewing natural stone and wood for whitewashed walls and fired clay tile roofs. A defensive wall had once ringed the city, but while it had stood unbroken against any number of foes, it was powerless against the relentless growth of the population over the centuries. An endless sea of structures stretched across the flat countryside, each grown to the height of the other like trees in a forest. Amphitheaters and arenas, statues and monuments, and temples of unrecognized denomination rose above the level of the common buildings to flaunt their magnificence. Nowhere among the rooftops could she find the familiar white marble of any temple dedicated to the moon.

Under different circumstances, Shalindra could have spent weeks exploring the newness of the place, but now she intended to be gone as soon as possible. Verelli planned to present their letters of reference to whoever currently ruled, secure the supplies they needed, and then make all haste to Tythir.

It was approaching noon when the group stepped off the ship, their destination the compact, largely rectangular fortress perched atop the raised central plateau near the center of the city. Though the rocky protuberance on which it stood lifted the fortification high above the city, the more mundane structures below would have easily eclipsed its height were they placed on equal footing. The most common of their edifices were decorated with elaborately carved stonework, and Shalindra marveled at municipal buildings whose grand scale rivaled that of any palace or keep in Actondel. Despite the seemingly impossible number of structures, the streets remained broad and the plazas spacious.

And everywhere there were people.

They moved about by the thousands on foot and by cart, some slow and others fast, like a hive of bees who had lost their singular purpose. Shalindra was thankful that Weeby, once more, knew his way. They passed streets that stretched like unbroken canyons for half a mile or more before arriving at another intersection. Every square and plaza contained a statue or fountain, and often both. The first floor of most buildings was given over to some kind of shop, and the aroma of stews, bread, and fish filled the streets. Exotic fabrics draped the open windows of tailors, and all manner of goods were available for sale, as if the entire city was a gigantic market. And Tythir was said to be even larger. Shalindra could only imagine the grandeur they would find in the capital city.

But for all the glory there were signs of distress everywhere. At least one shop in four was shuttered. There were as many people wandering listlessly past the vendors as there were buying, and on every corner in poor sections and rich alike, there were the despondent, sitting with a hand out for help.

Of the many buildings that had caught her eye, the church of Amalthee was one of the most striking for both its size and contrarian architecture, and Shalindra was thankful that their route carried them past the imposing grey stone edifice. A pair of soaring, squared towers dominated the front face, and the high arched ceiling of the rectangular church was lined on either side with flying buttresses to support its weight. Every visible piece of its construction was carved and ornamented, an undeniable monument to the goddess of knowledge. A library of only slightly smaller stature stood beside it. Familiar banners of deep blue hung from the towers and flanked the oaken doors, but Shalindra slowed as she spotted similar blue sashes draped across the chests of the guards who stood aside that threshold. Honarch noticed as well.

"Treven?" Shalindra asked him.

He nodded. "I can think of no other who would warrant those guards. We need to see him."

"We do," Shalindra agreed, unwilling to bypass telling one of Tormjere's closest friends of what had happened.

"Weeby and I can continue to the fort," Verelli said. "I will make certain that they anticipate your arrival. You should attract less attention here than in Actondel. However, parts of this city are just as unsavory as any in your homeland. Do be careful."

Weeby's eyes sparkled. "If you get lost, just tell them you're a member of the Conclave and need to reach the fort."

"I'll go ahead with Verelli," Fendrick said, surprising everyone. "You need to see the priest more than I do," he said in response to her look. "I'll just be a distraction."

She did not understand his meaning but accepted his choice. "We will meet you there when we are done then."

The group began to separate, each half heading in their chosen direction.

"Wait," Fendrick's voice stopped her. "Tell him he was right about..." He searched for the words, then glanced around in sudden embarrassment.

"I will," Shalindra promised, wondering if there was anyone Treven had ever met whose life he had not altered for the better.

She drew stares as she crossed the plaza with Enna, Honarch

and Birion, but those reactions had more to do with her armor than who and what she was. The absence of adulation in this foreign land was freeing, and the most normal she had felt in a long time. The doors of the cathedral opened as they approached, but it was not the guards who addressed them. Talley, the young acolyte who had visited the valley of the Three Sisters with Treven the prior summer, awaited them.

"Welcome," he said with a bow. "The Legitarso asked that I await your arrival. Please, follow me."

"How did you know we were coming?" Shalindra asked.

"Father Treven knows many things," he said. "But we also spied you walking through the square. There is an excellent view from the balconies near the top, particularly when the sun is out."

"What brings the Legitarso here?" Honarch asked as they turned down a hall into one of the towers and began climbing a circling set of stairs.

"I think that Father Treven should be the one to tell you," was all Talley said.

Shalindra's stomach churned with every step. Honarch would likely assume the burden of telling Treven of Tormjere's death, but how would she explain the depths of his sacrifice? If anyone in this world deserved to know, it was Treven.

They found the Legitarso of Amalthee, appropriately, in a library. The blind priest sat in a comfortable chair close to the fireplace while an acolyte read aloud from an ancient tome nearby. Treven looked somehow wiser, if that were possible in such a short span of time, but his sandy hair and ready smile were as youthful as the last time they had been together. The acolyte paused at their approach, and Talley announced them.

Treven rose, his hand finding Talley's arm for guidance. "It is good to see you all once more, though I feel that the news you bring would be best relayed in more private surroundings."

"You know," Shalindra said in surprise, before she could stop herself.

Treven turned back to the chair he had been sitting in and reached towards the small table beside it. The surface was bare, but his hand gripped something unseen before depositing the invisible object in his battered haversack. "The world is filled with information, sometimes more than we wish to learn."

* * *

Shalindra's retelling was long. She had spoken without reservation, as she always did around Treven, and related far more of the circumstances around Tormjere's death and her subsequent struggles than she had intended. But it felt good to have someone willing to listen without trying to fix things or offer advice. Apart from the two of them, only Honarch remained, with Birion and Enna long since excusing themselves to allow them their time alone with Treven.

Treven sat quietly in thought, his fingers turning a crude knife in a battered sheath back and forth, exploring every edge and scrape as if it were a divining stone. The knife she had— No, *Tormjere* had given him, long ago.

"An incredible journey," he said at last, his already soft voice further dampened by the deep mahogany walls, "though I still held out hope for a different ending. I owe him everything. He taught me so much, though he never knew it." He grinned. "Or maybe

423

he did. He was more aware of the consequences of his actions than anyone I have ever known."

"He always seemed to know what he was doing," Shalindra said.

"I can hear in your voice that it was not an easy past to revisit, and it's unlikely that your trials will become any more gentle." His milky white eyes sought hers. "Thank you for telling me."

It had been less difficult to speak of it this time than any other. Rather than reviving her sadness, it had only left her weary.

"My own route to here was more sedate but no less interesting. As fate would have it, we stayed in Kirchmont only a short time after returning from your valley. It has been requested that I make an appearance in Rappastall for years now, but something always managed to delay it. Now seemed as good a time as any to make the pilgrimage. The journey was straightforward but lengthy: travel downriver to Tythir and take a ship across the Mardrian Sea back to the island of my birth. But, as with so many people, our lives were interrupted by the incursion that now threatens all of us. Amalthee watched over us, for had we not decided to accept an extended invitation here, we would have been in Tythir when it happened."

"That delay is a blessing to us all," Shalindra agreed. "Would it not be safer to return to Kirchmont?"

"While we are not a militant order and do not produce warriors such as yourself, we can still devote ourselves to better understanding the threat. It is curious that, in all my research, Amalthee remains vague about the demons. Clearly, She sees a different role for us in this conflict."

Treven returned the knife to his ever-present haversack and replaced it from within with the invisible Book of Amalthee. His hand moved through the empty air as if he was opening the tome and turning the pages. "I tend to pass my time reading, as you might imagine. Sometimes, my investigations are related to a specific question or area of expertise; at others I simply peruse what She is willing to share with me, trusting that it might be of use some day."

He looked up suddenly, his sightless eyes locking onto hers as accurately as if he could still see. "What do you see when you look at the Book?"

Shalindra stared at the space between his hands. "I do not see anything."

Treven made a curious sound and seemed to derive some insight from that. "One of the things that caught my attention quite by accident was a passage about friendship."

Shalindra blinked, caught off guard by the shift in context.

"In the time of our greatest need, those willing to stand beside us are often the most critical to our success."

Treven closed the Book and returned his gaze to her. "I believe that is intended to be a message, but, if so, I pray you understand its meaning far better than I."

Shalindra did understand, or at least she thought she might. It seemed a clear sign that she would need her friends with her at the end, but only increased her worry at how to keep them alive.

"You have given me much to think on, as always," she said. "I wish that I had brought more comforting news." She paused, wanting to say something that would make sense of all that had happened, but Treven's calm smile said that he already understood.

She rose to leave, but Honarch remained in his seat.

"I'll be along later," he said, his voice betraying more emotion than she had ever heard from him. "You don't need to wait."

* * *

A light snow was falling as they wound their way up the side of the escarpment, riding horses supplied by Amalthee's priests.

"We shouldn't see this kind of weather for another month," Talley told them from the head of the line. Treven had volunteered the acolyte to guide them to the fort known as Iscarra Cannan, and Talley had taken it as his duty to inform them of every bit of potentially useful information. It was a thoughtful gesture from them both, though the main thoroughfares were so straight and wide that Shalindra could have found her way easily enough.

The walls of the fort were ancient and modest yet as durable as the granite they rested atop. A quartet of soldiers watched over the open gate.

Fendrick waited there for them as well, propped up against the wall patiently working a piece of wood with his knife. He put both away when he saw them coming.

"Master Hammerstrike," Talley said with a small bow. "It's a pleasure to see you again."

"Good to see you're learning," Fendrick replied with a glance at their mounts.

Shalindra had no idea what that was about, but it brought a smile to Talley's face.

"Don't worry about the horses," Talley said, sliding off and collecting their reins. "I can manage. The Legitarso is quite fond of knots and owns a thoroughly complete book on them that I was required to learn."

Talley finished his work and bade them farewell, and they followed Fendrick into the fortress.

The guards at the gate drew themselves to attention as Shalindra entered.

"Where is everyone else?" she asked Fendrick.

"Inside that way," he said, waving his hand in a gesture which encompassed half the compound. "They were going to meet with the commanding lord or something."

"You had no trouble getting in?"

"Not a bit. Didn't even need that letter. They knew Verelli by name and almost fell over themselves offering their comforts."

Enna made an unpleasant noise. "These Ceringions are more accommodating than your own family."

"It is strange to be more welcomed by those we considered our enemy," Birion agreed.

The thought did not bother Shalindra as much as it might have. So much had changed so rapidly that the contradictions now outnumbered the normalities. They had not made it to their target building when they encountered Verelli walking the other way.

"How'd it go?" Fendrick asked.

"As well as I had expected, but not as well as I would have liked," Verelli said. "They will not divert anyone to escort us to Tythir. From here, we are on our own."

"Is there anyone else we can turn to for help?" Shalindra asked.

"The Conclave still has resources, though the ones I would most like to avail myself of are elsewhere. I can secure horses and supplies, but likely not any reinforcements."

"None of your wizard friends would care to join us?" Fendrick pressed.

"No. There are roughly a dozen working here to aid in the defense. The Conclave is doing its part."

"Maybe the commander here needs a stronger suggestion," Fendrick said.

Verelli indicated the walls. "You're welcome to try, as he's now touring the battlements. In fact, Her Highness is already acquainted with him."

Shalindra raised an inquiring eyebrow.

"Lord Donatuc. I believe you defeated him outside Adair when your father was injured. He actually spoke quite highly of you, so it may be that you can convince him again."

"It would be worth the attempt," she said. "Where can I find him?"

"When we parted, he was headed for his tour of the walls here."

"Then I will seek him out and look for you back at the gate we entered when I am done."

Given the small number of walls and that they were short enough to see along their tops from the inside, it took little time for her to find the commander.

"Your Highness," Lord Donatuc said with a polite bow. "I'm surprised to see you here. When I was informed that you were headed this way, I scarcely believed it. After what was done to your kingdom, I half expected you to be leading an army of conquest."

Why did people always assume she wanted to rule everything? "I am more interested in saving both our nations. Demons care nothing for our borders."

He regarded her thoughtfully for a moment. "You've at least got the right perspective, but I should expect that of you. I suppose Verelli sent you here to change my mind?"

"I believe that was his hope."

"Well, it won't work. I admire you both for going, but we've already lost enough men and we're going to need every single person we can muster here."

"Having just completed our own travels here, I know the road was anything but easy. How was your journey home?"

Donatuc chuckled. "Much more eventful that I'd have preferred, but thank you for allowing it to happen. We had only made it to Braunton when word reached us of the invasion, and so we hurried our pace. It didn't matter, because by the time we changed course and arrived here, everything east of the city was under demonic control. We led one sortie towards Tythir, which was an unmitigated disaster. The carnage of it is also why I happen to be in charge."

"What became of your wizard?"

"Master Allisade? He left our care the moment we crossed back into Ceringion territory. That was the limit of how far I agreed to take him, after all."

"Thank you for keeping your word."

"My family prides itself on its honor. I'm certain it's not so different in Actondel. Regardless, it seems that I managed to escape one war only to land in another. I warned you that magic would be your undoing. It seems that now it may mean the destruction of everything we know."

"I intend to prevent that outcome," Shalindra said.

"Perhaps you can, but it is more likely you cannot, and we will have to deal with them here. I've faced demons only twice before coming here: once outside Tiridon when our fool wizard lost control of his beast and it slaughtered half of my army, and the other when your companion tore his way through my troops like they were children. I'll not waste what's left trying to reclaim what is lost, only to fail and lose the entire kingdom. The home I seek to protect is far closer to this than yours."

"A sentiment I understand."

"Speaking of which, what is Actondel's plan for the army your brother is attempting to raise? A bold move in the middle of winter. Tell me, will he stop at Braunton or seek to claim the entire Small Sea?"

Shalindra almost laughed at the thought of the handful of soldiers he had been able to accumulate being able to lay siege to anything more sizable than a tavern. "Prince Kentrick is not leading an army of conquest."

"For now," Donatuc said, not believing her.

"Actondel has its own troubles of late, and you need fear nothing from my brother. I can speak to King Gymerius on behalf of my family. I am certain that—"

"Gymerius is dead, as is every member of his family in the line of succession. I'm told that your king is less than he used to be, but at least you have one."

It was difficult to argue that point. "How many demons do you think there are?"

"Our conservative estimate is in the hundreds, but it's

impossible to know for sure. Any scout who has gotten close enough for an accurate appraisal has not returned."

That number did not surprise Shalindra. Indeed, it seemed almost low.

"Another way to say it is that we exist at the suffrage of the demons right now. If they wanted us dead, we could not have stopped them." He regarded the fortifications being built along the edges of the city. "We may remain unable to, no matter what efforts we put forth."

"Are things so despondent?"

"Oh, we've seen a minor victory or two. We managed to catch one in open country with our cavalry, but we lost more than a third of our number during the battle. We also killed one after a lucky shot with a ballista. We're making more of the siege weapons as fast as we can, but those are static defenses and will do little to help us reclaim what we've lost."

His appraisal was disheartening, and Shalindra searched for some ray of hope. "Verelli said that the Conclave was helping as they could."

"They are, to a degree, but we cannot get any of them to risk their necks by going into battle." He paused and rubbed at his eyes. "To be fair, most of them aren't cut out for that sort of work. Tell me, when you arrived here, what did you think of the city?"

"It is an impressive place," Shalindra said, "though there were clear signs of distress."

"That's an understatement. Our population has tripled in just a few short months, and with Tythir's stores lost, there is not enough food for everyone. People are bickering over commonplace items that we normally have in abundance. Soon, they will be killing each other for scraps." He shook his head. "I know Verelli sent you here to ask for my help, but we need every man here. If not to protect us from the demons, then from each other. I can give you horses and food, and weapons should you need them, but that is all I have to offer. I'm sorry, because you deserve more."

Shalindra looked out over the city. She would win no concessions that Verelli had not already achieved, because there were simply none to give. It was impossible to stand here and come to any other conclusion, no matter how much more difficult it would make her attempt to reach the portal.

"I must also apologize for being so blunt," Donatuc said, suddenly weary. "This was not what I expected to come home to. Return here tomorrow afternoon, and I will have our pathfinders brief you on everything we know about where the demons are and what they're doing. I'd love nothing more than to strike at these beasts with you. The least I can do is aid your attempt."

* * *

The reassembled group guested that evening at a house owned by the Conclave for just such a purpose. There was food, drink, and comforts aplenty that would have put to shame the hospitality of the richest Actondel lord. But it was not relaxation that Shalindra was now in search of. Tonight, she sought an answer for something that had been bothering her since they arrived in the Reginum.

Shalindra knocked on the door to Verelli's room.

"Your Highness," Verelli said as he opened the door.

"I prefer Shalindra."

Verelli dipped his head in acceptance. "Do come in."

Befitting his station within the Conclave, the magician occupied a suite rather than a single room, and he led her to a small study complete with books, a desk, and several comfortable chairs. He offered her a seat, but she remained standing.

"You never intended to bring Actondel's armies here, did you?"

Verelli blinked at the directness of the question. "No, I did not. Your kingdom had been diminished to the point of uselessness, by design. It amassed only around fourteen thousand men for the assault on Ildalarial, and more than half of those were Ceringion."

"And everything you said to my brother when you came to Merallin?"

"I will have to apologize to him for my antagonism, should I ever chance to meet him again. I had hoped to convince you to venture here while also ensuring that he did not. The last thing I wanted was to wait until spring for him to assemble a token force."

"I do not know if I should be flattered or disturbed that you felt that I alone was important. Why not simply ask me from the beginning?"

Verelli chuckled. "I did. You got up and stormed off the first time we met, which *was* an accident by the way."

"And today? You did not push very hard to gain assistance from the Ceringion forces here."

"What would any of them do for us?" He asked, waving a hand dismissively. "How many will you watch be slaughtered before your eyes while you stand at the rear and march them towards thousands of demons?"

She did not answer, because they both already knew.

"I can close the portal between our realms," Verelli continued. "We know it is there, and we know that it is their bridgehead. But I do not believe that I can get there alone."

"Why?"

"Because if it were possible, it would already have been done. Do you think the entire Conclave simply ran away when the demons began appearing? Do you think that you are the only one willing to risk everything for the sake of ending this invasion?"

There were so many layers to what he was saying and, despite the fact that his organization had attempted to kill her, she wondered how badly she might have misjudged them.

"I have been given many gifts," she said, "but I am a poor judge of how special that might make me."

"Very," he answered for her.

She accepted his words as truth, even if she did not entirely want to believe it.

"Now," he said, "one of those gifts you possess is the ability to forego sleep. As I remain bound by the fatigues of the day, I would beg your leave to retire for the night. I doubt we will have many opportunities for a relaxed slumber any time soon. Tomorrow, we'll begin to find out how accurate your prophecy really is."

Chapter Thirty-Three

Into a Wasted Land

The half-frozen hinges of the heavy oaken gate groaned in protest as the massive portal swung shut, an action punctuated by the ominously heavy thump of the inner bar falling into place. Shalindra resisted the urge to turn in her saddle and look back at the walls encircling Avalta. There had been no farewells or festive partings. Hardly anyone had even seen them go, and none of those who had knew their purpose. A dusting of snow was falling, frosting the world in white and obscuring everything with a blank fog. The effect was not unlike that of the amphitheater where she had met Lithandris and Eluria, save for the hues of color and the chill in the air. The horses produced clouds of steam with their breath as they trudged along a twisting route through ditches and berms planted with sharpened stakes. It would have been a daunting defense against a conventional foe, but against the demons, it would be next to worthless.

It was just over thirty miles by road to Tythir, but their pace would be slow and careful, and they would likely travel half again that distance as they took a more circuitous route north, one that Weeby promised would offer better cover from watchful eyes. And all of those eyes would be hostile.

The gate they had just left was like a line separating friend from foe, that much had been made clear the day before. Shalindra was under no illusions of the danger she was placing her friends in by continuing. Each and every one of them was there for a different reason, yet they had all committed themselves to seeing her quest succeed, even as she continued to hide its entire path. It was loyalty she did not deserve.

I will see them returned to safety, somehow.

Avalta faded into the hush of snow behind them, and though they now travelled through the most populous stretch of the Gold Road, there was not a soul to be seen. The terrain was sparse with forests, having long ago been given over to fields and crops, yet every farmstead and village they encountered was empty and cold.

Weeby guided them in a northernly swing away from the river to avoid any towns. Such structures were said to attract demons, and so they kept to the trees when they could, and when forced to cross open ground, they did so quickly and with fearful looks in every direction.

The snow increased in intensity throughout the day, with the flakes becoming larger and wetter. They stopped frequently to rest the horses and warm themselves at small fires, but there was a lack of conversation. It had nothing to do with the hostility they had once held for each other, stemming instead from the gravity of their situation. Each of them recognized the danger of what they were doing, and it required no discussion. While the signs of animosity had faded, Shalindra hesitated to describe it as camaraderie either.

The already frigid temperatures plummeted as the sun faded, but they did not risk the light of a fire no matter how much they wanted its warmth. The snow was too wet to create an enclosed shelter as they had employed in the mountains, so they piled it into low windbreaks as best they could and huddled side by side for warmth. They saw nothing during the night, but the rustle of leathery wings could be heard in the clouds above.

Morning came none too soon, but it brought relief from neither snow nor cold.

"That was utterly miserable," Weeby said, stamping his feet in an attempt to restore circulation. "A few more days of this and I'll welcome running into a demon."

They held up blankets to hide Honarch from view as he used the flame spark in his hand to heat cups of tea. The hot liquid was gulped down eagerly, restoring warmth to numb fingers and toes.

"What about speeding our travel now?" Enna whispered as they prepared to remount. "We're not likely to encounter anyone here."

Creating the mist gates had been a matter of necessity before, but Shalindra agreed that now was a similar urgency. "I can get us there faster," she announced.

All eyes turned towards her expectantly, though Fendrick looked like he would be sick.

"How?" Honarch asked.

"By using mist gates."

"Do you intend to bounce between our world and theirs

somehow?" Verelli asked.

She shook her head. "I can make them between any two points I can see." She created one as proof in front of them, having it emerge a short distance away.

"That would have been helpful up in the mountains," Weeby pointed out.

"I did not know I could do it then," Shalindra said.

Verelli studied it, impressed. "You are a woman of a thousand surprises."

"Are you sure it's safe?" Birion asked, looking only slightly more excited than Fendrick.

Enna walked through as proof, emerging at the opposite end.

Birion gathered his courage and tried to lead a mount through, but it bucked and shied away. The other horses appeared just as skittish. The gate began to resist her control after being held open so long, and Shalindra allowed it to collapse.

Enna stomped back from where she had been stranded and glared at them all crossly.

"Those gates are definitely an advantage over trudging through snow," Honarch said.

"Nice to see some helpful magic," Weeby added with a sideways glance at Verelli.

"I'm not willing to leave the horses," Birion said. "Should we become separated, they could be our only escape."

There was consensus on that, and so the group continued on horseback. Shalindra allowed herself to drift from the present, contemplating how she might be able to accomplish her part in the coming battle. It was a thorny question without a clear answer, and one that had previously resulted in great debates amongst the various *hers*. But those versions of herself had grown increasingly quiet of late, and today only two joined her.

Eluria had promised her help. Maybe she intended to provide the additional strength Shalindra needed to weaken Mergolath. It was a convenient hope but seemed unlikely. Eluria was not whole, and the short span of time that had passed since their meeting was insufficient to replenish her. But she was also a god, so there was no point in guessing at what she was capable of doing.

Neither of the *hers* had anything substantial to add on that point, beyond mentioning that she needed to figure this out rather rapidly. Both dwelled on recollections of their Ascensions, which had resulted in a similar fate for Eluria but had been less painful to endure.

The parallels between that damage to Eluria and how she meant to debilitate Mergolath floated to the surface of her thoughts. The two actions were similar in scope, but vastly different in the amount of effort required. Tormjere had mentioned in passing that demons did something similar by... What was it?

It's called the Rending, and they slaughter thousands of themselves during every one.

It saddened her to even think along those lines. Mindlessly killing every single demon was not something she would care to do even should she be capable, which she doubted she was.

She recentered herself on Tormjere's focus in an attempt to avoid such unhappy ruminations. At least the snow had stopped, and there was enough variation in the clouds to confirm that the sun still existed. The woods they rode through were no more cheerful: dark and silent, and draped in a mottled blanket of whites and greys. The narrow road they picked their way along was rutted and torn from thousands of travelers, but as empty as the open ocean.

It was through those dark trees that a sound filtered to them, so faint it almost failed to carry above the sodden clump of the horses.

Shalindra heard it first and swiveled her head side to side to ascertain the direction. It came again, off to the left, and heads turned towards the sounds of combat. She kicked her horse to a gallop, racing through the trees towards it.

The forest faded as she reached the top of a hill, and she paused at the edge of a wide vale. On the far side, a handful of men struggled to fend off a pair of demons. They wore no house colors, and their weapons were woefully insufficient. The men raced for the shelter of an abandoned farmstead, but they were being slaughtered one by one as they ran.

"It will be over by the time we get there," Verelli said, emerging from the trees with the others.

"He's correct, Your Highness" Birion said. "There's nothing we can do for them"

Shalindra was off her horse, ready to send a mist gate tunneling to the desperate defenders but could settle on nothing clear enough to anchor the other end.

Birion edged his horse in front of her, obstructing her view. "We need to leave before we're spotted."

One by one, they turned sadly from the scene, but Shalindra

did not look away until the last man fell.

It's the right choice. Nothing you did would've mattered.

I have made too many 'right choices,' and I long for the day when I can forget them.

You never do.

Chapter Thirty-Four
A Fractured Plan

Fresh snow lay atop old, lending a muted hush to the world that swallowed even the clomp of the horses as they trudged through it. The air sat as still and lifeless as the thin woods around them, unmoving as it hung above a frosted landscape without light or motion. The horizon faded into an impenetrable grey, lost in the morning mists and drifting snow. Only the broad flow of the river to their south gave any indication that they were not trapped in an artist's rendition of the scene instead of the real place.

It was in that pensive silence that Shalindra finally spied the faint outlines of the city through the fog, and beyond that, the smooth, open waters of the Mardrian Sea. The land before them sloped downwards in fits and starts, shedding its forests as it descended gradually eastwards onto a stretch of flatlands before meeting the ocean.

She could only image the sweeping panorama which would be revealed from this position on a clear day. Tythir, situated beside where the Haliestos River at last escaped its distant origins in the

Small Sea, was the eastern terminus of the Gold Road. That oft-contested route stretched all the way across the continent from Merallin—two cities joined by commerce but made enemies by greed and history. In Tythir's fabled streets, one could find luxuries from the edges of the known world, and purchase delicacies from passing caravans before they boarded one of the tall, three masted ships bound for distant ports. Its wealth was said to rival that of the greatest cities that any of the Three Great Empires had ever created.

Or it would have, had it still stood.

Tythir, once proud capital of the Ceringion Reginum and home of the Conclave of Imaretii, now lay like a blackened smear across the landscape. Shattered stubs of its graceful towers protruded at odd angles like shoots of wheat after a harvest. Dwellings, temples, markets, and even the old wall of the inner city had been reduced to rubble with such inescapable ruthlessness that it was difficult to tell from this distance where the city ended and farms began.

The outer wall appeared largely intact, as did a portion of the fortified palace. The morning mist which had obscured their view was thickened by the smoke of giant fires burning throughout, fighting against the snow that covered everything. On the highest hill stood the eight towers of Solor-Majalis, the fortress of the Imaretii. All had been spared from the destruction save for the largest, which was missing the top floors.

Shalindra signaled the group to a stop beneath a copse of trees bordering the edge of a farm, the last vestige of cover between them and the city. A small sound of denial escaped Honarch's lips as he dismounted and sagged against a tree.

Enna slid from her horse and placed a comforting hand on Honarch's shoulder.

The anger burning inside Shalindra warmed her more than any fire ever could, but she couldn't tell if that anger was directed at the demons who had committed such destruction or at herself for not being there to avert it. As so many had tried to tell her, her place had been here all along. "This is the fate that awaits every city of every kingdom, should we fail. I am sorry that my decisions delayed our arrival so long."

Verelli took a deep breath and let it out slowly, but his words held no malice. "Unless you had been standing here beside me, watching it the day it happened, there was nothing you could have done. I knew the city's fate when I turned my back on it and went to find you. Some things simply cannot be changed."

"Pretty obvious where we're to go," Fendrick said, looking to the future rather than the past. "Whatever's here can only be in one of two places."

"One fortress or the other," Birion agreed. "And there's no way to get into the city unnoticed. The land is so bare we'll be spotted before we get within five miles."

Weeby gave Verelli a questioning tilt of the head. The wizard seemed not to notice at first, then he turned away from the scene. "There are no secrets left to protect."

There was more pain in that admission than Shalindra would have thought possible.

"I suppose not," Weeby agreed. "Anyone who wishes is free to storm the walls, but there are other ways in. We'll have to go on foot from here, though."

"Should we hobble the horses?" Birion asked.

"Better to just release 'em," Fendrick said. "There's barely a blade of grass to be found, and their smell may bring demons searching where we don't want them to."

"We set them free," Shalindra agreed. It did not matter which option they chose—the horses would not be here when they returned. Better to give them a chance at living than consign them to being eaten.

Saddles and bags were quickly removed, and anything they couldn't carry was hidden in the bushes. By the time they were done, the light was beginning to fade.

"Faster, please," Weeby said. "If we don't find it before dark, we might have to sit out here all night."

Shalindra could only guess at what 'it' was, but the group followed in silence as Weeby hurried through the snow and deepening gloom to a sheltered, rocky draw not half a mile away. His pace slowed as they descended into the notch, continuing downward until the steep sides blocked the city from view. He finally came to a stop before the darkened outline of a door made to look exactly like the rocks around it. Had it not been ajar, it would have been almost impossible to see.

Weeby inspected the edge of the opening with his fingers, testing the gap, then glanced back at Verelli.

"I left it fully closed," the wizard answered.

Weeby drew his long knife in one hand and tugged at the door with the other. The portal swung open on silent hinges, revealing a dark tunnel that curved sharply down into the earth. He listened for a moment, then shrugged. "Everyone inside. We'll not unravel any mysteries standing here in the snow."

Fendrick entered first with shield and spear at the ready. Verelli and Honarch went next, then Shalindra and Enna.

"Go ahead," the halfling said to Birion, who had remained last. "I'll tidy up out here and then we'll be on our way."

Weeby stayed outside only a few moments before slipping back inside tunnel. He pulled the door almost shut, then stopped.

"No lights?" he asked.

With the closing of the door, the tunnel had gone almost completely black, but Shalindra could clearly see Verelli as he knelt and searched along the floor. His hands came across a small, amber-colored stone tucked against the wall. He turned it over in his fingers twice. "The spells were functional when I escaped."

He straightened and placed the stone in a pocket thoughtfully.

"Are there torches?" Fendrick asked. "Or are we going to stand here in the dark until tomorrow?"

"I'll take care of it," Enna said. She moved forward until she located Fendrick's shield by feel, then called forth a small globe of soft light attached to the boss.

Enna's prayer had been granted by the other her Shalindra had appointed to that task, but so attuned was she to the signature of her request that she felt the tingle of its arrival. Enna's prayers would always see an answer.

You'll have to tell her eventually.

I know. But her faith is so strong, and I do not have the heart to shatter it.

The pale light attached to Fendrick's shield illuminated only a short distance ahead, but it revealed a passage through the stone that was clear and free of moisture.

"How far?" Fendrick asked quietly, his eyes fixed on the impenetrable blackness ahead of them.

"Close to a mile before we come to an intersection," Verelli answered.

Fendrick led them forward at a steady pace. The tunnel was cool and empty, descending for a time before leveling out. Though wide enough that they could have walked two abreast, the party remained in single file. Every scrape of their boots or brush against the walls echoed in the unnatural silence.

It was difficult to judge distance, but they could not have gone more than half the expected length before the silence ahead was broken by a soft sound. As one they stopped, ears straining as they held their breath.

It came again, and then once more in a regular pattern that could only indicate the soft patter of dripping water. Despite the innocuous nature of it, Weeby and Verelli exchanged worried glances.

The wizard leaned close to whisper in Shalindra's ear. "The tunnel should be dry all the way in. Something isn't right."

"It's a long way out should we need to retreat," Fendrick mumbled.

Shalindra readied Shining Moon and motioned Fendrick forward. They crept ahead slowly, the sounds of dripping water growing louder with every step. A glint of metal threw a dim flash of reflected light from somewhere up ahead. Fendrick waved them to a stop and edged closer. She could not see past the dwarf's hunched shoulders, but he relaxed and straightened, then called back softly.

"It's nothing to worry over."

Shalindra continued forward to meet him, this time brightening the scene with her own light rather than suffer the guilt of allowing Enna to do so again. The metal they had seen revealed itself as a ring, still secured around the finger of the mage who owned it, and who was now sprawled across the tunnel floor in an unnaturally stiff posture.

Verelli pushed forward and knelt beside the body.

The unknown wizard's robes were slashed and torn by dozens of cuts made from every angle, and whatever blood had been in the man's body had leaked out to stain the rocks weeks if not months before.

Fendrick stepped around Verelli but continued only a short distance before he came to a stop and cursed. "He's not the only thing that ended here."

Shalindra flared her light, revealing a solid wall of rubble blocking the tunnel. Water dripped from a slender crack along the ceiling to puddle on the tunnel floor.

Fendrick put his ear to the stone and tapped it with the butt of his spear. "It's solid. There'll be no getting through it."

"Is there any other way?" Enna asked.

"There is always an alternate," Verelli said without looking up. "The closest is in Palbon."

"One of the smaller towns just north of here," Weeby added in response to their blank looks. "There's another tunnel beneath a smithy. We should be able to make it there before sunrise, if we hurry. It's at least an hour to the town with little in the way of cover, and I'd not care to be out in the daylight this close to the city."

"Nor should we spend the day sitting underground," Birion said. "We're all tired, but it would be best to push through tonight."

"Give me a moment," Verelli said.

Everyone looked at Shalindra as if it were her place to approve.

She nodded. Why wouldn't she? Verelli knew or at least recognized the dead man, and a short pause would change nothing. They allowed Verelli his space, then hustled back up the tunnel when he rejoined them.

While they walked, Shalindra's mind raced. This was far from the first setback she had experienced and nowhere near the worst, but for some reason she found her anger bubbling to life once more. She did not want to be here creeping through tunnels—did not want any of them to be here, suffering through a battle that was hers to fight. They all thought that the conflict lay ahead, but if history had been manipulated to place her on this path, could their lives have been any less ordained? Were they simply victims, unwilling pawns in a cosmic game they were unaware they even participated in?

She struggled to contain her roiling emotions, unsure of why they flowed so uncontrollably. Her mind circled Tormjere's focus, trying to distract herself from this surplus of emotion that threatened to explode from within her. He had always been uncharacteristically good at hiding his own anger—if he even felt such emotions. She should do a better job of controlling herself, but the magnitude of what would be lost should she fail drove her to…

She stopped so abruptly that Enna ran into her from behind. Everyone else came to a halt as well.

"What is it?" Enna asked.

Shalindra sought Honarch's attention in the dim light. "Did you ever see Tormjere angry?"

Honarch blinked, looking baffled.

"Is this relevant right now?" Verelli asked.

Shalindra ignored him and moved to stand before Honarch. "He said, once, that I had never seen him angry. But you have."

"We went through a number of difficult situations together," Honarch said guardedly. "Everyone gets angry. I doubt any of us are in the best mood right now."

"But one time was different than the rest, was it not?"

"I fail to see why that would make a difference to our current situation," Honarch dodged.

"I believe that it may matter a great deal." Not to what they were doing, perhaps, but certainly to her.

"Digging through the past without the context of having been there is a fool's errand."

"All of us have done things we regret." Shalindra's voice lowered. "I know who he was, better than anyone here. Whatever he did, it will not change my opinion of him."

Honarch looked down at his hands as he wrestled with his thoughts, then met her eyes. "It was the day we lost Gelid."

That was all Shalindra needed. She plunged into Tormjere's focus, and the memory came rushing to greet her.

Chapter Thirty-Five

Final Escape

Tormjere peered through the trees and cursed. The group of goblins they were shadowing had joined with others, and now at least fifteen blocked the exit to the pass. He glanced back to where Honarch and Treven had collapsed to the ground, both breathing heavily. Their frantic flight from the valley had brought the three survivors into a narrow draw between two steep slopes, stifling their options.

There was no way they could turn back the way they had come without running into an even greater number of the green-skinned creatures. Though not close enough to be seen, his senses burned with the feeling of their presence. The three men were trapped, but he would never entertain the thought of surrender. He had failed to save Gelid, but Tormjere vowed he would not repeat that mistake again. By Amalthee, or Eluria, or Lithandris, or Remulus, or whatever other god cared to listen, he was going to get Treven and the precious Book of Amalthee home, no matter what it took.

Honarch said something to him, but he did not hear the words, nor would they have altered his path if he had.

"I am tired of being hunted," he said coldly. "The ones on the left are yours." He drew his sword and slipped into the trees.

"When?" Honarch whispered.

"When you hear them screaming."

Tormjere stalked towards the goblins with as much stealth as he could muster. To his own ears, he was as noisy as a flock of geese taking flight but given how loudly they were arguing amongst themselves he could have walked without care.

A goblin a full head taller than any of those around it stood in the center of the group, either berating them or giving orders, or perhaps both. He assumed it to be the leader given the deferential manner in which the other goblins treated it. Every one of the goblins' attention was turned inward, and a hasty plan formed in Tormjere's mind. There was only one way to deal with these goblins, only one language they would understand.

He repositioned himself behind the closest pair of the creatures, both standing with their backs to him. He could have taken one of their heads off with a single stroke—goblins had surprisingly weak necks, he had discovered—and left his blade in position to strike at the next. Or he could have pulled his cut shallow and hit them both with one long slice. Either way would have taken them out of the fight and maintained the element of surprise for as long as possible.

But he did not.

I have to get them out.

Tormjere launched himself upward, ramming the point of his blade through the closest goblin's back, forcing it all the way in until the hapless creature was propelled into the air.

As the creature's feet left the ground, it screamed. The horrid, bone-chilling shriek of terror echoed through the mountains and caused the other creatures to jump in fright. Tormjere barely freed his blade in time to strike the second goblin before it recovered from the shock, slashing it across the face and leaving it to die with the other as he leapt forward.

I have to get them out.

Goblins might have been considered cowardly by most races, and as individuals it was an apt description, but they were vicious creatures by nature and reacted instinctively when threatened, falling back into defensive clusters. It was a perfectly valid strategy against a lone swordsman, but a poor choice when facing a wizard. Honarch's twisting mass of magical flame exploded in their midst, setting clothes and skin alight and flinging their small bodies outward. The wave of heat singed Tormjere's skin as it sent flaming splinters zipping through the air, but he kept running forward.

Fire will not stop me.

A burning goblin stumbled to the ground in front of him. He stepped on its neck to ensure it stayed down.

The goblins were in a panic now, charging about in every direction. Tormjere hacked down two more before either creature could mount a defense. Then he was through the outer knot of the creatures, and the large goblin stood momentarily alone before him. Undaunted by the chaos around them, it raised a wicked looking axe and roared at him like a cornered animal.

By any measure of his own abilities, Tormjere should have been terrified. The creature was almost a match for his height and far heavier, and it bore the scars of a veteran fighter. But he was beyond the point of caring.

Felzig will not stop me.

The goblin was going to die, and Treven was not. Some of that reckless determination must have projected on his face, for the goblin's arm wavered, delaying his swing just long enough for Tormjere to close. An angry snarl twisted the goblin's face, but a sharp cut across its arm sent the axe flying away. It lurched at him with its good arm outstretched, but Tormjere's two-handed slash split the unarmored creature from waist to neck. Tormjere left it lying in the dirt as he advanced on the creatures still standing.

Joloff will not stop me.

Another goblin died, impaled on his blade.

These mountains will not stop me.

He struck the next goblin so hard he almost cut it in two.

And I will be damned if these goblins will stop me.

He continued, relentless in his need to slaughter every single one of them.

Tormjere's senses burned at the approach of the larger contingent of goblins. Too many to fight, but he needed them here. Needed them to see. There was only one goblin left before him. It turned to flee, tripping over a rock and casting aside its knife as it scrambled away. He caught the creature and drove it face first into the ground. Yanking the dazed goblin to its knees, he jammed his sword through its back. It screamed, a pitiful cry of terror that ended abruptly as Tormjere kicked it away.

Honarch came running forward, and Treven staggered out of the bushes not far behind, barely on his feet. Tormjere would probably have to carry the acolyte soon, but there was still one message he needed to send. He drew his axe and returned to the large goblin, who now lay in a pool of its own blood, struggling to draw a breath. Using his body to shield Treven from the fact it was still alive, Tormjere seized the goblin by the scraggly hairs atop its head.

Its eyes widened in abject terror, as only a creature about to die in unimaginable pain can. Tormjere hacked its head off like he was chopping firewood, then seized a discarded spear and jammed it into the ground. On the top, he impaled the severed head, the goblin's fearful expression permanently frozen on its face. The other creatures would be here soon, and they would see.

Honarch and Treven looked on silently, but neither offered protest at the grisly display.

"They will leave us alone or they will die," was the only explanation he offered, but the rage that had driven him to do it had already begun to dissipate, and he wondered if he had gone too far.

The disappointment in Honarch's eyes gave him more of an answer than he wanted, and he motioned them towards the way out. "More will be drawn here by the sound of the fighting. We must run."

Run they did, following him through the remainder of the pass and down a steep descent. Treven tried to keep up but began to fall behind.

Tormjere slowed them to a jog, but the acolyte struggled with even that pace. When he next looked over his shoulder, Treven's eyes had become unfocused, and Honarch had taken him by the arm to help him along. At the bottom of the hill, Treven collapsed against a rock.

"I want to lay down," he said. "Just for a moment."

"Treven, you must keep going," Tormjere implored, so tired that he could barely get the words out. "Not for yourself. Do it for Gelid."

A small spark lit in Treven's eyes, and the acolyte forced himself to his feet once more.

Their desperate flight through the woods continued, past the point of exhaustion and well into the night. When Tormjere judged it unsafe to continue in the dark, they collapsed as one and huddled together to ward off the damp cold of the night.

Well beyond the point of exhaustion, Tormjere struggled to remain awake as the others slept, determined not to repeat his earlier mistake of falling asleep, but it was not long before his eyelids began to droop. The night was quiet and peaceful, with nothing but the gentle melody of insects to disturb the silence, and like a moth his eyes drifted towards the brightness of the moon.

His stomach twisted itself into a knot that had nothing to do with hunger, demanding that he face the thoughts he was intentionally avoiding. His hands shook as the image of the goblin's terrified face returned, every detail of its yellowed eyes clear in his mind as his axe bit deep into its neck. Even though it would have done far worse to him had their roles been reversed, there was nothing that felt good about it. A wave of revulsion washed over him, but he clamped down on it before his shivers woke Treven or Honarch. He was not proud of what he had done, but neither was he ashamed. It had been necessary and, as it had worked up to now, it was what had been needed. Safety and freedom from fear were concepts foreign to this wilderness. Goblins could be and likely were everywhere between here and the gates of Kirchmont, as were any number of more dangerous creatures. There was no one to turn to for help, no salvation beyond what they could attain for themselves.

If I have to kill every living thing between here and Kirchmont, every wyvern, goblin, ogre, and mystical moving tree that gets in my way, so be it. I will see Treven safely home.

His eyes locked onto the moon once more.

And I don't care what it costs me.

* * *

Shalindra's eyes opened, returning her to the darkness of the tunnel she was now travelling through. She resumed conscious control of her body in midstride, so smoothly that her immersion within his memory might never have happened. As she walked between Fendrick and Enna, she pondered what she had just been shown. She understood why he had never allowed himself that anger again, though he had fought constantly to suppress it, keeping it hidden not only from those around him but from himself. Even though he knew the violence he was capable of, he had given himself to his self-appointed mission, first with Treven and later with her, because no one else was willing or able. It had never been about the power he gained or the status he might have achieved, but how far he would willingly go to protect the people he cared about.

There was a lesson to be found in his choice, though the two remaining *hers* differed on what that was. Was his constant struggle to avoid that loss of control a cautionary tale of what could happen? Or was it a projection of what she had already succumbed to? The illusion that she could accomplish Eluria's tasks without becoming the warrior it required was one that she had stubbornly clung to, but the truth hit her as hard as it had him.

A hollow void of helplessness welled within her. This was not the fate she had wished for herself, but if this was what it would take to keep her world safe, she would do it. Because he had. Because Enna had, and continued to.

Because there was no one else who could.

Her only regret was the time and lives that had been wasted waiting on her to come to this realization. She could bring none of those people back, but she could ensure that no one else gave their lives for this prophecy.

The only sacrifice left would be hers.

Chapter Thirty-Six

Tunnels and Terrors

A blast of cold air sent powdery snow rushing to greet them as Weeby cracked open the hidden door. He slipped out into the night, and Shalindra took station at the entrance, no longer willing to let another assume that risk. Her senses—Tormjere's awareness, really—extended into the open spaces beyond the door. She felt her way up and down the draw, taking note of every rock and bush but finding nothing. It should have bothered her that she had unconsciously appropriated another piece of his focus to do it, but the thought only left her numb.

It wasn't given to be locked away.

And still, I will not allow myself to take everything.

She clung to that belief as a final act of defiance, the one piece of her humanity she might be able to preserve.

Outside, Weeby had completed his reconnaissance and was turning back towards the group. Shalindra took the opportunity to check over her other selves she had created and tasked with answering prayers. They continued to perform as she wished, allowing a steady trickle of requests to be fulfilled. The area beyond her mental defenses, and from which those prayers arrived, remained an unruly place in spite of these efforts, but she no longer feared it.

"It's clear, for now," Weeby called. "Come on before that changes."

She led the way out, alert for anything despite Weeby's reassurance. Their decision to wait for nightfall would not offer the same amount of concealment as it would against human foes, but even the slightest advantage was worth pursuing. The group followed the halfling up and out of the draw, emerging at a place close to their earlier vantage point. Just enough moonlight leaked through the clouds to illuminate the landscape, and the flickering glow of giant fires gave shape to the crumbled ruins of the city.

"Horses are gone already," Fendrick stated.

"Demons?" Birion asked. "Or did they have the good sense to run?"

"I haven't seen any other tracks," Weeby replied, "but who knows? We're headed there." He pointed across the snowy fields northwest of Tythir, towards a darkened set of ruins. The destroyed town occupied a large enough area to be called a city in its own right, even as it was dwarfed by its larger neighbor. "That's where we'll find another way in."

The wind was picking up, and to the west the clouds grew dark and thick above an impenetrable wall of white. They crossed the fields at a jog, the snow hampering every step. It was a race to avoid being caught by demons or snow, one which they were going to lose one way or another. Thankfully, it was the storm that swept over them first, plunging them into a snowy darkness before they were halfway there and slowing their pace to a crawl.

"The weather may kill us before the demons get the chance," Birion said, more an attempt at encouragement than a complaint.

It was impossible to see more than a few feet ahead, but Weeby's sense of direction was true. The dark silhouettes of ravaged buildings emerged from the swirling snow, and they took shelter in the first structure sturdy enough to remain standing. The door was gone and half the windows were broken, and piles of snow accumulated beneath them. The upper floor was collapsed, but enough of the first was intact to protect them from the wind.

"We'll have to wait until morning," Weeby said.

"There's risk to being seen once the sun comes up," Birion said.

Weeby shook his head. "I'll never find it in the dark. I doubt one building in ten is still recognizable, even in the daylight."

Fendrick poked his head into the fireplace to inspect the chimney. "Fire's risky, even if we didn't have to worry about being seen."

"Block the doors and windows as best we can," Shalindra said. "The space is small enough that our bodies will warm it."

A table was turned on its end to serve as a makeshift door, and the windows blocked with whatever stones and debris they could cram into them. They shivered together in the driest corner and awaited the dawn, which came none too soon. The clouds thinned in the wake of the storm, but the wind that had driven away the snow had also dropped the temperature. Patches of sky brightened with the colors of the sunrise, teasing at warmth that would never reach them. They forced numb arms and legs into motion to begin their search for the other tunnel.

They moved cautiously down empty streets, weary from the sleepless night but alert for signs of danger. An occasional spear or broken wagon protruded from the thick frosting of snow, but the ruins were devoid of life. Even the animals that lived on the detritus of the city had fled.

Weeby picked his way through, muttering to himself and pointing in differing locations as he tried to establish his bearings. He would often begin in one direction, then make a sharp turn as he recognized a feature or landmark.

Following Weeby onto a wide thoroughfare, Shalindra experienced a discomforting tug on her spine as a ghostly premonition pulled away from her body. Its appearance was as unexpected as it was uncontrollable, but certain to be worthy of attention. She drew to a stop, watching her translucent doppelganger continue down the street, followed by the incorporeal copies of her companions. Not three blocks away, they all jumped sideways in alarm and began a frantic retreat.

"Hide!" Shalindra warned in a piercing whisper.

The group scattered at her command, with Weeby and Fendrick taking shelter with her in the shell of a burned-out shop while the others ducked into the remnants of an ally on the other side of the street. There was no time to disguise their tracks in the snow, which pointed clearly to their hiding locations.

No sooner were they concealed than a rippling tap of spikey feet against cobblestone reached their ears, approaching at a steady clip. Shalindra pressed herself tight against the wall and peeked around the corner. The demon she beheld crawling down the street towards them was unlike anything she had seen on this world. Its long, segmented body was as thick around as a cow, and the plates of its carapace knocked together as it crawled over and through the rubble of the shattered town on dozens of thin legs. Disproportionately small eyes were sunk deep beneath the sharp ridges of a flattened head whose only purpose was to serve as a base for the trio of spikey mandibles protruding from its jaw. It slowed as it drew near, its antennae wiggling back and forth as if to taste the air.

Hands tightened on weapons as it drew perilously close to where the group was hidden. Shalindra could dispatch it easily, but even one screech could bring untold numbers of demons down upon them. The demon paused to sample their tracks in the snow, then twisted its head towards the building they sheltered in, like a dog following a scent.

Across the street, Verelli extended his arms and made a sharp pulling motion. The snow atop the roof dislodged, sliding down onto the demon in a clumpy, wet avalanche. The creature leapt sideways and gave a shudder that rippled up and down its body as it attempted to escape the snowy mantle that was already melting to steam against its hot body. It twisted about in one final shake before hurrying on down the street.

Shalindra looked back at Fendrick, who gave a sigh of relief and relaxed his grip on his spear. They waited for the demon to travel far enough away, then Shalindra waved Weeby onwards.

The halfling resumed his search, but progress continued to be slow.

"We cannot wander forever," Enna hissed after Weeby doubled

back for the second time in as many blocks.

"Do I look like I'm on a pleasure stroll?" Weeby shot back. "It's a little different than last time I was here." He paused to examine a sign which had once hung above the door of a burned-out shop, then moved quickly to the next pile of rubble, and made a small "ah" of discovery. "We're close."

"There." Fendrick pointed down the street towards a ruined structure. "I can smell the metal."

Weeby hurried over to what remained of the forge. The chimney and bellows remained intact, but the anvil had been knocked over and a master's set of tools strewn about on the ground.

"Yes, this is it." He scrambled over a pile of stone and into what had once been a small yard behind the forge. "It's under there," he said, indicating a partially buried storage bin.

Fendrick and Birion set to moving the debris as quietly as possible, uncovering a slanted door into the ground. The hinges squealed as Birion heaved it open, causing everyone to freeze in panic. They remained frozen, listening, but only the sounds of the wind reached their ears. Birion eased the door fully open, revealing a darkened interior.

Fendrick disappeared down the steep, rickety steps, then called softly from the darkness. "It's fine."

The group descended one by one, with Birion pulling the door shut behind them just as the snow was beginning to come down again. With luck, it would mask any sign of their passing.

Fendrick had already located and lit a pair of candles, and they found themselves in a small cellar beneath the forge. Rough shelves full of wrapped cheeses were stacked floor to ceiling along three of the walls. It was a tight space, more suited to a pair of cheesemakers than a group of their size. Shalindra thought it an odd place to store cheese, given the heat generated from the work above.

Weeby ran his fingers along the brick walls until coming to a specific one, which he leaned against with some force. They heard a muffled click, and then a section of the wall swung silently inwards. It lodged against the sagging ceiling, but the gap was sufficiently wide for Weeby to wriggle through.

A small, amber stone on the floor inside began to glow softly as he entered, then dimmed as he moved past. A few steps ahead of him, a similar light appeared.

Shalindra looked at Verelli.

"It's a base enchantment that younger students practice," the mage answered.

Honarch stepped in behind Weeby and retrieved one of the glowstones, this one a nondescript piece of quartz. "I remember enchanting my fair share of these. I always wondered where they went."

"A convenient skill to master while learning the fundamentals of spellcasting," Verelli said, "one which can be put to any number of uses. More importantly for us, it indicates that this tunnel may have remained undisturbed."

"May have?" Shalindra asked.

"We don't know why the stones were not working in the other tunnel. For so many to have been rendered ineffective would require a powerful nullification."

"Undisturbed or not, it's as risky as any other way," Fendrick said. "Best to get on with it."

"Now might be a good time to rest," Birion countered. "None of us slept last night, and we'll need to be ready for anything."

"We're all tired," Enna agreed.

"How far from here to the citadel?" Shalindra asked.

"Five, six miles?" Weeby estimated, rejoining them in the storeroom. "This tunnel connects to some of the natural caves, so it winds around a bit. If you want a secure place to stop, here is as good a place as any."

"Then we will rest and take time to gather ourselves."

"Same watch rotation?" Birion asked.

"You may all sleep," Shalindra replied. "I do not feel the need."

* * *

They woke hours later, not knowing what time of day it was and not wanting to risk a look outside to find out. They wolfed down a cold meal, made more palatable by the abundance of cheese, then it was time to go.

Weeby squeezed through the secret door, and Shalindra and then the others followed, each person's entry into the tunnel an unspoken pledge to their success.

Their pace through the featureless passage was rapid, measured by the glow of the guide stones that illuminated briefly with their passing. Eventually, the walls and ceiling grew damp, and there were places where dripping water had carved tracks through the stone to puddle on the floor. Weeby exhaled in relief when the seemingly endless tunnel finally opened into a hollowed-out chamber, one containing only a single exit blocked by a door of sturdy oak.

"Here's where things get interesting," Weeby said. "There will not be lights, or any clear direction marked ahead."

"I assume you know the way," Shalindra said.

"We can hope I remember," he replied with a grin.

"The caverns we will pass through are natural," Verelli advised, "though many have been expanded over centuries. A considerable number have been cataloged, but many more lead into depths that have seen no living creature."

"I can understand why nothing would be down here," Enna said, repressing a shiver.

"I said no living creature," Verelli corrected. "The caves are not empty."

Charming thing to build a city above.

"Let us continue," Shalindra said.

* * *

The chamber lay hours and many winding turns behind them, lost in the maze of hollow spaces beneath the earth. Enna's glowing orb was once more attached to Fendrick's shield, the edges of its dim glow a defining line of the limits of their world. The rock above them hung in pointed shafts which defied gravity, or cascaded in rippled sheets of stone down the walls. Sharply tipped columns rose from the floor to meet them, sometimes joining into a single column. They were painted in whites or shades of brown, and the smell of minerals permeated the still air. There was absolute quiet within this subterranean world, save for the infrequent drip of water and the occasional scuff of a foot on the stone.

"I've seen caverns like this in the mountains," Fendrick

whispered, "but never so close to the ocean."

Verelli shot him a warning glance, and the dwarf returned to silence. Though the group had encountered neither demon nor beast and the caverns gave every indication of being empty, they did not feel uninhabited.

They wove their way around the stalagmites and squeezed through narrow, uneven passages. The ceiling descended so low at times that even Weeby had to duck, and the others were forced to crawl on their knees.

Sometime later they came to a chasm wide enough to be called a canyon, and while the bottom could not be seen, the rush of water rumbled far below. It was a rare open space, one that eased the claustrophobic press of stone around them. A narrow, arched bridge of seamlessly interlocking stones spanned the divide. The structure was clearly engineered, but the minerals deposited over and around it by eons of water droplets made it seem to have grown naturally from the stone on either side.

"Who built this, and how?" Birion whispered.

"We did," Verelli answered. "Recall that some of the structures we will pass date from the time of the Three Empires, when magic was better understood."

"Are we sure it's safe?" Fendrick asked, eyeing its slenderness.

"It did not collapse the last time I crossed it."

That endorsement was enough for Weeby, who scampered across without hesitation. Verelli traversed the span at an unhurried pace, and the rest followed more slowly. The crevasse swallowed the echoes of their footsteps within its dark depths, and even Shalindra's exceptional vision was insufficient to see the bottom. The bridge was slick with water, and the low railings offered little reassurance in case of a fall. There was a collective sigh of relief when they had attained the far side and continued on more solid footing. The ledge descended slightly, then turned into a man-made tunnel that emerged into a second, much shallower chasm with another bridge. This crossing was no less nerve wracking than the first, depositing them on a landing with three tunnels leading into the rock. Weeby chose the rightmost one without hesitation.

They were not far along the tunnel when Shalindra felt a burning twinge at the back of her neck. She was about to stop the group to determine the cause when Weeby came to an abrupt halt and held up a hand for silence. At first there was nothing but the sounds of their own breathing. Then something ahead moved—something much too large to belong here. Whatever it was produced a cold feeling of dread within her. There was a familiarity to what her senses were trying to tell her, but Shalindra could not make the identity come.

"Is there another way?" she whispered to Weeby, who just shook his head in answer.

Shalindra directed them forward as she took the lead, her steps slow and silent. The tunnel merged with a cleft in the rock, a place where the floor had been worn smooth not by flowing water, but by the passage of many feet. Stalagmites lay like trampled grass along a trail, the edges of the breaks still sharp. A foul smell overrode the musty dampness, a pungent, rotten odor of death and freshly turned earth that wormed its way through the still air.

Shalindra held a strong suspicion of what might produce that stench, and it had no business being in these caves or even on this world.

"Shade the light," she commanded, "and wait here."

The tunnel plunged into near-absolute darkness as Enna dimmed her light to that of a smoldering fire. Shalindra allowed her sight to adjust, then tiptoed forward. Though beyond the glow of the light, the tunnel was as visible as the forest in twilight, and she moved with assurance. The dull echoes of sound coming from ahead indicated a sizable space, and the temperature intensified with every step. Soon the tunnel branched and widened, hooking left around a tight corner into a domed cavern large enough to encompass a small village. The center was filled by what resembled a pond, but instead of water it held a dark, viscous fluid of unwholesome greens and blacks.

A birthing pool.

The vile liquid emitted a faint, greenish luminescence, just bright enough to reveal the dark outlines of massive, bulbous creatures moving within it. Wharudroks. Easily the height of a castle rampart, they lumbered through the pool, stirring and agitating the liquid with their wide, ribbed legs. The heads of the massive, four legged creatures were so flat and lumpy that they all but disappeared above the oversized orifice at the base of their shoulders where a neck should have been. Those mouths, large enough to swallow a horse and cart—or another demon—whole and filled with row after row of spikey teeth, were only the most visible of the defenses each creature possessed. Shalindra knew that there were two beady black eyes just above those mouths, but at this distance they were too small to see.

Immense stone troughs were positioned around the pool, smoldering red and radiating heat like massive forges to incubate the life that grew within. On the demon world, the pool would have been filled with pieces of defeated demons mixed with blood and flesh supplied by the living. There were tinges within the stench that put her in mind of human battlefields, and she shuddered at the thought of what this one might contain.

She turned away in revulsion, searching for another exit from the cavern. A huge tunnel bored its way into the earth on the far side, but it was another darkened recess some fifty paces along the right-hand wall caught her attention. Just tall enough for a man like Birion to walk through and barely wide enough for him to stand side-by-side with another, it more closely matched the dimensions of the tunnel in which she stood. Whether it was the exit or not, she did not want to risk their lives fighting their way across the cavern. She hurried back to the group to relay what she had seen.

"Is there no other way but through?" Birion asked.

"No," Weeby answered. "Pretty much every route to Solor-Majalis leads to here."

"Why not burn all of it now?" Honarch asked, his eyes smoldering. "They destroyed an entire city. Maybe we should return the favor and kill their children."

"There is too much risk," Shalindra said. "The wharudrok are vicious, single-minded creatures that might take thirty or more demons to bring down."

"We came this way to avoid fighting our way into the city," Verelli said.

Honarch clenched his fists tight but held his tongue.

"Enna," Shalindra said. "Just enough light to see, please."

Enna brightened her light, and Shalindra led them back to the cavern. Pausing at the mouth of the tunnel, she beckoned Weeby forward. "Is that it?" she whispered, pointing to the assumed exit.

"Yes," Weeby confirmed. "From there it's only…" His voice trailed off as he spied the massive demons tending the pool.

Enna's sudden intake of breath signaled her alarm, and Fendrick muttered an unwholesome curse.

Shalindra ushered them back into the tunnel. "They will die to defend that pool, but they will never leave it. Not even when the new demons begin eating them alive as they emerge. If we make no move towards them, they will likely ignore us." She was repeating it from memory, no longer caring whose it was, so long as it held true.

Weeby took a deep breath to compose himself. "Well, the ground's pretty clear between here and our exit. If all we have to do is tiptoe across, it should be easy enough, right?"

No one seemed to believe it, and Shalindra was uncertain enough herself. But there was no other way.

"Follow me," she said.

Slowly, she moved into the open expanse of the cavern. With every step she took, the dark hole marking their way out seemed to stretch further and further away. She placed each foot carefully, resisting the urge to run, and kept a nervous eye the wharudrok.

They were noticed almost immediately. First one and then another of the ponderous demons shifted to face them, tracking the group's movements in the manner of a mother bear turning a wary eye towards an unexpected visitor. They were not supposed to do that, and whether they were staring at the entire group or just her, the weight of their gaze caused her to question the wisdom of crossing the cave. Her weapons would do no more damage to the massive creatures than to a castle wall, and not even she could outrun a monster who could cover a city block in a single stride. Every muscle in her body screamed at her to flee, but she forced her pace to remain steady. She was beginning to think they might succeed when the closest wharudrok took a lumbering step out of the pool, shaking the cavern like an earthquake as it planted its thick, pedestal-like forefeet wide. Its sides began to expand as it drew in a huge breath.

Shalindra had forgotten about that.

"Take cover!" she shouted, even though there was none to be had.

The wharudrok's body contracted like a bellows, spewing a jet of turbulent bile towards them. Enna's shield manifested simultaneously with Shalindra's own, sparing the group from being engulfed. The noxious liquid splattered everywhere, dissolving everything it touched with a hiss of acrid, yellowed steam. Birion cursed as he yanked his helm from his head and cast it aside, the steel now eaten full of holes and his hair singed.

"Run!" Fendrick shouted as a second wharudrok lumbered forward.

Puddles of the regurgitated offal smoked and hissed on the floor all around them, the smell they emitted so strong that it left an aftertaste of vomit in Shalindra's mouth. She abandoned the cavern wall and raced straight towards the exit tunnel, hopping from stone to stone to avoid the liquid still on the ground.

"Again!" Verelli shouted.

They huddled together between Shalindra and Enna as the women manifested their shields, but the streams shot over their heads to slam into the cavern wall they had just abandoned. There were cries and curses as the acidic liquid rained down on them. The wall behind them hissed and cracked as it shifted unwillingly from solid rock to a boiling froth. Chunks began to crumble away, threatening to bury the group as they crashed to the ground.

They made a dash for the tunnel, tripping and scrambling over the irregular floor, just as a new burst slammed into the space they had just vacated. Another blast of burning liquid chased them into the exit, but they did not stop running until they were well away from the birthing pool and its guardians. Enna brightened the light attached to Fendrick's shield enough so that they could all see clearly.

"They don't leave the pool, eh?" Fendrick gasped, his armor still smoking from the drops that had struck it.

"They never have," Shalindra said. "At least they cannot follow us in here."

"A small victory," Birion said, examining his scarred and pitted shield. With a grunt of disgust, he cast it away. "Is everyone…"

His voice trailed off as the clicking of spikey feet on stone echoed up the tunnel from the direction of the birthing-pool. He leapt with Fendrick to block the tunnel, almost completely obscuring Shalindra's view. Over their shoulders, she beheld a flood of centipede-like demons surging through the tunnel in a writhing mass of snapping mandibles and twisting bodies that slammed into the two men with the force of a battering ram.

Fendrick was bowled over by the impact, plunging the tunnel into darkness as he and his shield were trampled beneath dozens of sharp feet. Shalindra rushed to his defense, but the demon ignored the fallen dwarf beneath it and launched itself directly at her. Shining Moon was already in her hand, streaking upwards in an uppercut that drove the demon's head into the ceiling like an egg struck against an anvil. Black gore splattered the walls, but another was upon her even as the husk of the first fell to the floor.

Birion stood pinned against a fold in the rock by one of the demons, straining with both arms to force away the mandibles trying to sever his head. The other demons swarmed past, seemingly oblivious to anyone but Shalindra. Shining Moon struck their segmented bodies again and again as she bludgeoned her way forwards. She felt Enna at her back, but in the tight confines of the tunnel there was no room for anyone to help. She knocked the centipede demon away from Birion, then crushed it with a blow from Shining Moon before it could strike back.

Shalindra spun, looking for her next target, but the battle was over as suddenly as it had started.

Fendrick moaned as he rolled over, attempting to push himself to his knees. Birion slumped down against the wall and wiped blood from his face with a shaking hand.

Shalindra moved past them both to guard against further attacks. Enna was already at Fendrick's side, her prayers of restoration surging into Shalindra's awareness. The request was answered with all Shalindra could give, and Fendrick gasped as her strength poured through Enna and into him.

If Enna was surprised by the speed of it, she gave no sign, spinning to press her hands against Birion's wounds. Shalindra answered her prayer almost before it was made, and the knight's lesions dried away like water in the desert.

"If they didn't know we were down here before, they certainly do now," Fendrick said, kicking at one of the centipede demons. "This attack was no coincidence."

"We should be below the old city now," Weeby called softly. "It's not far."

"Then let's hurry," Birion urged. "This is not a good place to fight."

Shalindra found Enna at her elbow as they hustled onwards, her elvish features creased with worry.

"They recognized you," Enna said.

"They did."

"What do you think it means?"

"I am not sure, but they all know who I am."

Shalindra did not know if that was true or she was just echoing what Tormjere had told her, but she could recall no demon whose path she had crossed that had not treated her differently. This time, the demons' fixation on her had very nearly cost her friends their lives. Was their forceful response a sign that they simply recognized her as a deadly enemy, or could they have been warned that she was coming for them, and she was now leading her friends into a trap?

It this deep silence of the underworld, her growing sense of dread began to affect her perceptions, and she found herself flinching at every flickering shadow or distant sound. She jogged now and then, as if she could outrace such thoughts, but soon pounding vibrations—the kind felt more than heard—reached them.

"Something else's coming," Fendrick called up from the rear.

"How much farther?" Shalindra asked Weeby over her shoulder.

"There's a deep ravine with a bridge somewhere ahead," Weeby panted. "Across that is a door, and then we're there. Keep bearing left at every fork."

Shalindra was off again, giving them no time to rest. Their flight brought them into a chamber created by the intersection of several fractures in the earth, their combined size large enough that Enna's light failed to reach the ceiling or the entirety of the walls. It was bone dry, and every surface covered in a fine dirt that rose in clouds as they ran. The air was thick with the sulfurous aftertaste of demons, but Shalindra did not slow, veering into the left-most fissure.

"No, no, stop," Weeby called, frantically bringing them to a halt. "This is the wrong way. Go back."

Curses flew unmuffled as they reversed direction. Weeby took the lead once more as they returned to the chamber, scrambling up towards a different exit farther across and a short distance above them. The natural stone of the steep slope was terraced so evenly that it could have been cut intentionally as steps, allowing what should have been an easy ascent. Water seeped from fresh cracks in the wall, however, rendering the surface muddy and slick. Birion slipped, crashing heavily to his knees. Honarch and Enna stopped to pull him to his feet. Shalindra achieved the top at the same time

Weeby did, stepping protectively in front of the halfling at the mouth of the tunnel. The corridor was cleanly cut, and empty save for amber lights that blossomed along the floor. Verelli and Fendrick pushed past them both.

"Yes," Verelli said, "almost there."

Enna's frantic shout yanked Shalindra's head around.

A furred demon with the tusks of a boar was upon them. Enna's shield blocked its savage attack, and it leapt sideways before attacking again. Honarch's blast of fire ripped across it, and Birion rammed his spear into it with all his strength. The demon tumbled down the incline, in a shower of dirt and breaking stone.

The trio took their chance, scrambling up to join Shalindra before it could come at them again. They had just reached her when another pair of demons burst into the chamber. Spying Shalindra, they charged.

Birion backed into the mouth of the tunnel, Enna and Honarch just behind him.

Shalindra drew her weapons, but a shout of alarm from farther ahead stayed her hand.

"We can handle this," Enna said over her shoulder.

Shalindra hesitated, unwilling to leave them, but Birion's shout spurred her to action. "Go!"

She turned and sprinted down the tunnel. Amber stones flashed by her feet as she flew through the snaking passage and into an immense cavern shrouded in murky gloom. A narrow ledge ran left along the near side, and close to the end a stone bridge stretched across the jagged cleft into the darkness. At the foot of the bridge, Fendrick and Verelli squared off against one of the grey goat-like demons while Weeby shouted encouragement from behind. Crackling energy pulsed from Verelli's hand, rocking the demon. It twisted away as best it could, ripping a stalagmite free and hurling it at the wizard. Shalindra never slowed. Her shield snapped into place in front of Verelli, shattering the projectile in a shower of stone.

Through the dust she charged, blasting the demon back with a solid strike of her hammer. Another blow sent it plunging over the precipice and into the darkness below.

"It shouldn't have been here," Weeby said, pointing to a freshly excavated tunnel at the end of the ledge. "That's new."

"I have to help the others," Shalindra said. "How much farther?"

"Across this bridge and we're inside," Verelli said. He extended his hands towards the pair of shallow bowls atop the end posts. With a short, sharp phrase, he caused flames to rise within, as if they had been filled with oil and set alight. Another pair of flames appeared farther along the bridge, and then another, springing to life in pairs all the way across. When it reached the abutments on the far side, two massive braziers flared to life, revealing carved stonework edging a pair of doors large enough to defend a castle gatehouse, each one a thick plate of solid iron marked with runes and symbols rendered in gold.

Yet one shadow did not retreat from the light of the flames. Dark, leathery wings unwrapped from each other, and from within that cocoon of darkness emerged a greater demon. Skin of mottled reds and browns covered its thickly muscled body from head to toe, and glowing red eyes peered down at them with unrestrained hatred from above a squashed snout. It stretched its arms apart, as if it had just awoken, and took an eager step forward.

Verelli gasped. "If it takes the bridge, we are doomed to a frontal assault on the surface."

"Then we've no choice!" Fendrick said, tucking his head tight behind his shield and barreling across the stone causeway. Verelli charged ahead with him, Weeby trailing not far behind.

Shalindra cast a worried glance back at the tunnel, wondering why Enna, Birion, and Honarch had yet to appear, then raced across the bridge. She had taken the measure of demons like this before and needed to do so quickly now.

A rustling of leathery wings from above was the barest warning they received as large, black shapes swooped down upon them. Onyx talons slammed into Fendrick from behind. The plates of his armor deformed as the force of the impact knocked him sliding across the stone. The bat-like creature that had struck him disappeared over the side of the bridge before she could even get a good look at it.

Another came streaking at them from the opposite direction. Weeby flung himself against the railing, narrowly escaping the grasping hind legs of the demon.

A third landed atop Fendrick's inert form, but energy arced from Verelli's fingertips, burning lines across its chest. Shrill screeches filled the air as it twisted away and plummeted over the railing.

Shalindra turned in a circle with weapons ready but could find nothing to attack. Weeby was crawling towards Fendrick, who shook his head and forced himself off the ground. A hint of motion in the darkness above them betrayed an imminent attack, and Shalindra manifested her shield, turning aside an assault that could have decapitated either of them.

Everyone scrambled closer, standing back-to-back in the middle of the bridge. A trio of shadowy demons circled in the air above them, almost invisible until they dove within the reach of the light. Shalindra cast a hurried glance towards the large demon blocking the doors, but it seemed content only to watch, for now. There was reason to its behavior, but she did not have time to seek the memory of why.

"What now?" Fendrick said.

"We can't leave these at our backs," Verelli said. "I can't see them long enough to do anything."

Shalindra could see them now but lacked the means to reach them. But the light on Fendrick's shield spoke of a way to make the demons visible to all. With a thought, she produced a trio of her own glowing orbs, each one attached to the torso of the flying demons. The creatures shrieked in unison, twisting and diving in an attempt to dislodge the markers.

Jagged energy snapped through the air from Verelli's fingertips, leaving an after image in Shalindra's vision as it coursed through one demon and leapt to another. Both creatures plummeted downwards, trailing smoke. The smell of burnt fur they left behind was as repugnant as it was oddly satisfying. The final demon wrapped its wings over the globe of light attached to it, free falling into the darkness below.

Silence returned to the cavern. The final demon awaited them at the end of the bridge, a welcoming sneer peeling back the corner of its mouth. Fendrick edged his way towards it, alert for any additional trickery, but Shalindra stepped in front of him. This would be her battle to win.

"Did you think to crawl into our domain without notice, shieldmaiden?" the demon mocked in a raspy voice, beckoning her forward. "Come then, little prophet, and meet the same fate as those who have failed before you."

Shalindra did not give it the satisfaction of a reply as she advanced. Talking was pointless now, and with hammer and sword she fell upon it. Fendrick roared a battle cry and lunged forward with her, but for all his good intentions, she found his presence more hindrance than help.

Verelli's magic lashed out, but this demon was not without defenses of its own, and the sizzling energies failed to do it harm. Its answering attack came so quickly that Shalindra was forced to defend those around her. Maneuvering in the narrow space was difficult, with the demon's bulk further hindering her options.

All of this was apparent to the demon, who exploited this weakness at every opportunity. It used its wings to buffet them, pushing Fendrick towards the edge and throwing dirt and dust in Verelli's face.

Magic hissed and flashed from Verelli's hands, illuminating the cavern in strobing colors. The demon turned the attack aside in a cascade of crimson sparks. It tore free one of the flaming braziers and flung its burning contents at Verelli. Shalindra aborted her attack to shield him from harm but recovered quickly enough to slash a deep cut in the demon's leg. It hissed in pain and struck at her, cracking the stone as she slipped aside at the last moment.

"Avoid me all you want," it spat at her. "Your time nears its end."

It came at her in a rush, and she dove to the ground to avoid being crushed against the cavern wall. She rolled beneath it, but its kick sent her tumbling into the metal doors. It hurt far less than it should have, but the taste of blood in her mouth fueled her resolve.

"Here they come!" Weeby yelled excitedly.

The demon turned towards the defenseless halfling, who had been all but forgotten. The distraction was what she needed, and she drove Shining Moon into the demon's hip. As it lurched to the side, she risked a glance across the chasm.

Enna, Birion, and Honarch raced desperately along the ledge towards the bridge, pursued by multiple demons. Honarch flung magical fire over his shoulder as they ran, but they could not possibly hope to outdistance the larger creatures. Enna spun just before they were overtaken, her symbol clenched tight in her fist. Shalindra turned her awareness inward, relegating her battle with the demon to a different one of her selves as she sought Enna's prayer. She answered the request with such an abundance of energy that Enna's shield rendered itself fully opaque, shielding them time and again, their only protection from being overwhelmed.

"Help them!" Shalindra shouted.

Verelli and Fendrick might have been willing, but their path back across the bridge was blocked by her own conflict with the demon. Shalindra forced the demon against the wall with a solid blow from her hammer, but its arms were long enough to still deny them the bridge.

Behind Enna's stalwart defense, Birion and Honarch backed

their way slowly towards the bridge. Enna's shield pulsed outwards, forcing a demon over the edge. But more demons were emerging from the tunnel. So many more.

Shalindra was knocked to the ground, tearing her attention back to her physical self. She slashed upwards as she rolled away, her sword cutting a deep gash in the demon's stomach. She kicked out with both feet, and it staggered against the doorway.

At the other end of the bridge, Enna raised her symbol, preparing to strike with divine energy. Still on her knees, Shalindra returned her awareness to Enna, flooding the elf with power. But Enna's eyes were no longer on the demons before her. Too late, Shalindra recognized her intent.

"No!" she shouted, but the prayer was already answered.

Enna's symbol swung down, sending a silvery blue arc slicing through the abutments anchoring the bridge to the crevasse wall. The stone fractured with an ear-splitting crack. For a moment, it seemed that the ancient stonework might hold, then the span began to buckle one section after another in a shower of rock and dust. With a ponderous moan, it ripped free of its anchors and plummeted into the darkened depths of the chasm.

Blue eyes met green across the divide, each saying to the other what words never could.

Then Birion was pulling Enna away, and they disappeared with Honarch up the newly bored tunnel.

Enraged by fear, Shalindra threw herself at the demon before her with reckless abandon. Sword and hammer struck again and again, battering the demon with a constant barrage that left black blood flowing freely. Unable to defend itself any longer, the demon succumbed and fell.

Unsatisfied by its death, Shalindra turned her ire on the demons still clustered around the far side of the crevasse. The ledge was now filled with demons roaring their defiance, but they were as powerless to strike at her as she was them. It was a small consolation that she held their attention enough that they did not all follow Enna and the others, but there was no telling how many already had.

Verelli and Weeby were already at the doors they had fought so hard to reach. The mage's hand pressed against a circular glyph in the center, and the clank of latches being released filled the cavern. Shalindra only half watched, instead searching desperately for a clear space on the far ledge. All she needed was enough room to create a mist gate across the divide and she could still rescue the others.

Fendrick, guessing her intention, gave her a shove towards the now open doors. "They'll find their way out. Now go!"

For a moment, she did not budge, even as the dwarf put both hands against her shoulder and strained to force her. She finally allowed herself to be steered away, even as her stomach twisted in fear at what would happen to them.

As soon as they were through, Verelli pressed his hand against another circle on the inner wall, and the doors slowly shut. The long hallway they were in was tall and as wide as any city street, lit by shallow braziers of fire. The weight of the arched ceiling rested on curving beams of worked stone which connected to stout pillars cut from the walls. Shallow braziers of open flames rested atop squat pedestals at the base of each pillar, lending an alternating pattern of light and dark that faded into the distance. It was artfully crafted but felt as old as the caverns they had just left.

"Where are we?" Fendrick asked.

"Within the walls of Solor-Majalis," Verelli said. "Very close to our goal. If we were to…"

Their exchange faded from her consciousness as Shalindra turned her awareness inward, searching for the familiar sensation of Enna's prayers. They were there, arriving in a pattern of rapid succession that could only indicate a continuation of the fighting they had just fled. Shalindra answered every request twofold, desperate to keep them alive.

"How can we get back to Enna?" she asked, cutting someone off midsentence.

"We can't," Verelli answered.

"There has to be another way across. Where does the tunnel they took come out?"

"Who knows?" Weeby asked rhetorically. "It was dug by the demons, but if they keep heading up they're bound to find an exit somewhere."

"They will make their way out," Verelli reassured her, "but there's no time to go looking for them. At this point, we must assume that everything here is alerted to our presence."

"Head for the vaults?" Weeby suggested.

"Yes." Verelli said, nodding. "There are devices there I can use to augment my powers, but only one way down. While there is risk in becoming trapped, the benefits are legion."

His words put her in mind of an endlessly spiraling staircase, and a hall of seemingly infinite length with uniformly locked doors along both sides. Yet she had never been to such a place before.

"Any advantage we can achieve would be welcome," she said. "Let us hurry to finish this." Shalindra tasked one of her selves exclusively to Enna's requests, vowing to do everything she could to keep them safe.

Fendrick hung his shield over his shoulder and took up his metal bow, shifting the quiver of bolts forward on his belt. Verelli directed them a short distance down the hall and then up a spiral staircase. How far up they travelled was difficult to judge, but by the time they arrived in a more normally sized room, she judged that they had to be near the surface once more. The chamber retained the stone walls of the stairwell, but soft rugs covered the floor and there were enough comfortable seats for more than a casual gathering.

Weeby crossed to the only door and put an ear to it. Hearing nothing, he carefully opened it and poked his head outside.

"It's clear," he said, turning back to them.

"Where are we now?" Shalindra asked.

"The third level of Crition's tower."

Shalindra wondered if Verelli had a tower named after himself. "How far to this vault?"

"The first tower clockwise from here," he answered. "Thankfully, we will remain inside the entire time."

The corridors they crept down were eerily quiet. Everything remained as it had been at the instant of the demons' arrival months before. Food lay rotting and uneaten, but without the first fly or maggot to be seen. Chairs had been overturned in haste, and doors to private quarters left ajar.

Verelli paused to look into a large room lined with beds along each wall, and he seemed to deflate at whatever memory it evoked.

"What was this place?" Shalindra asked Weeby.

"The initiates' dormitory," the halfling answered softly. "Verelli spent a lot of time here with the apprentices."

The hall they were in turned at a sharp angle as it passed through a set of double doors, which she took to mean that they had moved from one tower to a building connecting it to the next. A colonnade leading onto a covered patio ran along the right-hand wall, while the left was solid and set with doors and windows. Something pulled at her curiosity, demanding she pause to look out from that terrace, but the sound of a stone striking against stone somewhere ahead kept her moving forward.

They slowed as another set of doors allowed their entry to the next tower. Plush carpet lined the floor inside, and the walls switched from stone to stained wood. Then, the floor simply ended, having collapsed into a cavernous hole scooped from the interior of the tower.

They crawled forward and peeked down into the ruined center of the structure. Torn masonry and shattered furnishings littered the floor. From their perch three stories up, they beheld half a dozen of demons digging down into the earth. They labored under the direction of another, far larger demon, one with wings that beat in annoyance with every given command. To their right, behind the winged demon, volumes of fresh air entered through some unseen opening.

She glanced at Verelli, but the mage just shook his head in frustration. Whatever he had hoped to gain from here would not be achieved.

The winged demon straightened suddenly, and its head snapped in their direction. Shalindra ducked away from the edge, but it was too late. There was a roar of warning and a flapping of wings rose from below, followed by a scramble of motion.

Shalindra rolled away as the demon's arms clawed long streaks into the floor she had just vacated. With both arms, the demon pulled itself onto their level. Verelli met it with a blast of magical energy, and Fendrick sent a metal bolt straight into its head. The demon slid back beneath the edge, but Shalindra doubted the wounds were fatal.

"Run!" Fendrick shouted. And then they were sprinting back down the hallway as the howling demons tore their way through the floor and surged after them.

Fendrick ran ahead, his stout legs propelling him faster than anyone so armored should have been able to move. Shalindra and Verelli ran close on his heels. The shrieks and howls of their pursuers echoed up the hallway after them.

"Left!" Verelli shouted as they approached the doors that would take them back outside the tower.

Fendrick barely slowed, careening off the walls as he took the corner. Then they were running down stairs that fell in perpendicular flights.

"Keep going," Verelli directed as Fendrick slowed at the first landing.

They descended until the steps ended, skidding to a halt before a door. Fendrick gripped the handle and yanked hard.

"It's locked."

"Stand aside," Verelli commanded. A hurried incantation was followed by a puff of acrid smoke, and the latch clicked open.

Fendrick shoved his way through. They found themselves in a rubble-strewn hallway that might once have been grand, but the carpet beneath their feet was ripped and soiled, and the opulence that once decorated the walls had been scattered about the floor.

Something caught Shalindra's eye out the window, and she moved closer to get a better look. At the base of the tower opposite theirs, the portal was a massive swirling vortex of purple black smoke, which occasionally spewed out flaming chunks of matter that streaked through the air to explode against the inner walls. The clouds in the sky above twisted, as if the very air rebelled against the thing that was there.

"I see it," she said. "The gate the demons are using to come to our world."

The others joined her to stare into the inner courtyard.

Four wizards stood on each side of the vortex, their bodies propped upright by slimy, slug-like demons whose tentacles were burrowed into their brains through their ears and eyes. Their tattered remnants of clothing were soaked by the drool dripping from their slack jaws.

"There are only a few demons at the gate," she said. "This could be the perfect opportunity to close it."

"She's got a point," Fendrick said. "The rest are all running around upstairs looking for us."

"There aren't enough of us to simply beat the portal into submission," Verelli said. "We need greater magics if we are to succeed."

"There are not any greater magics to be had," Shalindra said. "If we cannot do this, no one else may ever get close enough to try again."

Verelli nodded wearily. "The door is that way."

Then they were moving once more. They ran down another hall, scrambling over stone and debris. Holes torn in the ceiling allowed brief glimpses of a snowy sky brightened by patches of morning sun. Verelli waved his arm, motioning them to a halt.

They did, then peeked around the corner through a large opening whose double doors had been torn from their mounts. The courtyard lay before them, empty and quiet save for the steady churn of mists wrapping the large mist gate on the far side.

"We can only hope this is indeed our chance," Verelli said.

"I will take those on the left," Shalindra said. "The rest of you to the right."

With that barest of plans, they rushed into the snowy courtyard. They were not even a third of the way across when one of the demons, a smaller one with a bulbous head and tentacles for hair, turned away from the gate to face her. She almost thought she saw a smile on its face, but it made no move to either alert its companions or defend itself.

"Stop!" Shalindra yelled to the others, skidding to a halt. It was wrong. All of it was wrong. The citadel, the demons, this portal—nothing was what it should have been. She was about to order them back when the entire citadel seemed to lurch into motion.

From the base of every tower, through shattered windows and torn doorways, and even from the mist gate itself, poured rank after rank of demons. First there were dozens, then hundreds, and then still more came. From every hole and crevasse in the ruined citadel crawled a demon, like ants from a disturbed nest.

Behind her, the floor erupted in a shower of masonry as burrowing demons broke through. From the gaping hole came still more of the creatures.

The demons shrieked and growled, roared and squealed in a cacophony of noise that echoed inside the hexagonal enclosure, as deafening as it was incomprehensible.

Into this writhing frenzy descended a massive demon, plummeting down from the ruined tower on massive wings that barely slowed its fall as it slammed into the ground in a shower of broken stone. It stretched its arms and wings wide, obscuring the gate as it rose to its full height, double that of any other demon.

Though Shalindra sought to maintain a brave face, her shoulders slumped. Her failure had consigned her friends to share her fate. There would be no statue of victory for her in the Glade of Guardians, offering wisdom to whoever next assumed that mantle. Eluria had squandered her precious strength on her, and she had failed.

There's always a way.

She looked around, but she could not even contemplate in what direction escape might lie.

You've held it all along.

A feeling of dread froze her body in place. In her hand, Shining Moon burned hot with unholy desire that twisted around her heart like a serpent. Her sword slipped from numb fingers and her hands trembled as she drew the sacred weapon of Eluria to her chest.

Time slowed to a crawl, trapping her in the moment between

one breath and the next.

Let it happen.

Shalindra's vision shifted.

Overlaid upon the entirety of the scene before her lay a tapestry woven in flaming sparks of reds and oranges, one of life and movement, knowledge and strength, hunger and desire. The embers burned bright inside each of demons before her, their flickering mesh rendered to her sight not as the fading aftereffects of death but the blazing torches of their life.

You were told, once, what it could do.

The hunger of a thousand days gripped her, a carnal desire that no food of this world could ever satisfy.

You promised you'd do everything to protect them.

The mighty demon's eyes met hers, and it raised its arm to signal.

No matter the cost.

Chapter Thirty-Seven

Triumph

Sulfaxrhu peered down from his place of concealment, as still as the stone of the tower he stood atop. As was foretold, they were coming. In truth, he still struggled to believe it could have been so simple. When his Attuned had devised this scheme, he had been justifiably dubious—how would these minor champions be so brash and so foolish as to come straight to him? But they had, drawn to this place by the will of Mergolatrhu like one of the Nameless to warmth.

Their approach had been clumsy, if creative. The catacombs would have to be more thoroughly explored, no matter how unpleasant. But that was a small matter for smaller demons, and one for another time. Now his enemies were exactly where they were meant to be, and his would be the name all would remember for snuffing their light once and for all. They would not simply die, as had the others before them. Twice now had he faced a champion of Eluria, and he knew how to beat this one.

Almost on cue, they ran into the inner courtyard, no doubt

hoping to close the gateway between their two worlds as if it were the only bridge to this realm. He scoffed silently at the notion. Like the mages who had once ruled this fortress that he now claimed as his own, they knew only what they had been told.

He recognized them each, even from this distance. The dwarf who sought desperately to absolve his failure. The enslaver, powerful in his own right but unaware of his irrelevance in this conflict. He was there for his own benefit and would betray the others in a heartbeat if it served his interests. Then there was the priestess. The Guardian, as they called her in their shrill little voices. Wielder of the foul weapon of a fouler god. Without the Veluntrhu at her side, she was diminished, incapable of attaining the destiny she sought to achieve. There were others nearby, but after these were broken, they would be simple to destroy. He knew them all, and he hated them as he hated nothing else.

They arrive.

The words of his Attuned reached him as clearly as if they had been standing together. Lacking the ability to send such complex thoughts of his own, Sulfaxrhu's response was, of necessity, brief, more a sensation of pleasure than a command. But it was all that was needed.

The Attuned issued the mental signal, and his demons streamed into the courtyard. They swooped through the air. They emerged from beneath the earth. They trod forward with enough force to shake the foundations of the world that would soon be theirs.

He leapt from his perch, using his wings to slow himself only slightly as he plummeted downwards. He landed in front of the world bridge with thundering force, crushing the weak stone covering the ground. He spread his arms and wings wide as he drew himself upright, forcing the reality of his might upon these four puny attackers. He stood twice as large as the tallest of the demonic horde between them, a testament to the power at his command. The fear in their eyes was as satisfying as the rending of their tiny bodies would be. This would be a sweet feast indeed, and then this world and its bounties would forever belong to him.

The priestess stood protectively before the others, a meaningless gesture of submission. There would be no words spoken to assuage her failure, no explanation to delay the arrival of her doom. Sulfaxrhu reveled in triumph as he raised a hand to signal his thralls forward. His gaze locked with hers, and in those disgusting pools of blue he beheld… pity? It stayed his hand, even as it repulsed him with its weakness. Why was she looking at him like that?

Her entire body trembled with fear as she clutched her hammer impotently to her breast like a shield. A sliver of red flashed across those unsettling eyes, and for the first time since he had crawled from the birthing pool as an Unnamed, Sulfaxrhu knew doubt.

From her came nothing—neither sound nor light nor energy. But he felt it. Something tainted and foul, as horrible as it was powerful. The Attuned spun as one to face her in alarm, their dismay rocking him to his core.

Sulfaxrhu cast his arm towards her, convinced the strength of that motion would somehow speed his thralls towards her and avert whatever black magic she sought to manifest. The closest of them were only a few strides from her and instantly sprang forward.

But they never reached her.

Their bodies jerked back as if pulled by unseen shackles, stretching in different directions all at once as they were contorted into horrible shapes. Gargled screams were torn unwillingly from their jaws, spewing forth alongside their entrails as their flesh was yanked inside out.

The contagion spread outward like an avalanche, sparing nothing. The living did not succumb to it so much as explode, their forms shredded from within and scattered in the air. Like an ill wind, it swept through the horde, a gut-wrenching vortex of peeled open bodies and tormented death that spared no one and nothing.

"Naishairru!" the Attuned screeched in panicked unison.

Sulfaxrhu's blood ran cold and his insides twisted, as if seeking their own escape. Naishairru—Eater of Life, Bringer of Oblivion. An unholy imbalance in the laws that governed all life. Even he, who had tasted the blood of thousands of his own kind and reclaimed the marhu of their unwilling deaths, even he could not believe their enemy would commit such vile heresy.

"Defiler!" he screamed at her.

But it was an impotent curse, the pitiful complaint of one whose destiny rushed inescapably closer. The Attuned invoked their defenses, mighty incantations that channeled their goddess into such a manifestation of dominance that it should have obliterated any and all who stood before them. Yet they were swept aside as easily as the lowest thrall, spattering him with the gore of their deaths.

The last thing Sulfaxrhu saw were those gods-cursed blue eyes, tears streaming from them as she destroyed him utterly.

Chapter Thirty-Eight

Through the Gate

Fendrick collapsed to his knees, his bowels twisting in the most unpleasant of ways as he fought to keep his stomach from hurling itself from his throat. Beside him, Verelli failed at that same effort, emptying whatever he had inside him onto the ground. Somewhere behind him, Weeby whimpered. When the wizard recovered enough to look up, his face was ashen. Fendrick kept his eyes on the ground for as long as possible, not wanting to see, but they were drawn upwards against his will.

There were no words to describe the carnage around them. Globs of dark flesh were spread together in a stew of bile and entrails eight feet high, making it impossible to distinguish where one creature ended and the next began. Nothing broke the silence save the dripping of black blood as it ran down the walls. The stench was as nauseating as it was overpowering, a rancid assault on the nostrils that made his eyes burn. He wiped at them, dragging his gaze back to the… *being* that had done this.

The air around Shalindra warped and distorted like ripples of heat above sand. Her outline was indistinct, blurred by the silvery glow encasing her in a nimbus of light. She was less a woman and more a creature of energy and force, and were Fendrick's mind thinking clearly enough to control his body, he would have cast himself to the ground and subjugated himself before her. He could not fathom what she had done and suspected that he would not understand even if it were explained to him.

Verelli wiped the dripping rancor from his mouth with a trembling hand. "How...?"

Shalindra offered the faintest of smiles, a gesture of consolation that was more an expression of sadness than a measure of encouragement. She stooped to retrieve her sword and returned both her weapons to her belt.

"I would ask one final service of you both before I go," she said, her words piercing Fendrick's ears like needles of burning ice, making his head swim.

The piles of dismembered bodies parted before her, moved by some unseen hand as a path to the portal was opened. He forced himself to his feet, but she was already moving towards the gate.

"You don't mean to close it," Verelli gasped. "You would return to Urtratu without us."

"No!" Fendrick heard himself shout. "I swore I would stay with you."

"Where I must go, you cannot follow," she said without turning.

"We will wait..." He tried to run after her, but his legs would not obey the command.

Shalindra turned to face him, a beacon of purity and strength amidst a sea of death. Fendrick felt his resolve melt to nothing beneath her gaze, yet when she spoke there was tenderness in her words.

"So long have you already waited. Find Enna. Even now, our friends approach an exit from the tunnels below what was once the alchemist's shop on Vie Kivaldus. Flee back to the Ceringion stronghold and keep her safe. Though she, too, has given so much, there remains one more task she must accomplish."

She gave them both a final glance. "Thank you."

Fendrick remained rooted in place as Shalindra stepped past the muck towards the mist gate, watching helplessly as she was swallowed by the swirling mists. The portal collapsed in on itself with a booming displacement of air the moment she was through, leaving the three men alone.

"We need to go," Weeby said, tugging at Fendrick's shoulder, "and I don't ever want to come back."

Chapter Thirty-Nine

What Was Bargained

Mataasrhu brooded in silence, ravenous hunger gnawing uncomfortably at him. There was nothing to be done for it, a situation foreign to every creature who inhabited this world. Sulfaxrhu had assembled his horde to pillage the human realm, and in so doing had drawn members from every wharra. Mataasrhu had been deprived of all his goats as well as his strongest demons, and even his Attuned had left for the promise of unending bounty. All that remained were eleven of the weakest thralls—far too few to defend his cave.

He snorted in disgust. Not that he would be attacked. The Edict of Servitude had been rescinded, ending once and for all the sham of their subservience to the human wizards, but it was replaced by something even more unpalatable: the Edict of Peace. It was a vulgar concept coopted from a disgusting people, and it had no place in this world. Yet the Attuned had decreed it to be so, and even the most powerful demons had bent to their will. And so it was that during the launch of the invasion into the other world, all raiding and conquering was banned. Mataasrhu had been forced to allow the smallest of his thralls to be killed—a bloody sacrifice to appease the others. It was a convenient way for Sulfaxrhu to gather more followers without angering everyone, for demons who sat idle would begin to waste away, and he promised an unending slaughter. But for those left behind, there was only silence and boredom.

It was in the midst of this misery that *she* returned to the world. The proclamation came as an unnatural stillness that settled in the air, a subtle vibration of sound felt deep in the bones. Some of his thralls noticed as well, though they had no concept of what it portended. Mataasrhu held himself still to disguise that he alone knew the significance of that sensation.

Her whispered call came to him instantly. Not a lowly thrall to be ordered about, he waited for a long count before taking any action. It was a childish reaction that altered nothing and offered only the illusion of control over a situation which was no longer his to command. With a grunt of disgust he stood, a move that drew the instant attention of the other demons.

"I am going to find suitable targets for our next raid. This Edict will not last forever, and when it ends, we will ravage everyone in our path."

The lie was believed but met with only listless enthusiasm. Mataasrhu did not care and wondered why he had even offered an explanation—he would never see this cave or anyone in it again, after all.

He strode outside and launched himself into the air. The source of her call was surprisingly close to where Sulfaxrhu's horde had established their bridge to the other world. It was impressive that she had found a way to sneak through, though her route through Sulfaxrhu's gate was surprising. Mataasrhu climbed higher, clearing the canyon rim and banking towards the gathering place. He kept himself close to the ground, unsure if those who hunted the skies would respect this new Edict or challenge his passage.

His flight was brief and uncontested, and he was soon swooping down towards a broad, flat plain ringed by craggy cliffs of striated rock that drew closer together the farther he travelled.

The dark reds and browns of the stone contrasted only slightly with that of the coarse sands of the plain, made of a lighter brown that swirled and shifted in the hot breeze.

But nothing was there.

No gate, no horde, no Attuned. The valley bore the tracks of thousands of demons who had marched towards conquest, but it was now as empty as if they had never existed. Mataasrhu saw a speck of white against the dull tones of the rocks and circled twice to check for signs of a trap before descending.

Stone crunched beneath his hooves as he landed, and his head twisted back and forth warily.

"I destroyed it," the shieldmaiden said in response to his unspoken question.

"You?" he asked, couching the query in condescending tones to mask his surprise. "So, you've returned for your revenge."

"It could be viewed that way."

"How you choose to view it is irrelevant. You are here to seek my assistance as was bargained, and I shall aid you in reaching your goals. So, tell me, how many demons will you kill to achieve your revenge?"

"Only one."

"Then perhaps you should name the target of your—"

"Mergolath." The name echoed hollow as it bounced between the rocks, drawing an ill-omened rush of air which stirred the sands.

Mataasrhu withdrew from her as if he had been struck by a lash. "Insolent fool!" he snarled. "To name the Mistress of Torments in Her own domain is unwise."

The woman's eyes seemed to burn with an inner light as she stared at him. "I shall speak of my equals as I see fit."

Mataasrhu did not like those disturbingly blue eyes, nor the way they seemed to peer inside him. What was this thing standing before him?

"Insolent," he repeated, but without conviction. The sheer audacity of her statement marked her as unstable, but should she be capable of causing even half the disruptions *he* had been able to stir… "And how do you intend such an impossibility? Do you think to simply challenge Her here on the plains and be done with it?"

"I seek a larger advantage than what can be found here. There is a specific place where you go to reclaim your god's power, and it is there that—"

"Golardrhu?! You seek to mount the spire of the ancients and pillage Her largess? You are not insolent; you are mad beyond any meaning of the word. You will find no revenge there, shieldmaiden, only death."

"You seem to have given this sequence of events some thought already," she countered. "Have you plots of your own in this area?"

"Do not put words in my mouth!" he hissed angrily, taking a step towards her. "And toy with my patience no longer. You mean nothing to me, as *he* meant nothing."

She tilted her head back to look up at him but did not retreat. "On the contrary. I will mean everything to you. You bargained your assistance and asked what I wanted, and it is this: see me safely to the top of Golardrhu."

"I am under no obligation to fulfil a bargain that leads to my own death."

"Have you not wondered what I am willing to offer?"

"I need no further amusement. No matter what promises you may—"

"Everything."

"That is not a bargain, only wishful thinking."

"I know where I need to go, and what I must do. But I do not care to reach the summit alone, and, attaining that, I do not wish to assume everything I will take and become your god. See me there, help me begin the ritual as you have only dreamed of being capable of. Do this with me, and I will not shower the plains below with her bounty for others to reclaim. I will bequeath it all unto you."

The sheer audacity of that statement brought Mataasrhu up short, no matter how impossible it seemed. "No being would turn away that much power."

The woman shrugged. "I have enough."

She was as mad as the most afflicted creature he had ever heard of, and what she offered was more fool's bargain than immortality. And yet here she stood, in a place which had hosted a vast assemblage of demons such as had never before been seen. Whether she had truly dispatched them or only succeeded in closing the gate, he could not deny her power. She would never survive long enough to reach the mountain, but she might cause enough trouble along the way that he could take advantage. "And what are your expectations of me in exchange?"

"Once you have been given your reward, you will cease attempts to take over my world, and you will allow me to depart in safety with everything that is mine to take."

Mataasrhu turned away to face in the direction of the spire. It was lost behind the dark sands of a storm, but he knew its appearance by heart. He was not alone in his desire to climb to its peak, to pass through the ceiling of clouds that no demon dared enter and emerge unscathed on the other side. To stand atop the pillar of everything and gaze into the eyes of the goddess Herself… Countless cycles would come and go before he could ever begin to take even the first steps upon Golardrhu, and every moment between that time and now could be the instant of his death. The shortcut she promised could not be refused, no matter how improbable.

"It is bargained."

She seemed pleased, but she should not have been. He intended to hide their association for as long as possible, and it would supply the needed time to prepare. "Your destruction of the bridge to your world is problematic, but there are other ways for us to return."

"Then we must be quick."

He directed her attention over the ridge. At the broad end of the valley, the sands swept down into a vast canyonland.

"Through the Broken Lands is the route that will keep you most hidden. Do you see the second canyon from the side of those stone pillars? Descend into that crevasse and take the left branch at each of the first three junctions. After that, always turn to the right. You will emerge at the base of Golardrhu and without attracting the attentions of any demons. There will I await you."

"You are not coming with me?"

Mataasrhu laughed without humor. "I agreed to guide you, not lead you by the hand. The way will be free of demons, but know that there are reasons we do not travel these canyons. You should pray for whatever luck your gods may grant you."

He launched himself into the air, hoping that he had not been seen with her. The time was fast approaching when he would have to honor without reservation the bargain he had made, and then there would be no turning back. He glanced over his shoulder, but she was already gone. As Mataasrhu banked towards his den, he did not know if he should hope for her success or failure.

* * *

Shalindra cut down the last of the worm-like serpents with a sharp swipe of her sword and looked around to see if there were any more. Shining Moon blazed hot in her hand, signaling its approval as she absorbed the embers of the creature's death, even as its gore still slid unhindered from her armor. It was an act as natural as breathing, and she would no sooner stop one than the other. Alharania's warning was a muted and distant memory, a futile plea against what she had already become.

The air along the canyon floor was thick and hot, and the smell was nauseating even without the added stench of this latest encounter. It was difficult to judge how much time had passed since she had descended into the chasm, as the perpetual twilight of the surface had been replaced by an equally consistent murky gloom. The clouds blanketing the sky high above never parted, and there was not even a bright spot to indicate the location of the sun. She was not even certain that a sun existed, though something above the clouds had to be providing the light, minimal though it was.

She slumped with her back against the rock wall, then slid to the ground. She was more alone now than perhaps any person had ever been, but she had no cause to fear such isolation. This was where she belonged, after all. What she was meant to be. Her only wish was that the mist gate's closure had obliterated the memory of what she had done to get here, but nothing could ever erase the tortured cries of the creatures she had devoured alive. The raw strength that heinous act had supplied now coursed through her veins, eclipsing all that had been given to her by Eluria. The sensation hung like a numbness on her soul, a mark that would leave her forever tainted.

She was so tired.

Not physically, though she had not slept in months. No, this was a different weariness, one that seeped into her mind as a dull, insistently throbbing reminder that she was as yet insufficient for what was required. Shalindra had torn the life from countless living creatures, and it was not enough. She had cut down every demon that had shown itself to her, and it was not enough. She had sucked the embers of power from the corpses of unnamed horrors within these canyons, and it was not enough. Nothing could stand in her way. Not the twisting maze of the canyons, not the worm creatures that scavenged the detritus of the demonic conflicts fallen here from high above, nor even the burrowing creatures that sprouted from holes in the rock walls. The giant worm, a slug-like beast the size of a castle wall, she had allowed to pass, for no other reason than it was quicker to sneak by.

None of it did anything to slow her down, yet it seemed a proper penance for what she had done.

You didn't think this would be easy, did you?

I would give much to see even one familiar face, yet never would I inflict this torment on anyone I held dear.

At least you're not alone.

Am I not? I do not even know who I am talking to.

When you no longer recognize yourself, it's a bad sign.

Shalindra put her head in her hands.

I am going mad.

Madness is often associated with greatness.

I do not wish to be great; I only want this to end.

You don't have a choice anymore.

Taking a deep breath, she gripped Shining Moon tightly in her hand and forced herself to her feet.

I wonder if I ever did.

Chapter Forty
An Uphill Climb

Shalindra might have considered it a relief when she at last pulled herself above the canyon rim and onto the rocky base of the spire, but she was beyond the comforts of any such emotion. There would be nothing to feel until she either triumphed or died, and as she gazed up at the impossible height of the climb that now confronted her, only the finest of margins separated her desire for one ending or the other.

True to his word, Mataasrhu was waiting for her. He looked larger and the textures of his skin more weathered than just days before. Or maybe it was weeks. Whatever he had done to ready himself for this, he had not been idle.

The spire rose like a twisted mountain before them, extending from the barren, windswept plains to pierce the perpetual storm clouds that swirled far above. Even the imposing peaks of the Ironspike Mountains would have been dwarfed by this solitary monolith.

"How high does it go?" Shalindra asked aloud.

"As high as you make it," Mataasrhu stated, his deep voice oddly devoid of its usual arrogance.

"It seems without life, and yet alive at the same time."

"It is assembled from the remnants of those who have tried to mount it and failed. A tomb bound together by magic and guarded by the products of Mergolath's own hands." Mataasrhu glanced over his shoulder at something, then returned his attention to her. "What you attempt has never been done. Eons pass between one Rending Reclamation and another. Not one in a thousand will survive to see it more than once, and the most recent took place when *he* was here. To attempt to initiate one again so soon after another has achieved it..."

It did seem impossible. The Rending required a demon to gather enough power to climb to the top of this mountain, defeating all who stood against them, and still maintain enough strength to attack their own goddess. Somewhere upon the spire lived a demon who had been strong enough to do just that, or perhaps it had reached the top and died in the attempt. But there would never be another time like this one, and she had to make it work.

"Do you think it now hopeless?" she asked. "Shall I release you from your bargain and allow you to save yourself?"

Again, his response was subdued. "I have crossed the line of deniability. Even now, eyes are upon us, and there is no chance for me to escape recriminations."

"Thank you for joining me." She was sincere in that sentiment.

"It is not for your thanks that I do this," he said, his superiority returning. "Do not forget your part in this bargain."

"I will not."

He glanced back at the canyons she had traversed. "Shieldmaiden is a description which no longer fits you. As we are bound in this, what do you wish for me to name you?"

It was a surprisingly difficult question to answer, and she debated the question with herself before supplying one. "You may call me Shalindra."

It was undoubtedly an uncomfortable word for him to pronounce, but she appreciated even that modicum of respect.

"And so, we begin," he said, and started their climb.

Shalindra had to jog to keep pace with his lengthy strides, but she did not object to anything that would hasten their speed.

"Could you fly us to the top?" she asked.

"Anything which circumvents the climb up Golardrhu is forbidden." He did not elaborate further, but his reluctance seemed more than ritualistic tradition.

The lower tiers of the mountain were as barren as every other part of this world, a rocky, steepening incline broken by patches of sand rather than grass. Ledges and cleared areas dotted the slope with the randomness of clearings in a forest, but each had been deliberately fashioned. A handful were being reclaimed by blowing sand and fallen rock, but most showed the signs of recent use. More than one of the reddish stones bore a striking resemblance to dead demons, and the dark discolorations on the surface could have been blood. If so, there was more of it than she cared to contemplate.

"You said the ritual was recently invoked?" she asked to break the silence.

"*He* was here to witness it, if that helps. By our measure, that is the blink of an eye."

"How do you measure time?"

"Time." Mataasrhu thought for a moment. "That is a concept unique to your world. Here there is only a sequence of events, and those that have already happened exert no influence on what is yet to come."

A sound from behind caused her to look back over her shoulder, down the slope towards the base they had so recently departed. Lesser demons were beginning to congregate, watching them.

Mataasrhu did not look back at them. "I told you that our passage would not be secret. They wonder if another ravaging is to occur, and they will join our climb soon."

A Rending was going to happen if Shalindra succeeded, but it would not be in the way any demon would expect.

The scramble of claws on rock told her that the boldest demons down below were now following them. She hoped that they would reach their place and stop but knew that she and Mataasrhu would not be alone much longer.

"How far up did you make it during the last ritual?" she asked.

"Not far enough."

That meant that what they would face was an unknown to both of them. She wondered if there would have been some way to better prepare, or some more capable ally she might have found, but there had to be someone beside her when she reached the top and he was all she had.

They continued in this manner for some time. Nothing appeared to oppose them, a fact which seemed to make Mataasrhu increasingly uneasy. The surface had turned exclusively to rock, and many of the stony protrusions resembled collapsed demons so closely that they might have been statues. Fewer platforms were carved into the surface, and there were no paths to follow.

Glancing back, she saw a sea of demons flocking to the base of the spire. Battles had broken out as they fought for dominance and the right to rise higher. Larger, winged demons swooped down to join the fray, wading through the lesser beings. Dozens of the greater demons had broken free and were racing up the slope after them. Several were stymied as they ran across one another, each meeting becoming a battle to decide who would continue higher and who would die. One of those who had avoided or perhaps triumphed in such conflicts barreled ahead on a collision course straight for Shalindra.

Mataasrhu turned to meet it with claws out. The wolf-like demon was head and shoulders taller than he, and it came at him in a blinding assault of claws and teeth. With animal savagery, they rolled across the mountain, each tearing flesh from the other. From the first blow, it was clear Mataasrhu was no match for his assailant. Shalindra joined the fray, but the ground was sloped and unstable, leaving her at a significant disadvantage to a demon with wide, clawed toes. It recognized her dilemma and positioned itself on the most uneven terrain nearby, kicking stones and debris to keep her at bay as it struck at Mataasrhu. By the time she closed, the two demons were locked together so tightly it was impossible to strike one without hitting the other.

The wolf demon gained the upper hand, pinning Mataasrhu to the ground. Its jaws sought his throat but snapped closed instead on his upflung arm.

Shalindra seized the opportunity, striking the wolf demon a glancing blow with Shining Moon. It was solid enough to drive it back but not enough to inflict significant damage. The attack left her slipping on the loose rocks, and she teetered on the edge. Seizing on her weakness, the wolf charged. Her shield snapped into the air before her, sparing her life, but the impact knocked her from her feet, and she tumbled over the precipice.

What happened then was instinctive, a remembered maneuver that had saved her more than once before. Her eyes locked on the ground just behind and above the demon, and she sent a mist gate tunnelling from the empty air just beneath her to that spot. She landed hard on her shoulder, not thousands of feet below but on the ground behind the demon. Ignoring the pain of the impact, she rolled to her feet and slashed her sword across the demon's spine.

"NO!" Mataasrhu yelled.

His good arm seized the demon by the throat, but he lacked the strength to end it. Shalindra drove her hammer into its head to finish the battle, but before she could say anything, Mataasrhu was already clawing his way desperately away from her.

A sharp crack of fracturing rock split the air with a deafening report, and the mountain shook with such violence that she was thrown to the ground. An avalanche of loose stone rained down from above, pummeling them both and sending Mataasrhu careening back down the slope.

With a ponderous groan, an entire section calved from the side of the spire, a thin but impossibly tall titan of stone. Clouds of dust and boulders careened down as it propped itself away from the mountain on one elbow, and its colossal head shifted towards them with a grinding rotation of stone that set her teeth on edge. Twin chasms of inky darkness fixated on her from its featureless face, and its mile-long arm drew back to strike. A fist half the size of a city hurtled towards them, so massive that it appeared to float slowly across the sky even as the air in front of it smoked and glowed red from the friction of passage.

There was no time to avoid it. Shalindra scrambled beside Mataasrhu and manifested her shield in a full bubble around them. She put everything she had into it, strengthening it with overlapping layers until it lost all translucency and blocked their view behind a haze of silvery white, which lit in red flames the instant before impact.

In the end, it was not her shield that failed but the mountain itself. The impact ruptured the face of the spire, driving her and Mataasrhu into the core like a nail. She felt the collision from every direction at once, crying out as blinding pain shot through her. Her shield collapsed, leaving them at the end of a long, erratic tunnel. Only a pinprick of light entered from the mostly plugged entrance.

She began crawling across the slick floor towards the light as loose rock fell from the ceiling in chunks. Mataasrhu followed her, his larger girth squeezed tight against the walls of the tube cut by their passage.

Shalindra pushed herself to her feet and tried to run, but she was knocked back to her knees by something heavy falling across her back. Her first thought was that the tunnel was collapsing, but it had been too soft to be rock. She regained her feet quickly, desperate to avoid being buried alive. Something slimy slapped against her face, and she realized that what she had taken to be the solid insides of the mountain was instead a mix of soil, crushed stone and a gooey mass of what could only be described as charred maggots, each one the length of her leg. Their circular mouths were ringed with blocky, blunted teeth designed to grind up anything they seized upon.

Shalindra thrashed her way forward, unable to swing either of her weapons with any force, as the tunnel began to constrict beneath the press of earth and demonic worms. They writhed in an agitated state until she was completely engulfed. Panic gripped her as she began to suffocate, unable to tell up from down. Her only point of reference was Mataasrhu's cries of pain.

At last, she kicked something solid. Planting her foot against it, she pulled her weapons up and twisted violently back and forth. The leverage was enough to allow her to carve out a small space free of the demonic grubs but left her soaked in the slime of their deaths.

Producing a small globe of light by her feet, she took aim at the wall of rock before her and slammed her hammer into it. Stone chipped and fractured, and she hit it again and again, hoping that the crust of the mountain was not thick. Her next hammer strike yielded a small hole of light and a welcome blast of air. Mataasrhu seized it with his massive hands and ripped it open piece by piece until they could wriggle out.

The burning hot air of the demon world filled Shalindra's lungs as she emerged. A turbulent wind whipped a fine sand across the spire, stinging her exposed skin and leaving a gritty texture in her mouth as it scoured the slime from her body. She never imagined such an atmosphere could taste so sweet. The entire spire shook with the crunch of the stone giant's fist as it smashed into the demons far below. If nothing, it would put an end to their pursuit, so long as the giant's attention remained away from her.

"Never do that again," Mataasrhu said. "It is forbidden to advance by any means other than walking." He was battered and damaged, with dark blood leaking from dozens of small wounds. He scooped up a handful of crumbled stone, ground it into a coarse powder between his thick fingers, and then rubbed it into his wounds, where it became a thick paste.

As he continued inspecting himself for damage, Shalindra sagged against the mountain and looked out across the desolation of the world.

Everywhere her gaze travelled, it encountered nothing but sand and rock. There were no rivers or forests, no castles or cities. The entire vista was painted in uniformly dull reds and browns, devoid of any semblance of vitality. The curve of the bleak horizon was less a demarcation of earth and sky and more a swallowing of the surface by the unbroken blanket of clouds.

She shuddered with the realization that her own world could one day suffer the same fate as this one. Her closing of the portal between the two realms would be a setback, but so long as Mergolath drove her followers to find a way, no nation or race would ever truly be safe.

The ground beneath her shuddered as the rock giant stepped further around the spire, swiping its arm across the stone to wipe it clean of thousands of demons. It could have easily reached her had it looked up, but it remained distracted by the swarming demons below. She wondered how long that would last.

"We must go," Mataasrhu said.

"What awaits us in the clouds?" she asked, looking up.

"Only the Attuned might know, for they can read the will of Mergolatrhu in their movements. Anything that ventures within never returns."

Shalindra repressed a sigh. "And of course, there we must go."

You didn't really believe it would be otherwise, did you?

No, I did not.

* * *

Shalindra stretched her arm up, letting her fingers brush against the bottom of the clouds. It had taken a significant span of time to reach them, though without the cycle of day and night to measure against, it was difficult to judge just how long. As with every place she had gone, they had left a trail of death to mark their passing. Four times more they had been forced to fight off challengers, the last of which had seen Mataasrhu lose an entire arm. It had almost regrown, a fascinating regenerative ability that she had never known demons possessed.

With each kill, she had insisted that he consume the fruits of their victory. Mostly it was because he needed it—the increase in his strength and size was clearly evident—but it also saved her from absorbing it herself. It was a symbolic gesture after all she had already taken, but it helped her feel human.

Taking a deep breath, she pulled herself upwards. The interior of the clouds was made not of water but of ash, a gritty, acrid mixture that stung the skin and choked the air from her throat. It flowed over and around her like a thing alive, its tendrils clinging to her as they flew past. The winds driving them blew like a gale, buffeting her as she struggled to stay upright.

"We must hurry!" Mataasrhu yelled, trying to be heard above the noise of the wind.

Shalindra tried to respond but received only a mouthful of ash for her trouble. She bent to spit it out, but before she could empty her mouth, sharp talons raked across her back from an unseen foe, deflecting off her armor with the ring of stone on metal. The impact sent her stumbling forward, but her attacker was gone before she could look for it. Mataasrhu had moved ahead only a short distance higher, but already his form had grown shadowed and insubstantial. She clenched Shining Moon tightly in her hand and scrambled after him.

She ducked instinctively as a gleaming trio of black talons materialized from nowhere. They grazed her hair before slamming into the spire, ripping a shower of debris from the surface.

Whatever manner of being it was, it was gone before she could even think to look at it. She felt more than heard their attackers as they flew past, dark patches within the darker clouds that swirled around her.

Mataasrhu bellowed in pain and stumbled to the ground, lashing out in every direction. After another attack that swept her legs from beneath her, Shalindra was soon doing the same. Every dark patch was met with hammer or sword, but she was attacking shadows, and the clouds remained unphased. Her shield was equally ineffective, materializing too slowly to defend her from attacks that materialized from nowhere. In frustration, she sent her shield pulsing ahead. It struck the same nothing as her weapons, but the wake of its passing briefly left a clear, hollow space devoid of clouds. She did it again, feeling the resentment of the clouds as they were forced away.

The speed of the clouds seemed to intensify, angered by her defense. Shalindra pulsed her shield faster. It was impossible to keep them all away, but Mataasrhu bore the brunt of the attacks that slipped through, using his body to protect her as they pressed forward.

The ashen clouds did not thin so much as they simply stopped, and Shalindra broke through like a fish leaping from the water. The clouds clung and pulled at her feet like soup. Her hand found a solid piece of rock, unwilling to surrender, and with a mighty tug she pulled herself free. Mataasrhu lay gasping a short distance away, every breath expelling grey ash from his lungs. Black blood oozed from dozens of wounds.

It was dark, and oddly quiet after the continuous howling of wind within the clouds. The night sky above was lit by millions of stars, but they were in arrangements foreign to her.

Mataasrhu's eyes were wide. "I beheld such displays on your world, once. It is incredible, and terrifying, to see such emptiness."

Directly above the pinnacle blazed twin stars larger than all the others, baleful and red, like angry eyes staring down. Mataasrhu tilted his head back to follow her gaze towards them, and he slumped to his knees.

"She knows."

Chapter Forty-One

A Sacrifice Made

There was no escape from that gaze. Nowhere they could hide and no way to avoid it. Mergolath would bear witness to their final ascent, and she would be waiting.

Shalindra steeled herself, but uncertainty continued to claw at her. She was strong in ways that were difficult even to describe, but she approached this conflict with only the slimmest of plans. No matter what conquests she prevailed in the mortal realm, she was a tiny thing compared to a divine being as old as time itself.

Mataasrhu pushed himself up and pointed towards the now-visible peak. "We are close. Hurry."

There was no trail here, no path marked by the passage of feet over the ages, only an ever-rising pile of hardscrabble stones. Yet the rocky ground was soft, almost spongelike in the way it flexed with every step, and it crumbled and cracked beneath her grasping fingers. Mataasrhu's claws and superior reach gave him an advantage as the pair scaled boulders and sheer escarpments, but even he struggled. The thinness of the air left her light-headed from the exertion. She asked for no help and he offered her none, though he did not stray too far ahead. Whatever lay in wait for them, they would face it together.

After pulling themselves atop one of the endless boulders, their way turned inward rather than up, and they achieved the plateau suddenly. The entire expanse was swept clear, as if some giant hand had scooped away the top of the mountain in a single swipe. The shallow caldera left behind was barren and unnatural but not unused. The marks of violence scratched upon it were as numerous as wildflowers in a field. What time and wind might have flattened and smoothed, giant feet had cracked and torn asunder. Swaths were charred and blackened, melted like wax before a bonfire. Chips large enough to sail a ship through had been knocked from the brim of the plateau, blown free by impacts from the inside. In a world painted by desolation and death, its bleakness somehow stood out as a monument of torment and despair.

Shalindra drew her weapons and descended to the floor of the caldera with a single leap, every sense tingling and burning, warning her to flee. Mataasrhu descended at a more cautious pace, his wings tucked close against his back and his claws curled expectantly. She had taken only a few steps onto the sandy floor when the stillness was disturbed as the wall off to their left began to move, peeling away like a scab torn loose from the skin of the mountain. What emerged from the shower of crumbled rock was a nightmare unlike anything she could have imagined.

Curled and twisted horns jutted in rows around the sides of its head, massive versions of the thousands of spikey protrusions lining its chin and the outer edges of its arms. Its lower body was bulbous, curving back from what should have been its waist to encompass four thick legs, each one twice her height. Both its hands were empty, but she doubted they would remain that way for long.

Dark mists exuded from every pore, wrapping it in a cloak of ash. It stretched itself as if just risen from sleep, unfurling wings wide enough to swallow a castle within their embrace.

That so large a creature of flesh and blood was capable of movement defied belief, but it advanced with a sloshing of its immense girth that spoke of barely restrained speed, every thud of its footsteps an earthquake whose shockwaves threatened to hurl her to the ground.

It spoke with a voice that rumbled and grated from a cavernous depth, emitting heat as much as sound.

"Mataasrhu. I might have known."

Venom wrapped those words, every syllable dripping such scorn as to drown the listener beneath a sea of despair.

Mataasrhu crouched so low he was almost on all fours, his teeth bared and every muscle coiled tight. Shalindra had never beheld a demon so cowed.

The massive demon stalked towards them with exaggerated slowness.

"This is an unholy alliance you have bound yourself to, Mataasrhu. Your stain upon our race will bring me satisfaction to cleanse." Its eyes shifted to her. "What has he promised you, little shieldmaiden? Your world? Your freedom? They are not his to give."

"Nor are they yours to take," she challenged, stalling as she tried to think of a way to assault the creature that would not lead to her instant demise. She would have welcomed the opinions of the *hers* that had filled her head for so long, but they were all gone. Hers was the only path to have made it this far, and this battle would be hers alone.

The monstrosity barked a laugh. "You are a puny disciple of an inconsequential god. Behold me, and witness what a true champion is meant to be! When we are finished with our contest, I will tear the fires of reclamation from your corpse as I stand in triumph above you, and then I shall feed them to you again, so that you may die once more. I shall amuse myself with your unending deaths for the eternity of my reign."

Mataasrhu's own passions flared, lending contempt to his words. "Your end is the only one to be met here. So is it fated, Zrahzaxrhu."

The labelling of the creature before her somehow made it more frightening rather than less, but it did nothing to alter the course they were upon.

"*You* seek to name *me*?" it roared. Anger twisted through its words, combining with vindictive hate at an ever-increasing velocity. "I am no longer like you. I am no longer of this world. I am no longer named. I am!"

Flame erupted from its open maw, a stream of molten rock that shot across the distance between them with blinding speed. Mataasrhu flung himself into the sky, barely avoiding incineration. Shalindra's silvery shield manifested around her, turning aside the physical substance of the attack but impotent against the heat. She stood engulfed by the inferno, its merciless touch singeing her exposed skin and warming her armor to uncomfortable levels. She sent her shield pulsing outward to repel it, then launched herself to the side. Angry coils of mist and ash were all that awaited her, slapping her from the air and sending her careening across the ground. She jammed her foot against the first solid object it encountered, using the leverage to right herself and strike upwards. Shining Moon impacted the demon's arm with brutal force. First blood had been drawn by each of them, and the battle began in earnest.

Time was stripped of meaning and measure, the past and the future lost to the chaos of the now. Their conflict carried them across and around the arena, Shalindra and Mataasrhu working in different ways to remain apart and keep this foulest of demons guessing. Their victories were as inconsequential as they were few, and it was Mataasrhu who began to tire first. As her ally took to the air once more, Shalindra stumbled to one knee in feigned weakness, a ruse which brought the demon's full fury down upon her. Her shield held back its onslaught—barely—but it had provided the opening they desperately needed.

Mataasrhu landed on the demon's back. Before he could gain the leverage to strike, spiny protrusions shot upward, piercing him through. Shalindra watched helplessly as the demon gripped Mataasrhu in one massive hand and flung him against the stone wall with shattering force. He crumpled to the ground, unmoving.

Shalindra might have been left alone, but she understood who and what she now was. She called back her other selves which had been tasked with answering prayers, reassigning that sliver of her consciousness to her own defense and giving it purview over the creation of her shield and the movement of her body. She carved off another segment of her awareness to analyze and anticipate the creature's next attack. As she readied herself, she was no longer alone but in the company of allies, each acting in perfect concert with the other.

Her core, that instance of herself still wrapped around Tormjere's diminished focus, pressed the attack, wielding her pitifully small weapons against a monster of rock and fire. Even driven by her inhuman strength, her sword failed to penetrate the stony skin. Shining Moon was more effective, delivering shattering blows which would have felled lesser creatures instantly. But the demon's reach was long and its assault merciless.

The battle ebbed and flowed as the two combatants fought across the caldera. Grievous wounds were given and received, but as time stretched on, Shalindra could feel the weight of Mergolath's favor upon her champion. Her armor singed by fire and her body bloody from the incessant pounding, Shalindra inevitably slipped. It was an innocuous mistake, a slight misstep on a loose stone. Her recovery was so quick that an ordinary opponent would have missed it completely. The demon capitalized on that mistake, driving a massive arm through the opening it provided.

Shalindra's shield manifested at the last instant and took most of the blow, but the demon's fist crashed through and struck her squarely. The impact knocked her through the air and sent her sword clattering across the stone. Pain shot through her on levels that surpassed mere physical damage, a wicked injury that addled her mind and blurred her vision.

She struggled to her knees, barely able to discern the outline of the demon rushing towards her, but as she focused on the night sky beyond it, she beheld a glimmer of hope. Shalindra felt the shift of Mergolath's attention away from her champion and towards this new arrival. The demon must have sensed something, for it slowed, turning this way and that as it sought this new threat.

The fabric of the demonic world twisted, disturbed in a manner as subtle as it was overpowering. Shalindra was the first to spy it, a streak of light across the sky. It grew larger as it approached, expanding in size and intensity until it blazed like the full moon on a cloudless night. The demon's skin hissed and smoked, burning beneath the purity of it and tearing a bellow of rage from its mouth.

Into the world the star slammed, the jarring force of its arrival hurling chunks of the mantle to cosmic heights. Jagged bolts of lightning ripped across skies filled with debris. Oceans burst forth, freed from their millennia of subterranean imprisonment, their waters boiling to steam within the inferno exploding outward at impossible speeds, though of such a scale that the cloud of destruction seemed to flow no faster than warm honey as it poured across the curve of the world.

A visible shockwave slammed into the mountain, throwing all to their knees and leaving Shalindra's ears ringing. A concussive wind roared in behind it, scouring away the brim of their arena. Shalindra crawled to her sword and thrust it deep into the stone, clinging to it like an anchor. Superheated rock rained down around her, smashing against the woefully inadequate barrier she sought to protect herself with. Even her divine defense, one which had held against the blows of the giant, began to collapse before the onslaught. Rocks the size of houses flew through the air like pebbles kicked from a path. Every muscle in Shalindra's body burned, begging for release as she clung desperately to her anchor.

And from within this maelstrom emerged Eluria, clouds clinging and rolling from her body like water as she rose to stand astride the world, a towering beacon of beauty, translucent yet edged in silvery light of painful brilliance. The layer of clouds it had taken Shalindra days to climb above reached no higher than Eluria's shins, and had Eluria stretched up with her arms, she could have plucked the stars from the sky.

Yet, for all her majesty, this was not her domain. Here, Eluria was an unwelcome visitor whose intrusion was to be answered in kind. Through skies of swirling ash and fire, Shalindra beheld Mergolath's arrival.

From the dark recesses of the night sky, those inky patches unlit by the multitude of stars, the demon goddess descended, an indistinct form of onyx edged in deep crimson with skin as smooth as polished marble. She expanded as she continued to take on substance, standing head and shoulders taller than Eluria.

Though once she had been no less striking than the fairer goddess, Mergolath's appearance had been corrupted by the world over which she ruled. Her hair writhed like the tentacles of the Attuned, the thousands of strands ending in wicked barbs. Her torso was distorted and beastly, lacking any semblance of the feminine shape it had one commanded, and where Eluria stood upon gracefully curved legs, Mergolath perched atop a scorpion's body. The dark goddess spoke no words as she confronted Eluria, for the fury twisting her features would allow no sound to pass. Her dark arms seized the smaller goddess about the neck, and their battle was at last joined.

Continents buckled and heaved as the two gods strove against each other, hurling mountains of dust and sand into an atmosphere already choking beneath the fallout of Eluria's arrival.

Shalindra felt Eluria's calming strength enter her, reassuring and strong. Invigorated by it, she yanked her sword from the rock and drew herself to her feet, leaning into the gale force winds that continued to sweep over the mountain. Her lungs burned from the heat and ash she swallowed with every breath, but her own battle was yet to be finished.

Lightning surged and crackled around them, and columns of ash and dirt obscured everything. Much of the plateau was hidden in the clouds, but she spied the movement of a dark shadow and flung herself at it. The demon was also just regaining its feet but facing the wrong direction, becoming aware of her approach moments too late. Even so, it spun in place so rapidly that it nearly avoided her. Eluria's strength pushed her forward faster than the eye could have followed. She flew below the demon's grasping hands and drove Shining Moon into one of its forelegs with such might that the knee bent sideways and snapped. Her sword plunged into the wounded appendage right behind it, but rather than withdrawing it, she used the embedded blade to twist, rending its lower leg as a wing would be snapped from a cooked bird.

Through the gushing wound she sent her awareness plunging, seizing the smoldering embers of its life and tearing them free. Like a cancer, her ravages spread up its leg, shriveling the limb as she tore life from the living.

It screamed. A hideous cry of tormented pain that curdled the blood, but she did not stop until its stony fist batted her aside. She lost her grip on the sword as she tumbled away, and she tasted blood. Her head hurt and her ears rang. Again, Eluria's magnificence flowed over her like a cooling salve. Shining Moon's thirst burned in her hands as she launched herself at the demon once more.

It struck at her with magic and flame. Javelins of dark mist were turned aside by flashes of silvery light. Whips of fire lashed at her, but she dodged aside to deflect each.

There was a flicker of motion behind it, and Shalindra prepared to defend against another attack. But the shape coalesced into Mataasrhu, his tattered wings flapping desperately to maintain control as he dove towards the demon. A flying rock struck him, deflecting his aim, but he landed atop the demon's head, his claws raking and gouging across its spiny face, squirming this way and that as he sought to avoid the demon's attempts to dislodge him. The demon bit down on Mataasrhu's leg, nearly severing it. As Mataasrhu's back arched from the blinding pain, the demon's hand found its way to his throat. It pried Mataasrhu away with a sickening crunch of splintering bone.

Shalindra felt something inside her tear open, a cold anger mixed with the fear of failure. It suffused her, channeling all the power trapped within her into a singular purpose. She felt her body swell with strength unimaginable as she launched her attack. Shining Moon no longer pulled her forward—it struggled to match its speed to hers.

Once, twice, and then again, her weapon slammed into the demon, the blows falling in such rapid succession that they could have been from the same continuous motion, splattering the ground with its thick, dark blood.

The demon staggered back, reeling from the blows. Shalindra launched herself upwards, and with both hands she brought Shining Moon crashing into its head. Driven by the strength of Eluria and the stolen force of a thousand deaths, the hammer travelled through the head and deep into the chest cavity. Molten fire and black blood erupted from within and gushed over her, scalding her skin and setting her hair and clothes alight. She flung herself to the ground and rolled away, snuffing the flames.

She separated herself from the agony of those horrific wounds, allowing her consciousness to flee from that of her mortal form to a place as yet unaffected by the pain. From this vantage point, she turned her attentions to the twitching corpse of the demon, drawing the fires of reclamation from its expiring body to repair her still smoldering flesh.

When she judged the pain diminished enough for her to tolerate, she returned to her true self, assuming command of her prone body once more. She retrieved her weapons and rushed to Mataasrhu's side, splashing through the blood pooling around him.

He was breathing—barely—and responded feebly to her touch. She tugged his wagon-sized head towards her, seeking her way into eyes as large as her head.

"Let me in," she demanded.

Mataasrhu forced his eyes closed in rejection.

"You must do this with me!" she screamed at him. "I cannot be a demon god!"

"Achieve your goal, so… may achieve mine."

"I do not know what to do. Tell me how to perform the ritual."

Mataasrhu gestured weakly. "Stand atop… what was Zrahzaxrhu." His breath rattled in his throat, and his head rolled lifelessly to the side.

Shalindra ran to the vanquished demon's corpse and climbed atop the simmering ruin, not having the first clue as to what was to be done.

And then she knew.

The memory came to her as it had to Zrahzaxrhu—from that of her vanquished predecessor. She turned her face upwards, manipulating the sky above with a mighty incantation not dissimilar to opening a mist gate, but one which this time granted entry to the inside of Mergolath herself. Her gate carved its way through the tumultuous riot of color that was the spectacle of the battling gods. Explosions of unrestrained energy cast dazzling light across all of creation as multitudes of differing realities battled for prominence, each with differing laws. Some folded together in a harmonic melding of space and time, while others collided with indescribable force, their very natures so diametrically opposed that they were incapable of coexisting.

Mergolath's gaze fell upon Shalindra then, those burning red eyes crushing her spirit beneath the impossible weight of her own insignificance. She could not fight a god. Not even if she consumed every creature on this world could she muster the will or the energy needed.

And in that crushing moment of all-consuming despair, when the bleak, inescapable reality of her failings dragged her to her knees, Shalindra uttered the one prayer that had never been refused—the only one which had ever held absolute meaning in her entire life.

"Tormjere, help."

Chapter Forty-Two

Where Only One May Tread

Released of any constraint, the swirling ball of Tormjere's focus exploded, surging throughout her body and infusing her with purpose and desire. She became complete, the missing pieces of their lives melded together as they should always have been. She knew everything that was his to know, possessed the wisdom that he should never had held, harnessed strength he should never have attained, and set her will on a path only he could have forged.

In that one brief moment, he was with her again.

Crushing hunger gripped her, and her eyes blazed red as she lifted Shining Moon in both hands and reached with it through the vortex in the sky with gleeful desire. Shining Moon sang as it wrapped itself around its most hated enemy and began to tear pieces from the demonic god with a hunger that bordered on insanity. Those chunks fell as flaming meteors Shalindra drew towards the mountain on which she stood, guiding them past herself and sending them streaking towards Mataasrhu. She had no idea if he was even alive enough to receive them, but she would deny them to herself, no matter the consequence.

It was not enough.

Mergolath spoke in a language never uttered within hearing of man or beast, yet Shalindra understood every word.

"Is this what you intended? You think her pitiful efforts will make a difference?"

Mergolath gestured. Time coiled around Eluria's arm like a serpent, and it withered to ruin. Eluria burned it to ash with a glance, then replaced her missing limb, but it came back smaller and weaker than before. A flaming whip the length of a river appeared in Mergolath's taloned fingers, and she struck Eluria across the face, sending her spinning.

"You destroyed my realm!" Mergolath screamed, striking her again. "You burned everything I cherished to ash!" Another lash. "You laid waste to all that I had created, just as I shall lay waste to yours."

Mergolath's hands became massive claws that dripped lava like venom. She plunged them into Eluria, impaling the goddess. Eluria was lifted from her feet, her wounds dripping starlight as she dangled helplessly from those talons.

Time slowed, as if it would be an eternity before Mergolath's fingers would clench and end that which had been Eluria. In the stillness that was an absence of movement, a postponed pain that could not be avoided, came Eluria's voice, calm and serene.

~ Ask ~

There is nothing left for you to give.

~ Ask, that I may answer. One last time ~

Even knowing the consequences should she not, Shalindra

sought an avenue to avoid making such a request, but the words tumbled from her of their own free will.

Forgive me, Eluria, but I must have everything.

The answer came with resigned acceptance, and a tinge of relief.

~ Then everything is what you shall have ~

Shalindra felt her connection to the being who had once been her goddess surge, the ordained and inviolate wall between god and mortal parting like curtains flung open before the dawn. Radiance bathed her, no longer a comforting warmth but a raging fire. She allowed it to wash over her, a thing of unimaginable majesty yet still constraining a might which she had only the smallest of ideas could exist. Echoes of her tumultuous Ascension whispered warnings in her ear, but Shalindra was no longer afraid. Had she been given such gifts before now she would simply have ceased to exist, her mortal form evaporating in its light. But now, she was well versed in how to categorize and contain it, and could exploit such a reservoir as it was intended to be used.

Upon the darkened mountaintop, Shalindra blazed with power, casting away the darkness shrouding both her mind and body.

Eluria was shrinking, growing smaller every second. Mergolath stared at the dying goddess as she slipped from her fingers, no longer substantive enough to be held.

"You may not!" she screamed. "It is forbidden!"

Mergolath's eyes turned towards Shalindra, filled with wickedness and hate, but this time, Shalindra knew no fear.

Doubts no longer plagued her. Her knees did not buckle

beneath that fiery gaze, for she now faced Mergolath as a true equal, if not her better. And when those burning red eyes locked onto hers, Shalindra sent herself plunging into them. She sought fears and failings, mistakes and transgressions. These she flung into Mergolath's path like insurmountable obstacles. The dark goddess reeled, seeking to repress and rebury the things within her that even she did not care to see.

But as formidable an assault as they were, such memories were only distractions, a screen of smoke and illusion to mask Shalindra's true target. And then she found within Mergolath what she ultimately sought, for she had been shown it within Eluria's dying gift, and she knew how the spectacle would appear. In those deep recesses of Mergolath's interior lay what could only be named the heart of a god. Where Eluria's had been radiant, pure, and warm, its dark twin was fiery and corrupt, twisted inwards by self-adulation and fear. Shalindra took pity upon it, even as she sank into it and began to tear it apart. Her assault flashed like flint struck to steel, transforming to the burning embers with which Shalindra was so familiar. She drew them to herself before casting them aside, reclaiming the life from the goddess of demons as Mergolath had stolen and hoarded it throughout her infinitely long life.

Mergolath gasped, a sound like the steaming hiss of a volcano, and she shuddered in agony. She tried to turn her gaze from Shalindra, but the goddess of the demon realm was trapped. So long as Shalindra swam inside her, she could not look away. Mergolath chose to flee then, seeking a return to her immaterial form, one that would free her from such torments. With rock and sand, Shalindra bound her, lashing Mergolath's essence to the world she both ruled and despised, erasing her ability to leave.

Yet Mergolath remained a god, and one who was no stranger to assaults upon her person. She had no intention of succumbing to this new restriction. Even as she bent and spasmed from the pain writhing within her, she came towards Shalindra with great strides of her spiked legs, and her barbed tail coiled in anticipation.

It was then that the flaw in Shalindra's plan was revealed, for she was now tied to her position as surely as Mergolath was to hers, and no defense of hers would stop Mergolath's charge.

Yet her awarenesses operated independently, and this contingency had already been explored. If one Shalindra tearing Mergolath apart was not enough, she would have more. Shalindra's mental fingers stretched into arms, and then those fingers segmented yet again. Like a parasitic organism, their claws tore and shredded, burrowing in every direction throughout the goddess.

Mergolath stumbled as she reached the plains surrounding the spire, her spiked legs crashing through the crust of the world like it was thin ice on a pond. Molten lava spewed from the rifts, burning everything it touched. She lurched forward, but such damage had been done that her legs failed to obey the command.

Mergolath's defenses broke, and with the might of an angry god, Shalindra seized her unprotected core. Yet her tenuous connection to Eluria chose that moment to flicker and dim, exhausted as the goddess of the moon traded her own life for the taking of another. Eluria's final words came from a great distance, a soft blend of regrets and farewells.

~ *I love you* ~

Shalindra's body snapped around, threatening to drag her eyes from their contact with Mergolath. She almost faltered, almost threw away everything for a chance to follow those words to their inevitable conclusion.

"Focus, godling!" Mataasrhu's voice boomed in her ears.

With an iron will, that part of her that was more Tormjere's than her own asserted itself. Though it tore at her very soul, the task she had been given held no tolerance for diversions or desires. Shalindra clenched her jaw and sent every shred of power hurtling into Mergolath.

The dark goddess dragged herself forward, trailing the ruined remains of her legs. She lashed at the spire with her fury, hurling curses and denials with the same invective as she slung her attacks. The desperate attempt churned and billowed as smoke, flaying flesh from bone as it obliterated the demons caught within its plumes on the surface far below. She reached desperately for Shalindra, her fingers clawing canyons in the earth. She screamed in her impotence, a cry that tore the heavens asunder and ripped open deep chasms in the world.

Mergolath made one final, desperate heave towards Shalindra before collapsing, her body crumbling across the hellish landscape like a range of mountains dropped from the sky. Shalindra severed her connection to the dying goddess at the last moment, staggering back as the thousand selves she had spawned leapt to reinhabit her body simultaneously. Her head spun and her knees gave way, but she refused to let herself fall. She would never be on her knees again.

Staggering to the edge of the caldera, she looked down. All the world lay consumed in the throes of cataclysm. Geysers of lava shot upwards from the holes of Mergolath's footprints. Fiery rocks streaked across the sky, the force of their impacts with the earth releasing massive bursts of energy which pocked the surface with craters. Wind and lightning ravaged all, driven by dark, billowing clouds of ash and steam that reached to the very edge of the atmosphere.

A deep rumble of dissatisfaction arose behind her, and Shalindra turned to find Mataasrhu appraising the same situation. Though she looked him in the eye, he was no longer standing atop the spire with her. He stood on the plains beside it. His once reddish skin was now a glistening black, defined in burning outlines of red and orange, suffused with all that she had stolen from Mergolath as she herself had been imbued with all that was Eluria. They eyed one another, each evaluating the depth of the changes they had undergone.

"Is it over?" she asked, already certain of the answer but still seeking the reassurance of confirmation.

"This conflict may be, but there will be others in which we will deal."

"Then we did it."

He gave a snort strong enough to send the clouds swirling away. "We? You were working towards your goals as I was working towards mine. That they chose to intersect means nothing. Our bargain is resolved. Do not make the mistake of assuming there is anything beyond that agreement. We are not partners. We are not allies. We are not... that word you use for sentimental attachments."

Shalindra did her best not to smile. "Friends."

"We are not that either. But neither are we enemies, for now. You have served my purposes as I have served yours, and we owe each other nothing."

"Then I shall collect what belongs to me and be on my way." She gestured, encompassing the entirety of the destruction around them. "I am sorry for all of this."

"The hearty will survive, the frail shall perish, and my race will grow stronger." Mataasrhu lifted his hand, now large enough to grasp a city, and above the tip of a finger floated eight slivers of sparkling purity, crystalline versions of the embers that would be expected from the death of a demon, yet they were from no creature that had ever called this realm home.

"Their presence here disturbs me, and no matter how justly they were won, I would have sent them away with you regardless of our agreement. Your final spoil awaits your claim. Take her and depart, and do not seek to return without my permission."

Shalindra drew the shards of Alharania's life to herself, securing them within a fold of reality inside her body. It was as natural an act as placing coins in a purse, but the familiarity of it would require some adjusting to. "Thank you."

The god of demons shivered, and a deep rumble of disgust issued from his throat. Then he spoke words never before uttered in his realm. "You are welcome."

Shalindra willed herself to where Eluria lay, travelling there with such speed that she might have appeared in the new location before she had even left the old. The once mighty goddess of the moon lay like a scrap of clothing discarded on the roadside, translucent and unmoving—a tiny, crumpled speck of white on the vast plains of raging destruction which they together had wrought. The sand surrounding her had melted to a glossy black, streaked in lines of glass and solidified rock radiating outward from the site of her impact. Eluria clung to the last vestige of life that had been left her, dwindling, evaporating to nothing even as she refused to let it go. Her life raft was a single mote of energy, a tiny blue pearl crossed with fiery streaks of red—the one thing Shalindra had wanted so desperately to find and which, now beheld, was a conundrum of such complexity and danger that it overrode her desire to possess it, if only just.

She gathered Eluria tenderly into her arms and lifted her from the dirt. The remnant of the goddess trembled at the contact, but if she knew who held her now, she gave no sign. Shalindra took her from the tortured, demonic realm of Mataasrhu with a thought, carrying her forever from this place that had brought them both such sorrow.

Chapter Forty-Three

To the Victor

The white marble amphitheater where they appeared was pristine and comforting, though Shalindra had not thought to ever return here. As always, the construction contained all that was necessary for its purpose. This time, in place of an elevated pool to serve as a window to the cosmos, the stage on which she stood was empty save for an ornately wrought bed with a headboard of pure silver.

Eluria's eyelids fluttered open as Shalindra laid her on the pristinely white bedding. The starfield in her eyes was dim and only a sliver of light traced the crescent of each iris. Through her fingertips, Shalindra provided her what succor she dared, imbuing the tattered fragment of the once mighty god with just enough life to respond.

"You should have let me die," Eluria moaned with as much passion as she could muster.

"It was a death which would have solved nothing," Shalindra insisted.

"The small seed I left behind would have been consumed and

divided, introducing compassion and love to that poisoned domain, a realm which would have come to be shared by a multitude of gods. You were to be their first."

"I am now the god you prepared me to be," Shalindra said, "but I have never sought to displace you."

It was Amalthee's clear voice which responded from behind her. "Desires do not carry the weight of actions, and your wishes cannot change destiny. There can be only one goddess of the moon. To attempt otherwise would invite strife such as your world, and ours, has never seen."

"It is a thing that must be," Lithandris agreed, appearing at the right hand of the goddess of wealth and wisdom, though his dispassionate demeanor was a façade impossible to maintain.

Filled as she was with almost every shred of knowledge Eluria had ever possessed, Shalindra recalled that the god of the forests had beheld the death of Vanirus—Amalthee's brother and God of Knowledge—at Mergolath's jealous hands. That terrible event eons ago had precipitated a chain of events sending all of those gathered here hurtling towards this exact moment.

"Eluria must end," Remulus stated, his mighty form appearing with his co-conspirators. No stranger to death and destruction, his was the most unsympathetic stance, yet one shaped by the practicalities of the situation.

Shalindra rounded on them, no longer willing to accept the road they had placed her on. Taking an angry step closer to Lithandris, she declared: "And do you not acknowledge the predicament before us? You, who have witnessed the treasure she bears inside her?"

Amalthee stiffened, and Remulus jerked his head towards Lithandris in surprise. "Of what does she speak?" he demanded.

Shalindra answered without taking her eyes from the god of the forest. "Should I choose to end Eluria now, to consume her and take up her mantel as you would have me do, I would come into possession of the very same self-love that set Mergolath on her path to ruin, for any who loves themselves above all others is doomed to repeat her fate."

Remulus gnashed his teeth together in fury, and Amalthee appeared shaken.

"Is there truth to this?" she asked Lithandris.

"There is," he answered. "It was an impulsive decision made to present catastrophe, but it seems to have only delayed the inevitable."

"We shall bear no repetition of these events!" Remulus bellowed, calling forth a flaming great axe within his clenched fist. "It will end here!" Then his axe was arcing down towards Shalindra, driven at blinding speed by thick arms capable of hurling mountains without strain, yet Shalindra made no move to avoid it.

She did not need to.

The weapon came to a jarring halt just before impact, shattering into a million pieces that rained like burning stars onto the world of her birth. Remulus was tossed backwards by the force of the cataclysmic release of energies, an explosion which blackened the stage and surrounding columns. Amalthee leapt before Eluria to shelter the dying goddess, invoking her own formidable defenses to protect them both. When the dust and smoke had settled, she placed a hand to her mouth in surprise at the sight of Shalindra standing unaffected.

Shalindra's voice turned as cold as the winds atop the Ironspike Mountains. "You whose blessings I carry can do nothing to stop me. Yes, I feel all that you gave him." Her eyes went to each in turn as she spoke. "A sense of the forests he loved so dearly. Strength and aptitude in battle such as he should never have known. The insight to choose when words are more powerful than weapons. The—"

"All here know the roles of the others," Eluria's frail voice interrupted. "There is no need to enumerate them all."

It was not surprising that these three before her had not been party to the other gifts Tormjere had been blessed with, ones of magical aptitude and a calm clarity of thought that betrayed silent partners in this conflict, and Shalindra was willing to allow Eluria those secrets. But she was not finished with her incriminations.

"None of you will be capable of halting my advances, for you are bound against self-harm. What was he but an extension of yourselves? And what am I, but all that he was? In time, I will steal your knowledge, burn your forests, and trample your armies beneath the might of my self-adulation, and you will only watch in impotence."

Remulus was upon his feet like an enraged bull ready to charge but was stayed by Lithandris' gesture of caution. "Such an outcome is not desired by any present here, least of all you. What, then, do you intend?"

"I shall complete the prophecy to which I have been bound, and, in so doing, forever free myself of its constrains."

"The corruption that was Mergolath is destroyed," Lithandris observed. "No further are the demands which shall be placed upon you."

"There is yet one task I am fated to perform," Shalindra corrected, glancing back at what once was Eluria. "It was given to me to raise the dead, and in that final measure of my success, we will all find our salvation."

Amalthee's golden ringlets bounced from side to side as she shook her head. "The dead cannot be restored, not even by us. Once a life is ended then that which they were becomes dispersed, assimilated and interlaced into the fabric of the future. It is a ritual as old as time, and one in which you have partaken on numerous occasions. What is required is impossible to retrieve, though many have tried. If even the smallest piece of what you seek to reconstruct is omitted, the results are… unfortunate."

"All that is required has already been given to me—all but one piece." Shalindra moved close to Eluria and ran her fingers down the goddess' cheek. "Strange, is it not, that the key which allowed your sacrifice for me is the one thing that I must gather."

"As it is the one thing you cannot be allowed," Eluria said fearfully, pulling away from that touch.

Shalindra's mouth curled into grin. "Have you ever bargained with a demon?"

Eluria's voice was faint, a mere whisper in the wind. "I have but one thing left to give, while you may not offer enough to…"

"Everything you were."

Silence greeted Shalindra's proclamation. Eluria attempted to shake her insubstantial head in denial, but the effort was more than she could manage. "I cannot surrender it, for I have never known such joy in all my existence. To ask for my life would be a kinder demand, though that currency, as well, is forbidden me."

"It is what I offer," Shalindra repeated. "The one part of him that I lack and your guidance in the restoration that is to follow, and you will be returned all that I should never have been given."

"You would deny your destiny for me? Cast aside all—"

"I am not doing this for you."

Amalthee interjected herself between them. "What you seek is far simpler in agreement than in transaction. While it may be true that you are not fully restricted by the laws of our nature, the rest of us remain so. She may not supply more than has been requested."

"I was told that I may ask of her anything," Shalindra countered.

Amalthee denied that. "A promise made when you were mortal. Such obligations we may not place upon one another, though many and varied are the problems that might be better resolved if we could."

"Then another shall do so on my behalf. Enna…"

"May not ask," Eluria whispered, "for she is no longer mine."

It took little effort for Shalindra to settle on another elvish woman who could fulfil the needed role in this exchange, one who would be more than eager to restore her goddess at Shalindra's expense.

"Yes," Eluria whispered. "She will perform as required. But you must hurry."

Chapter Forty-Four

A Way Out

Enna ducked as Honarch's fiery blast of magic slammed into the demon, hurling it back against a tree and setting branches and fur alight. The impact shook free large clumps of snow that joined the heavy flakes falling from the sky onto the combatants. Birion followed the magical assault with his spear, stabbing it into the stunned creature. The demon bellowed in pain and knocked him aside as it righted itself, the spear still protruding from its chest. It charged towards Fendrick, who stood his ground with only shield and axe. Enna manifested her shield, deflecting the creature's assault. It twisted and thrashed in a cloud of disturbed snow, flailing about in an attempt to reach any of its assailants. Honarch dove away, sparing him the worst, but the demon's claws slashed across his back and sent him spinning to the ground. The demon paused for the slightest moment as it sought its next target, but before it could attack again, Verelli sent bands of energy wrapping around the demon's legs, dropping it with an ungainly flop. Fendrick was atop it before it could recover, his axe biting deep into the demon's neck and ending its life.

Birion regained his feet without apparent injury, but Honarch lay in the snow as he had fallen, angry streaks of crimson torn across his back. Enna rushed to him, taking her symbol in hand as she covered the sticky wetness of his wounds with the other. She quickly mouthed the words to her prayer, and… nothing happened.

Afterimages of a rocky, barren mountain engulfed in flame danced across her vision and the taste of acrid smoke filled her mouth, both sensations a jarring contradiction to the damp cold of the forest around her. Her strength drained away as if poured onto the ground. A wave of vertigo swept over her, and she slumped backwards, Fendrick's strong grasp the only thing which prevented her from collapsing completely.

A stab of panic shot through her at the failure, but she was so far beyond tired that she could rightly be considered delusional. She took a deep breath as she righted herself and began again, certain that some fault lay in her request. But her symbol remained as cold in her hand as the snow she knelt in, and no tingle slid down her arm as it should.

Honarch moaned in pain as he tried to roll over.

"What's wrong?" Birion asked.

Enna stared at her hand as if it were afflicted. "She's not there," she whispered. A cavernous emptiness filled her, a feeling of utter abandonment. This could not be happening. Not now.

Someone placed a reassuring hand on her shoulder, but she jerked away. "She's not there!" she cried.

Enna thrust both hands against Honarch's wounds and

shouted her prayer, but the words drifted impotently on the wind.

"No!" she screamed as Birion pulled her away. "Shalindra, no! She can't be gone!"

Fendrick took charge of Honarch, packing snow over his wounds to numb the pain and wrapping strips of cloth tight around his body to stop the flow of blood. A proper dressing would require removing his cloak, and there was no time. Honarch's face was white as they pulled him to his feet.

"Can you walk?" Fendrick asked.

Honarch gamely attempted a nod, but the action sent him tumbling to his knees. Fendrick slung his shield across his back, then lifted the mage in his arms.

"Are we all together?" Birion asked.

"Everyone's here," Weeby answered. "Which direction should we head?"

"Southwest," Verelli said. "We will encounter the road or river eventually. They will show us the fastest way out."

"That would be…" Weeby spun helplessly in a circle as he sought the correct compass point, but it was impossible to see more than a few feet in any direction. "I don't know."

Still held fast in Birion's grasp, Enna only half listened. No matter what they accomplished now, it would not matter.

"Into the wind, then," Birion said. "It usually comes from the west, and we won't get out of here by sitting still."

He eased his grip on her, making sure she would remain upright. Enna could not meet his eyes, continuing instead to stare at the ground as he gathered everyone and headed in their chosen direction. Her feet refused to move, rooted in place by the emptiness within her.

"Enna, we cannot stay here," Verelli said gently.

She nodded numbly, wondering if they were only delaying the inevitable. For her goddess to be gone…

Enna wrapped her cloak tightly about herself and trudged through the snow in a daze. She could imagine very few things which would disrupt the connection to her goddess, a touch she had known since before her birth, and each of them were so terrible to contemplate that they filled her with dread. She could only pray that Shalindra was safe, wherever she was.

The snow barely let up, and as darkness overtook them, they constructed a shelter from a combination of downed trees, branches, and snow. Once they were all packed inside it, Verelli lit a fire. It was kept small to prevent the walls from melting, but in such a confined space, even the tiniest of heat sources was a blessing. They drank heated water without tea or any other flavoring, simply to get warm.

Enna tended to Honarch as best she could, cleaning and rebinding the wounds, which had already begun to fester and blacken at the edges. He managed to swallow only a few sips of water, and his skin was warm to the touch. Unable to produce even a simple globe of light, she did not attempt another restoration. Never in her life had she felt so powerless.

She fell into an exhausted slumber, unaware of even whose shoulder she was propped against. Her dreams were disjointed, a strange mixture of the past and present that was uniformly unpleasant. She startled awake more than once, certain that danger was about to befall them, but each time there was nothing. It was in many ways a relief when she was jolted from her tormented nightmares by someone frantically poking her awake.

"Something's outside," Weeby warned in a tense whisper.

Enna caught a glimpse of Fendrick's feet as the dwarf scurried beneath the branches serving as a door.

"Who goes there?" Birion's shout sounded from outside.

"Friends of yours, so long as you're not a demon," was the bemused answer.

The voice was surprisingly familiar, and she scrambled from the shelter into the frigid air outside. The snow had slacked off and there was some direction to the light, and she judged it to be early morning.

Approaching Birion and Fendrick were a trio of men who might have been woodsmen or sellswords, two of average size and one larger, and all three carrying staffs tipped with a wide, curving blade. Each man was familiar to her in some way, though she struggled to place how until they drew close enough that she could peer into their hoods. Their faces seemed jarringly out of place without their traditionally red robes, but she recognized all three monks from different places in her past: Eljorn, Martyn, and Shiran. The shock of seeing them together was barely more than the surprise of seeing them here.

"Many are the paths we walk," Martyn said in answer to her surprised look, "but that is for another time."

"How did you find us?" she asked.

Eljorn grinned. "I should say that the gods guided our path to you, but, in truth, we simply saw your camp from the road."

"What road?" Fendrick asked.

Eljorn gestured over his shoulder. "Not ten paces that way. You're fortunate you chose this spot—we were close to turning back."

Martyn interrupted them. "And we should still do so. Soon."

"Honarch's wounded," Enna said.

Eljorn glanced at Shiran, who tossed his spear to Martyn before crawling halfway into the shelter to check on the injured mage. He pulled back quickly. "We'll need a litter."

The three monks fell to the task with industry, scouring the forest for suitable branches and producing a sturdy frame faster than Enna would have thought possible. They took the shelter apart to retrieve Honarch rather than pulling him through the small entrance, then placed him gently on the litter and wrapped him in blankets. Martyn and Shiran lifted him, and Eljorn led the way along the snow-covered road.

"Where is Shalindra?" Eljorn asked as they walked.

"Facing her destiny in the demon's world," Fendrick said. "She allowed no one to go with her."

"To know one's path is to walk it alone," Martyn intoned.

Eljorn nodded thoughtfully. "We must hope that she is successful. So many fates depend upon hers."

The statement seemed far more knowledgeable of the situation that it should have been, but he lapsed into silence once more as he concentrated on what lay ahead.

The road was distinguishable only by the absence of trees along a relatively straight line. The snow lay undisturbed without any sign of footprints, so the monks must have come a different way or somehow disguised their passage. Speed outweighed the need for secrecy at this point, however, and the group forged ahead with no concern for the trail they were leaving. Only the occasional rotation of those carrying Honarch marked the passage of time. The weather was their only adversary, but it could not have been the only danger. The woods, already muffled by the falling snow, were eerily silent, and not even a hint of wind gave motion to the branches. It was as if they were the only people left on this world.

Forests turned eventually to fields, and Eljorn called them to a halt at the edge of the trees.

"There should be a town just ahead," he said. "It was abandoned when we passed through yesterday, but there is no guarantee that it remains so. We will check first."

He signaled to the other monks, who continued ahead and soon faded away in the falling snow.

"I'd give anything to get out of this snow, even for a night," Weeby said, "though that's not a complaint about your caution."

Time stretched as they waited. Enna was freezing, but all she could think about was Shalindra, alone in the hellish world of the demons. The helplessness of her situation was overwhelming. There was no way for her to aid that battle—she could not even give assistance to those with her now. If Shalindra reappeared in Tythir, there would be no one there to help. Should she not find some way to return, they might never discover what had become of her, and Elurithlia's gifts would be lost forever. She shrugged off such depressing thoughts, advising herself to have faith. But she wanted to help so badly.

"Some battles must be fought alone."

Enna looked up to see Eljorn watching her.

"Do not fear for those who face their destiny as they must," he said, squatting down in front of her. "Reserve your distress for those who knowingly turn away."

"I don't know why hearing that makes me feel any better," Enna said, "but it does."

"This conflict is bigger than any of us. We all have our parts to play."

Enna suspected he knew his own role far better than anyone else, but before she could ask him about it, Birion stiffened.

"Something's coming," the knight said.

They scrambled to ready themselves, but relaxed when the shadowy outline of the two monks appeared.

"We saw nothing," Martyn said. "But heavier snow is coming. If any demons are wandering about, they too will seek shelter within the town."

"We need to get out of this weather," Fendrick said. "I'd be willing to face one of the beasts for the chance at a dry bed."

There was general agreement, and they proceeded to the town and took shelter in an abandoned tavern.

The building was cold, and a mustiness hung in the stale air. Tables and benches were ready for patrons that would likely never come, while ample wood was stacked near the fireplace.

"Honarch needs to be kept warm," Enna said before anyone could suggest another cold night.

"I think we all do," Birion agreed. "The wind's howling and it's impossible to see through the snow. Nothing's going to find us by the smoke."

They collected bedding from the rooms and laid a more

comfortable camp close to the fire, but any food left behind by the original owners had been carried off by rats. The monks shared what was left of their supplies, but by tomorrow hunger would become a larger threat than weariness.

Though it was still several hours before nightfall, sleep came quickly as soon as they stopped moving. They had been settled only a short time when the continuous hum of the wind was broken by an immense crash, like that of a siege stone impacting a castle wall. Loud roars quickly followed. There was a mad scramble as hands sought weapons.

"I'll see what it is," Weeby said, slipping out the door.

Enna could easily guess at the source of the disturbance, and almost screamed at the injustice of it all.

"Be ready to move," Birion said, clearly sharing her thoughts.

Weeby burst through the door. "There's a bunch of demons fighting each other. I couldn't see much, but they're headed this way."

Fendrick let loose a string of curses that would have curled the toes of the most profane sailor.

"I agree," Eljorn said in a more subdued manner. "These walls will not provide sanctuary. We must flee."

Shiran was already snuffing the fire. Enna held Honarch's hand as he was placed gently into the litter once more. He moaned as Martyn and Shiran lifted him from the ground but did not open his eyes.

Birion and Fendrick led them out into the snowy streets. Everyone hurried to follow, Enna trailing just behind the monks and Honarch. If they were lucky, they would be able to—

~Enna~

Jets of warmth coursed through her body, banishing her cold and misery and wrapping her soul with bliss. Her eyes closed and her body ceased moving as her mind reveled in the holy touch of her goddess, thankful beyond words that She was still there.

Yes, Mistress?

~ I require of you a service ~

"Enna!" Birion's piercing whisper was muted and sounded far away.

Anything.

~ You must retrieve the Manalathlia and bring her to me ~

By your light, I will do so. But she is so far away.

A hand gripped her arm, but she refused to yield to its insistent tug.

~ There are ways to take yourself home much more quickly. Picture the place where you promised yourself to me ~

The hand on her arm was joined by another, and she felt herself being dragged forward. She kept her attention focused on her conversation with her Mistress, certain that it was more important than anything happening around her. The location She spoke of was one Enna knew better than any in the world and one of the most distinct memories of her childhood: the Glade of Guardians.

I see it, Mistress.

~ There exists a connection between where you are and where you wish to be. Open the door between ~

Did She mean for her to create a mist gate?

I have seen it done, but how…?

~ All you need do, is ask ~

Something slammed into her from behind, knocking her to the snowy ground. Enna's eyes flung open as she rolled to her feet, and she instantly wished they had not.

Birion and Fendrick stood shoulder to shoulder between her and a goat demon, struggling to hold it at bay with their polearms. A flash of heat shot across her back, and out of the corner of her eye saw Verelli's magical fire explode into another demon off to the side. Martyn and Shiran faced off against a third, their bladed staffs whirling and slicing in a flashing wall of steel. Eljorn stood calmly before another as its massive fist descended towards him, but by the time the demon's hand reached where he should have been, the monk had twisted to the side, as if pushed away from the blow. His arms swung up in the air, and the demon was rocked back as the entire force of his own attack was turned against him.

No matter what direction Enna turned, all she saw were demons.

"Over here!" Weeby screamed at her from the broken shell of a building. Honarch lay helpless on the litter at his feet, awake now but unable to even sit up. Enna scrambled across the snowy ground, unable to add anything to their defense.

Snow, cobblestones, and parts of nearby buildings catapulted themselves suddenly into the air, as if they had sat on the skin of a drum struck hard. Just as gravity took hold and the crumbled debris began to descend, Verelli thrust his arms down violently, sending it bursting outwards in every direction.

The unmitigated violence of the explosion sent demons and buildings flying, leaving the group standing in a shallow crater scoured clean down to the dirt. Verelli staggered sideways, blood dripping from his nose.

"I can't do this forever," he said as they regrouped in the momentary calm.

Birion began pushing them down the street. "Hurry before they come back."

Fendrick and Weeby had already hoisted Honarch, and the group surrounded them as they ran.

~ Hurry. My time becomes shorter than yours ~

Enna was given no chance to act, as a demon tumbled from a side street and came crashing onto its back in front of them. Unlike the goats they had just faced, its skin was textured and leathery but torn open in countless places. Black blood flowed freely from its wounds to stain the snow. A wolfish demon clawed its way over a house and leapt atop the first before it could rise. The wounded demon thrashed desperately as it sought to escape, but its assailant was joined by two more, and it rapidly succumbed beneath their attacks.

Enna dove with everyone else towards the nearest cover, trying to avoid being seen by the battling demons. The snow drift she had aimed herself at proved to be a pile of stones dusted over. Her shoulder struck stone just below the snow, and she bit her lip to avoid crying out.

"That shop, there," Birion hissed from behind a demolished cart, pointing at a mostly intact structure with stone walls on the first floor.

Enna sprinted through the snow behind Fendrick and Eljorn. They were only steps away when the building exploded towards them in a shower of wood and stone. A goat-faced demon burst onto the street, pursuing the same conflict she sought to avoid. It froze in surprise as it caught sight of them, then launched itself at Fendrick. Verelli's magic flared, scorching the demon with multihued energies. The goat demon fell back with a shrill howl of pain as the smell of burnt hair filled the street. Fendrick struck at it, but it scrambled to safety behind another building.

Alerted by the sounds of battle, the trio of demons abandoned their kill and turned their attention towards the group. They spread across the street as they advanced, like a pack of dogs that had cornered their prey.

"Circle up!" Birion shouted.

They regrouped, forming a circle around Honarch where he lay moaning on the litter. Enna rushed to his kneel at his side, unable to face the snarling advance of the demons behind her. She needed to get them out, but she was a jumble of doubts and fears.

~ Hurry ~

Enna stood, and held her arm out towards the street in front of her as she had seen Shalindra do.

"What are you doing?" someone shouted at her, disrupting her thoughts.

"I can make a way out, just give me time!"

Verelli was beside her then, scooping both hands together, causing a massive spray of snow to shoot into the air. Another motion sent the snow spinning like a snowstorm around them, driven by a wind Enna could not feel.

Enna tried to concentrate on where she wanted to go, but the image disappeared as one of the demons emerged from the twisting wall of snow right in front of her. Martin and Shiran forced it back with a series of deft cuts, but the shadow of its dark form remained visible.

With a gesture, Verelli tugged at the cracked remnants of the buildings on either side of the street, ripping free stone and timber and adding it to the churning vortex surrounding them. One of the goat demons tried to force its way through, but its grey arm barely made it past the elbow before it was beaten bloody, and it withdrew.

"Whatever you're going to do, do it now!" he yelled.

Flaming orbs appeared in the wizard's hands, growing in heat and intensity until the sleeves of his robes began to smolder. He cried out in pain as he flung them at the spinning wall of debris. They struck it like a spark to oil, setting the whirlwind alight with a painful flash of heat.

Enna closed her eyes and forced the conflict from her thoughts. Resummoning the memory of the forest temple in Ildalarial, she prayed as she had never prayed in her entire life. It was not a prayer of words but one of emotion—a plea of desperation wrapped around textures and smells of the place she knew better than anywhere.

And, somehow, it worked.

The air in front of her began to ripple and tear, shimmering in shades of white shot through with sparks of blue and silver. The seams of reality parted, replaced by a window to a sunny clearing ringed with statues and bathed in the colors of autumn.

"Go!" she shouted.

Weeby had one end of the litter on his shoulders and was desperately dragging Honarch towards it. Eljorn lifted the other end, and then they were through. Martin and Shiran followed a step behind.

Birion hesitated, an anguished expression on his face as he turned back to her. Fendrick put his hands on the knight and shoved him through.

Lost within the efforts of his magic, Verelli seemed unaware of the need to flee. Enna grabbed him by the arm and dragged him into the gate with her. Her vision flashed white as she crossed the threshold, and then she was lying in the grass gasping for breath with everyone else, surrounded by statues of the prior Guardians. The gate snapped shut behind her with a soft pop, and the chaos of the battle was replaced by the tranquil sounds of birds objecting to their unexpected arrival. The late fall air was crisp, and she blinked against the brightness of the late afternoon sun.

"I hate those things," Fendrick muttered as he picked himself up from the grass. He looked around to get his bearings, then froze as he beheld the statue of Alharania.

Enna did not wait for them to sort themselves out. Throwing off her now stifling cloak, she sprinted from the Glade and up the path that led deeper into the temple forest.

When the path branched, she turned without hesitation towards where her mother was most likely to be at this hour: the Glade of Atonement. She burst into the small clearing, disrupting the ritual taking place within and sending the attending Sisters leaping to their feet in alarm.

"Ennathalerial?" Her mother asked, rising in surprise at the far end of the pond around which they had been praying. "What is this? Why are you here? And where is—"

"Mother, we are summoned to our goddess," Enna cut her off.

A murmur of surprise rippled through the assembled clerics. Some fell to their knees, wailing, and others clasped their silver disks of their faith and begged for salvation. As Enna rushed to her, Elothlirial took a half step away, doubt marring her normally assured features.

"Summoned to where?" she asked.

"I do not know," Enna said breathlessly, taking her mother's hands in her own, "but it will be wonderful."

Chapter Forty-Five

For Love

Shalindra brought both women to the amphitheater of the gods with a thought, placing them gently before her on the platform. Having never seen the two side by side, she had never noticed how closely Enna resembled her mother. Elothlirial clutched at Enna's hand, disoriented, but as she beheld the deities whose presence she now shared, she fell to her knees, abasing herself before them in mute terror, eyes firmly on the floor.

If Enna was intimidated by standing in the face of so many holy entities, she did not show it. Her eyes were alight, remaining on Shalindra alone as she bowed her head. "How may I serve?"

Chosen so well, Amalthee's silent communication echoed in Shalindra's mind.

Enna's outstanding fortitude was a small reassurance that did nothing to lessen the hollowness of Shalindra's guilt. The thought of Enna idolizing her, as so many already did, was unbearable. It reinforced her decision to turn from this path, but even though the choice was made, the end state was still far from complete.

Shalindra's eyes fell on Elothlirial, wondering if she would be strong enough to do what was needed. Enna caught the look and gently pulled her mother to her feet.

Shalindra addressed them both: "A bargain has been achieved between Eluria and myself—an exchange of what we each have been given but the other so desperately needs. I will spare you the particulars of how we have arrived at this juncture, because it holds no relevance to how either of us will emerge. Know that our choice is one which seeks to avoid catastrophe for all. From each of us, however, is required a request which neither may make of the other. And for that, we turn to you.

"Elothlirial, you who place your goddess Elurithlia above all others and have served her faithfully for so long, will you seek for her to release the part of Tormjere she carries inside her, and in so doing enable her continued existence?"

Elothlirial cast a fearful glance at the wisp of Eluria laying on the bed. "For Her, I would do anything."

"Enna…"

"You're going to give this up, aren't you?" Enna asked, her voice saturated by turbulent emotions. "For him."

"Yes."

"I would have been yours," Enna whispered, her eyes wet. "In all ways, forever. I committed myself to you long before I ever realized it, and it is a decision I would never change. Yours would have been the greatest church this world has ever known."

Moved deeply by such devotion, Shalindra came to stand close before her. "And I could have asked for no more passionate a champion. Will you accept my blessing and make this request of me as my Manalathlia, to return to Eluria all that is hers, for it is what I desire more than anything."

"Your desires are, and always will be, mine."

Shalindra pressed her lips tenderly to Enna's forehead.

Her green eyes dried instantly, and a low moan of rapture escaped her lips.

"Promise me," Shalindra said, stepping back. "No matter what."

"I swear it on my life, Mistress Shalindra."

"You are in alignment," Amalthee said, coming to stand between them, "and time draws short."

She held out her hands to Shalindra, and upon those delicate fingers where her golden book normally resided, a crystalline decanter of exquisite design appeared. Shalindra accepted it, but the goddess of wealth and knowledge did not surrender it without a warning.

"Should you falter in this attempt, should you fail to return even the tiniest piece of what you must divest…"

"His gift was absolute," Shalindra said. "I know him as I know myself, and there will be no mistake."

Amalthee's eyes held hers, and her golden words echoed in Shalindra's mind.

You are stronger now than Eluria ever can be, unique in ways not given for her to attain. Are you prepared to do without all that you will surrender, knowing that one day such abilities may be required?

I do not care what it costs.

There was a level of admiration in Amalthee's eyes as she released the decanter.

Shalindra turned to the elven women, each now the supreme mortal representative of their chosen goddess. "You must ask with all your heart, for the sake of everything you have or ever will hold dear. Do so now, and may the future that we all desire come to pass."

She saw the affirmation in their eyes, and Shalindra turned her attentions inward as the soft tones of elvish prayers filled the air around her. Centering herself on what was left of Tormjere's focus, that fraction of him she had not taken into herself, she drifted from the bright and sterile whiteness of the amphitheater into the dark and shifting orb of his protections. Here, there was no floor or ceiling to constrain her motions, no walls or trees to obscure her sight. Everything that she was spread itself evenly about her until she resided within a bounded sphere of her own device. There was no need for her to go looking for Enna's prayer amongst the multitudes which sought her blessings, for it blazed bright within her awareness, a silver beacon within the multi-hued realm of her mind.

She accepted it as she turned all the others away, drawing it near, allowing the light of that fervent request to cast itself throughout her and access all that it sought to retrieve. Those pieces answered with shimmering sparkles of their own, tiny stars being born, spreading across the sphere of *her*, like rain at the edge of a cloud, until all was alight. It was almost frightening how much more of Eluria there was than of herself, and she shuddered to think of the consequences of that imbalance had she remained a god. There might not even have been a Shalindra left.

With the task only half done, the silver manifestation of Enna's prayer tingled with anticipation, demanding the rest of its answer. Shalindra did not hesitate. She held no regrets, and no matter the cosmic power arrayed before her, she was not tempted. She plucked one of Eluria's stars from herself and sent it towards Enna's prayer. The pain of its removal surprised her, like a partially healed wound torn open.

Shalindra sent another, and then another. Every memory, every ability, every ounce of what Eluria was had to be removed. She might have toiled at this effort for decades or centuries, and so she began duplicating herself to speed the process. It was not so dissimilar to her assault on Mergolath, if more selective, but no matter how willing Shalindra was, the effect upon her physical self was the same. The fibers of her body pulled apart, stretched in unnatural ways as they were forced to release the energy held within. It burned with an agony that surpassed rational thought, every flickering mote of Eluria separating from her like a needle being dragged through her tissue.

You must not fail.

Amalthee's words supplied resolve, but nothing more. This was Shalindra's domain, a reality in which she was the supreme being, and visitors to it could only watch events unfold.

Shalindra became aware that she had collapsed to her knees, gasping for breath. Her sight was filled with the hazy outline of Enna's face held close to her own, the elf's lips moving in prayer even as her eyes teared in anguish.

Shalindra struggled to form words that might provide reassurance that all would be as it should, but only one emerged: "…promised."

She shook, whimpering softly as she was slowly dissected, cut apart so that all which did not belong inside could be removed. Blood seeped through her pores, leaking in rivulets from beneath her armor to stain both her garments and the ground beneath.

Her eyes squeezed shut in an attempt to reject the all-consuming pain burning throughout her body. It was not a solid black she now beheld but rather the absence of light which lent darkness to the night sky. Across that empty canvas, stars began to flicker into existence. First one, then a handful, and then a thousand. The purity of their light bathed her, flowing across her skin like water and washing away the pains and burdens she had carried with her for so long.

It was against this backdrop of infinity that Eluria came to be before her, not as the crumpled fragment of a god who had been snatched from the realm of her enemy, nor as the titanic juggernaut who had stood astride a world. She was of a size with Shalindra, slender and beautiful, edged in a silvery nimbus of radiance. Above her outstretched hand floated a bluish pearl of light, one streaked with red with surging with unknown energies.

"I understand, now, your decision," Eluria said, "for I feel I would rather perish than return this to you. It seems the cruelest of fates that only by its possession am I able to give it up." She averted her gaze, unable to bear the sight of it any longer. Her words became distant as Shalindra drifted away. "It was a wonderful thing to have known, and I envy you in ways you cannot imagine."

Shalindra fought to stay, her consciousness clinging to that piece of Tormjere like a cork bobbing on a stormy sea until, at last, it was time to surrender that too. She did not release it so much as push it away, returning it to where it was meant to reside. She gave and gave until there was nothing left to be given, until only the fragile sliver of herself remained, and the crushing weariness of a hundred sleepless nights descended upon her.

Her vision faded slowly to darkness, and in the nothingness in which she floated, she was, finally, free.

Chapter Forty-Six

A Prophecy Fulfilled

Shalindra awoke, standing in the Glade of Guardians beside Enna and Elothlirial. She looked around to ascertain if it was real or a dream, but before she could speak, Enna flung her free arm around her. Trembling like a caught rabbit, Enna's words spilled out.

"I thought I had killed you."

Shalindra squeezed her tightly, disregarding the hard edges of Amalthee's decanter pressed uncomfortably between them. "I feared the same for you."

"Was it real?" Elothlirial asked, directing her question more to the statues surrounding them than the women standing beside her.

Enna stepped back looked down at the precious decanter clutched protectively in her hands. "There can be no doubt, Mother."

Shalindra took a deep breath that emerged more as a sigh of relief. "Enna, I am… me. Just me. The voices, the images of other people's lives, they are all gone."

"And Tormjere?"

Shalindra searched inside herself for his familiar touch, but there was nothing but her own thoughts. "Nothing. You hold the entirety of his life in your hands."

Elothlirial regarded it with wonder. "I viewed its creation, and still, I can scarcely believe. I will give you the privacy this task deserves. Truly, you have earned it." She bowed her head to Shalindra, then addressed Enna. "When you are finished, find me. There is much to discuss."

Shalindra and Enna watched her depart the glade, and then they stood alone. They hurried to Tormjere's side, each taking their place opposite the other as they had when they left him in this position. The wood encasing his body melted away at their approach, and he looked exactly as he had the day of her Ascension. The contents of the decanter swirled rapidly in Enna's hands, eager to be rejoined within their proper vessel.

"Do you have any idea of what do to?" Enna asked.

"I do not." Shalindra closed her eyes and took her symbol of Eluria in her hand. "But I have faith in Her guidance. Pour it slowly onto him."

Enna unstoppered the vessel and held it close above Tormjere's chest, then tipped it just enough for the contents to slide from the container like clouds rolling down a mountain. Flickering pulses of bluish light danced as it was absorbed into Tormjere's body.

Shalindra concentrated as she rested a hand on him. At first, she felt nothing from his motionless form, but then, slowly, familiar patterns began to emerge. She had felt every extent of his body, healed every bone and muscle within him so many times, that she knew where everything belonged. With her memories as a guide, she sought to nudge his spirit back into place, channeling the disorganized tangle into a more orderly position, forming it as a sculptor would a block of clay.

There was a spark as his mind fought for awareness, groggy and frightened as it flailed about in a disconnected state. His body spasmed, and she hurried to reassure him with pleasant thoughts. The last of what was needed was once more inside him, and she rushed to align it, reminding him of himself and his movements, and prodding his stagnant body to resume its natural functions.

Tormjere sucked in a ragged breath, coughing as he rolled onto his side. He would have continued right over the edge had Enna not caught him.

He gripped her tightly as he forced himself into a sitting position. The jerky motion left him teetering, and Shalindra added her hands to Enna's in keeping him steady. He blinked and rolled his head around to look at her.

"Did it work?" he mumbled, frowning at the reluctance of his jaw to move in the proper fashion.

There were so many words he could have said upon waking from what he had endured, but it was no surprise that his first thoughts were for her. Shalindra smiled, then found herself laughing with pure joy. Finally, she was able to speak the words she had feared would never be said. "I love you, too."

She took his startled face in her hands and pressed her lips to his, and she would have remained that way in his arms forever if she could have.

No sooner had she stepped back than Enna flung her arms around him and kissed him fiercely, almost knocking him backwards over the dais and causing his face to burn a bright red. He disengaged from her clumsily and looked at them both as if they were crazed.

"I'm enjoying all this affection, I think, but will someone please tell me what happened?"

"What is the last thing you remember?" Shalindra asked.

His face twisted as he worked the stiffness from his back. "Standing with you during the ceremony, and then… a lot of unpleasantness. Clearly, I missed something."

She smiled at the understatement. "'Something' will take quite a while to convey."

"Maybe we shouldn't," Enna said mischievously. "I enjoy knowing so much that he doesn't."

Tormjere's eyes went to the sword on Shalindra's hip, and he raised an eyebrow.

I missed a lot, didn't I?

She smiled once more, happy for the first time in forever, and took his hand in hers.

I have so much to share with you and, by Her light, we finally have the time.

Epilogue

Tormjere placed the rounded stone atop another, watching as the clear water flowed over and around it to continue its burbling path down the mountain unabated. The coldness of the creek had rendered his toes numb some time ago, serving as a pleasing counterbalance to the warmth of the spring sun blazing down from a cloudless sky. He gauged the size needed to plug the next hole, then filled it with another stone pulled from the creek bed. Eljorn worked silently beside him, his red robes soaked through from the knee down. Though his brother's stones were arranged in a more orderly pattern, they were no more effective—or ineffective, depending on how one judged such things—than his own. Tormjere grinned as he shoved a handful of pebbles into the crevices of their makeshift dam—the creek was always going to win, but that was part of the entertainment.

A splash by the shore drew his attention. Blackwolf stood chest deep in the water with his head cocked to one side, no doubt wondering how the fish had managed to elude him. The effort at providing his own meal seemed to have been all the old dog could muster, and Tormjere scooped him from the creek and deposited him in a sunny patch of grass. After a shake that sent water flying in every direction, Blackwolf wandered over to where Shalindra sat and plopped to the ground. She ran her fingers through his damp fur, and he quickly rolled over and closed his eyes contentedly so she would rub his belly.

"As pleasant as this is, do you intend to continue hiding here all day?" she asked Tormjere. "Lord Cheldiff expects us for dinner, and it would be best if we arrived in a decent appearance."

The damp moss and dirty stones of the creek bed had done her white robes—sleeveless, of course, in the elvish fashion—no favors. Her armor would have done a better job at resisting dirt, but it was secure back at his parents' house. Shining Moon remained at her side, as always, but Tormjere would have been more enthusiastic about tonight's formal dinner were she to arrive bedecked in her Guardian's armor. He really wished he had not missed seeing those events during his... nap.

"I'd rather stay here and eat with my family," he said. Why would anyone sit with a room full of people they only pretend to like when the ones they did love were so close by?

"They will be joining us, if you recall. Your mother was thrilled to finally have an occasion to wear that yellow dress she's been holding on to for so long."

Tormjere slogged his way back into the creek to resume his work. "Then we'll stay at least until Enna and Fendrick return."

The dwarf had been less interested in building dams and more inclined to visit the local smithy, claiming that his time away from a forge was causing his bones to ache. Enna had offered to go with him, ostensibly to stretch her legs, but she had probably used the opportunity to learn more about his time with Alharania. As they had wintered in Ildalarial, she had pestered the dwarf constantly in an attempt to set the record straight on the lost Guardian's fate. Fendrick had relented only a week ago, likely because Enna was perhaps the only person in the world more stubborn than him.

Eljorn paused his work. "I agree with Blackwolf's decision that this seems sufficient effort for now," he said before climbing atop his favorite rock, where he sat facing upstream.

"You always left most of it to me," Tormjere chided, though he did not mind today. Despite months of refamiliarizing himself with the proper functioning of his body—an effort that each of his friends had contributed greatly to—he continued to feel out of sorts, as if everything was not quite where it belonged. The simple task of stacking rocks in the creek was soothing and allowed him to remember how his muscles were supposed to move.

I did the best I could.

Mind you, I'm not complaining. I enjoy not being dead.

He would certainly be the last to fault Shalindra or any of them for their efforts. If the gods had no idea how to resurrect someone, he could not criticize how it had turned out. And it definitely beat the alternative. His memories also remained out of sequence, and revisiting places where the events had occurred was as helpful to his mind as stacking stones was to his arms.

At least his more recent memories behaved as they should, including the recollection of when he and Eljorn had returned home. Their mother had fainted straight away the moment they walked through the door, and it had taken more than a little convincing once she was awake to make her believe they were really there. He had yet to mention the bag of gems that would make them rich enough to never need to work again; arriving with the legendary Guardian of Eluria and Princess of Actondel had already been enough to put her completely over the edge.

I am not a legend.

Fine, you're just excessively well reputationed.

She ignored him and returned to petting Blackwolf. The old dog had been far more vocal in welcoming their arrival, though the frantic expenditure of energy had caused him to collapse into sleep the moment Tormjere lifted him into his lap. Everything was as it should have been.

Except for him.

No matter how happy he was to stand in this creek once more, or how much he wanted to stay and mend fences and help with the kennel, he no longer belonged here. There was good mixed with the bad of that realization, but it was a fool's errand to try to alter the past, and he would have changed none of it even were he able to. With a shake of his head, he went back to stacking rocks.

He was still toiling away when Fendrick and Enna came walking up the trail. The dwarf carried a pack slung over one shoulder and a typically stern expression on his face, but Enna practically skipped through the forest, her green eyes as bright as the sun. Blackwolf peered at them both through a half-opened eye, but as Shalindra continued with her attentions, he promptly returned to his nap.

"Time for me to go," Fendrick said without preamble.

"So soon?" Shalindra asked. "Are you sure there is nothing else you need?"

"Eljorn's going to walk with me a ways." Fendrick put a hand to his vest, above where the fragments of Alharania's shattered soul were securely hidden. "You've already accomplished more than I ever could have thought possible, my lady."

"It was the least I could have done for another Guardian, and I pray that she will finally achieve the peace she deserves. Her sacrifice will never be forgotten."

Tormjere sloshed his way out of the water and offered his hand. "Safe travels, Velantriar."

"That's your title now," Fendrick said, shaking it. "Just make sure to knock the sand out of your ears every now and then, and don't go doing anything stupid. Again."

Eljorn left his contemplations to join them and placed his hands on Tormjere's shoulders. This parting was less traumatic that their last, when Eljorn had left to become a monk, but Tormjere still felt it keenly.

"Try not to stay away so long this time," Tormjere said, echoing his brother's motions.

"I won't," Eljorn said with a laugh. "Try not to die this time, eh?"

Fendrick shouldered his pack and turned to leave without further ceremony.

"Travel safely," Shalindra called. "You are always welcome, no matter where we are."

Fedrick hesitated, then waved a thank you as he and Eljorn continued down the trail.

He's not coming back.

I know. His path, at last, nears its end.

And ours has so much farther to go.

"If you two are done?" Enna asked peevishly. "Honestly, I'm going to have to come up with some form of punishment for leaving me out of the conversation."

"It's still her fault," Tormjere said with a chuckle. "I was just commenting that the two of you should have gotten rid of *all* the demons before waking me up."

Enna graced him with the look he deserved for that. "I think it's you who'll need to work harder to catch up."

"We'll have plenty of opportunity," he said, though his cheerful mood dimmed. He did have much to reconcile, not only with what had occurred but within himself. Those demons still loose in the world would be the whetstone he used to resharpen his abilities and set himself back the way he should be. "Are you certain you don't want to go back to Ildalarial, and retire to a nice, quiet life?"

Enna shook her head, her answer unchanged. "I will return there, one day, but not until things are… more settled. Is our plan still the same, or will you stay here and play in the creek for the rest of the summer?"

"Tempting, but once we're done pandering to the frivolous extravagance of His Lordship this evening, it's off to Kirchmont."

"We are not pandering," Shalindra said, "but I do look forward to seeing Treven once more." The Legitarso of Amalthee had sent word that he had aborted his pilgrimage for the time being and returned home to escape the chaos in what was left of the

Ceringion Reginum.

"And after that, more demons," Enna said with a mock sigh. "Maybe someone else will have cleaned them up before we get there."

"We could track down Honarch first," Tormjere offered. "There's no telling what trouble they've gotten into by now." Both wizards and the halfling had departed not long after Tormjere's… rebirth? Waking up? He had yet to come up with a good way to refer to his months of being dead that did not sound either childish or melodramatic. Regardless of what he called it, the magicians had headed east, convinced that they could salvage something of what the Conclave had left behind, and perhaps do so with a more responsible charter. Then there was the halfling. "Besides, Weeby still owes me a drink."

Enna rolled her eyes.

Tormjere had said it in jest, but it was really more of an excuse. Compared to defeating a god, the path they had charted for themselves appeared disarmingly easy, but if he could have anyone else with them it would be Honarch.

I feel the same. It is my burden to drive the demons from our world, but I thank Eluria that you and Enna will both be with me.

It doesn't matter how difficult this will be, we'll see it finished.

Enna stamped her foot. "Out loud, or by Her Light I will throw you both into the creek."

Shalindra hung her head. "We should find some way to let her join our conversation."

"Absolutely not," Enna said. "We were given the capability of speech for a reason."

It was Tormjere's turn to roll his eyes heavenward, but as he did, they came to rest on the pale disk of the full moon painted against the perfectly blue sky. As his attention returned to their eyes, one pair green and the other blue, he was struck by just how profoundly these two women had altered his life. Whatever else happened, ensuring their success at whatever task they chose was exactly where he was meant to be.

"Come on," he said. "Let's go set the world straight."

"History records those who achieve greatness.
Rarely does it speak of those who
helped along the way."

—*Honarch*

GUARDIAN'S PROPHECY: BOOK FIVE

SHADOWS
OF
PROPHECY

Arriving Fall 2022